CASIDDIE WILLIAMS

Elliot's Empowerment

# Contents

# Foreword

Content Warning:

Thank you so much for picking up Elliot's Empowerment. I am so honored that you have chosen this contemporary romance as your next read. However, I want to make you aware of a few triggers and heavy topics that run through this book before you dive in.

This is an 18+ contemporary romance with on page sexual activity. Scenes range from exposition to explicitly detailed. These characters go through an emotional journey together. This novel in no part is a guide on how you should take care of your mental health. How the characters deal with mental trauma in this book may differ from how you or someone you know has dealt with the same trauma. Your mental health matters and this novel is not here to lessen that fact. I hope you enjoy reading Elliot's Empowerment as much as I did while I was writing it.

Substance Abuse and Mental Health Services Administration: SAMHSA (800)662-4357

Potential triggers include but not limited to:

1. MMF/MM
2. Dome/sub roles
3. Pregnancy
4. Polyamorous side characters
5. Anal play
6. Spankings
7. Pegging
8. Character death
9. Orgasm denial

# Preface

In case you need a little reminder of who belongs to whom, here is a helpful cheat sheet of everyone's spouses and children that have been born coming into this book.

*Hazel's Harem*
Hazel Gibson-Committed to:
Malcolm "Mac" Harmon
Phoenix Graves
Jude Sanders
Children:
Rowyn "Wynnie" Harmon
Gideon "Dean" Sanders
Alexander "Alex" Harmon
Delilah Jane "DJ" Graves
Piper Sanders

*Dellah's Delight*
Dellah & Collin McLain-
Children:
Elliot
Finn
Paige

*Wynnie's Wishes*

Wynnie(Harmon) & Scotty Langford-
Children:
Victoria "Tori"
Eleanor "Ella"
Archer "Archie"

*Annie You're Okay*
Annie, Blake & Cole McGrath-
Children:
Rory & Ruby
Rosie
Ruthie

*The Rescuer's Heart*
Justin & Nicole Webb-
Children:
Hannah
Miles
Seth
June

*Never Run Again*
Spencer Coble- Committed to:
Tucker Bennett
Lincoln Reed
Miller Smith
Axel Garrison
Children:
Katy Rander

*Never Fear Again*

Katy (Rander) & Viktor Dempsey
Children:
Owen
Justine
Emory
Lexi

# Acknowledgments

Where do I even start?

Are you okay? I know I'm not. That was rough, but a road the characters needed to take to get them where they needed to go.

These books began my journey into writing, and here I am, a little over a year later, completing their stories. Eight books that took me to places I never knew I could be. I've explored and done more research into things that I never even knew existed.

I started this with a Chromebook and a TikTok video, and it became two beautiful worlds filled with characters that we laughed, cried, and cringed with.

While their stories are over, the characters aren't gone. How do we feel about a second generation of Tipsy Penny II? (Thank you, Elliot)

It's no surprise that my characters were rabbits with the amount of kids they had, so have no fear; they will get their stories, too. If you paid attention between the tingles (there were some HOT scenes) and tears, I dropped a ton of Easter eggs at what's to come.

Thank you. Thank you, thank you, THANK YOU. Yes, you. If you're reading this, you've supported me, whether with this book, one of the other seven in this these series, or my novellas. Without my readers, these would just be mindless words on a piece of paper.

"Hear me out." My eyes roll every time I see my Alpha, K.K. Moore, write that to me in a chat, buuuuut, I can't deny she has some good ideas...*sometimes*. LOL. From a random ARC reader who loved my book to an annoying pain in my ass, Alpha reader, you're invaluable to me, K!! Thank you for sticking by me and becoming so much more than a friend.

My Beta and Arc readers have expanded and grown over the last year. Some coming and going for only a book or two, but I value every piece of advice and critique that you've offered. Without you, I wouldn't have expanded and grown as much as I have as a writer.

I wish there was a greater word to express my deepest gratitude to everyone who's joined me on my journey and exploration into these amazing characters. Please know that I love each and every one of you, and I will continue to write about the crazy people in my imagination!

# 1

# Elliot

Four years of college, six boyfriends, two girlfriends, a best friend with three beautiful babies, amazing parents, determination, and perseverance that I had to push through every day. All of that has gotten me to this point.

I stare up, up and up even more. The building in front of me towers over all the others. All around me, the sidewalks are busy, filled with early morning people heading to work. I look down at the fountain beside me and place my hand on the plaque.

*Griffin Woodlyn*
*Beloved Husband and Father*
*"There's no expiration date on the love of a father."*

A petite hand with a beautiful wedding band and a diamond ring lined with yellow stones wraps over mine.

"Are you ready for orientation?" Wynnie leans her head

on my shoulder.

"Am I ready to follow in both my fathers' footsteps and conquer the business world? Yes." I turn and pull her into a hug. "Am I ready to live eleven hours away from my best friend, nieces, and nephew? Absolutely fucking not. Doesn't Scotty want to franchise and open a Tipsy Penny here? I can fund it."

"This is hard on me, too."

"I know. I can't thank you enough for coming out here with me. I know it's hard to be away from your littles for so long." She scoffs into my chest.

"Trust me, Scotty has it under control. And if he doesn't, Tori's favorite pastime is bossing around her brother and sister."

"Or anyone at the mini compound you live on, for that matter." When Wynnie got pregnant with her second child, Mac insisted their house was too small. He cleared several acres of land, and they all built Wynnie's family a home. Hazel is trying to wear my Dad down to build another house so Mom and my siblings can also live there.

"You're going to be late if you don't go in."

I hug her close again. "Are you sure you'll be okay alone until I'm done with orientation?"

"El, I'm a big girl, and it's only four hours. I'll be fine. I looked up coffee shops online, and there's this one nearby called S'morgasm. I *have* to check it out."

I touch the plaque one more time.

"Uncle Griffin and Aunt Zoey are proud of you, El. I just know it."

I sniff and blink away the tears threatening to form.

"Dammit, woman. You're gonna make my eyes leak, and I

have to look fabulous on my first day. *Stop it.* Tell me you love me, and go get your orgasmic coffee. If you're a good girl, maybe I'll take you to the aquarium to see the fishies when I'm done." I pat her head, and she reaches up and kisses my cheek.

"I love having a best friend, sugar daddy. Be good, El, or be good at it." She blows me a kiss as she walks away. I'm going to miss the hell out of that woman.

I take one last look up at the sign for MAD Gaming Inc. and walk toward the building. Ready or not, my future is on the other side of these revolving doors.

As I walk through the doors for only the second time, I try not to look like a tourist and swivel my head, taking in the incredible architecture of the building. The beautiful young woman at the front desk asks for my ID, and I hand it to her. She smiles at me while printing my temporary sticker for the day and directs me to the human resource office.

When I came a month ago for my interview, I got the same sticker, but instead of the word "visitor" it now says "employee" under my name. Elliot McLain, employee of MAD Gaming Inc.

Toward the end of orientation, which included a tour, taking my picture for a permanent ID, and several videos on sexual harassment and proper workplace behavior, I was handed a note.

*Please come to the top floor when orientation is over.*
*Danika Poulsen*

I've been a nervous wreck since reading the note. I've never met Ms. Poulsen, or does she go by McGrath? I know she's married now. I've googled her more times than is probably acceptable over the years.

I shake the hand of the generic-looking businessman who led my orientation and make a mental note to never look that bland.

"I have a note to see Ms... Mrs... Pouls... Annie?" He looks at me awkwardly like the stumbling idiot I'm acting.

"Ms. Poulsen is on the top floor. It requires special access. You'll have to go back down to the lobby and collect your ID for clearance.

"Oh, okay. Thank you."

The pretty lady at the front desk smiles when she sees me again. "How can I help you, Mr. McLain." *Whoa.*

"You remember my name already?"

"It's my job to remember." Her smile brightens. Is it your job to flirt, too, front desk lady? "What can I do for you, Mr. McLain? Was everything alright with orientation?" She's not just pretty. Fuck. She's gorgeous with bright brown doe eyes and wavy brown hair halfway down her back. Her navy dress disappears under her desk, but I can still see her petite figure that I would wreck if—

"Mr. McLain?" *Shit.*

"Sorry. I'm supposed to see Ms. Poulsen. The guy who ran my orientation told me I had to start here and get my ID."

"Lucky me." She winks and my dick appreciates it. Definitely flirting... with a ring on. *Dammit.* The prettiest ones are always married. She opens a drawer and pulls out my ID, inspecting it. "Nice pic." She smiles as she hands it to me. "You have full access to the top floor with your card."

"I do?" I look at my ID as I attach it to my suit jacket

4

pocket and read it carefully. In the bottom corner is a green check mark, and the words "Full Access" are written in bold letters. "Um, I had no idea. Thank you. Do I need to do anything special?"

"When you enter the elevator and press the top floor, it won't move until it scans your card. Just swipe it over the scanner, and you'll be good to go."

"Thank you..." I try to peer over and read her name tag.

"It's Alaina, but you can call me Lainey." Her smile goes straight to my dick. *Calm down, boy.*

"Thank you for your help, Lainey. I'll see you again soon." I walk away before I jump over the counter and take her under her desk. Shit. I need to get laid.

Once in the elevator, I follow her instructions and take it to the top floor. The doors open, and I immediately step off.

"Holy fuck." My loud curse echoes through the room as I'm blinded by the floors. "What the hell?" I look up at the ceiling, hoping to regain my eyesight and hear a laugh. No, there are two laughs.

"Walk forward about six feet. There's nothing in front of you to bump into." I do as I'm told, and when I look down, I feel like I'm blinded again. Why is every woman in this building stunningly gorgeous?

I hear more laughing.

"I highly agree with you, Mr. McLain." The brunette smiles at me and looks at the blonde beside her. *What? Oh shit.* Did I say that last part out loud?

"Please call me Elliot."

"All right, Elliot. Yes, in case you were wondering, you did say that out loud. Do you usually have issues with your

5

internal monologue?"

The brunette continues to giggle, and I want a hole to open up in the floor so I can step into it and disappear from this entirely embarrassing encounter.

As my vision finally comes into focus, I recognize the blonde as Ms. Poulsen.

"Shit. I mean. Sorry. No. I don't usually have trouble. I'm normally much better at—" I stop my rambling because the more I talk, the more I sound like an idiot.

"I'm not sure I've heard anyone stumble over their words this terribly since Cole." I know who Cole is. That's who Ms. Poulsen married. I'm not entirely sure who the brunette woman beside her is, though. I've seen her in a few pictures online, but there's never any mention of her name.

"I'm BlakeLynn Rogers, you can call me Blake." She extends her hand for me to shake. "This is Danika Poulsen, but please call her Annie, despite what she might tell you." Blake turns to Annie. "I'm grabbing coffee at S'morgasm, and I'll be back. Would you like your usual?"

"Yes, please. Thank you, *Mijn Diamant.*"

"Oh, my best friend just went there. Brown hair and the brightest blue eyes you've ever seen. They're hard to miss. Her name is Wynnie."

"If I see her, I'll say hi. Would you like anything, Elliot?"

"No, but thank you for the offer, Blake." She kisses Annie on the lips and walks past me. I'm speechless because it was a little more than a friendly kiss.

"Elliot, BlakeLynn is my wife for all intents and purposes. This floor is part of my inner circle, and as your ID tag says, you are now a part of that. What happens on this floor stays here. You've signed several NDAs. Do you understand?"

6

I raise my hands in surrender. "I'm a card-carrying bisexual. And my best friend's mom has three husbands. Love is love." She nods and extends her arm to the hallway behind her.

"Glad we are on the same page. Let's continue this conversation in my office."

# 2

# Lainey

I f I wasn't already hot and bothered by Sawyer's text this morning, the gorgeous brunette certainly did me in. Elliot McLain is young and good-looking, and I can tell he has a sense of humor just from our small interaction.

Sawyer: Profile set up. Want to approve it?

Sawyer and I have been together for three years. We have an incredible sex life and like to explore. A few months ago, we decided to make bucket lists of things we wanted to do or add to our bedroom adventures. To say it's been fun would be an understatement.

"You're awfully smiley today, Lainey. Care to share with the class?"

"Oh, hey girl. Heading out for coffee?"

Blake leans over the counter with a curious smile on her face. "Yes, but tell me you met the new guy? He's far too young for my liking, but I know you and Sawyer were

8

talking about spicing up the bedroom."

"Blake, even if he weren't young, you're happily married. Times two. And yeah, I met the dreamboat. He was pretty hard to miss when he was eye fucking me."

She slaps her hands over her mouth and giggles. It's hard to believe she's the wife of such a powerful CEO. While Annie is great, Blake is so much fun and carefree.

"Eye fucking?" she whispers, and her eyes light up. "Tell me I get aaaaall the details tomorrow night."

"Of course. Did we decide who's hosting?"

"We are. Bring your bathing suit. We're swimming, and Annie hired a cook for the evening."

"Oh, I bet Cole doesn't like that very much. I know how protective he is over his outdoor kitchen."

Blake shrugs. "There were words. And make-up sex. And a promise to hire a team of babysitters so the guys could go out tomorrow night too. Sawyer should have gotten the invite. If he didn't, I'll make sure it gets passed along today."

"*All* the guys?"

"All. Did you want coffee? I have to go so I can get back soon."

"I'm good. Thanks."

Blake wiggles her fingers at me as she floats out the revolving door.

*All.* There are a lot of kids in our friend group. Sawyer and I are the only childless ones, but there are a dozen kids between their three households, and it sounds like some aren't done. I know Katy and Vik plan on more.


Sawyer: Is that a no?

*Shit.* I forgot about Sawyer's text.

Lainey: Don't activate it yet. We can look at it together later. Love you.
  Sawyer: It's a plan. Love you too, Jitterbug.

I can feel my cheeks blushing, and I need to calm down. I have a job to do, and I need to not let my mind wander to my sexy husband or the flirty new hire. Besides, Elliot McLain works for Annie, and I know her dislike for intercompany dating. Although he isn't my superior, so technically…

🖵 🖵 🖵 🖵 🖵

"Okay, show me. I'm ready." I flop on the couch next to Sawyer, curl my feet under me, and tuck into his side. He pulls me in closer, and I inhale his fresh ocean scent. His cologne always reminds me of summer days on the lake.

"I used the pictures you told me to, and I went with funny for my profile with a touch of seriousness."

"As you should."

Through his bucket list, Sawyer admitted that he was curious about being with a man. I'm secure enough in our relationship that I want him to explore his sexuality. On his list was to experience being with a guy, and I encouraged him to make a profile on a dating site and see what's out there.

He hands me his phone so I can look over his profile. I'm glad he chose the vacation photo for his main picture. He's sitting on a towel with his arms back and legs out. Sunkissed skin is on full display, and his naturally light hair is streaked blonder from the sun's rays. I called his name, and he looked back at me and smiled when he saw me holding the camera. Sawyer looks carefree and gorgeous, but I know he's the opposite behind closed doors. My husband is mouthy and dominant in the bedroom, just how I like him.

"So, let's see how serious you got in this profile." I briefly look at the screen and back at him in confusion. "Wes? You don't want to use your first name?"

He shrugs. "I thought I'd use my middle name for some anonymity. This is all experimental anyway, right? Might as well go all out."

Sawyer's middle name is Wesley. If he wants to use Wes as his online name to make him feel more comfortable, I'll support him. Uncurling myself from his side, I straddle his lap, and he smiles while caressing my hips.

"Hey, Jitterbug."

"Hey, handsome. You know you don't have to do this if you don't want to." He sighs as I gently massage his shoulders. "It's just a bucket list."

"I do. It's just hard to believe you're so okay with me... stepping out on our marriage."

I cup his cheeks and kiss him with passion and appreciation. "We're good, Sawyer. It's not stepping out if I allow it, and you come home to me. Did you explain everything in your profile?"

His hands glide up my thighs, and I know exactly what he's thinking without words. "Is that what you need right now, Sir."

"No," he insists. "I just need you." His hands continue up my thighs, grabbing the hem of my dress. The thin, stretchy material easily slides up my body, and I'm left sitting in his lap in my navy blue bra and panties.

His eyes drink me in, and seeing him staring at me never gets old. Sawyer's lips feather kisses along my collarbone and chest, and I love my gentle giant as much as my fierce Dom. I peel his t-shirt off his chest and run my hands over his sharp ridges. He loves the gym almost as much as he loves me, and I love his body for all the effort he puts into it.

"You're so fucking beautiful, Soy Sauce."

He nips at my collarbone at the use of his silly nickname. On our first date, we went out for Chinese food. When he picked up the soy sauce to add it to his rice, the top fell off, and the entire bottle spilled in his lap. To say it made for an interesting date would be an understatement.

"Nothing compares to your beauty, Alaina."

He only calls me Alaina when we are in a scene. "You said you didn't want to play?"

"I don't, but I wanted you to understand how serious I am about how breathtaking you are."

"I see." My hands dip to his pants, and I quickly tug them open while I devour his sexy words with my tongue. He moans into my mouth when I pull out his already-hardening cock. Sawyer's thick fingers move my panties aside and run a line down my core. He hums his approval when they slide straight to my entrance and dip in. It's no surprise to him that I'm already wet. My body is so in tune with his that I'm ready anytime he is.

Sawyer doesn't even bother removing my panties, only pushes them aside before lifting me and sinking me onto his length.

His name spills from my lips, and I make quick work of removing my bra so he has full access to my body.

Using the back of the couch for leverage, I ride his cock and allow him to twist and turn my body for his pleasure. His thumb slips between us, and he uses our movement to tease my clit.

"I fucking love you, Lainey."

"You're just saying that because my tits are in your face."

With his free hand, he grips a breast and squeezes, his fingers indenting my flesh. "I love these too, but I love you more."

He growls as he sucks my nipple into his mouth, and I giggle as I bounce harder onto him.

"If you find someone special, Soy Sauce, I want you to bring him home. I want to share him with you."

He pops off my nipple and looks at me with curious eyes. "You do?"

"I do." This isn't something we've discussed. As close of a relationship as Sawyer and I have, it took him a while to admit his desires to me about being curious with men. He was ashamed to confess to me that his mind had been straying and thought he was betraying me. It took a lot of convincing to get him to act on it.

His hands cup my cheeks, and he looks deeply into my eyes. I stare back into his stormy grays and can see he's looking for something from me.

"Why haven't you ever said anything to me before?"

"A few reasons."

Sawyer's hands shift back to my hips, encouraging me to continue moving. "Tell me."

"I wanted you to make the decision for you alone. I was worried that if you thought it was something I wanted, you'd try to find someone for us, for me, and the experience wouldn't be for *you*. You were so brave to admit your desires, and I don't want to take it away from you. It's hard for someone who craves dominance to admit his needs. I'm so fucking proud of you, Sawyer. That's why I said someone special, because if he becomes special for you, I know he'll be special for me. But if that's not a dynamic you want, I'm okay with that, too."

My world spins as he flips us around, and I find myself lying on my back with Sawyer pounding into me.

"Something I said?" I playfully smack his chest, and he buries his head into my neck.

"You're so fucking perfect. I want that. I want to show you all the love you deserve." His thrusts are deep and full of his confession. "But I don't want to share you…"

I don't understand. "Sawyer?"

He slows his pace and kisses me passionately.

"I don't want to share you, Jitterbug, I want to *be* shared by *you*. No matter our dynamic, you're always in charge. I want to find someone who understands and is willing to commit to that."

"You want to find us a third? Someone to share our life with? Not just a hookup?"

"Only if you do too."

I'd never thought about that before. This entire situation is for Sawyer. I only wanted to join in and share the experience with him. To share his happiness if he finds someone. I was okay with him having a boyfriend.

"So, in this scenario, I would get a husband and a boyfriend? And you would get—"

"A wife and a boyfriend. But only if that's something that you want too."

Do I? It's not a life I'm unfamiliar with. I've had two men before, but we always knew it would be temporary. Patrick and Chip were-*are*-incredible men, but we were never meant to be long-term, and we knew it from the start. My boss, Annie, her husband Cole, and their girlfriend Blake, are an amazing example of how a throuple can work, and my best friend Katy's family lives an incredible polyamorous life. Her adopted mother, Spencer, has four wonderful men.

"I think I do, but can I have some time to think about it? You're kind of scrambling my brain with your dick right now."

He thrusts his hips and smirks. "Fair enough, Jitterbug. You don't need to decide right this moment. Orgasm now, decision later."

"You drive a hard bargain, Baby."

# 3

# Sawyer

Being the only non-dad in this sea of men is intimidating. I'm always one lingering look away from the question, "When are you going to have kids?" Lainey and I are still young, and while we both put kids on our bucket lists, there's plenty of time before we need to start. Until then, we practice. A lot.

"How's that wife of yours, Sawyer," Cole, Annie's husband, asks me while slinging his arm over my shoulder. The guys are gathered at Spencer's house since the majority of the men live here.

"Beautiful, spicy, fucking tempting."

"So, just the way we like our women. Excellent." He clinks his beer with mine, and I have the urge to tousle my fingers through his shaggy blond curls. Cole is a good-looking guy with bright blue eyes and a winning smile. It's no wonder he won Annie over despite her hard outer shell. I shouldn't be checking out my friends and their partners, but I'm still learning what I like in a guy, and it feels safe to linger a little

16

longer on their features rather than a stranger's.

"Can I ask you a question, Cole?"

"Anything. Whatcha got for me?"

I open my mouth to speak but stop. I thought I was ready, but maybe I'm not. I look around at everyone hanging out and laughing, and chicken out. "Actually... never mind."

"Nope. You can't do that." Cole backs me into a lounge chair next to the pool where we're all hanging out and pushes me to sit. This is your typical guys' night with beer and meat on the grill. Judging by Cole's face, I don't think he's going to let me get away with not having a serious discussion when we should be having fun.

"You can spill it now, or I can grab the whiskey and probably get more out of you than you want to confess."

Fuck. Maybe whiskey is a better idea. "Can I choose the whiskey?"

"It's your word vomit." Cole stands and cups his hands to his mouth. "Who's game for some shots? Sawyer wants to chat and needs loose lips to do it. Anyone want to join us?"

Hands raise and grunts are heard. Cole attempts to take count before giving up.

"Fuck it. I'll bring out the whole bottle and plenty of glasses."

Several rounds of shots later, and I know it's more than I should have had. Instead of having a quiet conversation with Cole, I'm about to bare my soul to the nine other men here. With the exception of Justin and Vik, the rest of the guys have all been in polyamorous relationships, so I'm in good company.

"I'm going to date," I declare, and the conversations around me go quiet. It seems those four words have caught

17

everyone's attention. Some of the looks I'm getting aren't the nicest. In fact, I feel like I'm a mouse in a den of lions.

All of these men know my wife through her best friend Katy, and everyone here is Katy's family. Vik the Viking, with his blond man bun and beard, is married to Katy, Lainey's best friend since high school. He's giving me the bodyguard stare I know he's perfected from being Katy's bodyguard for years before becoming her husband.

Justin rescued Katy from her neglectful mother when she was a teenager and was raped and later found out she was pregnant. Lainey talks highly of Justin and everything he's done for her bestie. His scowl confuses me.

Patrick and Chip are Lainey's ex-lovers when she was still Meghan, a lifetime before I met her. They are still a couple and have adopted a little girl together named Violet.

Cole is married to Annie, who employs both Katy and Lainey. Then there's the four other men—Spencer's men. Spencer is Katy's adopted mother, and they are her pseudo-dads. If looks could kill, I'd be in pieces right now, probably roasting on the grill.

"Sawyer," the cowboy hat-wearing Tucker, the oldest of Spencer's men, speaks up. "I'm going to hope there's more to that sentence because Lainey might not be ours, but she *is* our daughter's best friend, and we'll defend her honor as quickly as we will Katy's."

My brows pinch as I consider what he said and what I said to cause his reaction. My statement was pretty clear. I don't understand the hostility.

"Would you care to give us more context?" Lincoln asks. Another of Spencer's men, the cop, the broody one. She has so many men. I don't think I want that many. Lainey is

18

already a handful, but I love her handfuls. "Sawyer," Lincoln clips. "Context." *Oooh. Cop voice.*

"I'm going to look for a date. A man. I want to explore mine…I mean men." *Waaay too many shots.*

"I hope you're not telling us you're planning to cheat on Meghan," Patrick growls. He's a brick house that looks like a modern-day G.I. Joe, and I see what Lainey saw in him. I also realize he called her Meghan, letting me know how serious his question is. Chip grabs Patrick's arm to calm him, and I marvel at his boyish looks.

"No. Why would you think that?"

"Context, Sawyer," Lincoln repeats.

I rub my fingers across my forehead, trying to figure out why an innocent conversation seems to be going south.

"Okay, let's take a breather." Axel stands and stalks towards me, and I stare in awe at his perfect brown curls. I want to run my fingers through his hair even more than I did Cole's earlier. Axel crouches in front of me and puts his big, strong nurse hands on my knees.

"You're pretty." He blushes a bit before rolling his eyes at me.

"You've had a lot to drink, so I'm going to ask some easy questions. Okay?"

"Sure." I can do easy.

"You said you're going to date, correct?"

"Yes." I've said it several times. Why are they struggling to understand it?

"Are you and Lainey separating?"

"What?" I stand and brush Axel's hands off me. "Why would you ask that? I love my wife. She's everything to me. I'd die for her." I feel like a caged animal as Axel stands, and we're almost chest to chest.

Axel raises his hands in surrender and looks at the other guys behind him.

"Okay. You love Lainey. Got it. Can you tell us why you're going to date then?"

"Is no one listening to me? I'm going to look for a man." I flop back onto the lounge chair. "This is going all wrong."

"Hey," Cole touches my arm to grab my attention. "We're here to listen. Could we start from the beginning? I think we're missing some puzzle pieces."

Missing pieces. Yeah, that's what it feels like to me, too.

"Okay." I run my hands through my light wavy hair and tug. Axel retreats back to his seat, and I try to find the puzzle in my hazy mind before I lay out all the pieces. "Lainey and I made bucket lists of things we want to do. In life, for our life, in and out of the bedroom—anything and everything. I... I've always been interested in men, but I have a very dominant personality and never felt I could explore it. Lainey encouraged me to do so, and I set up an online profile to try it out."

There's a collective feeling of relief that lightens the air around me.

"So Lainey has agreed to allow you to explore your sexuality?" Miller, Spencer's firefighter asks. From what I remember of his relationship, he was straight until he wasn't with Lincoln. They were an item before Spencer. Maybe having a group conversation is exactly what I needed.

"Encouraged it. She even said she's interested in opening our relationship to include a third." After our couch sex last night, we talked more about what my dating someone would mean for us and what I hoped for our future. Hearing her say she was all for it made me feel excited but also a little guilty, and we had another round of sex so I could solidify with her that I want to add to, not replace what we already have.

"Well fuck yeah, Sawyer!" Cole slaps my back and grabs the bottle of whiskey. "A round of shots for adding to our happy family." Grumbles and cheers are heard as Cole pours golden liquid into tiny glasses. I shouldn't drink anymore, but this is a celebration. The beginning of a new future for me and my incredible wife.

"Hey, Sawyer. Did you say you made a dating profile?" Axel asks with a mischievous look on his face.

"Yeah, why?"

Tucker groans and runs his hands over his face. "Behave, Axel."

"Where's the fun in that, Grand Daddy Tucker?" Axel pounces over to me, narrowly missing Tucker's grabbing hand, and swipes my phone. He pushes a button on a wall, and a projector screen slowly rolls down.

"No," Vik protests.

"Yes," Axel retorts and sticks his tongue out.

Before I realize what's happening, my dating profile is large and in charge on the screen in front of us, and we're scrutinizing other guys' profiles.

"Let's find you your throuple." It's hard to argue with Axel when he's this excited, but I'll admit the thrill of the men I respect most in life helping me do this, is gratifying.

21

# 4

# Lainey

I want to tell the girls about the conversation Sawyer and I had last night. If anyone would understand, it would be them. Everyone knows about the little affair I had with Patrick and Chip, but I was barely an adult then, and now I'm a married woman. Happily married, might I add.

"Hey, what's wrong?" Katy can always tell my moods. She looks so carefree tonight with her long brown hair in adorable space buns high on her head. It's her daughter Justine's favorite hairstyle, and while she says she does it for her, I know she secretly loves how she looks with them.

"I have a little secret I want to share, but I'm nervous, even though I know I shouldn't be."

Katy's face lights up, and she whisper-shouts, "Are you pregnant?"

Heads turn, and her voice drifts through the crowd despite the low music and conversations around us. Blake squeals and splashes toward us from the step she was sitting on in the pool.

"Did I hear the word pregnant? Lainey, are you pregnant? I want potential redheaded babies running around." Her comment reminds me that despite dying my hair brown for the last three-plus years, my natural color is strawberry blonde. With Sawyer's light hair color, having a redheaded baby is possible. But still...

"Not. Pregnant."

The drippy brunette before me, in a bright pink bikini, pouts like a toddler who was just told no more sugar.

"You're no fun. We need more babies around here." Blake bats her eyes at Katy and then turns to Nicole.

Other than myself, Katy and Nicole are the only two who can have more kids. Spencer's traumatic past with her ex left her unable to have children of her own, but she's happy with her men and Katy. The car accident that shattered Annie's pelvis and killed her driver severely damaged her reproductive organs. Their twins, Ruby and Rory, were a miracle, but they didn't want to tempt fate again. Blake carried their next two girls, Rosie and Ruth.

"Don't give me those baby-making eyes, Blake. Give my uterus a break." Nicole points a finger at Blake, who pouts again.

"But you and Justin make the cuuuutest nieces and nephews. Four is not nearly enough, and you once told me you'd give your breeding kink husband a football team worth of kids."

"Sure, and my OB has been on vacation for six months with the amount of money we've already paid her for the first four." Nicole's gorgeous blonde curls dance around her shoulders while I watch her banter with Blake in amusement.

"It's Katy's turn anyway." My best friend's jaw drops at Spencer's statement. I know Spencer lives vicariously through Katy and steals her four grandbabies away whenever possible.

"How is it my turn? I was the last one to have a baby. Shouldn't it be Nicole's turn?"

"You're younger. Your vajayjay bounces back quicker." Blake crosses her arms as she makes her matter-of-fact statement.

"Woman, look at you. You'd never know you've had two kids. You don't even have a stretch mark on you," Katy protests.

She's right. Blake looks fantastic, and I'm silently thanking the universe for diverting this pregnancy conversation away from me.

Annie walks up behind Blake and wraps her hands around her waist, kissing her shoulder. Blake melts into Annie's touch. Their relationship is special and complicated. While she legally married Cole, her position as a female CEO leads her to live a secretive life regarding her relationship with Blake. "*Mijn Diamant*, you're gorgeous inside and out, and I'd love you even if you had stretch marks."

Blake spins in Annie's arms with a huff. "Don't lie to me. You like my tight little bo—"

"Lalalalala," Katy shouts with her ears covered, and I giggle, turning her attention back to me.

"Oh no. You had a secret, and now you have to spill it to the group."

"But—"

"Nope. Talk."

"You're the worst best friend, Katy."

She blows me a kiss, and I know she's not going to let me off the hook. And judging by the looks of the rest of the women around me, I don't think any of them will.

"Fine. I feel like this group is uniquely qualified to understand me anyway. Sawyer and I have decided to open our relationship to a third."

"Guy or girl? Guy or girl?" Blake bounces with excitement, and Candy, their old Doberman, approaches her to see what's happening. She reaches down to pet the dog while she eagerly waits for my answer.

"Well, I'd honestly be open for either, but this is for Sawyer, so it's another guy."

"Interesting," Nicole says as she sips her wine, giving far too much thought to the situation. "Are you sure another guy would be for Sawyer and not you?"

I open my mouth to respond, but I don't have any words. I hadn't thought about it like that. All along, this has been something Sawyer has wanted to explore. He wants to see if his interest in men is purely intrigue or something he would actually want to pursue. I've been supportive of him through all our conversations because no matter what happens, I know he isn't trying to replace me, only enhance himself. And after our conversation and sex last night, I know he's trying to enhance *us*.

"I guess it would be for both of us. But I'm not interfering in his search. That's all for him. If he finds someone special, then I'll get involved."

"Do you think that will work? Blake and I discussed Cole right away. I wouldn't have made a decision without her. Although we weren't actively looking to add anyone to our relationship."

Blake curls into Annie's side. "We certainly weren't. Especially not a young, pole dancing, dog walker that dommed his way into our hearts and our bedr—"

"BROTHER!" Nicole yells before Blake can finish her sentence. "Cole is my brother, and I don't need to hear about your bedroom activities. At least not before I'm less sober." She chugs the rest of her glass, and one of Annie's servers hired for the night quickly refills it.

I often forget that Cole and Nicole are siblings and what a small world it is. Nicole was Annie's hairdresser, and recommended her brother to walk Candy when Annie's dog walker suddenly quit on her.

"Anyway," Katy interjects. "Tell us more details."

"There really aren't any. At least not until he finds someone worth discussing. I'm open to any advice, though."

"You should tell Sawyer to talk to Miller and Axel," Spencer suggests. "They both had bi-awakenings and would probably have insight for him."

"Oh, I'm sure he's already talking to them about it. He's pretty excited. His dating profile is good. I helped him clean up some of the details of what he's looking for."

"Did he mention you in the post?" Katy's question has a hint of concern.

"Of course he did."

She sighs in relief and takes my hand, resting her head on my shoulder. "I just don't want my best friend to get hurt. Putting it all upfront so someone can make an informed decision is better than springing it on someone."

"He was very specific that he's a married man looking to explore and potentially add them to our relationship."

"Did he happen to mention his specific affinities in the bedroom?" Blake's Cheshire Cat smile tells of our late-night conversations and confessions. Sawyer is a dominating man in the bedroom, and I love it. He eased me into the things he likes, and I confided with Blake on several occasions. Before she and Annie were lovers, she was Annie's submissive.

"He brushes upon it. While it's obviously going to be a part of our bedroom life, he also didn't want people to think that's all their relationship would be. We want a partner, not a sub."

Blake throws herself at me, and I groan at getting wet from her bikini.

"I'm so excited for you both. I'm always here to talk whenever you nee—"

"Stop trying to steal my bestie," Katy adds herself to the hug Blake is forcing on me, and we all tumble off the chair in a fit of laughter.

I'm glad I confided in them. Each of these women can give me a unique perspective into their relationships that can help me grow mine. I give Katy an extra smile as she offers her hand to help me up, and I wrap my arms around her tightly.

"Thank you for being the bestest, best friend. Thank you for inviting me to the girls' night, where I met Patrick and realized my life was shitty and I deserved better. And thank you for all the love and support you've given me over the years. You can't understand how much it's meant to me."

"Ugh." Katy pulls away and stares into the sky, rapidly blinking her eyes. "Don't make me the crying girl at the drinking party."

She gives me a shove away, and my foot catches on the leg

of a chair. I tip from the lack of equilibrium and the alcohol, but I'm not going down without a fight. I hold onto Katy and throw my weight into the fall, and we both splash into the pool.

When we come up for air, Katy tries to dunk me again. "You bitch. You've ruined my hair. Now my buns are floppy instead of fluffy."

I bark like a dog and lull my tongue out of my mouth, panting. I swim away before she can try to dunk me again, and she takes chase. These girls' nights are good for my soul, and so are these women.

# 5

# Elliot

Annie hired me to be her personal assistant. I applied to be a gofer, and this is like the gold star of gofers. This isn't what I ultimately want to do, but I'm not naive enough to think I can just walk into a board room still wet behind the ears from college. Every foot in the door is the right direction, and this was a giant leap.

It's been two weeks, and I'm already homesick. Daily phone calls with my mom and dad help, but I haven't made any friends here yet, and despite her being married, Wynnie and I were practically inseparable when I wasn't at college.

Elliot: Any movement on a Chicago chapter of Tipsy Penny?
Wynnie: If I even smell a hint of consideration, you'd be the first to know. You lonely already? I miss your face.

How do I answer? I'm lonely as fuck, but I don't want her to worry about me. Ever since my parents died and Wynnie took me under her wing, she's been my saving grace.

29

The first months were hard. I fought and rebelled, but she was patient and understanding. Constantly reassuring me, Dellah and Collin, my parent's best friends whose care we were left in, were amazing people. I was such an asshole kid back then, but losing your mother and then five years later losing your dad makes you a cynical teenager.

Elliot: I miss your face too, and Tori and Ella and Archie. Apparently, I'm not cool enough for Finn and Paige. They reject my video calls.

My phone rings, and I smile when I see Wynnie's picture on the screen.

"Hey."

"Hey, El. No reason to miss my face when you can see me on a little screen."

"But how can I pick on the gray hairs you're growing if the screen is so little? Hold on, let me hook you up to the big screen so I can get a better look." I make a show of playing with the remote, and she scowls at me.

"What's that, Elliot? I can't hear you. I think our connection is fuzzy. I might need to hang up and call you back later."

"Nooooooooo." I huff and flop onto my couch. "Don't be mean to me. I'm lonely and desperate for a friend. You left me for that little town to fend for myself in this big city. You're the worst best friend, Rowyn Juniper Langford."

Her face instantly softens, and she puts on her mom voice. "Is it that bad already?"

"Yes. No. Maybe." I roll my head to the side and groan into the pillow. "I never thought I'd hate the quiet. I went from a rowdy household of kids, to college, where there were no noise curfews. The dream has always been to have my own place with peace and quiet. Who knew I hated silence?"

"You don't hate silence. You hate solitude. Come home and visit next weekend. The flight is only two hours."

The perk of not having to worry about money is that taking a two-hour plane ride home is just as easy as a two-hour car ride, and the only way I convinced myself I could take this job and leave my family.

"You don't think it's too soon? I don't want anyone to think I'm copping out already."

"Is that even a serious question? Your mom is one blubber fest away from my mom convincing her to finally clear more land and build the house she's been begging her to build. I secretly think it's already happening without Aunt Dellah's permission. I've seen some suspicious construction equipment lately."

"Knowing your dad, that wouldn't surprise me."

"Which one?"

I shake my head and laugh. "So true."

Wynnie has three dads. One is her biological father, and the other two are amazing men her mother Hazel collected. Aunt Hazel's relationship with Mac, Jude, and Phoenix ultimately gave me the courage to come out to everyone. Needless to say, no one was shocked. It wasn't until college that I realized I like women too, just not as much as I like men.

"So you'll come home next weekend? Everyone misses you, and it will help give you something to look forward to. Maybe even raise your spirits a bit."

"Twist my arm, why don't you? You might as well go full best friend guilt trip on me and tell me what a struggle life is without me there."

Wynnie puts her hand over her heart, and her jaw drops. "I'd never put that burden on you, no matter how bad my heart hurts for your return home."

Her serious face lasts all of two seconds before we're almost in tears laughing. I missed this. I needed to goof off with my bestie. My rock.

"Hey, Wynnie? You know I'm going to need to find a duplicate, right?"

"A what?"

"A duplicate. I can't find a replacement Wynnie because there's no replacing you, but I'm going to need to find a body double. I can't be lonely forever."

"It would be easier on my heart if you found yourself a husband or a wife. Or hell, be like my mom and find yourself a harem."

"I *am* a lot to handle, and many hands make light work." She smiles into the camera at me, but it doesn't reach her eyes. "Talk to me."

"I worry about you all alone. It's hard to forget your early days, and I don't want you to think that just because we aren't across town, we aren't still here for you in a heartbeat."

"Fuck. Why do you have to say shit like that?" I swipe at a tear that's threatening to fall down my cheek. "You're making me leaky."

"Because you know I love you, and I need you to *know* we are all here."

"I know. I really do." We stare at each other momentarily before the screen whirls away, and Tori appears.

32

"Uncle Elliot! I need you to come back right now. These kids you left me with are crazy, and my parents can't control them like you do."

"Okay, okay, Spunky girl. Can you hang on until next weekend? I'll come put them in their place and have a stern talking to with your parents."

"Oh, thank goodness. Yeah, I think I can survive that long, but don't be late."

The phone jostles around again, and I laugh at Wynnie's expression when she appears on the screen. I mouth "Drama Queen" and she nods in agreement.

"If I didn't know any better, I'd think I birthed that attitude. Now you definitely have to come home next weekend. I can't be subjected to the wrath of a spiteful pre-teen if you don't."

"I value your life too much to let your demise be at the hands of a child who hasn't even hit puberty yet."

"Well, thank goodness for small favors. Are you good? You seem better now than when I first called."

I do feel better—lighter. Talking to Wynnie always does that.

"I do. Thanks, bestie."

"I wish they had like a dating app, but for friends. 'Coffee companion wanted to sit across from each other while staring at our laptops, pretending to be social.' Maybe you need to get your fancy boss to develop that."

"That's actually not a terrible idea."

"Okay, but I get thirty percent of the profits because it was my idea."

"Damn, woman, just take me for everything I'm worth."

"All I want is your heart, and your Starbucks card, since

you now have S'morgasm."

We say our goodbyes, and I decide I need to stop my pity party. I'm in a new city with a new job. I'm young and handsome and—Dammit. I'm young and handsome, and I know how to use an actual dating app. Why didn't I think of that sooner? I've used them in the past. I haven't even updated my location from college yet. There's a whole new world out there for me to explore.

# 6

# Sawyer

This is intimidating. My first date with a man. I realize this shouldn't be as big a deal as it is, but I'm nervous.

"You look so sexy. Maybe I won't let you go, and I'll make you stay home and have your way with me."

I pull Lainey into me and look into her hazel eyes. Some days they're brown, and other days green. I love the changes they can make.

"Jitterbug, if you want me to stay home, I can. You're allowed to have doubts. This is a big deal for both of us."

She cups my cheeks and places the gentlest kiss on my lips. "I'm okay. You're okay, and you're going to go out and have fun. Or maybe he'll be a dud, and you'll come home and take it out on me. Seems like a win-win to me."

A growl of possessiveness rumbles through me, and Lainey lays her head on my chest.

"See, you like that idea too. He looks great on paper. He's an attractive guy, and you're meeting him in a public place.

Do you need me to give you the thirty-minute emergency call?"

"The what?"

"The emergency call. I give you thirty minutes to get to know him, and then I call and fake an emergency so you can leave. It's a classic girl move."

"I thought that only happened in the movies?"

"It's a thing. I'm happy to fake a sick dog or a fall down the stairs." Lainey goes limp in my arms and flops the back of her hand over her forehead. "Oh, Sawyer, I mean Wes, I've fallen, and I can't get up. I need you to come help me. Oh, and I'm naked, and I fell on a butt plug."

"Naked, huh? Oh my. I hope before you fell on the butt plug, you were slipping on lube. Otherwise, that fall would be shocking."

"But, of course, my white knight." Lainey stands and straightens my collar. "You look handsome. This blue shirt makes your gray eyes pop. Now, get out of here before you're late. I'm going to miss you. Update me if you can."

"I'll update you."

"If you can. I don't want to be a cock block."

Grabbing her chin, I press my lips to hers. "You can do whatever you want to do to my cock, any time you want."

"Go." Lainey playfully pushes my chest, and I peck her cheek before I leave.

🙂🙂🙂🙂🙂

Johnathan and I decided to meet at Midnight Moonshine. Well, Lainey decided that's where we were meeting. Spencer's cowboy, Tucker, owns the club, and there's a restaurant where we can start. If we want to prolong the evening, we can dance. It seemed like a good choice. It put Lainey at ease, knowing if there was any trouble, Tucker has cameras everywhere.

I put in my profile I'm looking to explore my sexuality, and I know that can bring out some salacious people who might only want to meet me to take my so-called virginity. Spoiler alert: I'm not putting out on the first date. I need to trust someone to let them take any control over me, and as I have a dominant personality, it takes a lot more trust than most.

The rideshare pulls up in front of the club, and I thank my driver before exiting his sedan. I've been here several times, but I didn't want to drive so I could enjoy a few drinks if I felt nervous and wanted to loosen up. But not as loose as the guys' night. That was a rough next morning.

I run my hands through my hair and remember the feel of Lainey rubbing her fingers into my scalp. Yesterday, I got a fresh haircut in preparation for my date, and she loves running her fingers over the newly shaved stubble of my fade.

When I step inside, I walk to the right through a set of glass doors leading to the restaurant portion of the club. A pretty brunette greets me at the host stand with a smile.

"Good evening. Do you have a reservation?"

"Yes, ma'am. Wes party of two."

"Oh, your other party just arrived. I'll take you to him."

"Wait"—I look at her name tag—"Ava. Is the gentleman tall, dark-haired, and handsome?"

She smiles and looks over her shoulder. "He's the one in the light green shirt over by the stage."

I follow her direction and see the back of his head. He looks slightly in our direction, and I breathe a sigh of relief. He looks like his picture.

"Thank you, Ava."

"Good luck."

I approach Johnathan from behind and place my hand on his shoulder. He looks up at me and stands, embracing me in a hug. We've been talking and texting for over a week, but I'm a little taken aback by his immediate tactileness.

"Wes, you look just like your picture. That's such a relief. You never know with these online sites."

I return the hug and smile back at him when he releases me. "I was thinking the same thing. It's nice to meet you." I round the table and sit across from him. Jonathan already has a glass of wine, and as he sits, he nervously takes a big gulp.

"Sorry. I've been here for about ten minutes. I hate being late, and I'm a bit nervous."

I give him a half smile in understanding. "Why are you nervous?" I didn't expect him to be nervous, too.

"I haven't been with a woman in a long time, but your profile piqued my interest, so I swiped."

*Oh.* I obviously put in my profile that I'm married and we're looking to expand our relationship, but I was also clear that the initial meetings would be with me.

"That's not really something to worry about yet. You have to pass my tests first." My tone is playful, but a sheen of sweat forms on Jonathan's forehead. He picks up his glass, chugging the rest of his wine. His head whips around, presumably looking for the server. "Are you okay?"

"Hmm? Oh yeah. I'm fine. Just nervous, like I said."

"About my wife?"

His fingers tap on the stem of the glass, and I slouch back into my seat. This is already not going well. Maybe I should have taken Lainey up on her thirty-minute fake emergency. I haven't dated anyone since her and if I can be corny, we fell in love at first sight.

*"Shit. Shit. SHIT!"*

*"Such a foul mouth for such a gorgeous woman."*

*"What?"*

*The beautiful, cursing brunette looks up at me from her crouched position outside the MAD Gaming Inc. building. Her hazel eyes, sparkling green in the morning light, look back at me in confusion and panic.*

*"Do you need help with something, beautiful?"*

*"Um..."*

*"I'm Sawyer. I own the coffee shop next door. I promise I'm not some weird creep thinking dirty thoughts about you being down in that position." Fuck, her cheeks just turned the prettiest shade of red.*

*"Um..."*

*I think I broke her.*

*"Can I help you up?" I offer my hand, and she stares at it until I wiggle my fingers, and she snaps out of her trance.*

*"Thank you." Her hand feels petite but solid in mine, and when she stands, I don't let go.*

*"Sawyer. And you are?"*

*"Oh, I'm Meg... Alaina... Lainey. Call me Lainey."*

*"A woman of many names. Very interesting. Okay, Lainey, is there something you need help with?"*

*She looks behind her and back at me. "You said you own the*

39

*coffee shop? As in, the one right here?"* Lainey looks over her shoulder again, and when she turns back to me, she looks hopeful.

"Yeah, that's me. Java Junkie." She grabs my arm like a lifeline, and I feel her body vibrating.

"I was sent to get a coffee order for the CEO, and I can't find the paper it was written on. Is there any chance in this entire shitty day that you happen to know what Ms. Poulsen drinks?"

*Ah, she works here.*

"You seem to already be hopped up on caffeine. I hope you don't plan to order yourself any coffee, Jitterbug."

"Oh, um." She removes her hand from my arm and I feel the void left behind.

"I know what she drinks. Follow me." She obediently walks beside me as we make our way to the front of my store. "I'll get you taken care of. Was she the only order on your list?" Panic strikes her face, and her responding "No" is high-pitched. "Okay, relax. How many were on the list?"

"Three."

"And who gave you this list?"

"A blond guy with curly hair and super blue eyes."

I open the door for Lainey, and she walks into my little coffee shop. I sell mostly coffee, but I partner with a local bakery who provides me with muffins, bagels, and cookies to sell. Java Junkie is small, with exposed brick walls and memorabilia from other local establishments hanging for decor, but it's all mine, and I'm proud of it.

"I've got you covered, Jitterbug. Have a seat, and I'll get those drinks made. You should have something to eat while you wait. Let Gus know what you'd like, and he'll get it for you." Gus nods at my subtle order, and I walk behind the counter to make their drinks.

40

*I quickly get her order ready for Ms. Poulsen, her husband and their partner. They've been my customers since I took over the coffee shop, and I'm eternally grateful for their patronage.*

*I grab a few cookies and bring the tray of drinks and the bag out to Lainey. She's sitting at a table, picking at a muffin with her crossed leg bobbing. Is she naturally this energetic, or was I right about her being over-caffeinated? I love that she listened to me and chose to eat.*

*"You're all set, Lainey." She practically jumps from her seat and bangs her knee on the table.*

*"Ouch, shit."*

*"Such a sailor's mouth, Jitterbug."*

*She looks up at me through dark lashes as she rubs the pain from her knee. "I know you know my name because you just used it, so why do you keep calling me Jitterbug?"*

*Sassy too. I love it. "Because you're jittery and cute." I swipe my thumb across her cheek, and her eyes flutter. She's receptive to my touch. "Why have I never seen you before?"*

*"I just started. I'm the new receptionist at the front desk. I was asked as a favor to get their coffee, but this isn't part of my duty."*

*"Shame. I'd love to see you more." Her cheeks redden again, and dirty thoughts cross my mind. Where else can I turn her red?*

*"How much do I owe you for everything? I was given the company card."*

*My eyes linger on her lips as she forms words that I can't hear. Her upper lip is slightly smaller than her bottom, and she has a deep cupid's bow on her dark pink lips.*

*"Sawyer? How much?"*

*"On the house if you let me take you out this weekend."*

*"Out? Like a date?"*

*"No, not like a date. A date. You, me, dinner. Maybe a kiss on*

41

*your doorstep because I'm a gentleman and will walk you to your door at the end of the evening." I lean closer to her ear and lower my voice. "Then maybe you'll invite me inside, and we can—"*

*"Okay." She jumps back at my whispered words.*

*"Okay." I give her a smile that speaks of promises to come.*

I walked her to the door at the end of the evening and didn't leave until I had to open the coffee shop two days later.

Jonathan finally flags down our server and orders us each a glass of wine without asking.

"I'm going to run to the bathroom real quick. I'll be right back."

"Yeah, sure. I'll order us an appetizer when he gets back."

I nod and walk away. Why didn't he just order something when he ordered drinks? I dislike people who make servers run in circles. As someone who works in the service industry, I know how taxing it can be.

The restaurant bathrooms are on the other side of the dining room, but we're seated close to the dance floor, so I open the doors and head toward the club bathrooms. As I reach my hand out to open the door, someone from inside opens it first, and I almost crash into him.

"Oh shit, man, sorry."

"Sorry." We speak over each other as my hand grabs his shoulder to catch my balance. I look up to apologize again as I upright myself, but words get caught in my throat. Bright blue eyes stare back at me, framed by dark eyebrows and hair that looks so soft, my fingers twitch to run my hands through.

"Are you okay? I didn't mean to almost knock you over."

"Yeah. Yes. I'm good. No worries," I stammer out.

SAWYER

"Good. Have a good evening." Blue eye's pats my shoulder and steps past me to head back into the club.

*Shit. Who was he?*

I probably look like a stalker standing in the bathroom doorway as I watch his ass walk away, but goddamn, he's hot.

# 7

# Lainey

I can do this. This is torture. I agreed to this. Why am I freaking out?

Lainey: 9-1-0

Katy: What the hell is 9-1-0

Lainey: It's an almost emergency... but not emergency enough for 9-1-1

My phone rings, and I know I should have just called her, but I never want to bother her if she's busy with the kids.

"Hel—"

"You're so confusing. It's either an emergency or it's not."

"Kaaaaaty. I feel like I've made a mistake, but also I don't. I want to drive down there, but I've had too much to drink, and it's a stupid idea, too. You need to talk me off the ledge before I do something stupid. And why hasn't he texted me with an update?"

"Whoa. Lainey, where are you?"

"I'm home." Grabbing a throw pillow off the couch, I bury my face in it and scream.

"Feel better?" She's laughing at me, but this is a serious matter.

"It's not funny. I'm panicking."

"Lainey, I can't help if I don't know what's happening."

"Blah. You need to catch up. Sawyer is out on his first date. They went to Tucker's club, and I know I agreed to him dating, but..." I scream into the pillow again because my thoughts are jumbled in my head, and I can't think straight.

"Do you need me to come over?"

*Yes.* "No."

"Lainey." Shit, that's her Mom voice. Dammit, she's on to me.

"I don't know what I need. No, what I need is to hear from Sawyer. I've never been insecure about our relationship before, and I'm one hundred percent behind him exploring his sexuality. But..."

"But?"

"But this part sucks. Can't we do this together too? We looked at his dating app together and picked this guy out. They talked for a while, and he told me all about the texts they exchanged. But I'm not there, and I know this part is for him, and I *shouldn't* be there, but...ugh!"

"Hold on."

"Sure." The line goes quiet, and I look to make sure we didn't lose connection. The timer is increasing, so she must have put me on hold. The silence isn't helping my anxiety, and I start pacing to burn some of the nervous energy coursing through me.

"Okay, I'm back. Tucker isn't working tonight, so I

couldn't get you any dirt, but I'm on my way over."

"No, you don't have to do that." *Even though I really want you to.*

"Lie to me again, and I'll turn around. Owen and Justine are having a sleepover at Nicole's house, so it's just the two littles. Viktor can handle them for a while. You need me."

The sigh of relief that my body exhales releases more stress than I realize I was holding. "You're the absolute best, you know that, right?"

"Do you need Blake too?"

Do I?

"No, just my bestie. And maybe the rest of the bottle of wine I'm drinking."

"Be there soon."

When the doorbell rings, I jump from my seat on the couch, but I know it's Katy when the door immediately opens. Ringing the bell is just a formality to give a heads-up if anyone is naked because we've walked in on each other more times than we need to talk about.

"Have you heard anything yet?" She presents me with a jar of honey-roasted peanut butter and a bag of mini chocolate chips and pushes me back onto the couch. While I open her goodies, she takes two spoons out of the kitchen drawer and grabs a bowl for dipping. When she sits next to me on the couch, I dump the bag of chocolate chips into the bowl, happily scoop some peanut butter, and dip it in the chips.

"Nothing. I've heard nothing," I say through a mouthful of goodness.

"Why don't you text him?"

"I'm twying to be suppowtive." My tongue sticks to the roof of my mouth, making me sound funny. I stick up my pointer finger and ask her to give me a minute. She nods while shoving her spoon in her mouth. "I'm trying to be supportive and don't want to bother him. But I appreciate you trying to spy for me."

"Of course. You know, I can always ask Tucker to check the cameras."

"No. I can't invade his privacy like that. He'll tell me what he wants to when he gets home. Right? Oh god, he'll tell me, right?" I shove another spoonful of peanut butter in my mouth to stop my panic from spilling out.

Katy picks up her phone and sends a text. I'm going off the rails, so I'm sure she's calling for reinforcements. Blake or Nicole will probably be knocking on my door within the next thirty minutes.

"Lainey, look at me. Is there a doubt in your mind about Sawyer's love for you?"

"No."

"Do you still want him to explore his sexuality with other men?"

"Yes?"

"Then what are you worried about?"

"What if he finds someone he really likes and I don't like them?" I can't believe I just confessed that. I pick up the bottle of wine and chug straight from the lip. Who needs a cup?

My phone buzzes on the table, and I nearly choke as I try to swallow and gasp at the same time. I'm coughing and trying to catch my breath as Katy hands me my phone.

Sawyer: Checking in, Jitterbug. This date is a dud, but I'm trying to be polite. I don't think I'll be here much longer. I'll text you when I'm on my way home. Love you, beautiful.

"It's Sawyer. He's miserable and will be home soonish."
Katy's smile tells more than her lack of words. "Did you do
that? Did you text him to give me an update?"

Her jaw drops, and she places her hand over her heart.
"Would I do that?"

"You absolutely would."

"Okay, yeah, I did. But don't you feel better?"

"Fuck, of course, I feel better."

Lainey: Love you too, Baby. Get home safe.

"Can you stop chugging wine and peanut butter now?"

I look at the bottle still in my hand and my abandoned
spoon in the bowl of chocolate chips. "Do I have to?"

⮂ ⮂ ⮂ ⮂ ⮂

"Jitterbug? Are you sleeping?"

"Hmm?"

"I'm home, beautiful."

"Home?" Sawyer's chuckle tickles the hair around my
neck, and I realize he's here. I roll toward him and almost
fall off the couch.

"Fuck." I must have fallen asleep from all the wine and
sugar. Sawyer catches me before my ass hits the floor and
scoops me into his arms.

"You're home. I missed you." I nuzzle into his neck and
inhale his ocean-fresh scent.

"I'm home, and I missed you too. Did you and Katy have

a fun evening?"

I almost forgot Katy was here. Wait. Katy was here. Date. Sawyer was on a date. I push at his chest and wiggle until he puts me down. I scan him from head to toe, not knowing what I'm looking for. *Does he look different?* I run my hands across his chest and broad shoulders. *He doesn't feel different.*

"What's wrong?"

"Your date. How was your date?"

Pulling me into his chest, he kisses the top of my head. "He spent half the meal talking about how long it's been since he's been with a woman while getting drunk. He was weirdly touchy-feely and rude to our server."

"Nooooo. Well, he's definitely a hard pass." *Why am I happy about that?*

"Exactly. But I'm a little disappointed."

Pulling away, I look into his gray eyes, which sparkle with mischief. "About what?"

"I was promised a naked wife with a slipped butt plug. Instead, I find a passed-out wife with"—his thumb swipes the corner of my lip, and he smells his finger before sucking it into his mouth—"peanut butter smeared on her face."

Tracing the corner of my lip with my tongue, I taste the remnants of my panic snack and feel ashamed. Sawyer grabs my chin and tilts my head to look up at him.

"I talked to Katy. You know you could and *should* have texted me. We're a team, and although the beginning part of this is for me, the end result is for *us*."

"I knew you were nervous and didn't want you to think I was second-guessing my choices."

"*Were* you second-guessing your decision?"

"A little," I confess. It's easier to admit my feelings to him than to myself.

"Alaina. Were you having doubts before I left?"

*Oh fuck.*

I can't lie, but I can't tell him the truth either. Tonight was a level of tough and complicated that I didn't know I would feel. I was, and am still, completely supportive of Sawyer, but until tonight, it was just abstract thoughts. What ifs and maybes. Tonight was real. My husband went on a date... without me... with a man.

"Alaina. You can answer me, and we can discuss it, or we can go into the bedroom, and your body can tell me."

A shiver runs down my spine at what his words imply. I don't say a thing. My lack of response *is* my response. I don't have permission to speak. He nods in understanding and releases me.

"Go to the bedroom. I'll give you a few minutes to prepare."

Sawyer turns his back on me, and I quickly rush to our room. I know I'm in for a rollercoaster of emotions, but my body needs the purge. I wasn't open with him about how I was feeling. I honestly didn't know I was feeling anything about it until the time was upon me. I don't have anyone to blame but myself. I should have been checking in with my mental health.

My affair with Patrick and Chip taught me more self-worth than I knew existed within me. Their affection started my journey to becoming the woman I am today. Sawyer is as thankful to them as I am.

Sawyer opened me to a world where I can feel and release my emotions in a healthy but controlled way. He knows how far I can be pushed and where my limits lie.

As I walk into the bedroom, I strip to my underwear and sit at the end of the bed with my head down and my hands in my lap. I did my research when Sawyer explained what he likes to engage in inside the bedroom. I'm no stranger to different kinks, but the Dom/sub world has its own set of rules, and at the top of them is trust.

Growing up in a household where I couldn't even trust if I'd have a meal to fill my stomach, let alone if the adults in the house even knew I was there, didn't lead me to an adulthood where I could easily trust anyone.

Sawyer saw those broken pieces of me, and through more patience than I knew was possible and many, many exercises of trust, he's earned every ounce that I have to give.

We learned early on that kneeling on the ground is too vulnerable for me. I understand that there is a level of respect for your Dominant partner being above you, and the compromise was sitting on the bed with my head down. I'm allowed to keep my underwear on so I can feel and freely give to Sawyer the last pieces of modestness before I'm fully naked.

Do I still need these accommodations/safeguards to feel safe and trusting of him after all these years? No. But having the routine helps us strengthen the respect we have for each other and reminds us how far we've come as a couple.

The bedroom door opens, and my heart rate spikes. The steady beat strums in my ears, and I close my eyes to try and lower it. With my eyes closed, my ears intently listen to Sawyer as he wanders around the room. He takes off his clothes, assumingly leaving on only his boxers per usual. I can smell him as he moves around, and the anticipation of knowing but not knowing what's to come has my nipples hardening.

His presence surrounds me as he stops before me. I hold my breath. Waiting. Wanting. Wondering.

Sawyer's fingers brush across my collarbone, and the simple feather touch lights up my body.

"Alaina, tell me why we're here."

"I was hiding my feelings, Sir."

"Good girl." I'm rewarded by a swipe of my nipple, and my breath hitches. "Since your eyes are already closed, we're going to keep it that way, and I'm going to blindfold you. Do I have your permission?"

"You do."

"Thank you, Alaina." My name sounds like silk on his lips, and that's exactly what I feel as the cool material wraps around my head. He ties the knot and kisses my forehead. "Do you need a pleasurable punishment or a painful one?"

If we were in a true scene, I wouldn't get these options, but we're here to serve a purpose. I'm struggling to voice my feelings on a critical subject. So, do I want to be edged or spanked?

"Pain," I whisper. I need to be reminded this is my safe space and I can talk to Sawyer about anything.

His stubble grazes my cheek, and I hold my breath. "I'll take care of you, Bug. I love you." He quickly moves away, and I bite my cheeks to keep in my smile as I fall in love with him all over again.

"Would you like to try your answer again, Alaina?"

*Shit.* "Pain, Sir."

"Much better. Bend over the bed."

I stand to spin and lie flat on the bed, but I have to catch my balance. I stood too fast for the amount of alcohol I had tonight. Sawyer grabs my waist with one hand and lifts my blindfold with the other.

"How much have you drank tonight? I saw the empty wine bottle, but Katy was here, so I assumed you shared."

There's a storm brewing in his eyes, and I have to answer him correctly, or he'll put me to bed right now and leave me wanting.

"What time is it?"

He looks at the clock and back at me. "A quarter to twelve."

Almost midnight. Let me math a second. He left at eight, and I opened the bottle shortly after. The last time I remember seeing the clock, it was around ten-thirty, and the bottle was empty. I know Katy helped, but I drank most of it myself.

"Jitterbug, punishment or not, we can't play if you're drunk."

"I know. The bottle was opened a little after eight, and I haven't had a drink in over two hours, but I did drink most of the bottle myself."

"Did you eat?"

"Peanut butter dipped in chocolate chips."

Sawyer's forehead drops to mine, and he sighs. "You have me stuck between a rock and a hard place. My need to punish you is warring with my need to nurture you right now, and I don't like it."

"I'm sorry." I caress his cheek, and he leans into my hand. "Make love to me, and I'll tell you how I feel while we do."

"That's not a solution, Lainey."

"No. It's a compromise." I bring my hands to his chest and pepper gentle kisses along his collarbone. "Please, Sawyer." I trail my hands and kisses down his body and sit back on the bed. "Please." His hard cock tents his boxer briefs, and I easily pull him out and lick his tip.

A low groan rumbles through his chest as I take him into my mouth, and his hands find my hair.

"Alaina, this is a form of coercion."

"Mmhmm."

"Fuck," Sawyer hisses through his teeth, feeling the vibrations of my response.

I love giving him head, but it's usually a reward for me since the act gives up the control he enjoys possessing. There's no haste or rush to my movements. I'm enjoying his body's response to my mouth on him. When his hips start to rock in time with my mouth, I know he's going to give me what I want.

"Fuck, you're a temptress. Get up here." With a handful of my hair, he tugs, and I slide up his body. "You can't tell me how you're feeling with my cock in your mouth, Jitterbug."

"Well, then put it somewhere it isn't so enticing."

Sawyer growls and pushes me onto the bed. I scoot to the top of the headboard, and he crawls after me.

"You're in trouble, Jitterbug. Prepare to talk."

# 8

# Elliot

"Uncle Elliot!" Tori screams out the window as Wynnie pulls up to the arrival curb at the airport. I step out the sliding doors, and Tori jumps out of the front seat, wraps her arms around me, and quickly gets in the back of the SUV.

I lean against the door frame and give my best friend a big smile. "Hey there, beautiful, can I hitch a ride with you?"

"Get your ass in here before the evil-looking woman in the yellow vest blows her whistle at us."

I look over my shoulder as the woman in question holds my stare with her whistle hovering inches from her mouth. I wink and quickly slide into the front seat. Wynnie is driving away before my door is even closed.

"I hate airports. I hate even more that they are going to become a necessary part of our friendship."

"Don't spew that curse word at me, woman."

"What?"

"*Friendship*. I'm your family. Your bestie. Your soulmate."

Wynnie reaches out and pokes at my head. I duck and swat her hand away, giving her a critical look.

"What are you doing?"

"Trying to see how your head fit through my door with as big as it is."

Her finger creeps towards me again, and I grab her wrist and direct her hand back to the steering wheel. "Keep away from me, crazy lady. Two hands on the wheel. There's precious cargo in here."

"Thank you, Uncle El?"

"Oh, and Tori is in here too."

"Uncle Elliot!" Tori screeches behind me.

"Okay, fine. Wynnie, no one wants to die in a fiery blaze of a car crash, so please leave both hands on the wheel."

Wynnie doesn't respond to my comment, but her knuckles turn white against the wheel.

"Hey, relax. I have to be able to laugh about it a little."

I love my best friend for considering my emotions. While my dad didn't die in a fiery blaze, it was still a car crash, and even bringing up something similar to it makes her cautious.

"I know. I'm sorry."

"So, where are you taking me?"

Wynnie is suspiciously quiet, and I already know what that means. I spin in my seat and face Tori.

"Spill it, Tater tot." She purses her lips, and her eyes dart to Wynnie's in the rearview.

Wynnie huffs, "Tell him."

"Everyone is at my grandparent's house."

"Who's everyone?"

"*Everyone*," Wynnie says with an eye roll. "You would think you've been gone for years and not weeks. You were away

56

for longer periods at college."

"Yes, but I wasn't eleven hours away then. How many times did Mom randomly pop up at my dorm? And don't be jealous that I'm clearly the favorite."

"Shit." Wynnie rolls down my window, and I'm really beginning to wonder if my best friend is losing it.

"What are you doing?"

"Making more room. I think your head is expanding."

I smack her thigh and cross my arms. "You're such a bitch. Why do I keep you around?"

"Because I make cute kids that worship you and make your head even bigger."

Tori giggles from the back seat, and I give her the stink eye.

"I've changed my mind. I don't need this abuse. Turn the car around."

"No can do, buddy. I'm under strict instructions to bring you to my mom's. You're welcome to jump, but you're too pretty to potentially mess up your face, so I think it's a safe bet you'll stay put."

"Grr, I hate you."

"I love you too, El."

Pulling up to the house, I stare out the windshield in shock.

"Woman, are you serious? Now I really hate you. Look at all these cars."

"The guys all went to an auction, and with Dean, Paige, and Alex being close to driving age, they bought each of them a car to work on together."

"I'm struggling enough with my little brother driving. Can we not bring my sister into this? It's only been a few weeks, but you're making it feel like years."

At sixteen, my brother Finn has been driving for a year, and although Paige is only thirteen, two years until she can drive really isn't that long.

"I'm going to guess the little yellow thing is for Paige?"

"Nope, that one is Alex's. Red is Dean's."

"Wait. Your brothers picked normal cars... the only other vehicle I don't know here is the lifted black pickup truck."

"Yep," she says, popping the P.

"Wynnie. They bought my sister that monster?"

"Your sister *demanded* that monster. They all went to the auction together. Paige had researched beforehand and knew what vehicles were up for auction. That's what she wanted, and Uncle Collin told Dad and Dad P. it was okay."

"Ugh. I'm going to have to beat the boys away, aren't I?"

"Dean and Alex pretty much have that covered."

"Good. I'm glad my sister has your brothers and mine around to watch out for her." My mom and Aunt Hazel are best friends, and although I was already a teenager when we came to live with my parents, my siblings were younger and grew up with Aunt Hazel's kids. I was the oldest, and Wynnie took me under her wing. I don't think I can ever express to her enough how much it meant to me back then that she took an emotional wreck of a pre-teen and befriended me.

Wynnie pulls into a spot amongst the sea of cars, and I can already hear the ruckus.

"*Shit.*" I duck when a barrage of foam bullets pelt the car. Tori pops up from the back seat and hands me a gun, and Wynnie pulls her own from under her seat.

"Do you always keep a loaded foam gun under your seat, bestie?"

"El, do you forget who my parents and siblings are?"

Tori opens the back door and yells to me before it slams shut. "Adults versus kids! Good luck. You're gonna need it!" She runs across the yard with her gun in hand, and I just stare as she disappears behind the house.

"You knew about this, didn't you? How is this fair? There's like twenty kids here."

"It's actually *un*fair. There are nine adults and only eight kids without Archie. Although Scotty gave him a gun, he doesn't know how to use it yet since he's only two. It's more likely if you see him, he'll throw a bullet or the entire gun at you."

"Is there any getting out of this?" Wynnie gives me a deadpan stare. It was a stupid question—the stupidest.

"So we're on the adult's side?"

"Yeah. They tried to add us to the kid's total, but I figured I'd be nice, so I fought for your honor."

Another several bullets hit the car, and I know it's someone's way of telling us it's time to get out and face the wrath of the children.

"Guess I'm not having a relaxing welcome home. Let's go kick some little kids' asses, bestie."

"How? How did we get our asses handed to us so badly?" I swipe the beer in my hand across my forehead, attempting to cool my overheated skin as we sit in the lounge chairs around the pool. The kids are still playing, but the adults have all tapped out.

"One word. Finn. He's created his own little army of sharpshooters, and Tori is his second in command."

"Of course." I'm not surprised to hear that Finn and Tori

have joined forces. She's always been sneaky and loves to play Finn at his own game when it comes to anything competitive. Finn getting Tori on his side would make them unstoppable.

"How's my favorite college graduate, now living in the big city boy?" I quickly move my feet as my mom sits on the end of my lounge chair. She leans forward and wraps her arms around me. I love hugs from my mom, and I feel a prickle in my eyes. I had no idea I missed this so much.

"Hey, Mom," I choke out before I clear my throat. She releases me but keeps a hand on my forearm. "I'm good. It's different, but I'm enjoying my job."

"We're so proud of you. Even if you're just making coffee for your CEO boss. Every foot in the door is a step in the right direction." Her hand squeezes my arm, and I couldn't be more appreciative of her. One day, she was a motherless woman with a husband, and the next, she had three traumatized kids, and she never batted an eye.

"I'm doing more than just making coffee. I deliver mail around the building, handle her schedule, and make appointments. I'm learning a lot."

Mom brushes her thumb across my cheek. "We're so proud of you." I smile at her sincerity, but it's short-lived. "But I miss the shit out of you." She pinches my cheek, and I swat her hand away.

"Mom," I whine and hear Wynnie giggling next to me.

"Your dad wanted me to see if you're coming to the house." She turns to Wynnie and smiles. "We offered to take Tori and Ella tonight, so Scotty would only have Archie if you wanted to come over. The two of you can spend the night in the garage apartment."

Wynnie jumps from her seat and kisses my mom's cheek.

"Aunt Dellah, you've always been my favorite. I'm gonna go find my husband and kids and say goodbye."

"Grab the tequila," I yell as she runs off. "You really are the best mom. You didn't have to do all this so Wynnie and I could hang out."

"You seem to forget that her mom is my best friend, and I value every minute of solo bestie time I can get. I can give this to you both, and it's not a hardship for me or your dad. Besides, Paige loves Tori, so it's really only watching Ella. Popcorn and an animated movie, and we won't even know she's there. It's a win-win because Archie will be in bed early, and Scotty can have a relaxing evening alone, too."

"Thank you, Mom."

"I'll make hangover pancakes in the morning. Come over when you're awake."

She kisses my cheek and walks back towards the house. Finn appears by my side as I sip my beer and wait for Wynnie to return.

"Hey, big brother."

"Hey, little brother. How is it being the big man in the house?"

"You've been gone for four years. I've been the oldest kid for a while." I tilt my head, waiting for him to finish what he really wants to say. "Okay, fine. It's kinda cool. Since you have your own place now, it's really official that you don't live there. Mom and Dad are getting used to not making extra food to freeze and bring to you at college."

I smirk at the memory of my mom showing up on my doorstep with freezer bags stuffed to the brim. She was always worried I'd starve or live off energy drinks if left to my own devices. When she had more people to feed than just her and Dad, she quickly realized that filling bellies was one of her love languages. Mom and Paige have taken many cooking classes together, and it's been a great bonding experience for them.

"I'm honestly surprised she hasn't figured out how to send me frozen meals in Chicago." He smiles, but it's strained. "What's up, Finny?"

He rubs the back of his head and looks uneasy. "How is it? Being places they've been. Looking at his plaque every day you walk into work."

Our mother died just after giving birth to Paige. Finn was only three and has admitted to me, he isn't sure if he really remembers her or if the images he has are just memories of pictures he's seen. He was seven when our dad died in a car accident, and I know he remembers him.

"Honestly, I try not to think about it too much. I say hi to him every morning when I walk by the fountain where the plaque is. I've driven past our old house. They've painted the brick white, which was actually comforting to see."

"How was it comforting?"

"Because it made me feel like the house had new life. Like the ghosts of our parents aren't hanging around being sad. Being back there makes me miss you and Paige a lot, though. You guys have to come and visit soon. It's only a two-hour flight." He perks up at the idea, taking some of the weight off my chest.

"I'd like that. I don't remember a lot, but maybe we could visit the aquarium and the big metal bean thing. I remember those places."

"I'd love that, Finny. You know you can call me anytime. I

may have a big boy job now, but I'm still your big brother, and my boss knows how much my family means to me." I see his lip quiver, and I feel the same emotions. Grabbing his shoulders, I pull him in for a hug. He firmly wraps his arms around me and sighs.

"I haven't wanted to bother you, but I'll reach out more. I really miss you. It was different when you were only an hour away. Even though I didn't visit you much in college, I knew you were close and could if I wanted or needed to. You're so far away now."

"Two hours by plane. That's it. And I'll pay anytime you want to come." Annie set up trust funds for all of us after she learned that our father died in her accident, leaving us orphans. Mom and Dad are in charge of the accounts until we turn eighteen. At that time, we get a small monthly stipend until the age of twenty-one or when we graduate from college. Whichever comes first. I was still in college when I turned twenty-one, but it had already been ingrained in me how to be responsible with the money. Finn has another two years before he can access his money without asking, but I know if he told them he wanted to visit me, his tickets would be paid for.

"Okay, I will."

I sit back from our hug and hold his shoulders so he can look at me. "I'm serious. Any time."

# 9

# Sawyer

This is the fourth bum date. I'm beginning to wonder if these guys are actually reading my profile or just swiping on a hot guy. This guy looks like he's just here for a free meal, and honestly, I'm happy he's stuffing his face and giving me a reprieve from his constant talking. Either he likes to hear his own voice, or he feels like he needs to fill the void of silence with mindless chatter.

I pick up my napkin from my lap and dab at the corner of my mouth. "I'm going to use the bathroom. I'll be right back." He barely looks up from his plate to acknowledge me before shoving the next forkful of mashed potatoes in his mouth.

This is the fourth date and my fourth time at Midnight Moonshine in as many weeks. I walk through the club doors once again, telling myself these bathrooms are closer, but in reality, I'm scanning the dancefloor for the bright blue eyes I ran into the first night I was here.

I realize I'm being pathetic coming here week after week

with different men, hoping to run into a random guy with whom I had a three-second conversation, but I can't get him out of my head and it's not doing any harm. The guys always love the idea of having our date here when I suggest it, and the last time I was here, we even made it out onto the dance floor. Unfortunately, he didn't understand that no means no and tried getting too handsy with me in the parking lot.

I sigh as I finish washing my hands in the bathroom, and no mysterious blue-eyed stranger catches me before I can fall. My eyes scan the bar area and the dance floor before I head back inside the restaurant to my glutinous date. I'm done with this evening. As I approach our table, I find it empty. Did he go to the bathroom?

Ava, my favorite hostess, comes over to the table, looking a little uncomfortable.

"Your date wanted me to tell you thank you for the meal, but he had to go."

"Oh, thank god." I flop into my seat and look at the massacre he made of his ribs.

"I thought you looked a little miserable over here."

"He ate half the menu. At least one of us left here happy."

Ava gives me a sympathetic smile. "You'll find a good one soon. I have a feeling. Did you want anything else, or should I send your server back with the bill?"

"I'll have another beer and the bill if you'll be so kind as to pass along the message, please. Thank you, Ava."

"Any time, Wes."

I need to blow off some steam. This dating thing is harder than I expected it to be. At least this date ended early for a weekday. My coffee shop is self-sufficient, and I rarely go in anymore, but I think I'll go in the morning and get the inventory started early. I need something to do with my hands.

⬚ ⬚ ⬚ ⬚ ⬚

"Hello?"

"It's me, Gus. I'm in the stock room." Gus, my manager, looks at me questioningly when he reaches the stockroom. He's been working here for over four years and runs the place for me. He started when he was in college and needed some spending money but quickly became a full-time employee when college didn't work out. His large frame with dark hair and eyes make him look intimidating, but as soon as he opens his mouth, you know he's just a big teddy bear.

"Did I know there was inventory today? I would have come in earlier to help you."

"You're good. I needed to do some busy work. I have a lot on my mind. Sorry, I should have texted you to let you know I would be here."

"No worries, Boss. It's your store. Do you want any help? I have some time before the pastries get here."

"Nope. I've got it. Do your normal routine and ignore me back here unless you hear a shelf fall on me or something."

"Let's hope that doesn't happen. The boss doesn't like paperwork."

I glance over my shoulder and give him the finger, and he walks away, chuckling to himself.

"I'll take a coffee whenever you get the first pot going." He grunts his response, and it only takes a few minutes before I smell the rich aroma of coffee in the air. A few minutes later, Gus places a mug on the shelf beside me and leaves before I can thank him.

I'm elbow-deep into a shelf counting flavored syrups when I hear Gus talking to someone. It's still too early to be open, and I try to strain my ears to make sure nothing bad is going on. Gus's boisterous laugh rings out, and I go back to counting.

"See you next time, Gus. Thanks as always."

My head hits the shelf above me as I jump at the sound of that voice. I can't get out of the stock room quickly enough to see the person attached to it. When I reach the counter, it's empty, and Gus looks at me with concern.

"You're bleeding."

"What?" I touch my hairline, where I feel the throbbing, and when I pull it back, there's blood. "Oh, shit. I hit my head on a shelf. Who was that?"

"Let me get the first aid kit. Do you need to go to the hospital?"

"Um," I recheck my forehead. It doesn't seem to be bleeding too badly. "I think just a clean-up. You know head wounds always look worse than they are."

I wait until he returns with the first aid kit before I ask him my question again.

"Gus, who was here? I heard you talking to someone."

"Here? Oh. He's a gofer for someone important next door. He asked me a few weeks back if he could occasionally get coffee early since he noticed I'm here around the same time he is. He comes in about once or twice a week. He seems like a good kid."

"He works next door at MAD?"

Gus dabs some gauze on my head, cleaning up the blood.

67

"Yeah, as far as I know."

Well, fuck. That place is enormous. If it's my mystery man, I have no chance of finding him unless I stalk my own coffee shop.

"Do you know his name? He sounded familiar." I don't want Gus to think I'm some weirdo stalker or anything.

"He told it to me the day we met, but we don't ever really talk much. I know what he drinks at this point. Occasionally, he'll order a few extra coffees, but that's usually if he comes in after we're open.

Shit. It doesn't seem like there's any pattern to when he comes in. It would look suspicious if I suddenly started hanging around here.

"This is going to sound weird, but does he have dark hair and bright blue eyes?

Gus' brows scrunch as he looks at me. "Can you see through walls?"

I chuckle, but it's really to cover up the anxiety I'm feeling. "No. I told you his voice sounded familiar. I think it was someone I know, but I didn't catch him in time to see. I was too busy mortally wounding myself."

"I think you'll live," he grumbles.

*I think I might not.* I'm fighting with myself not to run to the office and pull up the camera feed, but fate has already brought him to me twice. We ran into each other in a club, and he frequents my coffee shop. When the timing is right, the universe will bring us together again. Or whatever bullshit I need to tell myself to not be a creepy stalker.

Sawyer: What's your ETA, Jitterbug? I'm feeling frisky.

I have anxious energy now and know exactly how I can release some of it. Lainey said she would stop by and get coffee before work. She looked so peaceful when I got home last night, and I wanted to ruin her sleep, but I know the underlying anxiety she still feels when I go on my dates, and I didn't want to cause her any more stress.

Lainey: Frisky sounds fun. I should be there in 5. Does frisky come with a latte?

Sawyer: Of course. And a happy ending. Hurry your ass up.

Lainey: There better be caramel and whipped cream...

Lainey: In my latte and on my tits later at home when we have a shower to wash away the sticky.

Sawyer: Your wish is my command, Bug.

"Oh, no. I know that smile. I haven't seen it in a while. How long do I have to find my noise-cancelling headphones?"

"About four minutes. Three if she listens and hurries like I told her."

"At least I get a heads up."

He's joking about the noise-cancelling headphones. In our early days, we perfected the art of quiet sex in small spaces. There's a janitor's closet in Lainey's building near the first-floor women's bathroom. We have many fond memories there, and I'm pretty sure my palms have some permanent bite marks from her teeth.

The bell dings above the front door, meaning Gus must have turned it on, and it's close to opening time. Lainey is cutting it close, but I can't say a word when I step out from the back, and she looks fucking edible.

Her sleek black dress hugs every curve of her body with tiny ruffles at her shoulders for sleeves. Her hemline may go down to her knees, but the slit up the side shows her thighs with each step. The bright red heels paired with her red lipstick means I don't get to kiss her, and that makes me both mad and feral at the same time.

She approaches me, and I gently take her hips in my hands and nuzzle my cheek to hers.

"You little brat. You did this on purpose." My voice is thick with my desire.

"Mmhmm."

"Are you wearing any panties?"

"Yes, but I have a feeling I won't be very soon."

"Correct. And you definitely won't be walking out of here with them, either. Office. Now."

Lainey smiles sweetly and says good morning to Gus before leaving for the back. Gus shakes his head and reaches under the counter, turning the music up.

"Have fun, Boss," he snickers while putting on imaginary headphones and bobs his head to a beat.

I step into the office and growl quickly, locking the door.

"You're fucking asking for it, Alaina."

My bratty wife is bent over, hands leaning on my desk, with her dress hiked up over her hips and her ass on full display. The red lace of her thong disappears between her perfectly round ass cheeks, and she's smiling, knowing exactly what she's doing.

I drop to my knees and bite her cheek, formulating a plan that won't be as satisfying for me right now, but the reward will be worth the punishment.

"Touch yourself?"

"What? I thought—"

"Are you questioning me, Alaina?"

"No, Sir." She instantly recognizes the change in our dynamic and complies.

"Turn around and sit on my desk and play with yourself." I unzip my pants and see her eyes drift to what I'm doing. "First one to orgasm gets to be in control tonight."

Her eyes light up. Not because I've pulled my cock out but because of my offer. I don't often offer to give up control. A blow job is enough relinquishment for me, but I know she enjoys the occasions when I allow her to take over. The first time Lainey pegged me was when I realized I truly had an interest in men. Not that enjoying being pegged meant I had to also want to have a man do it, but it was already on my mind. As much as I love the thrill she gets from the experience, I realized there was something missing. Something that I knew could make the experience better.

Her fingers move feverishly around her clit. She lifts them to her mouth and sucks, adding wetness before she returns them back between her legs.

"I want some of that." Taking a step forward, I stop when I'm inches away from her pulsing hand. "Spit."

Lainey's jaw shifts as she gathers saliva in her mouth. She bends forward and allows it to slip past her lips. The warm liquid lands on my cock, and I moan as the lubrication helps with the friction of my pumps.

Her eyes are determined, and although I may look like I'm putting up a good fight, I'm not. I want her to win. My wrist moves furiously, but there's little pressure on my cock, and it won't get me to release.

A surge of desire spikes through me as I watch her

breathing increase and know she's getting close. "Are you going to come for me? Think you can beat me, Alaina?" Her fingers slide vigorously up and down, and her knuckles wrapped around the edge of the desk turn white. "Let me help you."

I abandon my cock and step between her legs, sinking one, then two fingers inside her. My other hand clamps over her mouth, and a moan bursts out when I glide over her G-spot.

"Show me what a good girl you can be, and come for me. Then I want you to get on your knees and make me come. Tick tock. You don't want to be late for work."

Her moans are muffled under my hand. When she leans forward, I move it away and pull her into my chest as her body convulses into me. Moans vibrate into my chest while my fingers inside her draw out her orgasm. My dick aches after hearing her release, and when she can't take anymore and pulls at my wrist, I step back, and she drops to her knees.

Without any instructions, Lainey takes me in her mouth and sucks me to the back of her throat. I shudder as the heat of her mouth engulfs my cock, and I fold over, bracing my hands on the desk. She knows exactly how to handle me. This is my appetizer to whatever she has in mind for tonight.

"Alaina," I hiss her name as teeth graze across my head. Her tongue swirls around in a figure eight before she sucks me back in again. "Finish me," I growl.

A sound that I can only compare to a purr vibrates around my cock before she pops off and rises.

"The fuck?" I grab her neck, and the defiance in her eyes as she stares at me is admirable. "Why did you stop?"

She lifts her thumb and dabs at the corners of her smirking

mouth. "You took too long."

I open my mouth to reprimand her, but her smart watch beeps, warning her that it's time to get to work. My hand slackens but doesn't leave her neck, and her smile widens.

"Love you, Sawyer. Thanks for the morning pick me up." She steps back from my hand, and I let it fall to my side. My cock stands straight up, red and angry from her edging. "Think about me while I'm at work, and I'll reward my good boy tonight."

She gives my erection a firm squeeze and stroke before striding to the door. She's adjusting her dress, ready to leave, but before she grabs the knob, I halt her movement.

"Alaina, stop." She freezes and turns on her heels. I extend my hands and make my demand. "Panties." I need the upper hand back, and as much as I'd love to let her leave with the smug smile she had on her face, I'm in control until tonight.

Her thumbs disappear under her dress, and she slowly skims her red thong down her legs. When she hands them to me, I bring them to my nose and inhale. This is the reason I wanted her to touch herself with them. The smell of her orgasm lingers on the lace. Lainey's eyes glisten as I bring the panties down to my cock and wrap them around my length, giving a few quick tugs.

"Kiss me before you're late to work." She steps into me, flattening my cock between us, and gives me a passionate kiss that pulls me closer to the edge. It won't take me long to come once she leaves, but I might punish myself and wait until tonight.

"I love you. Bye, babe." With one last peck to my lips, she saunters out of my office with an extra pep in her step.

Inhaling a ragged breath, I stick her panties into my front

pocket and begrudgingly tuck my straining cock into my pants. If she's already this sassy now, I'm in trouble tonight.

# 10

# Lainey

There's nothing more empowering than being able to top my Dom husband. I knew exactly how much time I had, and I also knew Sawyer would let me win his little competition. He doesn't often allow me to take charge in the bedroom, but he wouldn't have offered it if he didn't want it for himself. I know it's hard for him to give up control, but everyone needs to every once in a while. Making it a bet still gave him some of the power to make the decision.

I may not be wearing any panties at the moment, but I'm no fool. I quickly walk toward the lobby bathroom to put on my emergency pair. I learned early in my relationship with Sawyer he has a pantie fetish and always keep an extra pair in my purse. I'm rummaging through my eternal pit, only half paying attention to my surroundings, when I find the tiny black g-string. It's not practical, but it's better than nothing and doesn't take up any room in my bag.

Just as I look up to walk into the bathroom, I slam into a

body. My hand jolts from my purse, and the g-string falls at my feet. I quickly bend to pick it up when a hand gets there before me, and I freeze.

*Nononononono.*

This can't be happening. Shiny black shoes. Tailored navy pants against thick muscular thighs. I look up at the person crouching before me and see the gorgeous new guy with a finger out, dangling my very tiny panties at the end.

"Are you missing something, Lainey?"

If my thighs weren't already slick from my orgasm, I might think it was because of my name passing through his lips. I grab the offending underwear from his finger and ball them into my fist, too mortified to do anything but mumble, "Thank you."

"Hey." Crooked fingers drag my chin up to look into ocean-blue eyes, and my lips part at his beauty.

"Mr. McLain. I'm so sorry I—"

"Don't apologize," he says sternly. "And call me Elliot. Please."

My body lights up from the edge in his tone, and I feel like an idiot because all I can do is stare and blink. The corner of his lip twitches, and I wonder if he can see what he's doing to me. No air moves through my lungs as his face leans closer to me. What is he doing?

"Elliot, I'm mar—"

"Married?" He cuts me off and pauses inches from my face. "I know. The rings on your finger are like a flashing 'Stay away' sign."

"Oh." Butterflies swarm in my stomach at the fact he's noticed me enough to pay attention to my rings. Elliot closes the inches between us, grazing my cheek to whisper in my ear.

"Breathe, Lainey." I gasp not realizing I was holding my breath. "Good girl." *Oh fuck.* "I just wanted to say thank you for making this the most memorable moment of my job since I got here." He squeezes the hand holding my g-string, and I swear his lips graze my ear before he pulls away. "Your husband is a lucky man." Elliot pushes a loose strand of hair behind my ear. "Damn fucking lucky." Before the words can fully register, he walks away, and the loss of his body heat sends a shiver down my spine.

"Fuck." I take a few cleansing breaths to get myself under control and speed into the bathroom to put on my panties. I ball up some toilet paper and clean myself as a pang of guilt washes over me because I know there's no chance in hell all this wetness is from my encounter with Sawyer this morning. I can feel how turned on Elliot made me. No man should turn me on except my husband.

I wash my hands and leave the bathroom, settling myself at the front desk. There's no room for guilt when I have an evening to plan with my husband. You did nothing wrong, Lainey.

Today was long. Every time my mind wandered, there was never any telling if it was gray or blue eyes I would see. The guilt I tried to compartmentalize was a nagging itch at the back of my mind that I couldn't reach.

"Baby, I'm home. It smells amazing in here. What are you cooking?"

I step into the kitchen and giggle at the warzone Sawyer

is in. Tomatoes, garlic, a cutting board, and some kind of powder litter the island.

"Sawyer?"

"Huh? Oh, you're home." He pulls an earbud out of his ear and smiles at me. I giggle as I see the splatter of red sauce on his light blue shirt.

"I hope there's more food in the oven than on your shirt."

Sawyer looks down and huffs. He reaches behind him and removes his shirt in the one-armed, sexy way that always makes me melt.

"I made pizza. Margherita pizza, to be exact."

"It smells delicious. How long until it's done?"

"Not long. Would you like a glass of wine while you wait?"

I nod as I step out of my heels and reach behind me to unzip my dress. Sawyer is too busy pouring my glass to notice me stripping. When he turns with my wine, he instantly growls.

"Where did *those* come from?"

I realize my mistake when his gaze zeroes in on the tiny black scrap of fabric between my legs. I meant to take them off before I got home to avoid this very situation. My only saving grace is I'm in charge tonight, and if he decides to punish me for it, he'll have to wait until tomorrow.

"It's my backup pair." My shirtless husband approaches me and stops when our chests are flush. His thumb wraps into the tiny string on my right hip, and he plucks.

"Explain?" His word has a growl of warning, but I won't back down.

"It's your fault. You have a habit of stealing my panties, so I started keeping spares in my purse. I haven't had to use one in a while since you aren't at the coffee shop as often anymore." I run my hands up his chest, and his pecs tighten under my touch.

I hum my approval and lean in, feathering light kisses around my hands.

"Are you trying to distract me from my disapproval of your lack of punishment?"

"You can be disappointed all you want. Feel free to air your grievances when I'm six inches deep in your ass."

I hear him hiss out "fuck" not knowing if it's from my statement or the sting of pain he's feeling from my bite on his nipple. Sawyer winds his finger into my hair. Something I know he restrained himself from doing earlier because he knew I had to go to work.

"Take your cock out." It's hard to miss his growling sigh as he undoes his pants, pushing them down onto his hips before pulling out his hardening cock.

Gently, I graze my fingers up and down his shaft, and his head falls back.

"Did you jerk off into my lacy red panties after I left you wanting this morning?"

"No," he whispers out. I'm stunned by his answer. I thought for sure he would have used them to his advantage.

"Why not?"

"Because my orgasm belongs to you."

I clamp my hand around his cock, and he gasps. "Damn right, it does. When you come, you'll be screaming my name, not holding back your moans because your employees are in the next room. How long until dinner?"

Sawyer looks at the clock on the stove, and I see the timer counting down the last three minutes. "Would you like me to lick you like a lollipop for the next two and a half minutes, or let you be for now?"

"Lollipop."

His hands stay in my hair as I sink to my knees and lick a line up the underside of his cock. My tongue swirls around the tip, and his fingers flex, tugging on my strands. I love how he's holding himself back. His hands aren't pulling my hair, and his hips are still. He's allowing me to do what I offered.

"You're so fucking perfect on your knees, Alaina."

I can't help but smile while I lick and suck along his shaft. I haven't taken in more of him than the head because teasing is the name of this game. His time is dwindling. Just as the timer on the oven beeps, I sheath his entire cock in my mouth and give him one hard, long pull, scraping my teeth along the bulging vein on the underside.

"Fuuuuuuuuuck."

His body constricts when I pop him out of my mouth, and I feel a swell of pride at his already blissed-out look that only two and a half minutes of sucking him off caused. Tonight is going to be so much fun.

While we eat our pizza, I sit beside Sawyer on the couch with my legs draped over his lap, allowing me to touch him everywhere and anywhere I like. Out of nowhere, a wave of guilt from this morning washes over me, and I know I need to confess my feelings to him before we go any further tonight.

I sit up and move to pull my legs away, but he grabs my thigh, stopping me.

"Where are you going?"

"I want to talk to you about something, and it will be easier if you aren't touching me."

Sawyer sits up straighter in his seat and eyes me cautiously. "I don't like the sound of this, but I'm listening."

"After I left you this morning, I quickly ran to the bathroom to put on my panties." He growls at the thought of me putting them on after he stole my original pair. Ignoring his possessiveness, which I love so much, I continue. "As I was about to walk into the bathroom, I ran into someone and dropped them on the floor."

His brows scrunch, having no idea where this is going. "O-kay?"

"He's someone I've seen before, and he's very attractive, and my body... *reacte*d to him. He called me a good girl, and I swear I had no control over—"

"Why?"

"Whhhhhy what?"

"What did you do that made him call you a good girl?"

I expect to hear that possessiveness in his tone, but it's not there. He's curious and asking a genuine question.

"Oh, um. Apparently, I wasn't breathing, and he told me to, so when I did, he called me a good girl, but he was speaking in my ear. Like I said, my body just reacted, and I'm not entirely sure because I was already wet from my orgasm, but I'm pretty sure his proximity and his words and the fact that he had my g-string in his hand well..." I stop myself from my rambling string of words because Sawyer is smiling. The opposite of how I expected he would react to my confession.

"You *are* a good girl." He brushes his thumb along my bottom lip, and my mouth falls open in shock.

"What?"

"Alaina Hayes, you're a fucking stunning-looking woman. I expect other men to see it, too. But the fact that your body

81

reacted to another man who wasn't me gives me hope."

"Hope?" Can I say more than one-word answers?

"Yes, hope, Jitterbug. One of my worries with adding to our relationship was that *you* would feel like it was cheating." His finger trails down my neck, over my collarbone, and down to my nipple, where he swirls it over my hard tip. "Your reaction to another man means your mind is open to it.

"I..."

"Shhh. Would you ever consider doing anything with someone *without* my approval?"

I pop up onto my knees and grab his arm, half panicking. "No! God, no. Absolutely not."

"Lainey. Relax." Sawyer pulls me over to straddle his lap and squeezes my hips in reassurance. "I know, Jitterbug. I know you wouldn't. And *you* know you wouldn't. Thank you for telling me what happened."

I couldn't have predicted his absolute acceptance of my feelings. This is why Sawyer and I mesh together so well. He understands me at such a fundamental level, and it's like he's always been a part of me.

Taking his face in my hands, I kiss him. It's fierce and brutal, and we're both panting when I pull away. I press my forehead to his and lock eyes with him. The gray is barely visible to the black of his pupils.

"Sawyer?"

"Yeah, Jitterbug?"

"Bedroom. *Now.*"

I slide off his legs as he mumbles, "Oh, shit," and hastily disappears down the hallway. I take my time cleaning the kitchen, and when I finally make my way into the bedroom, my very gorgeous and very naked husband kneels at the bottom of the bed, waiting for me.

My hands run through the short waves of his hair when I pass him to go to the closet so I can prepare myself. Fond memories of our relationship pass through my mind as I strap on the harness and make sure it's secure. The love. The trust. The acceptance. All things that took time but are solid between us because we nourished and watched each piece grow and bloom.

Sawyer hasn't moved when I finish and step out of the closet. He's the perfect fake sub. I say fake because I know every nerve in his body is vibrating with need to get up and turn the tables, but he won't. He's dedicated and respects the power in a scene. He's offering himself to me, but I need to strip him down emotionally to find out why.

I approach him, and his chest rises and falls in a slow, controlled intake of breath.

"Safeword."

"Apple."

"Very good. Suck." I push my hips forward, and he lifts his head and opens his mouth. It's erotic to see his lips stretch around the black silicone dildo. This one is specifically for him. We shopped together to find what he was comfortable with when he first decided he wanted to show me his trust.

Sawyer sucks and licks around the cock until I pull back. "I want to see you. Get on your back. Knees up." He hesitates. I see the vulnerability on his face and cup his cheek in my hands. "Sawyer, I want you to talk to me. I know something is going on, but I'll give you the choice. If you want to talk, lay on your back; if you don't, bend over the bed, and I'll take you from behind."

83

Backing away, I turn around so he can make his decision without me feeling like I'm influencing it. The bed rustles behind me as he gets situated with his decision.

"I'm ready, Alaina." I know when I turn around, he'll be on his back. Open communication has always been as important in our relationship as the trust we give each other when we step into this room.

"You're so fucking beautiful, Sawyer." He's waiting, legs spread apart and propped at the edge of the bed, exposing himself fully and utterly vulnerable to me.

Stepping between his legs, my hands roam up his body, and I lay on top of him to reach his lips.

"Thank you."

His smile is radiant as I lean in to take the last sweet kiss between us before I defile his body for our pleasure.

Standing, I grab the lube from the nightstand and rub a generous amount onto the dildo and between Sawyer's cheeks. He instinctively grabs the back of his knees to give me better access, and I know he's more ready to unburden his mind than I thought.

I line up and take my time, slowly slipping into him. Sawyer closes his eyes and keeps his breathing even. The only indication of any discomfort is the slight twitch of his brows.

# 11

# Sawyer

Lainey is all power and love as she sinks into my ass. I prepared myself earlier by wearing a butt plug. We don't do this often, but I wanted it to go smoothly, and I know she hates the thought of me being in pain.

I concentrate on breathing and the thought that the pleasure comes quickly after the initial pain. I can do this for her. For me.

"You're doing so good, Baby," she croons. I had no idea I liked to hear her praise until the first time I let her enter me. It's natural for her to give words of affirmation in her everyday life, and it's spilled its way into the bedroom and our sex any time we aren't in a scene.

When she's fully inside, she pauses to look at our connection. I understand what she's seeing. It's incredible to see what someone's body can do. How it can stretch and mold to fit another's body.

A low moan escapes me as she pulls out and slowly sinks back in. She's watching my ass, but I'm watching her. She's fucking incredible. My heart almost leaps out of my chest, taking all my air with it when she looks up and locks eyes with me. There's a raw vulnerability in her expression. I know Meghan was abused mentally as much as physically as a child. Meghan is the woman who derives pleasure from the dominance she has right now. The control a position like this allows her to take from her emotions. But there's a downside to a scene like this as well. A downside that Lainey will have to deal with when she comes down from the adrenaline and lust. Her after will have to rationalize and deal with her before, and I'll help her. I'm always here to help her.

"Alaina," I grunt. The first snap of her hips catches me off guard, and her lip twitches at my reaction. I want to rub the smug smile off her face, but I'm not the one in charge. She is.

A warm hand slides up my chest and lands around my neck. I see her pupils dilate at the thought of squeezing. She liked the occasional breath play but has never tried it with me. All she would have to do is ask, but she's not there yet. I'll always go at her pace.

"Talk to me."

I blink several times as she looks down on me. Her question is so vague I can't even focus my mind to pinpoint a single statement to give her.

"Why do I have a dick in your ass, Sawyer? What's troubling your mind?"

I close my eyes. Now, she's asked a specific enough question that the negative thoughts take root.

"I'm... not good enough."

Her hips pause, and the hand around my neck brushes my

cheek.

"Say that again."

"I'm not good enough."

A noise rings out, and my cheek stings before I can even comprehend she's slapped me. Lainey's eyes are full of fire as she dares me to protest. She's never slapped me before. I know it's something that she likes. Her father would slap her across the cheek for the most minor infractions as a child, but as an adult, a slap gives her power.

"Say. That. Again," she seethes. Each word is slow and calculated.

Will she slap me again if I do?

"I'm not good enough."

*Slap.*

She hits me harder than the first time. Knowing it was coming doesn't make it any easier.

"Why?"

*Fuck.* For so many reasons. Why now? Because I feel like I'm failing her. She's expecting me to find us our perfect third. After hundreds of swipes and four failed dates, I'm not even close to finding someone for me, let alone someone halfway good enough to meet her.

"I can't do it."

Her eyes scrunch, and her head tilts. "Do what?"

"Find someone for you. No one is good enough. I'm not good enough."

*Smack.*

Fuck, that stung. I didn't predict that one. Tears well at the corner of my eyes from the intensity.

Lainey's petite hand wraps around my jaw, and she bites my bottom lip before sucking it in and controlling our kiss.

As quickly as she kissed me, she stands, pushing on my thighs, bending me in half.

Fire rages in her eyes, and she pumps her hips into my ass. She's furious. I can tell by the scowl turning down the corner of her lips and the blanch of my skin under her white knuckles. I know I'll have fingertip bruises when she's done with me.

She pauses and stares at me. "You're supposed to be doing this for you, not me." She resumes her punishing thrusts, and her words cut me deep. "You're the only one that's perfect for me. Take me out of the equation, Sawyer. That's why you feel like it's not working. This is *your* bucket list."

My cock swells more with each thrust, and pre-cum coats my abs. She's right, and I know it. I needed her to remind me; this is the only way my mind would allow it. Self-doubt isn't something I naturally have, but when it comes to Alaina, I want perfection, and dating hasn't been going well.

"You're fucking amazing, Sawyer, and when you find someone that's right for you, he'll be right for me."

Lainey leans back over me and stops inches from me to stare into my eyes. "And if you don't, that's okay too. But"—she snaps her hips hard, making me gasp—"you better find a bottom because this ass is mine and only mine unless you get my permission. Understood?"

"Yes, ma'am. Only yours."

"Good." She stands and steps back. Her fingers fiddle with the buckle on the harness.

"What are you doing?"

"I'm done being in charge. Fuck me to sleep, and then wake me up and fuck me some more."

I growl as I sit up and pull her close to me so I can get the harness off her and my cock into her quicker. She knew I had something on my mind, and together, we worked it out. Now she's done and doesn't want to play anymore.

"I fucking love you, Alaina." I stand, towering over her, and grab her hips. A moment passes through us where she gives up control, and I take it.

"I love you, Sawyer."

"Now get your ass on the bed. I want you on all fours, and you're getting two smacks for everyone that you gave me." I squeeze her neck and watch the pleasurable fear flash through her eyes. "And if you ever smack me again, it will be three for every one. Do you understand?"

"Yes, Sir."

"Good girl. Ass up. Now."

# 12

# Elliot

No. No.

Hmm. Nope, hates kids.

No. No. *No way.*

Oh, who are you? Good looking, likes animals, *oh*. He's hatfishing. Eight pictures in and he takes the hat off. Why does a hat make a guy look so much sexier?

"Uuuuugh. This is impossible."

Am I too picky? I have to have a standard, right?

Gah! I need a pick-me-up. I scroll through my call log, trying to decide who I should call.

"Hey, Elliot. How's it going?"

"Uncle Phoenix. I'm drowning."

"Drowning? In?"

"In dating app hell. Help me."

His laugh, even if it's at my expense, is comforting. It reminds me of home.

"I'm not sure how I can help you. I fell in love with my best friend. And considering my *other* best friend already fell in love with *your* best friend, I don't see that helping you either."

"Why do Wynnie and Scotty have to be so adorably perfect? Think they'd mind a third?"

"Ellio—"

"Don't. Yeah, I heard it too. Gross. Let's blame it on temporary insanity and never speak about it again."

I hear rustling on the line, and another voice joins the conversation.

"Elliot, why does Phoenix look like that? What did you say?"

"Trust me, it's not worth repeating. How are you, Uncle J? I miss everyone."

"We miss you too, kid. Two nights wasn't enough time to see you. Seriously, what did you say to Phoenix?"

I sigh because I know Jude's curious nature won't allow him to stop asking until he knows. "I was complaining I was lonely and joked, asking if Wynnie and Scotty would want a third." Silence. "See, I told you it wasn't worth mentioning. Are you both broken now? Have I mortified myself enough for a lifetime?"

"Don't ever mention anything like that to Mac. Even after well over a decade together, I'm not convinced he couldn't make a body disappear, and I like you, kid."

"Got it." My police officer uncle is not someone to be messed with on a good day, but mess with any of his kids, and I have no doubt he'd make you disappear.

"So are you having man problems? Woman problems? What's up?"

Besides Wynnie, Jude and Phoenix were the first ones I came out to in high school. Everyone already knew, of course. And if I'm being honest, I think I knew I was only hiding from myself. I grew up surrounded by people in a polyamorous relationship who I knew would never judge me for my sexual preferences, but as a teenage boy, I was scared. I had already been through enough life-altering experiences. Feeling rejected wasn't something I wanted to add to my list.

"Dating problems in general. I never realized how much I would hate not having my siblings around. Making friends here has been tough, and the dating scene is intimidating. I know I grew up here, but my puberty years were spent in a small town. I feel like a small fish in a big pond."

"Because you are, and that's not a bad thing." Glad to hear Phoenix's shock has worn off. "When you came out to us, you thought you only wanted to be with men, but then you went to college and realized you liked both men and women. You were able to stretch your wings and discover yourself. Now's your chance to do that again."

"But I liked my little bestie nest with my nieces and nephews and obnoxious cousins and siblings." I'm being so whiny, but the trip back home, which I had hoped would help, only made me more homesick.

"Elliot, you're a social butterfly. You haven't made any friends?" Jude questions.

My mind wanders to the very tiny panties I had in my hand and the way Lainey's nipples hardened when I leaned into her ear. I know I shouldn't pine after the married receptionist, and it makes me feel a little icky to think about, but it's just thoughts. It's like wanting a sugary dessert when you're on a diet. Tempting, but you know you can't have it.

"I haven't tried very hard. It's easier to live in my self-pity

92

bubble. The online dating sites haven't been very appealing in their selections either."

"Alright, kid, I have homework for you."

"Nooo. I called Uncle Phoenix, not Mr. Graves."

"It's a good thing they are one in the same. Find someone in your ginormous building and have coffee with them. Or what about your boss's husband? Could you ask him out for a drink?"

Could I ask Cole out for a drink? Would that be weird? I'd rather ask the sexy receptionist at the front desk, but she's off-limits. I've seen Blake have coffee in the lobby with several women before. Maybe she'll let me join.

"Fine. I'll find someone to have coffee with."

"Good. Now go be a twenty-something guy and find some trouble to get into. You're too good sometimes. We love you, kid."

"Love you, El."

"Love you guys, too. Thanks."

I feel a little more refreshed after our conversation, but now the nerves of having to make friends settle in my stomach. Wynnie and I have such an easy relationship, and my college roommate and I became friends because of our proximity. Making friends as an adult is hard.

☺ ☺ ☺ ☺ ☺

Today, I'm going to ask Blake if I can join her coffee date. I know she has them several times a week, and she's invited me before, but I always decline because I figure she's only asking to be polite. Not today.

The office is quiet as I step off the elevator. The sun is

barely up, so I don't need to shield my eyes from the glare of the white marble. Not being blinded when I walk off the elevator took some time to get used to.

I'm usually the first one in the office. My parents taught me the importance of work ethic, and while being the first in isn't necessary, I like knowing I have everything together before anyone else shows up.

I'm checking Annie's schedule on the computer when I hear a commotion from the other side of Annie's door. My desk sits in an alcove across from her office. It gives me a bit of privacy, but I'm still easily accessible to her and anyone who comes for appointments.

Standing quickly, I rush to Annie's door but pause before my hand grips the doorknob.

Is that?

*Oh shit.* That's not commotion. That's...moaning.

I take a step back and look in all directions. My mind is misfiring, trying to figure out what I should do.

*"Fuck, Danika. Fuck."*

Fuck is right. Blake moans in pleasure, and I freeze at the ear porn. This is wrong. So fucking wrong. I need to walk away, but holy fuck does it sound hot.

Taking a step back toward the door, I can hear more than just Blake moaning. I assume the other female is Annie, but it's muffled, and my imagination whirls with reasons why.

*Walk, the fuck, away, Elliot.*

If there was an Angel and a Devil on my shoulder right now, the Devil would be having a dance party, and the Angel would be trying to beat it over the head with a frying pan.

This is so wrong.

*"Danika. May I come. Pleeeeeeease may I come?"*

94

Blake is asking permission to come? I've heard office rumors about their relationship, but this makes me feel like they may be more than rumors.

*"Not yet, BlakeLynn."*

Fuck, what are you doing, Elliot? Without realizing it, I'm rubbing myself over my pants. I spin on my heels and head toward the elevator.

Coffee. I'll get coffee. Gus will let me in a few minutes early. *Fuck.*

I wait fifteen minutes before I head back to my desk. I'm almost late for work, which isn't me at all. When I step off the elevator again, I shield my eyes and take the calculated steps I know by heart to avoid becoming blind. I nod at the floor receptionist, an elderly woman with spunky grandma vibes, and quietly slink to my desk.

My ears strain the entire way, listening for any rogue moans or groans, but all I hear is the hum of the air conditioner and a copy machine in the distance. I'm sure they're done by now. People are roaming the hallway and starting the workday. But Annie's office and my desk are the only people at the end of this corridor, so they could potentially do whatever they want at any time of the day, and my discretion is the only one they would need.

Fuck. Is this my life now? Listening to my boss and her partners rail each other whenever they want. I'm cool with it, but I might need to get some noise-cancelling headphones if I don't want to sport a tent in my pants. Annie, Blake, and Cole are all fucking gorgeous, and I can't help biology.

Annie's door clicks, and Blake steps out. She sees me, and a bright smile lights up her face.

"Hey, Elliot. Good morning."

"Sounds like it was." Fuck. *Fuckfuckfuckfuck.* Did I really say that out loud? Oh my god, I'm fired. That's it. I'm done. Burying my face in my hands, I feel my ears heating up from embarrassment.

I think I'm imagining things when I hear Blake giggling. There's no way she's laughing at me. I'm sure she's pissed off that I would make such a blatant statement.

"How long have you been here, Elliot?"

"I just got here?" I mumble.

I hear her heels click on the marble floor as she approaches my desk.

"Maybe I should ask a different question. How much did you hear, Elliot?" There's no malice in her voice like I expect. She almost sounds amused, and I take a chance to look up and see a smile on her face.

"I got here about thirty minutes ago. I heard... things. But I signed an NDA. I'd never speak of what I hear or what happens in Annie's office."

Blake raises a hand, stopping my rambling, and I'm grateful because I'm not sure I could have stopped myself.

"Elliot, we trust you. No one steps onto this floor without Annie's full trust. I'm sorry you had to hear that, but I'm also going to say that it probably won't be the last time. With four kids at home, we sometimes sneak away here for some private time." She looks over her shoulder at Annie's closed door, and a blush spreads across her cheeks.

"I'm sorry."

"Please, don't be sorry. You did nothing wrong. Let me make it up to you. Come to lunch with me this afternoon. I'm meeting up with some of the girls, and I bet they can tell you some stories about me that are even more embarrassing and make you feel better." She sweeps her long brown hair over her shoulder, and I see a red mark on the base of her neck.

"Um, you might want to…" I motion to the base of my neck, and her hand shoots up to the spot on hers.

"Dammit, Annie." She moves her hair back and shakes her head. "So, lunch? I happen to have an in with your boss and can get an extension of your lunch break." She rubs the spot on her neck. "And she owes me."

I chuckle because I've envied their relationship since I started, but this just makes me love it even more.

"I was planning to ask if I could join you for your coffee date. My uncles say I need to make friends, and it's usually easier for me to bond with females."

"Well, then it's settled—lunch with the ladies. I'll send out the invites and be back here at 11:45 to get you. Don't worry about Annie. I'm sure you already know she has a lunch meeting."

I do. I had already looked at her schedule before the moaning started.

"You're adorable, Elliot. Whatever you're thinking about, your cheeks just turned pink. See you in a few hours."

I really need to work on my facial expressions and, apparently, my inner monologue. But at least I accomplished what I wanted to—an invite to dine with the ladies and hopefully make some friends.

🙂🙂🙂🙂🙂

"When I tell you living with them was torture, I'm not kidding. They fuck like rabbits. Constantly." Nicole's blonde curls dance around her shoulders. She really could be Cole's twin: same color hair and eyes, only softer features.

"Come on, Nicole. It couldn't have been that bad." Nicole pins Blake down with a deadpan stare for several seconds before they burst into laughter. Lunch has been fun and carefree, and despite my protest, I'm on glass of wine number three.

I've met Nicole several times and seen them have lunch with the brunette beside me, but I haven't officially met Katy until today. She's my age and fucking adorable. I can already tell she has a take-no-shit attitude, but she's fun and playful. I see a lot of myself in her.

"Okay, but from what I understand, none of you have terrible sex lives. How many kids are there between you?" I make a show of counting on my fingers and lift my leg, pretending to take off my shoe so I can count my toes. Katy slaps my arm, and I like her even more.

"There's a dozen. For now." Katy's eyes dart between the other two women, who both have wide eyes.

"Not me." Blake raises her arms in surrender. "My baby factory is closed. My vag is ruined enough."

"Justin is wearing me down. It's hard when he keeps telling me how beautiful the babies we make are."

"I knew it!" Katy exclaims triumphantly.

"Excuse me, youngster," Blake scolds Katy. "You have the snappiest vagina between us with your youthfulness. I expect at least two more nieces or nephews from your baby breeding Viking."

"Excuse me, trophy wife of a bazillionaire. You have the deepest pockets between us. Annie may pay my Viking husband and me very generous salaries, but babies are expensive."

"Pfft." Blake waves her hand, dismissing Katy. "If money is your only excuse, I'll get you a raise in the next hour." Katy's jaw drops, and I get dizzy from the ping-pong of their conversation. This is exactly what I needed—some fantastic girlfriends.

"Speaking of babies, can we hound Lainey instead of the women who have already popped out four." Nice deflection, Katy. And I'm all ears about the delicious receptionist. Are they friends with her, too?

"Who's Lainey," I ask, playing dumb. I'd love to get more info about the woman who haunts my thoughts more often than I want to even admit to myself.

"She's the pretty brunette at the front desk. My best friend from high school." So they do know her, and very well, it would seem.

"Oh yeah. I've seen her." And had dirty thoughts about her. And held her panties in my hand while she practically panted in my ear from our proximity.

"She's great. We invited her today, too, but she said she was skipping lunch so she could leave early."

In unison, which is entirely creepy, they all sigh, "Sawyer."

"Context?"

"Sawyer is her husband," Nicole offers. "They are pretty obsessed with each other, and it's cute in the suffocatingly obnoxious 'makes you want to puke' kind of way. But he's incredible to her, so we have no complaints. We just like to tease her about it."

So, the husband is Sawyer.

"You might have met him before. I know you get coffee from Java Junkie. He's the owner." Blake takes the check from our waitress and hands over a card while I process her words.

"Gus?"

"Who? Oh, no. Gus runs the place most days, but Sawyer owns it."

What a relief. I sigh heavily, not meaning to have such an outward reaction.

"Hmm." What is Blake humming about?

"Do you think?" Nicole questions.

"Maybe." Katy grabs my chin and turns it toward her. "You like guys *and* girls, right?"

"I... um... yes?" I'm so lost. They're all looking at me like a margarita they want to inhale.

"I'll talk to her," Katy states, dropping my chin. They begin talking, and I'm so lost in whatever just happened that I can't keep up with their conversation.

# 13

# Elliot

With newfound friends and a sense of renewed confidence (and alcohol), I'm determined to find someone special... or a date... or a hookup. Hmm.

I'm determined to find someone *other* than my hand.

Okay. That one I can commit to. Maybe I have too much liquid courage.

*Nah.*

On the way back to the office, I questioned Blake about the weird silent conversation the three of them had at lunch, and she promised me it was nothing terrible and that she would let me know if anything came of it.

I settle into my oversize, comfy chair that I love reading in and open the dating app. I have a good feeling. Something is better than nothing. I'm looking for happily for now, not happily ever after.

Okay, that's enough cheesy clichés.

The app loads and the red banner across the top of the

first guy says, "Perfect Match." I wonder why the algorithm says Clint and I would be a perfect match. Non-smoker, within my age range and location proximity, wants kids, occasionally drinks but doesn't do drugs. Likes kids and animals.

We're off to a good start, but there's no way the first one is the best one. Let's look at pictures. He likes cars, I'm good with that. Looks like he has a dog in several pictures.

"My baby Fred," reads the caption on this pic—

"Oh shit!" I throw my phone into my lap like the picture could jump out at me and attack.

It takes several deep breaths to work up the courage to pick the phone up with my thumb and index finger and swipe left without even giving the screen another glance.

Spider.

*Fuck that.* That wasn't a spider. It was a tiny baby-eating monster crawling on Clint's arm. I looked at the caption before the picture because it was the only one with words attached to it.

I can't get involved with someone who actively participates in cuddling with a creature with eight legs. I'm good.

Damn. He did look like a good match for me. Is there a way to eliminate spiders in my profile? I'm cool with a little house spider hanging out in a corner, but that thing has hair and teeth and eyes I could see. *So many eyes.*

My searching continues with an occasional swipe right of potential matches. They don't have to all be perfect. Happily for now.

The bar at the top tells me what percentage each match is based on how compatible we are. I've watched the number go up and down to as low as 83%. I have the lowest set to eighty. I feel comfortable with that number for now, but if I need to, I'll change it.

I'm feeling hopeless again when a pop-up appears on the screen and offers suggestions for matches outside my criteria.

"Great. I've looked at everyone, and I'm being too picky."

Elliot: Tell me I'm pretty and not high maintenance.

Wynnie: I never want to lie to you that big.

Elliot: Bitch.

Wynnie: You're gorgeous and have standards that can sometimes be...picky. But you're worth it.

Elliot: Fine. I'll take that. And you're stunning, and I love you.

Wynnie: Thank you. What's going on? Do you need more text validation?

Elliot: No. Just alcohol and dating app woes.

Wynnie: Ah, the dynamic duo. Don't beat yourself up. You can be as picky as you want, but make sure to give every profile a chance before you swipe. There's a diamond in all that coal.

Elliot: You're getting wise in your old age. Kiss my babies for me. I miss your faces. Thanks for the pep talk, Bestie. Love you.

Wynnie: Anytime. Love you too.

"I can do this." *After I refill my wine glass and get into my PJs.*

With a full glass, my blue flannel pants, and no shirt, I curl back into my chair and throw a blanket over my lap.

Sometimes, I wonder if I should get a cat. Especially when I curl up like this, having a furry companion join me would be nice. Then I remember I sometimes work twelve-hour days, and it seems cruel to leave an animal home alone for that long.

"Let's do this." I click the button to expand my search, and the page reloads.

Brent- Nope, too far.

Zaden- Cute, but as much as I don't mind an age gap, he's closer to my dad's age than mine. While that totally works for Wynnie, I already have daddy issues.

Terry- No.

Allen- Nope.

I'm trying not to be too picky regarding looks, but if there's no initial attraction to draw me in, it feels pointless to look further.

Chris- Potential. He's a little farther than I'd like, but doesn't look bad. He'll get a swipe right, and I'll see what happens.

Sean- Is beardfishing. I can't tell if he does or doesn't have one right now, but when he does have one, he isn't very good at grooming it, and that's a turn-off for me.

Wes- Okay, cutie. Nice beach picture. Tanned and toned. I like it. It says we're 92% compatible. Why didn't you appear in my previous search?

"Oh." I've been looking at pictures first and bio after. Now I see why he didn't pop up.

Wes- 28 -Chicago area

*I like animals, and kids, and long walks on the beach... Yeah. Let's be real. I like all those things, but I'm also a happily married man, and my wife and I are looking to expand our relationship. I'm looking for someone comfortable enough to get to know me first before introducing you to my wife. I realize it's a unique situation, and I'm happy to DM with you for more details.*

*A little about me. I own my own business. Running is a hobby, and I'm addicted to coffee. I'm going to be honest here, I'm a dominant. My wife likes to submit to me in the bedroom, and we have an excellent relationship. The end goal isn't necessarily for you to also take on that role, but it's something that you need to be okay participating in when she's involved.*

*Please don't message me if you have no interest in women because the ultimate goal is to add to our relationship.*

*If you've gotten this far, thanks, and maybe I'll chat with you soon.*

A couple. A *married* couple. Could it be true? I know lots of married men who lie just to get some, and they're actually cheating on their wives.

Besides the fact he could be lying, he openly admitted he's a Dom. That's... I'm usually a top myself. It's not outside my personality to allow my partners to occasionally top me, but it's not what my bedroom activities typically look like. If he's a Dom, he has a strong personality, and we could clash.

*Holy shit, am I actually considering this?*

Yes. Yes, I am because he's hot, and everything else fits what I like in a partner... and I'm probably too tipsy to give this any real consideration. The worst that can happen is we decide we aren't compatible, and I'm out the money for a meal.

*Swipe right.*

Well, that feels like a good way to end my swiping for the night. Wes may not even swipe back, so there's no use overthinking anything for now.

*Buzz Buzz. Buzz Buzz.*

"Five more minutes, Mom. Too much wine."

*Buzz Buzz. Buzz Buzz.*

"Noooooo. Shhhh."

*Buzz Buzz. Buzz Buzz.*

"Okay, I'm up." I roll to my back and slowly blink my eyes open.

*Buzz Buzz. Buzz Buzz.*

What the hell!

Rolling over, I grab my phone and realize I've been added to a group chat that's currently blowing up.

Blake: I already need mimosas. With an S. Plural.

Nicole: I may need a pregnancy test.

Katy: I need some aspirin, and mimosas, and a pregnancy test. I hate your faces. And Uteruses.

Blake: What the actual fuck! I can't take you hornball, baby-popping women. Where's Elliot? I need backup.

Oh hell. Group texts are one thing, but girl group texts are a whole different ball game. I'm in trouble. We exchanged numbers before we left lunch, and everyone in the chat is saved in my phone except one number who hasn't responded.

Blake: Eeeeeeeeelliottttttttt! Come out and play.

It's too early for all the girl talk, but I have a feeling Blake isn't going to leave me alone.

Elliot: It's too early for mimosas, and pregnancy tests, and anything else before nine a.m. for anyone who doesn't have kids. The wine I drank last night says I need eight more hours of sleep.

Blake: And the three shots of espresso I've had already this morning say to get your butt up and come over. ALL OF YOU!

Nicole: Grumble, grumble. Hiss, hiss. Who's stopping for breakfast? And the pharmacy?

Blake: There's already food on the way. I sent Cole out. I can't ask him to stop at the pharmacy, though. He won't believe me if I say it's not for me.

Elliot: I'll stop. It will make me feel like I'm contributing as the non-uterus having member of this chat.

Katy: You're the best, El! See everyone soon.

I shoot up in bed, realizing what I just agreed to—drinking at my boss's house. I need to be on my best behavior.

# 14

# Sawyer

Lainey looks so fucking peaceful and beautiful, curled up on our bed. I had some accounting work to take care of, and she fell asleep while waiting for me. As I crawl into bed, I get a notification that I have a potential match on the dating app. I don't feel like dealing with the next disappointment before bed, so I hit the side button to turn off the screen and curl into my sleeping wife.

I wake before Lainey. My body is still used to the early morning at the coffee shop, but it seems that someone has woken up before me. My rock-hard erection pokes her in the hip, and I'm shocked she's still sleeping.

She looks too fucking delicious, and I decide I need a snack, and she needs an orgasm. Dipping below the blanket, I gently push Lainey onto her back and spread her legs. Her pink panties stare at me in the dim light of the rising sun through the thin blanket. I rub my thumb over the satin material several times, teasing myself more than my still-sleeping wife.

Slow and gentle, I pull her panties to the side and dip my mouth to her core. My tongue is tentative and feather-like as I rouse her body before her mind. Her arousal begins to coat my chin as I strengthen my strokes, and soft whimpers caress her lips.

She's waking.

"Sawyer," my name whispers from her mouth. She's still not entirely awake, and her mind catches up with what her body is enjoying. When hands fist my hair and her hips buck, I know she's awake.

I lift my mouth long enough to say good morning before diving back in and devouring her like I want to. Relentlessly and with the ferocity of a starving man, I feast. Lainey's hands tug, and I have to place a hand across her abdomen to stop her from thrusting off the bed.

She's always the most sensitive when I wake her like this, and it doesn't take long before she's chanting my name and coming. As her orgasm subsides, I lick every last drop before she pushes me away, giggling.

"Mmm. Good morning, Baby. Can I return the favor?" Her smile is sleepy and sated, and I think she'll fall back asleep if I let her.

"It's still early. Go back to sleep. You just looked too tempting, and I had to have a taste." Lainey runs her fingers through my hair and tugs for me to come to. I carefully climb up her body, and we kiss a lazy, passionate good morning.

"Okay. More sleep. Love you." Her eyes stay closed as her head drifts to the side, and sleep succumbs her. With a final kiss to her forehead and a whispered "I love you, too," I head to the bathroom to prepare for the day.

As I pick up my phone from the nightstand, I unlock it to see the notification from the dating app. I might as well check it out and see the latest disappointment.

Sitting on the edge of the tub, I swipe the app open to see a gorgeously handsome man staring back at me. Dark hair, blue eyes, and a young, innocent smile that I instantly want to corrupt…because it's him. I don't even think before my finger swipes right to confirm the match.

It's. Him.

My Midnight Moonshine guy.

The face I've been obsessing over for weeks—the voice in my coffee shop.

My hand drifts to my hairline, where I cut it on the shelf, trying to get to his voice. The universe brought him to me. I realize my hands are shaking as I swipe through his photos. The adrenaline coursing through me from the sheer dumb luck that he found my profile appealing is both scary and elating.

He… not he. Eli. His profile name is Eli. Fuck I could get lost in his blue eyes. A picture of him with his arm around a smiling brunette and several kids with the caption, "Best Uncle Ever" appears. She doesn't look like his sister, but genetics are crazy, so she could be. The next is Eli, with a foam gun in his hand and the most devious smile I've ever seen, and my dick twitches.

I bite my knuckles as I swipe through more pictures. He's obviously a family-oriented man, as several pictures have various kids in them. He's a college graduate based on the picture of him in his cap and gown surrounded by at least a dozen equally happy-looking people.

Eli - 22 - Chicago area

*Does anyone ever really read these things? You saw my cute face and swiped through my pictures, and you're making a snap judgment based on physical looks alone. Be honest. I know I'm hot. You know I'm hot. If that's all you're looking for, please swipe left.*

Damn. I like him already. Funny but straight to the point.

*Life is hard out there, and I'm in a new city. I'm not looking to settle down and have your kids (although that is the ultimate goal) but I'm not looking for a one-night stand either. Beers, trivia, maybe some ax throwing if you have decent aim. Hospital bills are expensive. ;)*

I laugh and quickly cover my mouth to stifle the sound. I don't want to wake up, Lainey.

*If you're still here, you deserve a cookie! If I haven't scared you off yet, swipe right, and let's chat. Oh, and PS: I'm not strictly dickly. Pussies are pretty too.*

Pussies are pretty too.

God, that sounds fucking erotic, and I know it's not.

It's early, but I pull up the messaging box. Since we matched, we can talk. Do I mention crashing into him in the bathroom doorway at Midnight Moonshine? Or that he regularly comes into my coffee shop? No. Definitely not the coffee shop. It will make me sound like a stalker.

My finger taps on the side of my phone as I contemplate what to say. My mind is blank. There isn't an intelligent word forming in my head except for "Hi, I'm Sawyer," except I'm Wes, and that definitely won't work.

Fuck it. I'm going with the truth. If it scares him off, it wasn't meant to be

Hey Eli,

Your profile is impressive, and yes, I read till the end.

111

Where's my cookie? I promise I'm not a crazy stalker (doesn't every crazy stalker say that) but I'm pretty sure I ran into you in the bathroom doorway at the club Midnight Moonshine a while ago. Your blue eyes are hard to forget.

I really promise I'm not a creeper. I hope you read through my entire profile and understand my situation. Any questions you may have, I'm happy to answer.

Have a wonderful day, Eli.

~Wes

Okay, well, that's done. Now I wait to see if he answers. Buck the fuck up, Sawyer. Your message could go nowhere, and if it does, it's fine. I have a beautiful wife, and I'm satisfied with her. The blue-eyed hottie would be an enhancement.

Every minute that passes by without a response feels like an eternity. I'm being foolish, and I know it. It's still early in the morning and a time for regular people to be sleeping. I busy myself with accounting work on my laptop, ordering supplies, and when Lainey appears next to me, I don't even hear her until she taps my shoulder.

"You okay, Baby? You look distracted."

*Do I? I'm not surprised.*

"I just have a lot on my mind." She runs a hand through my hair and massages the nape of my neck.

"Wanna talk about it?"

"I'm good, Jitterbug. I'll let you know if there's anything notable."

She assesses me for several long seconds before conceding to my words with a small smile. I push my laptop to the cushion beside me and pull her into my lap.

"I think I found someone good on the dating site, and I'm

a little anxious to see if he responds. But I was thinking. Do you want a code name?"

Lainey wraps her arms around my shoulders and tilts her head. "Code name?"

"Like how I'm going by Wes."

"You haven't asked me that before, and you've been on several dates. What have you been calling me up to this point?"

"I haven't. If I spoke of you at all, I referred to you as my wife."

"Hmm." Her eyes squint as she stares. I rub circles with my thumbs on her bare thigh as she considers me.

"What?"

"You haven't spoken about me to any of your dates. I come out here, and you look...nervous. Then you tell me you're waiting for a message back on the dating app. You must have found someone interesting. I'm intrigued, but I'll let it go for now. You'll share when you're ready." She places a gentle kiss on my lips and pulls back. "Lane or Meg. I'll let you choose." She giggles, and it lights up my heart. "I like the idea of an alter ego."

Lainey jumps from my lap and starts chopping her hands through the air. She kicks left, then right, making huffing and puffing sounds, does a ridiculous spinning jump, and finally lands with a hee-ya.

"Jitterbug, who are you planning to grace with those smooth moves?"

She plants her hands on her hips, taking big gulps of air from her exertion. "You don't like my mating dance? Should I do it again? Maybe it didn't work the first time."

Before she can hurt herself, I grab her by the waist and

pull her back into my lap again.

"Don't worry. It worked." I wiggle my hips so she can feel my growing erection.

"Too bad you'll have to wait. I need to get ready for work." Lainey slides off my lap before I can protest, and she blows me a kiss while wiggling her hips back toward our bedroom. Teaching yoga classes on Saturday mornings is just as good for me as it is for her.

*Fuck she's stunning.*

"You'll pay for that later."

"I sure hope so."

While I adjust myself in my pants, since she teased me and left me wanting her, my phone buzzes next to me. My eyes dart to the cushion, and I swear my heart skips a beat. Could it be him? It's still early, but I know he's an early bird, at least during the work week.

My hand shakes from adrenaline as I pick up the phone. The notification on the screen tells me I have a new message from Eli.

*Fuck.*

He swiped on you first. He's returning your message. It's a good sign. Relax shithead.

Hey Wes,

Or should I say... Hey, creepy non-stalker? ;)

You earned your cookie. Will you take an IOU? Last I checked, my name isn't Willy Wonka, and I can't materialize one through the internet. I'll work on that for you.

I do have a vague memory of running into a very attractive guy in the bathroom doorway. I'm sorry I don't specifically remember it as you though. I wish I did. After browsing your pictures, I wish I had realized it was you. We could have been talking for weeks.

Speaking of talking, if I could be so bold, I'd like to give you my number. Talking on here can be tedious, and I don't always see the notifications right away.

I have questions; maybe we could meet at Midnight Moonshine sometime soon to discuss? Hope to talk to you soon.

Eli

I read through the message four times before saving his number into my phone. Lainey comes back into the room with a shit-eating grin.

"He messaged back, didn't he?"

Her outfit distracts me from her question. It's skin tight from her crop top sports bra to her leggings. The color is a pale pink and almost makes her look naked.

"Earth to Sawyer," she giggles.

"What? Oh yeah. He did."

"Good. Message him back quickly and set up a date. I haven't seen you look this excited...ever about a match. I can't wait to hear all about it. Love you, Baby."

I stand to kiss her as she leaves our apartment on her way to wiggle her tight ass for her class of about twenty.

Lainey didn't ask to see the message or the match. We decided after the first failed date it's easier not to get her involved with every match. It's like house hunting. Every house you visit, you picture yourself living in and growing old in. You put in a bid, it gets rejected, and you're crushed. Your imaginary future is over before it even starts. So now, to avoid that scenario, I don't tell her anything about the guy until I feel I'm ready to introduce her. Or, like the first many failed dates, when it's over.

Lainey told me to message him back quickly, and I learned a long time ago to listen to women when they talk.

Sawyer/Wes: Hey Eli, it's Sawyer. I'll take the cookie IOU, and I'd love to set up a time to meet and answer your questions.

Hit send, Sawyer.

I scrutinize every word before I—*shit.* I quickly change the text to say Wes instead of Sawyer and hit send before second-guessing myself.

I should have offered a time and place. He offered Midnight Moonshine, but I should have confirmed it was good.

Three little dots dance on the screen, and I'm hyper-aware of every breath I take as I wait for the message to come through.

Eli: Soooo, I mentioned I'm new to town and don't have any friends yet. I'm free tonight if you are. But I don't expect you to be on such short notice. We can plan for next weekend if you have time.

Sawyer/Wes: I happen to also be free tonight... and next weekend. Let's go back to the scene of the crime. How's 7 for you? Dinner first, then maybe the bar or some dancing after?

Eli: It's a date. See you at 7.

# 15

# Elliot

The one time I've been here, I came alone in a desperate attempt to convince myself I could do things without an entourage. I ended up texting Wynnie the entire time and had to take a rideshare home. That's probably why I don't remember the stunning man I'm meeting tonight.

I'm fifteen minutes early entering the restaurant; I want to make a good impression. Walking up to the host stand, I notice a smiling brunette waiting to greet me.

"Good evening. Do you have a reservation?"

"Oh, um. I'm not sure. I'm meeting someone, but I'm early."

Her smile brightens. "Bright blue eyes and handsome. Are you meeting Wes?"

"Uh, yeah, actually. How did you know?"

"He told me who to look out for. Right this way, please."

I nervously follow the hostess toward the back of the restaurant. I thought I was early, getting here fifteen minutes before our date, but apparently, he got here earlier. As we approach the table, I recognize the man from his pictures: dirty blond hair and muscular shoulders. Even sitting, I can tell he's tall. Taller than me.

"Wes, Eli is here," the hostess announces.

When Wes looks up, his gray eyes sparkle as bright as his smile. He stands and extends his hand to shake mine. His grip is firm, and I like that. I can feel the touch of dominance in his hold that he mentioned in his profile.

"Nice to officially meet you, Eli." He releases my hand, and I sit at the table across from him. Wes is dressed casually in a dark green polo shirt and khaki pants. I chose a pale blue cotton button-up because it's light and if we end up dancing, I know I'll get hot.

Looking at him in the dim light of the restaurant sparks deja vu.

"Maybe I do vaguely remember you. This lighting helps." I look up at the ceiling and back at Wes. He seems hopeful by my statement.

"Either way, we're here now. And this might be a better introduction to tell our grandkids than bumping into each other near a urinal." His eyes widen when he realizes what he's said. I momentarily let him stew in his thoughts before allowing my laugh to spill out.

"You should see your face. I'm sorry. I don't mean to laugh at you, but it's priceless." His worried expression melts, and he half-heartedly laughs with me. "Relax, Wes. I knew it was a joke. Besides, we can't discuss grandkids until we discuss kids first. I want at least a dozen."

His laugh pauses, and a look of horror spreads across his face. I have to give him credit for how quickly he can change emotions, but I need to fix this. It seems my humor isn't quite landing right.

Standing, I watch as the emotions play on his face once again, but this time it's worry. He thinks I'm leaving. Sorry, Wes, no such luck. I step to the side, place a hand on his jaw, and lean down and kiss him. He's shocked for a moment before something snaps inside him, and he grabs the collar of my shirt and takes over the kiss. His mouth is soft, but his motions are forceful. Neither of us use tongue, just tangling lips.

With much restraint, I pull back, but his grip on my shirt doesn't allow me to go far. There's a feral look in his eyes as they ping-pong between mine, and he's practically panting.

"As much as I'd love to continue this, we *are* in the middle of a restaurant."

His sharp intake of breath lets me know he had forgotten about our surroundings, and he instantly lets go of my shirt, smoothing a hand over my chest to reduce the wrinkles his fist made.

"Fuck, I'm sorry. That was…"

"Incredible? Sexy? Terrible?" I throw out adjectives as I sit because, once again, his face shows all his emotions, but I can't quite decipher this one.

"No," he says, but I'm not sure it's in response to me.

"Okay, none of the above. So tell me what it was, Wes. I apologize if I completely read the situation wrong and overstepped."

"No," he says again. His hand reaches out across the table and grabs mine.

"That was… my first." My head cocks to the side. *His first.* First what? "My first kiss… with a guy." Oh. *Oh. Ooooh.*

119

His hand squeezes mine in a silent plea not to leave, but I won't. "I have a lot more questions now than I initially came here with."

"Questions are good. I have answers. Lots of answers. And my wife didn't give me a curfew, so I'm all yours." I arch an eyebrow at him, and he returns my gesture with a smirk. "I don't say things I don't mean, Eli."

"Noted, Wes. Now, before you tell me about your wife, it seems I have a lot more to learn about you. I'm all ears."

We spend the next several hours talking and drinking, and eventually make our way into the club and sit at the bar. Wes tells me about the bucket list he made with his wife, Meg, and I grow fonder of her and him as I learn about their dynamic and the love they have for each other.

I apologized for taking a kiss from him that he might not have been ready for, and he brushed it off by kissing me. I'm intrigued by the relationship they have and their desire to add a third. I've never thought about entering into this type of a relationship, but I must say it's appealing.

"So, Eli, what interested you about my profile that made you swipe?"

I'm surprised it took him this long to ask the question. It's usually asked within the first few "getting to know you BS questions" on a first date.

"Your honesty was first. You put it all out there. It was refreshing to not have to play any guessing games. I'll be honest, though, and say I thought maybe your profile was a catfish for someone who just wanted to be sneaky behind his wife's back."

"Do you still feel that way?" I pause for too long while contemplating my answer, and he pulls out his phone. "Give me a word."

"A what?"

"A word. Any word."

"Um." Why is this so much pressure? It's just a word. "Um... butt plug."

Wes bites his lips as he types out a message. It doesn't take long before he spins his phone around, and my mouth goes dry. Wes grins like a kid in a candy store.

A pair of toned legs lay on a navy comforter. Not only is the word 'butt plug' written on a piece of paper, but an actual butt plug sits in the crease of her leg just above her knees.

"Holy shit. Okay, I believe you. There was no way to predict that. And that's Meg?"

"That's my Meg." He turns the phone around and looks lovingly at the picture. "Do you want to—"

"No," I cut him off before he can offer me more pictures of her. "Am I curious after that picture? Hell yes. But to my understanding, this is about you and me first. The two of you seem to have a process, and I don't want to ruin it. Although that's one hell of a tease."

"That she is," he says through a chuckle. "I don't know about a process because this is new for both of us. But you're right; it's about you and me first. And honestly, this is the best first date I've had so far."

He smiles, and I return it. His gray eyes seem to sparkle silver, but there's still reservation behind them.

"What are you thinking? Something is holding you back?"

Wes runs his hand through his blonde hair, and it looks so soft I want to run my fingers through it, too. He blows out a breath before locking eyes with me, and the nervous look is back.

"Does it bother you how inexperienced I am? I feel like a fish out of water, having no clue what I'm doing, but you're making it so easy. Almost too easy."

"Is that a bad thing?"

"Fuck no," he says almost forcefully and immediately backs off. "Sorry. I'm not used to feeling like this. I'm always in control. Nothing I said in my profile was an exaggeration. I... occasionally I give up control in the bedroom to La-Meg." He stumbles over his wife's name, and his eyes flash to mine.

Reaching out, I take his hand. "Wes, it's okay if that's not your actual name or your wife's. Eli isn't mine either, but let's keep it this way for now. Roleplaying is fun, don't you think?" He squeezes my hand and gives me a curt nod. "And as for the other thing. No, it doesn't matter to me. I'm a switch anyway, and I'm happy to teach you... if we get that far. I don't get the impression you're just looking to get your rocks off. You wouldn't have included your wife in your profile or been so detailed about your wants. Does that put your mind at ease at all?"

"Fuck," he hisses. "This is all so foreign to me. Not the guy part, although that's obviously new, but this feeling of... inadequacy? Incompetence? Virginity?" He laughs on the last word, and I nudge his knee with mine.

"You're going to tell me that butt plug in Meg's picture was hers? Because I could have sworn it screamed, 'Take me big boy.'"

Is he blushing? That's fucking adorable. I brush my hand across his cheek, and he closes his eyes.

"That was mine," he confesses.

"I knew it," I whisper, my lips inches from his. Wes' eyes

pop open at my closeness, and they drift down to my lips. I see his Adam's apple bob as he swallows hard. We've already kissed twice tonight, but something feels different in this moment, as if each piece of information we've shared tonight has led to this moment.

I initiated the first kiss and him the second. But this kiss? The kiss, currently lingering on the precipice seems monumental, like it will seal an unspoken fate.

My thumb brushes his jaw, and he makes a decision. I see it in his eyes. Wes closes the distance between us and presses a gentle kiss to my lips. I'm impressed with his lack of concern when it comes to PDA. I've been out long enough that I couldn't care less what others think, but Wes is new to anything with another man. As his tongue brushes my bottom lip, asking for entry, all worries about his modesty fly out the window.

Spreading my legs around his so we can get closer between the bar stools, I part my lips and let his tongue sweep mine. He tastes like the sweet and smoky bourbon he's been sipping on since we moved to the club side, and I wonder how much it's helping him with liquid courage. I can tell he isn't drunk, so I won't concern myself with him making the decision to kiss me in his inebriated state.

Wes places a hand on my thigh as he deepens the kiss, and he moans into my mouth. The vibration on my tongue shoots straight to my cock, and goddamn, was it a sexy sound.

With reluctance, I pull away. "Wes," I whisper as he tries to chase my lips. "Wes, we're in public, Doll."

His eyes flutter open, and he stares back at me with a dreamy look. "Sorry," escapes his lips in a breath, and I smile.

"Don't be sorry. I don't *want* to stop, but we should. You're making me hard, and I want to do things with you that shouldn't happen on a first date."

The hand on my thigh flexes and his eyes dip to the growing bulge in my pants.

Wes' lip quirks. "Did I do that?"

"Your lips did, and I'm not complaining, but you deserve to have things taken slow." I glance down at his lap and see a very similar situation happening in his pants. "And we don't want to scare anyone." He sees my gaze and attempts to shift, but his legs are caged between mine, so he has nowhere to go. "Hey, don't be embarrassed."

"I'm not—"

"You are, but you shouldn't be. Our bodies reacting to each other is natural. If you let me, I'll teach you everything you need to know, and then I'll happily let the student surpass the master. I've tended to be the top in my past relationships, but I'm eager for someone to take my body to the next level."

Wes growls and crashes his lips to mine in a quick but dominating kiss as he shows me what he could do to me, and I allow it. Bask in it. When he pulls away, I can't stop the smile that slowly creeps up my cheeks.

"Fuck, exactly like that, Doll."

"We should probably go home."

"Yeah," I agree.

"Separate."

"If that's what you want." Even if he asked to go home together, I'd tell him no. I can already sense there's more to him than a quick fuck. There's something between us that will surpass a one-night stand.

Wes sighs heavily, and the exhale is shaky. "I've had too much to drink. I'm going to call a rideshare home."

"Let me." I take out my phone and pull up the app. He takes my wrist and shakes his head.

"Eli, you paid for dinner, which was a change for me. Let me pay for my own ride home."

"No." I'm tapping away while he continues to protest. "Done."

"Eli."

"Wes?"

"I'm supposed to take care of you. That's how this is supposed to work."

"Well, it's a good thing *supposed* to ends in E-D—past tense. I can take care of you for a change. Say, thank you, Eli."

He stares and stares. And stares. "When I get my hands on you—"

"I'll enjoy every fucking second of it. For now, your ride will be here in fifteen minutes. Let's go wait outside."

Taking his hand, I slip off the stool, and he follows me without protest. We exit the building, and I walk toward a set of benches against the exterior wall. Before we reach them, Wes tugs on my hand, and my back hits the wall, with my arm pinned above me. I look up to see the veins in his arms flexing, and as my eyes travel lower, I see the fire in his gray eyes.

When he pinned me, my free hand went to his hip and his mine. I should be nervous or cautious that a man I don't know has me pinned to a wall, but the outline in his pants leaning against my thigh frazzles my brain from thinking anything but dirty thoughts.

"This is a position you should get used to, Little Eli.

Pinned beneath me and at my mercy."

A dark chuckle escapes me, and I hum my approval. "There might be a *little* problem with that, Wes."

"And what's that?" There's a challenge in his eyes. Challenge to disobey him, to deny what we're both clearly feeling. But I'm not denying anything. On the contrary.

I slip my hand between us and cup his erection. He gasps when I apply light pressure. I lean forward and whisper in his ear. "You see, Doll, there doesn't seem to be anything *little* about either of us."

Any distance between us is eliminated when he crashes his lips to mine. This kiss is all dominance and challenge, but I don't give in like I did earlier. I push back. Our tongues don't mingle; they battle. Teeth nip, and lips suck. The stubble on his chin grazes mine continuously, and I feel the rash forming from the friction.

Wes abruptly pulls away and leans his forehead on mine.

"Fuck. Eli, you have to stop." His voice is thick with lust.

I'm not sure why *I* have to stop when we were obviously both kissing each other.

"Fuck Eli, please. Your hand," he pleads, and it's strained. *My hand?*

I look down at the tiny bit of space created when he broke our kiss and realize I'm massaging his cock through his pants. I quickly move my hand to his hip, and he breathes a sigh of relief.

"I'm sorry," I rush out. I hadn't even consciously been doing it.

"Don't. Don't be sorry. I'm going to have to go home and fuck my wife, hard, to make this erection go away." He shifts his hips, and the outline of his cock rubs against my equally as hard one.

"Will you think of me?" *Fuck*. That was a bold question that slipped out before I could even think.

"In general or while I fuck my wife?"

"Both."

"Can I see you again?"

"I fucking hope so." I lean in and press a gentle kiss to the corner of his mouth. Wes turns his head so our lips fully touch. This kiss is slow. There are no angry tongues, only sweet pecks, and gentle licks.

"Good. Then I expect you to do the same while you take care of this." He cups me over my pants, and I can feel his hesitation, but holy fuck does it feel good.

Something beeps at our crotches, and I look down with a confused look. Wes chuckles and removes his hand, showing me his wrist.

"Elevated heart rate. I'm a runner."

I smirk. "Nice to know I can have that effect." A car pulls up to the curb with a lit sign in the front, designating it a rideshare. "I think your ride is here." My pocket buzzes, presumably from the app letting me know my driver has arrived. "Get home safe, and I'll talk to you soon. Text me when you get there?"

"Okay. Thank you for tonight. It was…"

"To be continued." I swivel my hips and rub us together one last time.

With a peck to my lips, he pulls away, adjusts himself, and heads to his ride. I stare at the retreating car until I can no longer see tail lights.

Walking back inside, I ask the kid at the entrance to call his boss. A few minutes later a cowboy hat wearing Tucker, one of Katy's fathers, walks out of a side door into the lobby.

I came thirty minutes early because Katy told me I needed to touch base with her father before my date arrived. The girls were concerned about me meeting a guy I knew nothing about but were ecstatic when I told them we were meeting here.

"That looked like it went well. Did y'all have a good time?" Tucker's accent is almost non existent except for the occasional y'all thrown into his speech.

"It was great. Thanks. You can report back to Katy that I wasn't kidnapped by a psycho stalker."

"That still remains to be seen, but I know that gentleman. He's been here several times, and he's never caused any trouble."

"Several?"

"Mmhmm. But they never make it past dinner. He liked you, Elliot." There's something hidden in his eyes as Tucker puts a fatherly hand on my shoulder and gently squeezes. The back of my eyes prickle from the simple gesture, and I have to remember to call my dad tomorrow. I miss him.

"Thank you, again. This place is great."

"You're welcome anytime. Admission will always be free for Katy's friends. Are you good to drive, or do you need a ride?"

There's that fatherly concern again. It tugs something in my chest that I know is more than missing Collin. I'm missing my first dad.

"I'm good. I didn't drink as much as my date. I sent him home in a rideshare. Will his car be alright here overnight?"

"Of course. There are lots of cameras out there, and I keep security on through the morning to watch over the cars left behind. It's a regular occurrence."

"Thank you again, Tucker." I hug him because it feels like the right thing to do, and I need one right now. Without hesitation, he hugs me back, and I thank the universe for bringing the right people into my life when I need them.

# 16

# Sawyer

reathe. Breathe, Sawyer. You're only fifteen minutes from home. You can survive fifteen minutes despite your dick feeling like it wants to burst out of your pants.

Sawyer: Please tell me you're awake, Jitterbug.

The dancing bubbles appear immediately, and I feel instant relief.

Lainey: I am. Everything okay?
  Sawyer: It is now. I'll be home in about 10. Be waiting.
  Lainey: Waiting or... WAITING?
  Sawyer: Strip and be ready, Alaina.
  Lainey: Can I ask a question first?
  Sawyer: Yes.
  Lainey: You're out late. Did you have a good evening?
  Sawyer: Very. Be prepared.

Lainey: Yes, Sir.

My finger taps on my thigh as I attempt to control my pent-up energy. Eli kissed me. I kissed Eli. He touched me. He did more than touch me. Fuck. I was ready to blow my load right there. I was worried my mystery man wouldn't live up to my memory from that night.

Maybe he wasn't as good-looking as I thought.

I was probably so bored with my date that I overhyped my three-second interaction with the blue-eyed God.

No. Fucking no. Everything tonight blew every memory I had of him out of the water. He was more... *more*. Funny. Charming. Considerate. I was shocked when he paid for dinner. I was barely able to slip the bartender my card and pay for our drinks after. It seems like his nature to take care of people, and for the evening, I allowed it, but going forward... Well, I guess we'll see.

I don't want to predetermine the relationship that he could have with my Jitterbug. I love to spoil her, and she loves to be spoiled. Who am I to stop Eli if he would want to spoil her. This was one date. A really fucking incredible one, but still the first.

Is there a chance I'm blowing things out of proportion because it's all new to me?

Sure, that's always a possibility, I guess. But tonight wasn't a one-way street. He gave as much as I did and didn't push me any further than I was comfortable. Although, if I'm being honest, I probably would have gone further. He made me feel comfortable. He has such an easy going personality.

I look down at my lap, counting the minutes until I can text him that I made it home safely. It's strange he's doing everything I would normally say and do for Lainey. It's nice.

No, nice is such a shit word. It's exhilarating. Lainey cares for me. She loves me. Eli had no obligation to do anything he did tonight. Especially not kiss me...or touch me.

I shift in my seat as my body reacts to my thoughts. Thank fuck we finally pull up to my apartment because I'm about to burst. My emotions, my energy. My cock.

"Thanks, man." I pull out a five-dollar bill and hand it to the driver over the seat. I'm sure Eli tipped him, but I don't want to make any assumptions. I exit the car, and it feels like I blink and I'm putting the key into our lock.

The apartment is dark and quiet. The lingering scent of soy sauce hits my nose, and I assume Jitterbug got Chinese for dinner. I smile as I walk the hall to our bedroom and remove my shirt along the way. I know I told her to be ready, but I don't think I want to scene with her. Tonight, I want to make love to my wife.

As I walk through the bedroom door, Lainey takes my breath away. She's so obedient, sitting quietly at the end of the bed, awaiting her next instructions. She's fucking incredible, but I don't want her obedience.

"Jitterbug." Her eyes snap to mine, and the use of her nickname lets her know where my thoughts are. A smile that lights up the room explodes on her face.

"Sawyer."

"Come here."

Without delay, she springs from the bed and launches herself at me. The moment she's in my arms, thighs wrapped around my hips, I'm on her. Kissing, sucking, biting. It comes from both directions. She's as needy for me as I am for her.

"Fuck, Jitterbug." Her hot mouth sucks on my neck while I walk her to the nearest dresser and plant her ass on top of it.

"Did Wes have a good evening?" she purrs in my ear.

"He did." Lainey moans as I dip down and take a nipple into my mouth. Her nimble fingers unbutton my shirt, and she greedily rubs them against my chest.

"Tell me about him."

I pull away and look into her eyes. A pang of guilt rushes through me. I kissed him. He touched me. Obviously, finding someone for us both involves physical activity, but I never expected it to happen tonight, and it hasn't happened on any other date, so we've never had anything to discuss until now.

A knowing smile grows on Lainey's face, and I feel hope.

"Something happened." Her eyes ping-pong between mine, and I nod. "Something happened!" she says louder and with more excitement. Her ankles lock behind my back, and she pulls me flush to her. "Sawyer, tell me right now."

"We kissed."

"Oh my god." She grabs my cheeks and peppers my lips with small, quick kisses. "How was it?"

"There's more."

She squeals against my lips. "More?"

I want to be ashamed to confess the next part, but her exuberance urges me on.

"There was making out." She hums into my neck where her lips have roamed. "I pinned him to the wall outside." She moans, and her hands move to undo my khakis. "He rubbed my cock over my pants."

"Kinda like this?" Lainey slips her hand into my boxers

and glides it across my length.

"Mmm, fuck. Nothing like that."

She grabs the head of my cock and pulls. "What else happened?

Reaching behind me, I tug at her legs to unhook me, and she pouts. "Let me get undressed, Jitterbug." She sighs and drops her legs to my sides. I'm naked and rubbing my cock against her wet heat in seconds.

"What else happened? Was he a good kisser?"

"He is. And he's a bit dominant too. It was a change from always getting my way. To be challenged. I liked it."

Lainey moans, and her head falls back as I run my tip back and forth over her clit.

"Sawyer," she moans out.

"Do you know what he asked me?" I line up with her entrance prepared for my next move.

"What?"

"If I would think of him" —I thrust into her to the hilt— "while I fuck my wife tonight."

"Oh fuck, yes." Her nails dig into my shoulders as she holds on. "Tell me his name. Tell me the name of the man who got you all riled up."

Perfume bottles clink together on the dresser from the thrusting of my hips. She wants to know his name. I never had a problem telling her the names of my dates after they were over because I knew they were one and done.

"I'm going to see him again," I pant out between thrusts.

"Yes," she yells, and I don't know if it's in response to my comment or because I hit her sweet spot.

I cup my hands under her ass cheeks and lift her from the dresser. I walk us to the bed without leaving her pussy and crawl us onto the mattress. Lainey relaxes her body under me while I reposition us. She keeps her eyes closed as I resume our lovemaking at a slower pace.

"You want to know his name?" I question, confirming she still wants it after knowing I plan to see him again.

"Please."

"Eli. His name is Eli. Although he confirmed it's not his real one and that mine isn't real either when I slipped up and almost called you Lainey to him." I lean down and softly chuckle into her neck. "I showed him your butt plug picture."

"And? What did he say?"

"I confessed it was mine, and he appreciated it."

"He sounds amazing. When do you see him again?"

"We didn't decide—*shit*."

"What's wrong?"

I look over my shoulder where my jeans lay on the floor. I have an idea if she'll go for it.

"I was supposed to text him when I got home. What if I sent him a picture instead?" Her smile is just as mischievous as my thoughts.

"What did you have in mind?"

I sit up, settle onto my knees, and look down. "This is a nice view." With my cock fully seated inside her pussy there isn't anything too provocative to see. It's more of a sexy tease than anything else.

"I like your thinking, Mr. Hayes. Let's do it."

I reluctantly pull out and quickly grab my phone before sinking back into her. We moan at the feeling of our reconnection, and I line my camera up to get the best angle. Before sending the picture, I show the screen to Lainey for approval.

"Fuck, that's hot. Send it to me, too."

I forward the picture to her and open up my text thread with Eli.

Sawyer/Wes: Made it home safe. Thank you for the incredible evening... and the inspiration. We're BOTH thinking about you. «insert picture»

Putting the phone down, I lift Lainey's knees to her chest and pick up my pace. I'm not surprised when my phone digs with a text message within a minute of my picture.

"Check that for me, Jitterbug. My hands are a little busy." I squeeze her nipples between my fingers, and she whines as her hand blindly reaches out for my phone on the bed. She finds it and her finger swipes across the screen to open the text.

Her eyes widen, and "shit" slips through her lips before she turns the phone to face me. It's a similar picture to the one we sent him, only solo. Eli's toned chest and slightly defined abs are on display. His hand is wrapped around the base of his cock, and the picture strategically cuts off before anything scandalous shows.

"What's it say?" I can't read the words through the movement of my thrusts.

Eli: Good. Because I'm thinking about you... and that butt plug. Glad you got home safe. Have sweet dreams, Doll.

"Doll?" she questions after reading the text out loud.

I shrug. Eli used the term a few times during the evening,

but I didn't think anything of it.

"It's cute. I like it. But I'll like it even more if you stop going easy on me and make me come."

"Fucking brat." I pull out and flip her onto her stomach. She giggles when I pull her hips up but it swiftly turns into a moan when I thrust back inside and smack her ass cheek. "If you want your orgasm, take it. Make yourself come."

Lainey adjusts her shoulder, and I watch her hand disappear. I wait to hear her moan when she touches herself, but instead, I feel her on my cock. Her fingers make a V shape at her opening, and they caress my shaft with each pump I make.

"If you don't want to come, that's on you, but don't come whining to be later when you're dying for release, Alaina."

I can't help my smirk when her hand moves to pleasure her clit. My hand traces up her spine. When I reach the nape of her neck, I grab a handful of her hair and arch her neck back.

"You better hurry. If I come before you, I won't let you finish."

Her pace increases, and I shift my hips to angle exactly where she needs me. With a few thrusts into her sweet spot and her fingers doing the other half of the work, she explodes. Her interior walls spasm and I have to hold myself back. I want to prolong her orgasm as long as it will go. When I feel her body relax, I grab her hips and slam into her until I find my own release.

We collapse onto the bed in a heap of sweaty limbs and labored breathing.

"You can go out with Eli every night if that's how you'll come home." She runs her nails down my spine, and I shiver.

137

"I like him, Jitterbug. I know it was only a first date, but it felt so simple and easy. He said he's willing to teach me whatever I want to learn, and in not so many words, said he's willing to submit for me once I'm comfortable."

"How do you feel about that?"

"I think I should be asking you that. But the image of both of you submitting for me is intoxicating."

"Baby, you know I'm happy if you're happy." Lainey kisses me tenderly, so I know she means what she says. "And there's enough of you to go around."

"I also get the feeling he's got a little bit of dom in him. How do you feel about *that*? Think you could handle two of us."

"Fuck. I think I would welcome that."

I roll over and hover over her body. "You're too fucking perfect, Jitterbug. I don't deserve you."

"You're right. You don't." She pushes me off her and sprawls out like a starfish. "Now clean me up, and let's sleep."

I chuckle and mutter "brat" under my breath as I get up and head to the bathroom.

# 17

# Lainey

ore. I'm sore. In the best way possible, but shit, it's been a while since Sawyer has taken so much out on my body.

"You okay over there, friend? You're wiggling a little, or a lot."

"Don't laugh at me, Katy. I'll tell Vik you're being mean to me, and you'll have the same fate."

I shift uncomfortably again in my seat, and Katy smirks. I was extra bratty last night and earned myself the paddle instead of Sawyer's hand. There are no regrets, except for maybe the need for a hemorrhoid donut to sit on.

Katy sips her coffee as we wait for the other girls to join us for our break. Her eyes drift above my head, and her smirk turns into a full-blown smile.

"What's that look for?" I peer over my shoulder and wince at the position change as Blake walks toward our table.

"Crap."

"She'll get the details out of you."

I hang my head because she's right. I'm not intentionally keeping anything from any of them; there just hasn't been anything to say until recently. But Blake? Blake is a bloodhound when it comes to getting the gossip. I swear she makes FBI agents shake in their boots when she wants information.

"Hello, ladies." She pauses, looks at me with scrunched eyes and pounces. "Oh, Lainey. Spill."

One look. That's all it took for her to know I have secrets. Well, not secrets per se, but things to divulge.

My shoulders fall as I huff and slump in my chair. A small grunt slips past my lips as my ass rubs against the seat. Blake practically vibrates, waiting for any crumb of information I'll give her. As if her sex life isn't more exciting than Katy's and mine put together with a wife *and* husband.

"Don't make me beg; I did enough of that last night."
*Point proven.*

"Sawyer found a guy he's interested in." Blake squeals, and I cup my ears.

"More. Tell me more. Have you met him?"

"Not yet. They just met this past weekend, but they've been texting regularly, and it's been ramping up Sawyer, then, in turn, our bedroom activities."

"What can you tell us about him?"

"Not much, actually. I want Sawyer to develop his relationship first then if and when he feels it's right, we'll meet."

"What's going on over here?" Nicole approaches us from behind, drawing all eyes to her. "Everyone looks like they're either waiting on the winning lottery numbers or an execution. I can't decide?"

I should have known she was coming. The smell of pumpkin spice and fall follows her everywhere.

"Lainey was just telling us about Sawyer's new boyfriend," Blake says with a big smile.

"Boyfriend?" Nicole plops down in an empty chair and rests her chin in the palm of her hand, ready and waiting for more details.

"*Not* his boyfriend," I correct while glaring at Blake. "Just the first guy he's been interested in. They seem to be getting along really well, and I've been getting the blunt of Sawyer's sexual frustration at night. All my parts are sore."

Katy takes my hand and looks deep into my eyes. "If you were any other person, I'd ask if he was hurting you, but I know you well enough. If that were the case, Patrick knows how to hide a body, and Chip could make someone disappear from the internet."

She smiles at her attempt at a humorous statement, but there's an edge to it. Patrick and Chip are the best at their jobs, next to her husband, Vik. Unfortunately, we all know how well because Katy was kidnapped by her adopted mother's stalker after he raped her and got her pregnant. We don't talk about it, but she shot and killed him in her attempt to escape.

Katy has come a long way in the years since the incident, but having lived it with her, I can still see the times when it haunts her. Despite the trauma it caused, it brought her the most beautiful baby boy, Owen, and her bodyguard, Vik, and they now have three beautiful children. Speaking of which…

"By the way, how are you feeling?" I ask the table in general, knowing one of them will answer.

"Bloated."

"Constipated."

Nicole and Katy answer simultaneously, and the table erupts into laughter. Our mimosa morning turned into a pregnancy party when Nicole and Katy saw double lines on their tests. We celebrated with ice cream floats and pancakes for breakfast.

Happy for the conversation to be off me, I press further. "Were they shocked?"

Katy looks around the room at anyone but us. She hasn't told Vik yet.

"Justin called the contractor already. He wants to add to the house, despite my insistence that our children don't each need their own rooms. But we all know there's no stopping him once he sets his mind on something."

She's right. Justin will do anything for the people he loves, almost to a fault. But his kids? They are his entire world, and Nicole is his sun.

"You're suspiciously quiet, Katy," Blake accuses. "Are you okay?"

"Five is a lot. How am I going to handle another kid?" She rests her hand on her lower stomach and looks down with sad eyes. "Can my love stretch that far?"

"Hey." I grab her shoulders and pull her into my arms. "You have so much love to give. Don't ever think that. There are so many people in your life willing to help you at the drop of a hat. Do you need a break? A date night? Have you even told Vik yet?"

With silent tears filling her eyes, she shakes her head.

"I know he'll be happy, and it's not that I'm *not* happy. I think I'm just... overwhelmed."

"Okay, you need a night off—a reset. We can split the kids. I'll take the littlest Dempsey. Who's taking the older three? Do you have enough stored breastmilk for me to take Lexi overnight?"

Blake and Nicole talk between themselves as Katy half-heartedly protests. She's the type of self-sacrificing person who doesn't want to ask for help even when she's underwater. Vik has helped her work through a lot of it and predicts the things she needs before she even knows she needs them, but it's clear this has slipped through the cracks.

"Is one night enough, or do you need two? I'll take my niece for however long you need."

"Guys, I can't ask any of you to do this."

"It's a good thing you aren't asking. We aren't even offering. We're telling." Nicole finishes typing something on her phone and places it down. "There. I told Justin, and he agrees, so now you have no choice."

Katy knows she's defeated now. She'd never go against him. They saved each other in more ways than one.

Blake takes a similar stance to Nicole except she flaunts her text from Annie. "The boss has spoken. Your and Vik's shifts will be covered on Friday. We will take the kids off your hands tomorrow night, and we don't want to see you until Saturday evening."

"Two days," Katy mouths, but no sound comes out. Tears begin to tumble down her face, and her shoulders shake. She buries her face in her hands, and I pull her back into me.

"You don't have to thank us. We're your friends, and we love you."

"I know," she sobs into my chest. "Fucking hormones."

143

"Stop that," Nicole whines and sniffles. "You got me going now too, bitch."

Blake pulls a crying Nicole into her shoulder and looks at me, mouthing, "babies."

□ □ □ □ □

"How did I get roped into babysitting?" My sexy husband leans back on the couch with a sleeping toe-head blonde on his chest. Lexi fell fast asleep in his arms after her bottle. He gently rubs her back, and her sweet little lip pops out.

"You're the baby whisperer." She was fussy and didn't want to take the bottle for me. I'm convinced it's because I have boobs, and she wanted straight from the source, not a silicone nipple. Sawyer took her from me, and she easily accepted the bottle from him. Katy warned me it might happen. Lexi is well over one year old, but they breastfeed for as long as possible. Mostly morning and night at this age. It doesn't help that Vik has a huge lactation kink. I'm convinced that's why he keeps her knocked up.

"Let me send Katy a picture to ease her mind." I quickly send her a text showing her sleeping youngest, and she likes the picture but doesn't reply. I'm going to take that as a good sign she's too occupied to type back.

"I'll take her to bed. Is the monitor turned on?" I nod, and he sits up, taking her to her room.

Our guest room has everything needed for any of the kids to sleep over, whatever their age—baby monitors, a pack-and-play, bed railings for the older kids so they don't fall out—lots of extra pillows and blankets. I love keeping the kids whenever my friends need help. I wish Katy had said something earlier before she was feeling overwhelmed.

Sawyer's phone chimes on the coffee table, and he looks back before leaving the room.

"Will you check that for me, Jitterbug? I might be a minute."

"Sure." Walking over, I pick up the phone and sit on the couch. Lexi is an easy toddler, but she's also high energy and used to lots of noise and stimulation from her older siblings. I'm exhausted.

Eli: Evening, Doll. I've been thinking about you today. Are you free tomorrow evening?

Oh, Eli. Should I respond for Sawyer? I don't know how long he'll be, but Eli can see that the message has been read. I'd hate for him to think Sawyer is ignoring him.

Sawyer/Wes: Hey Eli, it's Meg. Wes is putting our niece to bed. He's free tomorrow. If you'd like to make plans, I'll let him know.

Eli: The infamous Meg. So nice to speak to you. Are you sure he's free? I'd hate to take him away from you on a Friday if you have plans.

Sawyer/Wes: He's all yours. I'll be babysitting another night, so we had no plans.

Sawyer/Wes: I like how you make him smile.

That was a bold thing to tell him, but if Sawyer likes Eli as much as I think he does, he should know.

Eli: He makes it easy. You make him smile, too. Maybe

145

someday soon, we can make him smile together.

"Who is it, and what is that huge smile for?"

I didn't notice Sawyer walk back into the room. Either he was quiet, or I was too engrossed in the text messages to hear him.

"I see why you like him. Eli is a smooth talker."

"Oh, is he? What did he say?"

"We were chatting."

"You were...you texted him back?"

*Oh shit.* "Should I not have? I'm sorry. I didn't want to leave him on read, and I didn't know how long you would be with Lexi."

Sawyer sits beside me on the couch and pulls me into his lap.

"It's okay, Jitterbug. What are the two of you talking about?"

"You, of course." I hand him the phone and let him read our exchange.

"Are you pimping me out now?"

I shrug a shoulder. "Maybe."

"You two are so much trouble."

Sawyer kisses my neck and moves to put the phone down. "Wait, one of us has to respond to him."

"Busy. You do it." He continues to nip and suck on my neck while he hands me the phone.

Sawyer/Wes: Apparently, I'm a pimp now. LOL. What are the plans for tomorrow so I can relay the message? Wes is a little (ahem) preoccupied at the moment.

Eli: Show me.

146

Show him? Okay.

I turn the camera on selfie mode and take a close up of Sawyer's face buried in my neck. My hair is up, so none of me is seen in the picture, and I hit send.

"What are you up to, Jitterbug?"

"I told Eli you were preoccupied, and he wanted to see."

Sawyer hums his approval as his phone vibrates.

Eli: Fuck, that's hot. For future reference, I'll gladly accept pictures any time.

Eli: Hey, Meg?

Sawyer/Wes: Yeah?

Eli: Let me do something special for you tomorrow since I'm stealing Wes away from you.

Sawyer/Wes: You don't have to do that. I'm happy to share him with you. ;)

Eli: I have VERY inappropriate thoughts about that statement... but for now, just let me spoil you a bit. Please.

Sawyer/Wes: How's a girl to say no when you beg so pretty?

I giggle because I realize I'm flirting with my husband's... not boyfriend because they barely just met, but Eli definitely has potential.

"You're getting awfully chummy with my phone. Care to share with the class?" Sawyer removes my shirt while he waits for an answer, and I accidentally drop the phone between us.

I open my mouth to tell him what we're discussing when the phone buzzes twice in quick succession, shocking me.

"Shit. Who needs a vibrator? I should just tell Eli to keep

sending texts." I pick up the phone while Sawyer taunts and teases my nipples. When I gasp, he thinks it's from his mouth, but I pull back, and he looks at me questioningly.

"What's wrong?"

"Um... I... look."

I turn the screen around so he can see the two notifications. One is a text from Eli, and the other is a notification from his bank. Money has been deposited into his account.

"What the fuck. Jitterbug, I was joking about you being my pimp. What did you say to him? What does the text say?" Sawyer swipes on the screen.

Eli: Wes, I'll treat you tomorrow night, and I want you to treat Meg on Saturday. Meg, order yourself a nice dinner while Wes and I go to a comedy show. How does that sound to you both?

Sawyer reads me the text, and I'm speechless. Eli sent two thousand dollars to our account. That's not pocket change. Eli sent that for *me* to use.

"What do I say back?"

"You mean, what do *I* say back? He thinks he's still talking to me. Sawyer, that's a lot of money." The phone buzzes again, and we both eagerly look at the newest message.

Eli: Meg, I hear you overthinking. I'm gonna be sappy for a second and tell you that Wes already feels like someone special to me, and by association, so are you. I like to treat the special people in my life. Don't think about it. Say, "Thank you, Eli," and decide whether you want steak or lobster for dinner tomorrow—or both. Buy yourself a pretty new dress and make Wes take you somewhere fancy because you both deserve it.

"I feel like I'm drooling. Am I drooling? This guy can't be real, right? Did you meet some Nigerian Prince who needs us to send him back the money?"

"Jitterbug, I promise he's real. I met him and kissed him. His hand on my cock was definitely not a figment of my imagination."

"Give me this phone. I'm going to reply to him, and then we're going to go have sex in our bed and pretend we're rolling around on the two thousand extra dollars in our account."

"Sounds good to me."

I squeak as Sawyer grabs the back of my thighs and picks me up. He heads towards the bedroom when I stop him.

"The baby monitor."

"Shit."

He turns and leans down so I can grab it.

Sawyer/Wes: Yes, Eli. Thank you, Sir.

I smile the entire way to the bedroom because I know if Eli has a dominant side like Sawyer thinks, the Sir will rile him up. And I think I like the idea of potentially letting two dominant men have me.

# 18

# Elliot

I took a risk that I think paid off based on Meg's last response to me. She called me Sir, which surprised me. I've been cautious with the way I've been handling things with Wes. I know he's an Alpha Dom. Anyone who knows could spot him a mile away. Even as nervous as he was at our first meeting, and knowing he has little to no experience with men, it's obvious he's trained Meg well.

I haven't mentioned my wealth. It's not something I talk about or really consider in my everyday life, but I wasn't lying when I told her I like to treat the special people in my life. Thanks to the trust fund that Annie set up for me and my siblings and having business-smart parents who taught us how to properly invest and save money, I have more than I'll ever need in a lifetime.

I'm sure Wes will have questions when I see him in a few hours, but I won't apologize. It won't be the last time I spoil either of them. At least, I hope it won't if things continue the way I hope they do.

Katy: Date number two tonight, right?

Elliot: Aren't you supposed to be on a break? Shouldn't you be sex-drunk or something for the next twenty-four hours?

Katy: A girl's gotta eat and refuel.

Elliot: Have you told him yet?

Katy: Yes. Hence the need to refuel. I swear he's trying to put another baby in me while there's already one in there.

Elliot: He's just making sure it's in there good and sticky. And to answer your question, yes. Date #2 is tonight. We're going to a comedy club. Then maybe…

Katy: Oh, I like … 's. He's a virgin, right? Eww, that sounds wrong, but I guess it's technically right. IDK how you men do things. :::throws up hands in exasperation:::

Elliot: Weirdo. It's the same way women do things, just a different hole. Although I've heard stories from you and Blake, I think you DO know how we do things.

Katy: Ugh. Drunk Blake and Katy need to stop airing out their bedroom laundry. ANYWAY! I'm excited for you!

Elliot: Me, too. I like him. And I texted with his wife last night, and she seems fun and flirty. And they've sent me a few pics that are H.O.T!!!

Katy: Dayum! I'd say I'm jealous, but I'm staring at a naked Viking wearing only an apron and flipping pancakes.

Elliot: If you don't want ME visualizing your naked Viking, don't paint pretty pictures like that, missy.

Katy: Imagination off my man, El. Have fun tonight, and don't get into too much trouble.

Elliot: I'll get into just the right amount of trouble for you
;)

An hour. I can leave my house in an hour. Wes and I are meeting outside the comedy club at seven. About half an hour ago, I got a picture of the feast Meg had ordered herself. I think she ordered half of an entire Chinese restaurant, and it makes me happy that she's treating herself like I told her to.

I took the longest shower possible. I've exfoliated, lotioned, and primped everywhere necessary. My closet has become the bane of my existence as I agonize over every piece of clothing I own.

With much debate, I settle on a pair of gray slacks that remind me of Wes' eyes and a black button-down. I fidget with the buttons on my cuffs as I roll up the sleeves.

Checking the time on my watch, I still have forty-seven minutes. This is going to be the slowest hour ever. All I need to do is fix my hair, and I'm ready to leave. My phone buzzes on the bathroom counter, and my stomach flutters when I see Wes' name on the screen.

Sawyer/Wes: I have too much nervous energy. I'm walking out the door, so whenever you get there, I'll probably already be waiting.

Eli: Oh, thank fuck. My house is so clean I think I might OD on the fumes if I stay here any longer. I'm leaving in 5. I'll see you soon.

Sawyer/Wes: Can't wait.

*Neither can I, Wes.*

I quickly fix my hair and grab my wallet. Within five minutes, I'm out the door, and if I could have made it three, I would have been out sooner.

The elevator takes forever, the line out of the parking garage takes forever, and the line into the next parking garage takes forever. I have so much nervous energy my fingers have tapped the steering wheel the entire way here.

The clock on the dash glows 6:37. It may only be twenty-three minutes early, but it's twenty-three minutes less I have to wait to see him again.

I finally park my car and forcibly stop myself from jogging out of the parking deck. As I walk down the street, I can already see him. He might as well be my very own Greek statue with how much I want to worship at the feet of his beauty. Wes looks casual with his hands in his pockets, wearing a pale yellow short-sleeve shirt with buttons. *I like buttons for easy access.* He's paired it with navy slacks, and I love his sense of style.

His back is to me so he doesn't hear me approach, and I like that I have the element of surprise.

"You look incr—*shit.*"

Wes spins at my words, and like a madman starved, his lips are on mine, and his hands are in my hair. I don't hesitate to wrap my arms around his waist and lean into the kiss. Once I finally came out to my family, I embraced who I was and never looked back. PDA doesn't bother me. I am unapologetically who I am, and if you don't like that, you're free to look the other way. This experience is new for Wes, and I never could have predicted he'd be so open about his affection.

When he finally pulls away, I feel a little drunk from his lust.

"Hi," he says timidly, and I pull him back in for another kiss. We're panting this time when I stop and rest my forehead against his.

"You don't get to kiss me like that, then say hi to me like you're shy. You owned that kiss; now own the greeting."

He chuckles and shakes his head. "Hi, Eli," he says with more conviction. "I'm going to make this weird and tell you I missed you. It's your fault because you said I should own my greeting, so there it is."

He missed me. Fuck I missed him too. We only met a week ago, but I feel like I'm becoming a cliché in a rom/com. What do they call it? Insta lust? I'll ask Katy, she'll know.

"Then I guess I'm weird because I also missed you." He smiles so bright he could block out the sun. "You kissed me."

"I did. Is that bad?"

I take his hand and weave our hands together. "Not at all, Doll. I'm on your timeline. If you want to kiss me in public, do it. If you want to skip the comedy show and go to my house, I'm all yours."

Fire sparks in his eyes at my last suggestion, and I squeeze his hand.

"I—"

"Let's go inside for now, and we can think about the other stuff later. Sound good?"

"Yeah. Yeah, sounds good."

I lead the way into the comedy club, holding hands the entire way. We have a table close to the stage, so we aren't able to talk too much during dinner, and when the show officially starts, we push our chairs next to each other to watch the comedian better.

Wes' leg brushes mine, and sparks light up my body. He's so warm. Or maybe I'm warm from his proximity. When his hand slides on my leg, I hold my breath. No. I'm lying

154

to myself. There's no air in my lungs. I want to ravage him. My thoughts this past week have been dirty and all directed towards this man.

I know a comedian comes up on stage, and I know she's funny because Wes smiles and laughs the entire evening. But me? I couldn't tell you a single joke she told. My attention is focused solely on him. His smile that tilts slightly higher on the left than the right. The way his eyes squint when he's laughing hard. How his shoulders bounce when he huffs at a joke that's funny but not quite laugh-worthy. His entire presence is overwhelming, and it feels hard to breathe being this close to him.

I know I'm staring, and it's probably super creepy, but shit, I can't stop myself. Without turning his attention from the stage, he leans his head next to my ear, and the electricity between us sizzles.

"You haven't laughed once. Do you not think she's funny? We can leave if you're bored."

Wes' breath fans across my cheek as he speaks, and I shiver. I've never had this visceral of a reaction to anyone before. What is it about this man?

"Eli?"

*Shit. I haven't answered him.*

"I'm a little distracted."

He turns to look at me, and I squeeze his hand.

"What's distrac—*oh*." I move our hands over my semi-hard cock so he can feel why I'm distracted.

"So, in answer to your question, I'm sure she's funny, but you're the only thing in the room I want to pay attention to. And do I want to leave? Yes, but only for naughty purposes, so we should stay."

155

"Should?"

"Wes, I told you I'm on your timeline. I've had hookups and one-night stands. I've had relationships and breakups. I'm here to help you experience whatever you want, whenever *you* want. Not me."

"I want you, Eli."

"You do?"

"I do. I want you to teach me. Let's finish watching the comedian. That means you, too. Eyes off me."

I sigh heavily. "Do I have to? This view is too good."

Wes shocks me when he touches his lips to mine. It's a slow kiss and doesn't last as long as I want it to, but I savor every second of it.

"Watch the comedian, then I'll let you take me home and teach me something."

"Something?"

"Anything you want, Eli."

"Fuck. Okay." I peck his lips, wanting more but knowing I'll get it soon enough, and turn my attention to the stage for the first time tonight.

I can't wait to get my hands on this man.

# 19

## Sawyer

The balls I somehow found to tell Eli I'd go home with him disappear as soon as his eyes are off me. I can't focus on the comedian on stage like I was before my proposition. I know anything I do with him won't technically be new. Unless he wants a blow job. Fuck, I didn't think about that. I've never gone down on a guy before.

"Hey," Eli's gruff voice whispers in my ear. "You suddenly look nervous. Nothing you said to me is set in stone. You're allowed to change your mind. Relax and enjoy the evening; we can worry about the rest as it comes."

He runs his free hand down my forearm, and the simple touch, paired with his words, calms me.

"Thank you." Eli rests his head on my shoulder, and we watch the rest of the set.

Despite my best efforts, when the check comes, Eli hands his card to our waitress without even looking at the total. He refuses to let me pay once again, and I still feel strange about it. I'm the provider. It makes me feel a way I'm not used to, and I can't really name it, but I know I don't like it.

Something in my demeanor must change because as we walk out, no longer holding hands, Eli questions me.

"Hey, Wes. If you're not okay with our plans, we can go our separate ways. No hard feelings."

"What?" I turn and give him a confused look. "No. Why would you ask that?"

"You seem... *off* all of a sudden. I just want you to know you have an out."

"No." I draw him to the side of a building so we're away from the exiting crowd. "Eli, no. Listen...*Fuck*. I don't know how to be vulnerable. It's not me. You keep doing shit for me, and I don't know how to react. *I'm* the caretaker. *I'm* supposed to be paying for meals and asking *you* out on dates. Your-your making me feel inadequate."

"No. Fuck. No, no, no, Wes." Eli huffs out a breath and leans his forehead to mine. "Fuck. I'm so sorry. I'm not trying to make you feel vulnerable or inadequate. I'm a nurturer. Gift-giving is my love language. Handing over my card to pay for things is second nature. Thank you for telling me. I'll make a more conscious effort not to automatically pay for things. God, I'm sorry. But I won't apologize for asking you out tonight. Maybe next time, you should be quicker at asking me."

Eli smiles, and it eases some of my tension, at least on this particular subject.

"I should be better at this communication thing."

"Wes, you're doing great. You told me how you were feeling, and we fixed it."

"Just like that?" It can't possibly be this easy.

158

"Yeah, just like that." Eli's hand moves to my cheek and places his lips on mine. We stay locked together for several heartbeats before he pulls away. "Just like that. Now, what would you like to do? We didn't get to talk much, and I'd love to do that, but it's late, so other than a bar, there isn't much open."

"A bar would be fine, but is your place still an option?"

Eli's blue eyes light up as a smile creeps up one side of his cheek.

"Yeah, it's definitely an option. Do you want to meet me there? I'm not sure where you're parked."

Eli gives me his address and we kiss again before we separate. My keys jingle as I put them in the ignition. I'm anxious and nervous. Am I really going to Eli's house to... to what? There was no discussion. There were lots of implications, but that's just flirting. Right?

*Fuck.*

I punch a few buttons on my steering wheel, and ringing permeates the air.

"Baby, are you on your way home already?"

Her beautiful, melodic voice instantly calms me. "Not quite."

"Is everything all right?"

"I'm perfect. I wanted to run something by you."

"Okay. But where are you? Are you driving? Where are you going?"

"Lainey. So many questions. Listen first, answers second." I'm already feeling more like myself when she doesn't respond. We understand each other. Can easily slip in and out of our roles. "That's what I like, Alaina. Thank you. I'm going to tell you why I called, and then you can speak freely.

Do you understand?"

"Yes, Sir."

And with those two words, all is right with the world.

"Elliot has invited me back to his house, which is where I'm going. There has been flirting and some insinuation that things may progress further than kissing. I need you to tell me if you're still okay and comfortable with me going through with... it, whatever *it* might entail. I don't want to hear you say it's up to me. Your opinion matters, and if you aren't comfortable, I'll head home to you right now. Tell me your thoughts, Alaina."

"Is this something you want? Do you still want to explore things with Eli?"

"Yes."

"Do you feel comfortable and safe enough with him to give him this piece of you, Sawyer?"

"Do you think it's too soon? Is that why you're asking?" I know it seems soon. But like Eli said, this could have been a quickie or a one-night stand. We've spent every day for the last week texting and talking whenever we were free. I do feel comfortable and safe.

"Not at all. That's not what I was implying. If the roles were reversed, those two things would be your first priority for me, and they should be yours, too."

"I fucking love you, Jitterbug."

"I know. I'm more than just a pretty pussy."

"Don't talk about yourself like that," I growl into the steering wheel speaker.

"Baby, I was joking. And yes, I'm okay as long as you always come home to me after."

"Always."

"And you know what?"

"What?"

"Tomorrow isn't promised to any of us; go be a ho today."

If I could bang my head on the wheel without crashing, I would. "You're incorrigible, woman."

"And you wouldn't have me any other way. Are you nervous? I'm kinda nervous for you."

"Yeah?"

"Why the question in your tone?"

"Because I'm equally as excited. You and I have done everything together that I could do with him except for a blow job."

"What? I give you blow jobs all the—*ooooooooh.* You mean giving, not receiving. Just ask him."

"Ask him? Ask him what?"

"Ask Eli what he likes. I'm sure he's received enough to know how he likes his dick sucked. Just ask, and he'll walk you through it."

"Hmm. Is that how you learned? By asking the guy you were about to blow?"

Lainey chuckles, and it's my own personal symphony through the speakers.

"Nope. I read magazines. '31 Techniques to Giving the Best Blow Job.' I read a lot and researched."

"You're serious?"

"Absolutely. Hey Sawyer. Or should I say, hey, Wes?"

"Yes, *Meg.*"

"Relax. Have fun. And don't rush home. Lexi and I will be here in an hour or eight. Oh, and if you feel so inclined to send pictures, I wouldn't be upset."

"I fucking love you."

161

"You said that already. I love you too, Sawyer Wesley Hayes. Go have fun. I want all the details when you get home."

I pull into a quaint neighborhood, and I'm shocked to see moderate-sized houses all around. I assumed Eli would live in an apartment being a single guy. Does he live alone? I know he's new to town. Maybe he rents a room from someone? I guess I'm about to find out.

My GPS tells me I've arrived in front of a smaller white house with black shutters and a white picket fence. An actual white freaking picket fence. There's no way this is where he lives.

Sawyer/Wes: I'm here. I think?

Eli: I see you. You're in the right place. Park in the driveway and come on in.

The front door opens, and Eli leans against the doorframe with his arms folded across his chest. He looks like a fucking god, and I park behind a white sedan which I assume is his.

"Hey, stranger," he calls to me as I step out and survey my surroundings. I smile back as I unlock the gate and walk the stone path to his porch.

"You live here?"

"I live here. Do you like it?"

Two black rocking chairs sit on the porch with lush green plants all around. It looks like something straight out of a magazine.

"It's unbelievable." Eli steps aside to let me in, and at the last second, he grabs my arm and pulls me into him.

"I'll remind you one more time before you step into my

house; this is a safe zone. There are no expectations, and you're in control. Talk to me, and I'll talk you through anything you need. Okay?"

I crush my lips to his so he can feel how okay I am. This situation may still feel slightly overwhelming, but he's easing my mind piece by piece.

"Okay. Now, are you going to let me in, or are we giving your neighbors a show?"

"Come on in, Wes. Welcome to my home."

# 20

# Elliot

Wes is in my house. He's wandering, looking at glimpses into my world via pictures. Wynnie insisted I hang as many as possible so I wouldn't forget their faces. Wes stops at one of us on her wedding day.

"Who's this?"

"My best friend, Wynnie. She's my cousin adjacent. Our moms are best friends."

"Oh, so you grew up together? That's awesome."

I rub the back of my neck, happy his back is to me. "Something like that."

Wes spins before I can steal my face, and his expression morphs into concern. "I'm sorry. I didn't mean to pry."

I take the few steps to close the distance between us and put my arm around his waist. With care, I stroke the frame of our smiling faces and sigh. I push him a few feet to the left in front of one of the oldest pictures hanging.

"These are my parents, Griffin and Zoey, and my brother

Finn. My mom is pregnant with my little sister Paige here. I'm the oldest." Before he can speak, I turn him to face the next picture taken within the last six months in my college cap and gown with the five of us. "This is my mom and dad, Dellah and Collin."

"I'm... confused." I watch his eyes bounce between the two pictures, trying to put the pieces together.

"My mom died from complications when Paige was born. Four years later, my dad died in a car accident. Collin was my dad's best friend and became our guardian and eventually our adopted parents."

"Wow. That's incredible."

A look passes across his face that makes me pause. "What was that? Tell me?"

"I have a confession."

*Well, shit.* "Okay." I drag out the word, trying to suspend whatever he's about to confess for just a few seconds longer.

"I know where you work."

*He does?* "How?"

"Java Junkie. I was there one morning taking inventory and heard your voice." Wes' hand drifts to his hairline and rubs at a small healing scar. "I tried to get out to see you, but I hit my head on a shelf and cut it open."

"Wait." That's the coffee shop next to work. I look at his face again now that we're in full light. No more recognition dawns on me than the first night we met at Midnight Moonshine.

"I promise I'm not a stalker. I don't even spend that much time at the store. I think you're familiar with Gus, the manager; he pretty much runs the show. He told me you worked next door, but he couldn't remember your name."

"Of course, I know Gus, but… is that how you found me on the dating site?" I don't want to question things, but he seems too perfect, and if he was looking for me, this could all be a cruel joke.

"Not at all. You actually found me first, remember."

"Fuck. You're right. Sorry. That was ridiculously accusatory. You're just—"

"Awesome? I know." Wes chuckles, breaking up some of the tension building in my chest.

Do I tell him? We're sharing, and I've already come this far.

"Do you recognize the name Griffin Woodlyn?"

I watch as he stares back at the picture of my father, trying to decide if he recognizes him. A crease forms between his eyes, and I want to run my finger over it and smooth it away. Finally, he turns to me and asks, "That's a subject change. Should it?"

"Maybe. Have you ever wandered around the fountain outside MAD?" I assume he's wandered a time or two since he owns the coffee shop right outside the building.

His eyes squint as he racks his brain, but I see it the moment realization dawns on him.

"The plaque. The name on the fountain. That's…" He turns back to the picture. "Oh, Eli. I'm so sorry."

"It was almost a decade ago, and I had an incredible life. Wynnie took me under her wing. I don't know what I would have done without her. I was a little shit teenager who was angry at the world."

"Rightfully so."

I shrug a shoulder. "Probably. But she never let me dwell on it. She was the first one I came out to. She's my best

166

friend."

Wes turns and pulls me into his chest. His embrace is warm and comforting.

"I'm so glad she was there for you. You've been through so much. Now I understand your need to nurture. I can't imagine going through all that. I bet you're the best big brother."

"They're pains in the asses, but I love them. Most days."

Just talking about Finn and Paige makes me miss them. I need to get home again sometime soon.

"Eli... or should I call you Elliot?"

My head snaps back as if I've been slapped. "How?"

"You put money into my account. You may have only needed my phone number to send it, but your name popped up as the sender in my account."

"Shit. I didn't think of that. Well, now you really know me. Sad backstory and all."

"Your backstory isn't sad. It's courageous. What would you like me to call you? Is Eli a nickname?"

"Not really. Everyone calls me Elliot or El."

"Okay, Elliot, I have a question."

"Me first. Do I get to know your name? It's okay if you aren't ready."

He signs and places his forehead on mine. "Are you sure? Because I think I'm not. I'd tell you right now if it was just me, but I also have my wife to think about. She works in the same building as you. I don't want to make things weird yet."

"She does? I wonder if I know her?"

This is an interesting turn of events. Now I'm curious.

"I'm sure you probably do, which is why it makes this a

little more complicated, and I don't want to take any chances yet."

His eyes close, and I can tell he's having an internal battle.

"Wes." He hmms his response. "Wes, it's okay. I've already told you I won't push you, and that includes this."

"Thank you." He tilts his head to kiss me his thanks. Wes' arms wrap further around me, and I melt into him.

"Elliot," he whispers into my lips. "Teach me to give you the best blow job of your life."

I choke on the air between us, and he lets me go so I can step back and breathe.

"I'm sorry. I—" Holding up a hand, he stops talking while I compose myself. It takes me a moment to get my shock under control. Of all the things he could have said, I never would have thought those would be his words.

"Damn, Wes. Straight to the point. I can do that if you want. I like it when you communicate with me."

"I remember you telling me you're a switch, but do you have a preference, Elliot?"

"I like hearing you say my name." I step back into his arms and gently push us toward the couch.

"I like saying your name, Elliot. It suits you better than Eli."

The back of Wes' knees bump the couch, and I push his chest so he falls. I drop to my knees and spread his thighs.

"What are you doing?"

My hands travel up his legs, and he licks his lips.

"I'm a visual teacher. I'd rather show you what I like so you can see it first hand."

My hands reach his belt, and I lock eyes with him. "May I?"

"Yes."

No hesitation. I like that. I hope that means he's getting more comfortable.

"Give me a safeword, Wes."

"Answer my question first."

I pause my fingers, zipper halfway down. Question. What didn't I answer? "Remind me of the question."

"Do you prefer to be a top or a bottom? Because I'm a top, Elliot. What you're offering to do for me is not something I usually give up easily, even to my wife. I know the power of a blow job. My body will be completely at your mercy. Before we cross this line, I need to know your preference. I like you, and I'm heavily leaning toward introducing you to my wife, but I need to know you and I are compatible in the bedroom first."

I sit up on my knees and lean my body between his legs to get closer. His openness right now is a sign of his dominance. He's putting me in my place—if I'll allow him. It's up to me if I'll accept or deny his offer.

"Wes, I say this as truthfully as I can. I will be whatever you want. I'm a pleaser, but not to a fault. Your pleasure is what I desire. Whether that means I'm giving or taking, I don't care. I know you're a power top, and that excites me. Are you interested in having a second sub? I can be that. Are you interested in running a scene together with Meg? I can do that, too." His lip twitches, and I'd love to know which of those scenarios he's thinking about.

I know my answer is a bit of a cop-out, but it's the truth. It goes along with the whole nurturing part of my personality. I like pleasing people. In bed, out of bed, in my daily life, all of it. I know how short life can be, and I like bringing joy to others' lives.

"Apple."

"What," I chuckle. I just confessed all that, and his response is a fruit?

"Our safeword is Apple. I have no idea; Meg chose it before we were together. It was a comfort word for her in a previous relationship, so we kept it. I think you and I should use the same word. Is that okay with you?"

"Ah. That makes sense. And you were okay with using a safeword she's used with a previous partner?"

"Partners, with an S. She was briefly with two men prior to me. We're all friends now. And yes. Meg had a lot of obstacles, but we learned to safely navigate through them together when we first started our relationship in the bedroom. Her safety and security were my first priorities. Apple was an established safeword for her, and she knew her boundaries within it."

"Fuck, Wes. You just made me fall for you even harder." Annnd I didn't mean to say that out loud. "Sorry. Oversharer sometimes."

"Hey." He tips my chin up so I look straight into his gray eyes. "Share everything. The good, bad, and ugly. That's how you develop healthy relationships."

I chuckle. "You sound like a Hallmark card."

"And I'm done playing your game."

Wes stands and manhandles me until we've switched positions. He's quickly on his knees, undoing my pants.

"I don't ask permission, Elliot. We've established a safeword. Use it if you need it."

"Fuck. Okay, yeah." I lift my hips to help him lower my pants and boxers. My already hard cock springs out and slaps against my stomach. There's no hesitation or tenderness when he takes me in his hand and firmly strokes. It feels incredible.

"I'm going to do what I know I like, and you tell me if there's anything else you want me to do."

Before I have time to respond, his mouth surrounds me. Hot, wet, and fucking... "Fuuuuck. You don't need any instruction. Keep doing what you're doing."

Wes takes me all the way into his mouth, and his tongue massages the underside. He's skilled. I know Meg must appreciate the things he can do because I'm greatly appreciating them. He uses his hand to cover what he can't fit in his mouth, and the added pressure makes my eyes roll back.

"Can I touch you?" My hands are itching to grab his hair, but if he's not comfortable, I'll hold back.

He nods and hums on my cock, and I take that as a yes. His hair feels like silk between my fingers, and I take a chance and give it a slight tug. Wes sucks harder, and in turn, I pull harder. A give-and-take power play happens between us, and without realizing it, I'm thrusting into his mouth, using him for my pleasure.

Grunts and groans fill the room, and Wes seems to be enjoying this blow job as much as I am.

I release my grip on his hair and slow my movements. "Wes, I'm close, Doll. You can pull away if you don't want to swallow me." He moans low and long, and my balls draw up.

"Okay. Oh god. Fuck. Fuck. Holy Christ, fuuuuuck." I hold his head down while I spill into his mouth. My breathing becomes labored, and I wait for any kind of reaction from him. I came in his mouth. Me. A man. He

171

swallowed a man's come for the first time.

As if it's the most natural thing in the world, he takes one last lick at my head, and my body shutters as he sits back with a smug look on his face.

"Fuck, Wes. I'd tell you what a good boy you are, but I'm afraid you'd try to suck out my soul again for punishment." He crawls up my chest and hovers his lips inches from mine.

"You'd be correct." Wes seals our lips together, and when our tongues mingle, I taste myself. "I should go."

"But—" He kisses me again before I can protest. I can feel his erection pressed against my stomach, and I'd be lying if I didn't say I was disappointed he wants to leave.

"Go out with us tomorrow."

"Us? As in, you and Meg? It's your special day."

"And I have an idea how to make it even more special. Don't say no."

"Okay. Yes."

Wes taps my cheek twice and grins. "Good boy." *Fuck that's hot.* "I'll text you when I get home, and tomorrow, I'll let you know the plans."

"I'll be ready and waiting. Get home safe."

He stands, and I move to rise and walk him out, but he stops me with a hand to my chest.

"I'm already using all the willpower I have to walk away right now. If you get up, I'll end up staying."

"Would that be such a bad thing?"

"No, it wouldn't. Which is why I'm leaving."

Wes bends down and kisses me one more time. When he pulls away, I see the turmoil on his face but also the resolve to leave. I won't stop him. I can tell he isn't second-guessing what he did. He's not running. He's making the decision to

172

leave, and I respect him for that.

"Thank you for tonight, Wes. I'll speak to you in a few and I'll see you tomorrow."

"Thank you, Elliot."

I stay seated on the couch until I see his headlights leave the driveway. I was too worried if I got up any sooner, I'd follow him outside.

What a fucking night. And I have a feeling Wes has something very special in store for tomorrow.

# 21

# Lainey

Should it feel wrong that I just told my husband to be a ho? Probably. Am I full of nervous energy to hear how his night went? Absolutely!

Lexi has been hard to settle this evening after video calling with Katy and Vik, so I took her into bed with me, and the cuddling calmed her to sleep. I'm lying with her, reading on my phone, when Sawyer texts me to say he's on his way home.

It's too early. Disappointment floods through me for him. He called when he was on his way to Eli's house, but he wasn't there long. I'm not unfamiliar with a quickie, but I know my husband, and that's not how his first time would be... unless it didn't go well.

Lainey: Everything okay, Baby?

Sawyer: It's wonderful. I have an idea I want to run by you when I get home.

Lainey: Lexi is in bed with me, so don't be too loud. See

you soon. Love ya.

Sawyer: «kissy face emoji»

I went from excited to disappointed to curious. We tried deciding what we should do with the money Eli sent us and how we should enjoy it, but we hadn't come up with anything. If Sawyer has an idea, I bet it's a good one.

Twenty minutes later, the sound of the front door almost makes me jump out of bed, but I'm pinned down by a sleeping toddler who is at an awkward enough angle it's kept me from bringing her to bed myself.

My gorgeous husband walks in the room, and the sex hair almost takes my breath away. I know that rumpled hair look. Someone who wasn't himself had their hands in his hair and pulled. Sawyer's hair is thick and will stay at funny angles if he doesn't brush it back.

I love the sight of him.

His smile beams as bright as mine feels. He gently kisses me and picks up Lexi from my arms without a word.

When he returns, he jumps on the bed, and I giggle when he stalks towards me. Sawyer blankets his body over mine and begins to devour my neck.

"Your hair."

He hums into my neck with question.

"You have sex hair, my wonderful husband."

"Mmm. Not sex hair," he mumbles into my neck. "Blow job hair."

"Give or get? Or both. I want all the details." I'm so excited for him.

"Give." Sawyer travels down my body with his kisses and lifts my sleep tank, burying his face beneath it.

"How was it?"

"Exhilarating. Fucking hot. Salty." He punctuates each word between kisses, and I huff a laugh at his explanation.

"Those are appropriate words. How do you feel?"

"Horny."

"Sawyer." I push the top of his head and try to scoot away from him. He growls, but relents, and his head appears. Resting his chin on my stomach, he looks at me with hooded eyes. I see the lust and wonder if it's from Eli or for me. "Talk to me. Tonight was a big deal."

"That's the thing. It wasn't. We talked, he tried to go down on me—"

"Tried?"

"I got impatient and dominant and flipped us around."

"Sounds like you."

"Brat." Sawyer nips at my nipple through my shirt, and I squeak.

"Tell me your idea for tomorrow."

"I'm ready for you to meet, but I have an unorthodox idea."

"Oh, I love unorthodox ideas. Tell me more."

I wake up the following day feeling disoriented and alone in bed. I look at my nightstand and see the baby monitor is missing. I realize Sawyer must be up with Lexi. Stretching, I think about our conversation from last night, and a rush of excitement tingles through my body.

Blindfold.

Movie theater.

Sex.

That's what Sawyer proposed. With the money Eli sent us, he wants to buy out the back of a movie theater and "introduce" Eli and me via our bodies. I'm not opposed to it. In fact, it sounds fucking exhilarating. One of my bucket list items is public sex. Of course, I assumed it would be with my husband, but I can't deny the thrill of what tonight will bring.

Sex, in a public place, with a stranger to me, while my husband watches.

*Fuck.*

I had no idea voyeurism should have been on my list as well.

I finish stretching as Sawyer steps into the doorway with an adorable blonde close behind him.

"A-Leelee!" Lexi yells and runs toward me. I reach over and scoop her up, gently tossing her onto the bed. Her giggles fill the room while Sawyer carefully places a cup of coffee next to me on the nightstand.

"Morning, Jitterbug. I thought I heard rustling in here, so we came to check it out. How'd you sleep?"

"Restlessly with excitement. Have you talked to him?"

Sawyer hadn't asked Eli about his plan as of last night. He wanted to talk it over with me first before offering the scenario to him. The idea was amazing to me, but I was concerned how *he* felt about it since he hadn't crossed that threshold with Eli yet.

As my ever-loving dominant, my pleasure is his pleasure. It's important to him that Eli and I are compatible.

"I have. He seems to be as early of a riser as this adorable little one here." He playfully pokes at Lexi's belly, and she giggles more.

"And?" Sawyer pokes at my belly and smiles.

"Is someone eager?"

"Yes. Aaaaaand? What did he say?"

"He was all for it and had a movie theater half booked by the time we'd finished talking about details. I protested at him spending more money, but he insisted the money he sent us was for *us* and tonight was just as much for him, so he wanted to pay."

Grabbing my coffee off the nightstand, I take a sip and stare down Sawyer. "Did you find us a sugar daddy?"

Sawyer opens his mouth to protest but closes it before any sound comes out. His face contemplates my question, and his posture deflates.

"Did I? Shit, maybe I did."

"Well, you went home with him last night. What's his place like?"

"It's an actual house in a neighborhood. It's one of the smaller ones, but he's only one person. He loves his family. There were pictures of them all over the living room."

"Unc Sowa. More nanas?"

"The princess beckons, Jitterbug. Go take a shower and get ready for the day." Sawyer kisses my forehead and grabs a wiggling, laughing toddler. My mind is reeling with the possibilities of what tonight could bring. Sawyer stops in our doorway and winks at me.

I've had so much nervous energy today. Even my morning yoga class couldn't tamp down my excitement. Sawyer finds me staring into my closet, feeling defeated, and chuckles.

"Everything okay?"

"What do I wear? This is so stressful." Sawyer comes up behind me and wraps his hands around my waist.

"I'm okay if you stay like this." Our eyes meet in the mirror of our closet, and I scowl at all of my wardrobe choices.

"Of course you are, but the general public might frown

on my walking around in just my black bra and panties."

His eyes roam my body, and I feel his heated gaze. "I disagree. But I told you to wear a dress. It's easy access." Sawyer's hand roams down my body, and he cups my core.

"Don't tease me." I swat his hand away and step out of his arms. "I'm nervous. Remind me of the plans again."

Sawyer turns me so I'm facing him and takes my shoulders in his hands.

"Eli emailed me the tickets. We'll get there and relax, eat, and have a drink. About forty-five minutes into the movie, I'll blindfold you, and he'll join us." My heart races at the thoughts of what happens after he joins. "What's our safeword, Jitterbug?"

"Apple."

"Good." He pulls me into his chest, and his warmth engulfs me. "Eli knows and will respect it if he hears it. You have all the power tonight, Alaina."

Sawyer trails his hands over my back as I listen to his heartbeat thump in my ear. It's calming and reassuring.

When I met Sawyer, I was healing. Healing from a childhood of abuse and neglect. He was gentle and caring with me. He understood my reservations and never pushed me into anything I wasn't ready for. The respect I have for this man is immeasurable.

Our safeword was the first thing we established, even before anything sexual started between us. He recognized all of my broken pieces and wanted me to always know I had the control to stop anything I couldn't handle.

"I love you. You know that, right?" I lean back from his chest so I can look into his eyes. "Tonight is as much about you as it is me. You're going to see me with another man, and if at any point you can't handle it, Apple is your safeword, too."

He smiles down at me, and I can feel the love emanating from it.

"I know you love me, Jitterbug, and I know our safeword. We're going to have fun tonight. Finish getting ready. We don't want to be late." Sawyer kisses my forehead and leaves me to figure out what to wear.

# 22

# Elliot

I'm here. It's almost time. The halls of the movie theater are empty as I wait the allotted time. Wes and I agreed to wait before entering.

I'm still floored that this was his idea. I stared at my phone for longer than necessary this morning, trying to determine if I was still dreaming when I read his text.

Sawyer/Wes: I have an idea. I've already spoken to Meg, and she is all for it, so now I'm giving you the option.

Eli: I'm all ears.

Wes proposed sex with his wife in a movie theater. I knew about their bucket lists because we discussed them on our first date. Hearing that public sex was one of Meg's items, and he was offering that to me, was shocking, to say the least.

I like fun and adventure in my life, but this is thrilling.

A notification buzzes my phone, and it's a text from Wes.

Sawyer/Wes: She's ready for you. Remember, the safeword is Apple, and it is to be respected 100%

Eli: Absolutely. Be right in.

My nerves are at peak height when I stand from my bench outside Theater Nine and gently pull the doors open. The action on the screen should begin in about ten minutes. I chose this movie because I saw it a few weeks ago and know there's a big battle scene about halfway through, and it will help mask any additional noise we might make.

As I turn the corner of the stairs and look up, I can see the empty rows and the shadows of my two targets. Meg is on Wes' lap, as we discussed, and he'll hand her over to me when I sit. He'll never be more than a few inches away so he can be there for her and know before she does if things are going farther than she can handle.

Wes told me enough about Meg's past to know this is a big deal for her, allowing someone she doesn't know to take charge of her body.

As I climb the stairs, their bodies become more focused in the dim light. Wes whispers in her ear, and they both smile. I know he said we work in the same building, and I probably know her, but I don't want to focus on that right now. If things go poorly, I'd rather not know who she is.

"He's here," Wes tells her when I approach them. Meg looks fucking stunning. A light blue sundress with thin straps and a ruffle on the end highlights her dark hair and full pink lips.

I nod at Wes while I sit beside them, and we exchange a silent offering. He crooks a finger at me, and I lean closer. He surprises me when his lips press against mine, and I greedily return it. It never dawned on me that I would get to taste him tonight as well. I thought it was all about Meg.

The woman in question moans when she realizes what we're doing.

"That's so not fair. You aren't allowed to make out without me seeing."

Wes chuckles against my lips and pulls away. "Is someone jealous, Jitterbug?"

Jitterbug? That's an adorable nickname. I'd love to know how it came about, but my eyes lock on them as their tongues tangle together. His hand moves possessively to her throat, and her body melts into him. I could sit here all night, watch them, and be just as happy as the event I came for. Their bodies mold and mesh together so well, like they're the only ones in the room.

A quiet "fuck" slips through my lips, and when they pull apart, I realize it's not as quiet as I thought.

"Maybe my wife isn't the only jealous one. Would you like a taste?"

I nod. We agreed I'd be silent on the off chance she recognizes my voice. There's a lot on the line if tonight doesn't go well, and we wanted to make things as smooth as possible.

My eyes dart to Meg's chest as she pants in anticipation. Wes tilts his head in her direction as an offering, and I reach up and grasp her chin. She gasps as I turn her toward me and press our lips together for the first time.

She tastes sweet, like the wine she must have been drinking. Her lips are light and hesitant at first, but as Wes shifts her to sit in my lap, they become more desperate. Eager.

Meg straddles me, and I can feel the heat radiating from

her core. I bet she's wet already. Is she excited for what we're about to do? The thrill of getting caught? Sex with a stranger? Fucking all of the above?

"Touch each other." Wes' encouraging voice cuts through the lust. I didn't realize neither of us had made a move yet to explore each other's bodies. "Let me help."

Wes lowers the zipper on the back of Meg's dress, and it sounds like an alarm going off in my ears when, in reality, I know it's barely making a sound. It appears all my senses are heightened, and that fact hammers home when she slips her hand up my t-shirt and runs her delicate fingers over my stomach and chest.

"I like abs." Fingers trace the parallel lines between the ridges of my body that I work hard to keep toned. I bite my lip in an attempt to keep in the noises my body wants to make.

Reaching up, I hook my fingers on the straps of her dress. I slowly pull them down her arms until she's forced to remove her hands from my shirt to take them off.

"My wife is gorgeous, isn't she?" Wes whispers in my ear as I stare at the absolute goddess before me. She wasn't wearing a bra under her dress, so she sits topless on my lap with her hands back under my shirt. Her breasts are full and proportionate for her small frame.

"May I?" I whisper back to him.

"Please." The response comes from Meg, and I notice her chest heaving with anticipation.

I lick my lips and trail my hands up her stomach to her breasts. She bites her bottom lip, and I stop myself from pulling the lip out of her teeth. I keep my hands preoccupied by engulfing her breasts in them. Her nipples are hard on

184

my palms, and I twist my hands to graze over the sensitive points.

A heavy sigh that's more of a silent moan takes over her entire body, and her hands flex on my bare chest. Meg pushed up my shirt in her attempt to have access to me.

I take hold of one breast and guide her nipple to my mouth. The first moan I hear is low and masculine, and I realize it's from Wes. I smirk into Meg's chest, knowing I'm turning them both on. As my tongue massages and my teeth nip at her tip, I'm rewarded by the rocking of her hips over my growing cock.

"She's so fucking ready for you. Do you smell her arousal? It's heaven." As if Wes' comment sparks something in Meg, her hands go to the button on my jeans, and her fingers frantically move to get me out of my pants.

"Stop," Wes demands, and Meg and I both freeze. His tone is so fucking hot, and I wait for his next command.

"Yes, Sir," Meg's melodic voice responds, and I'm internally warring with the dominant and submissive inside me. I can be whatever my partner needs me to be. Wes said stop, and I did, but hearing Sir come from Meg's lips. *Fuck.*

"I want you to turn in his lap. I want access to the rest of your body while he fucks your pussy."

If I wasn't hard before, I'm fucking rock now. The image of what he wants is enough to make me come, but knowing I'm about to participate in it has me thinking of poor fashion choices and stained clothes to calm myself down.

Wes helps Meg turn so her back is against my chest, and I love the new position. I have easy access to her breasts, and with a devious smile, he disappears under her dress. I know exactly what he's doing when she moans and reaches behind her, grabbing the back of my neck.

Fucking bastard is eating her pussy, and I'm jealous. I want to tell him to give me a taste, but I'm already struggling with not speaking. If I start, I'm worried I won't be able to stop. I'm not a quiet person by nature, but praising my partners is in my blood.

My jealousy doesn't last long when Meg is being shifted up my body, and I feel hands on my jeans. Meg is still gripping my neck as Wes pulls my cock out of my pants. I lean forward and suck Meg's neck into my mouth to contain the loud moan that threatens to escape me when his hot mouth takes me in. For a man with little experience, he's playing us like his perfect little puppets.

Wes pops me out of his mouth, and I feel the slick wet heat of Meg's pussy as he rubs me against her. I'm slowly going mad with the need to possess her, but I'm not in charge. I'm a pawn in this master game of Chess, and Meg is our Queen.

"Jitterbug, do you need to tap out?"

He's checking in with her before this goes any further. I fucking love that. The fact he can still keep his head in this lust-filled scene shows how good of a dom he is. My patience is on thin ice, but it's because I don't know what role I'm supposed to be in, and I'm pleasurably overwhelmed.

"No."

"What's our safeword?"

"Apple," she breathes out.

"Eli, what's the safeword?"

"Apple," I whisper into Meg's ear so she knows I'm aware and will respect it.

Wes pulls a condom wrapper up to his mouth and rips it open with his teeth. My stomach muscles contract when he gently rolls it down my shaft. It's the oddest sensation to feel but not see someone else put a condom on my cock.

He grips my base as he lines me up and instructs her to move down my body. Every move she makes sinks her further onto me, and I close my eyes and just feel.

"Jitterbug, are you good?"

"Yeah. Fuck. So fucking good. Eli, please move."

My eyes lock with Wes' and he nods. "You heard our girl. Show her how well you can please her."

*Our* girl. Does he realize he said that?

I slide down a few inches in the seat and plant my feet firmly on the ground before thrusting up into her needy pussy. My hand quickly moves to her mouth as the moans she was containing so well earlier break through. We want the idea of getting caught, not the actual act.

Meg's breath comes out in short, quick puffs over my hand, and I feel the vibrations of the sounds she can't contain bouncing on my palm. My abs scream at me from the position we're in and the workout they're getting from the upward thrusting motion, but I don't fucking care.

I have even less care when Wes disappears again, and not only is he teasing her clit, but every time I pull out, his tongue extends to my base, and he licks me too. Where the fuck did this man come from?

Meg must be getting close because her moans are becoming more frequent and longer.

"Are you going to come for us, pretty girl?" I couldn't help myself. Even if she does know me, my voice is so gruff with lust even I barely recognize it.

The "um hum" she whines under my hand is enough that I'm ready to blow, but she needs to go first. I can't leave her unsatisfied.

My hand slips, and her teeth dig into my palm. I growl at the pain but relish in the pleasure.

"Bite if you need to." She does, and instantly, her walls pulse around my cock. She feels so fucking incredible it pulls me over with her. My cock pulses, and her pussy squeezes, and I can't imagine we aren't making enough noise to cause attention, but she feels so good I'll gladly get kicked out or spend the night in jail to repeat this night over again.

Meg's body goes slack in mine, and she comes down from her release. My eyes focus on her gorgeous tits as they rise and fall under her labored breathing.

Wes appears smiling from between our legs, and his chin glistens with her arousal. The spike of jealousy comes again, but this time, I reach forward and grab his shirt. I pull him over Meg and lock my lips with his. I taste her on his tongue, around his lips when I venture off, and on his chin, where I lick her off him.

"She tastes like a meal you never want to give up, doesn't she?"

Meg giggles between us as we make out until I step in shit.

"You taste fucking phenomenal, Meg."

She stiffens up, and the air around us changes.

"Apple. Fucking Apple."

Wes snaps up, and I pull my hands away from touching either of them. Meg scrambles off me and jumps into Wes' arms, burying her face into him.

I have no idea what happened, and by the look on his face, neither does he. We have a silent conversation of nods as I take the condom off and get myself back in order.

I open my mouth to say... something, anything. He shakes

his head and tips it towards the exit. I nod in defeat and confusion. I mouth "sorry" and he scrunches his eyebrows and shakes his head again. It gives me minimal relief that he doesn't instantly blame me for whatever reaction she's having.

Finally, I motion for him to call me, and he gives me a curt nod before turning his attention back to his wife, whose shoulders appear to be shaking as if she's crying.

I have no idea what I did to cause such a reaction from her, and I know my stomach will be in knots until I hear from Wes. *If* I hear from him again. Our relationship moving forward was contingent on tonight, and everything was perfect until a few moments ago.

I should have known better. Nothing in my life is ever perfect.

# 23

# Sawyer

Lainey isn't talking to me. After Elliot left the movie theater, she fixed her dress and turned her back on me. I followed like a lost puppy.

She used her safeword. I don't understand why, and she isn't in the right mind for me to ask her. We established that word for her right from the beginning, and although she's used it with me before, it was never during sex or a scene. No is a word that was hard for her to use at first, so when we would talk about things to do or try, she felt more comfortable saying Apple instead of no.

She told Elliot Apple. Something triggered her, and it's killing me not to know what it is so I can help her work through it. The husband and Dom roles inside me are tearing each other apart. One wants to nurture, and the other wants to burn the world down. The problem is, I can't tell who's who, and it's confusing as hell.

I offered my hand to her when we first got in the car, and after some hesitation, she took it. Besides that, she's been staring out the window deep in thought.

*What the fuck happened?*

The deafening silence continues as we take the elevator up to our apartment. I'm dying inside. We are a couple that talks through everything. It's been that way since day one, and I don't know how to handle a silent Lainey. I could make Alaina speak to me, but I don't think that's what she needs right now, and part of my role as her dom is knowing her emotional needs.

By the time I unlock our door, every nerve in my body feels like it's misfiring. I click the lock and turn towards her with my mouth open to speak, and she already has her hand up to stop me.

"You have a million and one questions. And rightfully so." *Goddamn right, I do.* "First, I want you to know that physically I'm good."

"Physically. Not emotionally? Mentally?"

"I'm... processing." She reaches out and takes my hand. A small part of me relaxes at her touch, but I know she has more to say. "Tonight was amazing. The meeting, the sex, you, all of it. I..."

Her gaze shifts to the ground, and I know she isn't going to say anything else.

"You're processing. Okay, Jitterbug, I won't push. Let's take a shower and go to bed. Maybe things will seem clearer in the morning."

Lainey huffs and releases my hand. "I'm going to sleep in the guest room tonight. I promise it's not you. I need to clear my head."

"Lainey." I don't have anything else to say. She's communicated her feelings to me, and I'll respect them, but I feel defeated. I want to know what happened.

"I love you, Sawyer. Nothing has changed. We'll talk in the morning." She reaches up on her tippy toes and kisses my cheek before retreating down the hallway.

Feeling beaten up, I walk in the opposite direction to our bedroom and strip as I walk to the bathroom. I take an unnecessarily long time standing under the spray of the hot water, running the events through my mind, trying to figure out her trigger. I know all of her boundaries and limits, and nothing was crossed. The sex was over. Elliot and I were kissing. There was nothing.

When I step back into the bedroom, knowing there's no way I can sleep, I hear my phone chime on the floor, where I dropped my pants. I'm not surprised to see a text from Elliot.

Eli: I waited as long as I could, but I feel like shit. If you don't respond, I'll understand. Meg is your priority.

Eli: I had an incredible time. I just wanted you to know that. And it's been a pleasure getting to know you.

Eli: Last one, I promise. I don't want to sound desperate or anything. Please let me know if there's anything I can do to help fix whatever happened. I won't reach out after this. I'll wait for a response back.

The last text was received ten minutes ago. How long was I in the shower?

I relax on the bed and consider what to text back to him. I have no more answers than when he left the theater, but I don't want to leave him hanging.

He's right. Lainey is my first priority, but unless she lets me in, I can't help her. Before responding to Elliot, I open my text thread with Lainey.

Sawyer: Jitterbug, I just wanted to say good night and I love you. I hope you sleep well. I'll be here when you're ready.

The icon changes from delivered to read, and then a little heart response pops up on the screen. I wait to see if she'll reply, but nothing else comes.

Sawyer/Wes: Sorry for the delayed response. I was in the shower. I wish I had answers that I could give you, but she didn't want to talk. She did tell me she was okay and that tonight was amazing, but she needed to process. I've gone over every moment in my head and can't figure out what triggered it. I'm sorry. I wish I had more info.

Eli: Hey. It's okay. I'm glad to hear from you. I'm sorry she didn't open up to you more. I can understand how tonight might have been a lot for her. We can put a pause on us until you get to the bottom of it. The last thing I want to do is come between you both.

Sawyer/Wes: It hurts me to say, but I agree, a pause might be best. As soon as I know what's going on, I'll let you know... either way. I had an amazing evening, too, btw. I genuinely hope we can do it again. I'll talk to you soon, Elliot. Night.

Eli: G'night, Doll.

# 24

# Lainey

Tonight was such a high and such a low. I had no idea that my body could have such a visceral reaction to hearing three little letters spoken to me by someone.

Meg.

*Meg.*

Eli called me by "my name." The one I told Sawyer it was okay to use as a codename. I haven't been called Meg since I was a teenager. Meghan is a life I happily left behind and probably should have thought about before I offered it as an option. Eli used it in text but it was a concept then—an alter ego. Tonight he called *me* Meg, and I reacted without thinking. No. I freaked out, and I feel guilty.

I know I need to talk to Sawyer about it. I can only imagine how inferior he's feeling right now. I don't ever shut him out, but this feels like something that I can't process with him yet. But I do know who I can.

Lainey: I'm sorry it's so late. I need you. Both of you. I'll be at our spot at 9am. I'll understand if you don't want to come, but I'll be there.

Neither of us slept last night. I heard Sawyer up and down several times, and around seven, I heard him leave the house.

I'm a fucking coward. He went for a run, and instead of facing him this morning, I quickly got dressed and left the house ninety minutes earlier than I needed to.

I'm lost in thought on my second cup of coffee when a large hand caresses my arm. My eyes flutter shut, not needing to see his face to know who it is.

"You came."

"We both came. You said you needed us." Another hand clasps my knee as the seat next to me rustles.

Of course, they came. They're my saviors. I place a hand over each of theirs and finally open my eyes.

"My guys," I sigh out.

Patrick takes a seat opposite Chip, and they give me weary smiles. I look around for a stroller, but they're alone.

"Where's Violet?" Two pairs of brown eyes stare back at me.

"With Katy," Patrick replies. His gruff voice sends a shiver through me, and memories of his whispered words come back.

Chip takes his hand from my knee and links our fingers together. "You never reach out. We figured it was a little more than a social call when you texted in the middle of the night. What's going on, Pixie?"

Calmness rushes through me at his use of my nickname. I was still Meghan when I was with them, but they never called me by my name. It was always a term of endearment. It helped me realize I could be someone new. I didn't have to live with my demons.

Patrick reaches out and takes my other hand. "Why do you look scared?"

Scared? I don't feel scared. Exhausted. Confused. Upset with myself. Those are more accurate to how I'm feeling. But Patrick was always so attuned to my feelings, so maybe being scared is accurate.

"Pixie. Talk to us."

I squeeze their hands and smile. "Thank you for coming. I need a judgment-free zone, although I'm pretty sure there won't be much anyway."

Looking between the two men who are complete opposites of each other, I can feel the love radiating off them. Part of me is happy I was able to bring them together and help them build their beautiful bond and their family. But a part of me will always feel terrible that I didn't stay to be a part of it. I was broken when we were together.

No. Meghan was broken. They helped me realize I didn't have to be that girl anymore, and as much as I wanted to stay warm and safe in their arms and the cocoon of life we had created, I needed to find myself independent of anyone else. Even the men who helped put some of my pieces together.

"Never." The sincerity in Patrick's single words glistens in his eyes. He's a man of little words, but when he speaks, they have meaning, and you listen.

"Sawyer and I—"

"What did he do?" Chip interrupts. He has such a soft demeanor, and hearing such a clipped tone makes me smile.

I lean forward and kiss his forehead. "Sawyer did abso-

196

lutely nothing. It was me."

I tell them about our evening and leave out some of the more racier details. I pause when I get to the pivotal point of the story. Looking back now, I know I overreacted. I could just as easily have had this conversation with Sawyer, but I don't think I would feel as at ease with him as I do with Chip and Patrick.

"He called me Meg, and it—fuck, I don't know, it freaked me out. I haven't been Meg or Meghan since, well, really, before you two. You never used my name. I loved it. I felt like a different person, and you pushed me to *be* that different person."

"We've always loved you for who you are and never asked you to be anyone else."

Chip's right. They love me, and I love them back, but it's not a romantic love. It's respect, friendship, and thanks that I'll never be able to fully repay them. I had to say goodbye to everything that was Meghan in order to become Lainey. The woman whose past was a complete piece of shit. These incredible men who came when I called are my in-between. They helped me see who I was and gave me the encouragement to go after her. My heart broke to leave them behind, but I would never give up the relationship we have now or what they have together.

"I know that, but I don't know him, and I guess it was something about a stranger using a name that's so dead to me that it triggered some hidden fear inside me."

"Little Bit, what did Sawyer say?"

My shoulders fall, and without saying it, they know I haven't talked to him.

"Pixie, that's not fair to him. Does he even know you're

here talking to us?"

I shake my head in shame. "I needed to get this out to someone who would understand how it's more than just a name. It's a past that I no longer want to associate with. You two helped me change from her to who I am now sitting here with you."

"No," Patrick objects. "We helped you say goodbye to Meghan. Sawyer helped you become Lainey."

I take my hands from theirs, pull my knees to my chest, and hide my face. It's fucking insane how words can cut so deep.

Patrick is right. I attribute them to being my saviors, but the journey after them was mine. They may have put my cracks back together, but Sawyer healed the parts of me that still had holes.

"Pixie, don't hide from us. You never have before, so don't start now."

I lift my head but rest my cheek on my knees, looking away from them. A hand grabs my chin and tugs it up.

"You're too beautiful to hide." The smile on Patrick's face makes his scar stretch, and my fingers twitch to trace it, as I've done so many times before.

"I'm not hiding."

"You are." Chip reaches out his phone, and I see he already has Sawyer's name pulled up to call.

"I hate when you gang up on me."

"That's not what you've said in the past, Little Bit."

My mouth drops open in mock horror. "I am a married woman, Patrick. You shouldn't talk about me like that. What would my husband say?"

"Thank you. He'd say thank you. Now call him, Pixie, or I

will."

"Fine, can't I use my own phone?"

"Nope. I want him to know you came to us first. It makes us more superior." Chip's boyish smile reminds me why he was so easy to fall for.

"Ugh. Fine." I hit the call button, and Patrick hits the speaker button before I can put the phone to my ear. I glare at him with squinted eyes, but the moment Sawyer picks up, every ounce of fight in me melts.

"Chip? Is Lainey okay? Why are you calling me." He sounds defeated and worried.

"It's me."

"Jitterbug? What-Why are you calling me from Chip's phone? Are you okay? You left."

It's the last two words that crush me.

*You left.*

You. Left.

I did. I walked out this morning, and I can't imagine how he felt when he returned from his run, and I was gone.

I must stay quiet for too long because he questions me again. "Are you okay, Lainey? Please, just-just tell me you're okay."

Am I okay? I should be. I have no reason *not* to be. But the words are stuck in my throat.

"Pixie?" Chip looks concerned, and I shake my head as the tears fall. His phone slips from my hand, and he catches it before it hits the ground.

I'm overwhelmed with emotion.

Shame. Guilt. Despair.

Everything floods me at once when Sawyer asks me a simple question.

Chip walks away with his phone, and Patrick picks me up from my chair and puts me on his lap.

"Little Bit, you're safe." His large frame cocoons me. I feel safe, but it's foreign. Almost wrong. Wrong because it's not the arms I want to feel safe with right now, but I just pushed that person away. "Shh. Calm down. I've got you."

I'm trying. The tears have taken over, and I can feel myself shaking. A warm body cloaks my back, engulfing me between Chip and Patrick. I don't deserve them, but I reached out to them for a reason, and this is it. They're the glue that holds my before and after together. My past happened, and I can't run away from it. I can change my name and dye my hair, but Meghan still existed. Chip and Patrick knew Meghan, and they know Lainey. Only their presence could ground me the way it is right now.

"Thank you." The words are weak, but they hear me and don't need any explanation.

I don't know how long we stay embraced with them whispering words of encouragement to me, but a hand sweeps across my cheek, and my eyes flutter open to see my wonderful husband.

"Hey, Jitterbug." I look over my shoulder at Chip, and he shrugs in answer to my silent question. "If you're not ready to see me, I'll go."

"No." I'm released from my safety net, and I dive into Sawyer's chest. The tears flow freely again, but these are relief.

Patrick and Chip each kiss the top of my head and say their goodbyes. I've already said thank you, but I'll reach out later to thank them again.

Chip obviously told Sawyer where we were, and he came.

I left, and he came. He's such a good fucking man, and I'm sure the last few hours were torture for him.

"I'm sorry. It was terrible of me to leave."

"Shh. You don't need to apologize, but I do hope you'll talk to me."

I pull away and look up into his beautiful gray eyes. "Let's go home, and we can talk."

When we get home, I pull us straight into our bedroom and strip us both. Sawyer tenderly lets me do whatever I need without protest. I crawl into bed, and he follows. We both know this is about connection, not sex, and neither of us makes a move toward anything physical other than molding our bodies together.

We lay, holding each other while I compose my scattered thoughts. I inhale a deep breath of Sawyer's chest and realize he didn't shower after his run. He smells musky and all man.

"Sorry. I was too worried to think about showering. You didn't answer your phone."

"I'm sorry Chip had to call for you to know where I was."

"He didn't." I try to pull back in confusion, but Sawyer holds me tighter. "I looked up your location on my phone and saw where you were. I had a hunch when I saw the coffee shop, which was confirmed by Chip's call. I was already on my way there."

He knows that the coffee shop was my spot with them. The three of us would meet there during the day when we first got together. It was a way to be with each other amidst our busy schedules and have some peace. I didn't have to pretend the world around me was pretty and perfect because they knew all of my dirty parts. I watched Patrick and Chip's relationship grow outside the bedroom, sitting in front of those same windows. When I decided I needed to leave to finish finding myself, I brought them there and urged them to continue what they had despite my presence.

Sawyer is grateful for everything they did for me. A lesser man would be jealous, especially finding me in their arms when he showed up, but that's never been an emotion between them.

Respect.

Respect is the word I would use to describe the relationship between the three men. Protective would be another. I'll never forget Patrick's threat to Sawyer if he ever hurt me. Without any challenge in his voice, Sawyer accepted his fate with a handshake. They've been good friends ever since.

"He called me Meg."

"What?"

"Eli called me Meg."

With confusion in his tone, Sawyer pushed further. "I don't understand. That's an option for what you told me to have him call you. Meg or Lane were the options, weren't they?"

"Yes, but up until that moment, no one has called me anything remotely close to Meghan in years. I'm not even sure why I gave it to you as a choice. When he said it…"

I do not know why it's harder to explain it to Sawyer than Chip and Patrick.

False. I know exactly why. Sawyer never knew me as her. I've always been Lainey. *His* Lainey. Sawyer was the first and last partner to ever call me by my new name. He never knew me as Meghan like they did, so it's harder to explain it to him.

"Take your time, Jitterbug."

"That's not me anymore. *She's* not me. Not even blind-folded having sex with a stranger. I freaked out. It's the only explanation I have. I should have said something as soon as it happened, but I'm not sure I understood it at the time. I just needed to detach myself from her. From Meghan. I'm not her."

"Jitterbug, shhh. You are not her. You're Alaina Hayes. My Lainey. A strong, beautiful, kickass woman with an even more kickass job. You've climbed mountains physically and metaphorically, and you left behind the scared girl you used to be. But I love you both. I love you no matter what your name is because I love your heart. Although, I do love you a little more since you have my last name."

"Jerk." I poke at his chest, and he fake pouts as if I could even hurt him.

"Are you upset I went to them?"

"No. I'm proud of you for realizing who you needed to help you through your tough time. I don't have some hero complex with a bruised ego because that wasn't me. They know that side of you personally. I know her through stories and memories. It's different, and I understand that."

*Fuck he's perfect.*

"You sure sound very hero complex-y Mr. Hayes."

"I'll be your hero anytime you need me to be, Mrs. Hayes."

# 25

# Elliot

S awyer/Wes: It hurts me to say, but I agree, a pause might be best. As soon as I know what's going on, I'll let you know…either way. I had an amazing evening, too, btw. I truly hope we can do it again. I'll talk to you soon, Elliot. Night.

It's been three days since the movie theater. Three days since my last text with Wes, and despite trying to keep my cool, I'm failing. I shouldn't be. I barely know him, or her for that matter. It hasn't even been two weeks, but my connection with Wes, or whatever his real name is, was there. We could both feel it.

I told him I wouldn't send another text, but the number of times I've typed something into our message window and deleted it is ridiculous.

"Earth to Elliot."

"What?" My eyes snap up and meet Katy's questioning glare.

"Where did you go? You've been staring at your phone like you can't decide if you want to smash it or make love to it."

That's an accurate representation of how I feel inside.

"Sorry. Just zoned out."

"Obviously. Care to share what's going on in that head of yours?"

I stare at the tiny open hole in my coffee lid, wondering what, if anything, I can share about what's going on in my head.

"I—"

"This week sucks." I'm pleasantly cut off by my gorgeous receptionist as she plops onto the chair next to me. A delicious smell wafts my way, sparking my senses.

"What's wrong with *you* now? Elliot is over her in Lala land. I can't handle two of you. I have enough children in my life."

"Elliot." Lainey perks up as if she didn't notice I was at the table. "I haven't seen you all week."

Because I've been wallowing in self-pity and avoiding happiness at all costs. "My week has sucked too." I shrug and chance a glance at her hazel eyes. As always, I get momentarily lost in the swirls of color. Some days they're more green and others brown.

"Great, now you're both going to complain. Such buzzkills." Katy throws her hands in the air, exasperated with us.

"Says the pregnant woman who can't even drink."

"Alaina Hayes. Don't be a meanie."

"Wow. You're going to full-name me. That's cruel. Those baby hormones must be raging."

I bite my cheek to stop the laugh I want to let out. Hearing their banter is lifting my mood.

"On second thought, *Alaina Hayes,* I want to hear about your issues. Let me bask in your misery."

Lainey sinks in her chair, all humor leaving her body. "I'm having boy troubles."

"Oh man. You just referred to your husband as a boy. That must be bad." Lainey shoots me a look for daring to have an opinion but shakes it off just a quick.

"I wish it were that simple. Sawyer is amazing."

"Of course he is," Katy says with a sigh.

"Shut it, preggo. You asked for details." Lainey points at Katy with the hand holding her coffee cup and squints her disapproval.

"I surrender." Katy raises her hands in defeat. "Geez. I may be the pregnant one, but you're sure testy today."

"Sorry. Like I said, Sawyer is great, although I'm not sure how because I'm pretty sure I messed things up with his boyfriend."

Katy reaches out to take Lainey's hand, and I internally sympathize with her situation. But...

"Boyfriend?"

"Um, yeah." Lainey and Katy exchange a look. To my understanding, they've been best friends for years, and their silent conversation shows it. I've spent plenty of time with Katy, but all the functions I've been to, Lainey has always been absent, so I don't know her nearly as well, despite the eye fucking I give her regularly.

"Maybe not boyfriend. Hookup or, I don't know. Either way, I think I screwed things up. I smoothed it over with Sawyer, but it's up to him where things go with the guy."

I guess I'm not the only one who had a crappy weekend.

"I'll leave you two to talk." I stand, and Lainey grabs my arm. Something about the feel of her touch makes me pause.

"You don't have to leave. I don't mean to bring down the conversation. We can change the subject."

I can't stop staring at my forearm where her petite hand holds me. The air lingers thick between us, charged with an energy I don't understand. My phone buzzes, breaking our connection, and Lainey removes her hand.

"I'll see you ladies later." I step away with the burn of Lainey's hand lingering on my arm and pull out my phone. The name on the screen stops me in my tracks. I change course and duck into the nearest bathroom. It feels ridiculous to hide in order to read a text message, but I'm far too excited to care.

Wes texted me.

Sawyer/Wes: Hey, Elliot. I'm sorry I've been quiet. I'd love to meet up and talk about this past weekend. Things are good with me and my wife, and I need to make them good with you... if you'd still like that.

Fuck yes, I'd like that.

My finger can't type fast enough.

Eli: I would love that.

I want to type more. I want to tell him how the last three days have been torture for me being in limbo. He said Meg was good with everything that happened at the movie theater, but she still used her safeword, and I need to know why so if things continue, I don't do it again.

Sawyer/Wes: Want to meet at Java Junkie?
    Eli: Or you could come over...

His answer will help me determine where things are going. If he still wants to meet for coffee in a public place, chances are slim things will continue between us. If he agrees to come to my house, there's hope. If he's willing to be alone with me I have a chance to fix whatever mistake I made. I'm a people pleaser, and it's been killing me to know I triggered Meg.

Sawyer/Wes: 6:30 and I'll bring dinner?

*Fuck*. He agreed to come over.
    The bathroom door swings open, and I jump, remembering my surroundings. I forgot where I was and quickly shove my phone into my pocket and exit the room. Once I reach the elevator and scan my card to access the top floor, I eagerly pull out my phone. I need to respond before he thinks I'm ignoring him.

Eli: Sounds perfect. I'll provide the wine.
    Sawyer/Wes: See you tonight. «kissy face emoji»

# 26

# Sawyer

Lainey has been encouraging me to reach out to Eli after I told her we agreed to pause our dating. Despite understanding why she used our safeword, I needed to know she still feels safe.

I quietly watched her for the last few days, confirming she wasn't wearing a mask. She came and went as usual, and I saw no signs of anything negative. With another push from Lainey, I finally reached out to Elliot.

I'm nervous as I drive to his house, with the smell of garlic and tomato sauce in the air. I figured Italian was a safe food choice. The porch light comes on as I pull into the driveway, and my heart races when Elliot's silhouette appears. Even cloaked in darkness from a distance, he's beautiful.

When I step out of the car, he approaches me to help with the food, and there's an awkward air between us. I want to kiss him. His lips call to me—pink and plump. My eyes trail to his Adam's apple, and I watch him swallow hard. It's clear he's as affected as I am at the moment.

Elliot leans in, placing a hand on the top of my car, caging me in.

"Fuck, Wes. I want to kiss you, but I know I have no right to."

"Kiss me," I whisper. At least, I think I do, but Elliot just stares at me, unmoving. "Elliot, please kiss me," I try again but a little louder.

His brows scrunch as if in pain, and he rests his forehead on mine.

"Not right now. Let's eat and talk first."

"But you said—"

"I said I *want* to kiss you, and that hasn't changed. But I need to know where things stand first, so let's go inside and eat. Okay?"

"Okay." He kisses my forehead and takes a bag from my hand. I can't help but feel a sense of disappointment and awe. He has more restraint than I do. I was ready to beg him to kiss me.

My eyes drift to his ass as I follow him into the house, and I want to chastise myself for looking. But if I never see him after tonight, I want to get my fill while I can.

We eat in silence. The sound of scraping metal on glass dishes grates on my nerves. I should probably speak first. It's the reason I'm here, but a feeling of impending doom sits heavy in my stomach.

Lainey sent him away with a safeword, but I ignored him for three days. The fact he welcomed me into his home shows a lot about his character. He's a good man, allowing us time to get through the events of the weekend.

"Did I hurt her? Was our kissing too much too soon?" The guilt lacing his words breaks me in two. I drop to my knees in front of him and take his hands. The fork he was holding clatters on the ground, most likely splattering me and the floor with red sauce, but I'm focused on Elliot. On his eyes. Eyes that should be as blue as a summer sky but instead are muted with concern.

"God, no. You didn't hurt her, and she thought the kissing was hot."

"Then what, Wes? What did I do that caused Meg to use her safeword? Fuck, I'm so proud of her for using it, and I don't even know what I did, but it's been eating me up inside not knowing."

I feel like absolute shit. I was so concerned with Lainey's mental health, it never dawned on me to think of the toll it might have taken on Elliot.

Releasing his hands, I cup his cheeks.

"Are you okay? I fucked up. I should have checked on you. There were three people in that scene, and I completely neglected you. Fucking rookie Dom shit. I'm so sorry, Elliot."

"She's your priority. I understood." His eyes tell a different story than his words. He's hurting.

I sit back and pull him from the chair into my lap. He comes willingly, and I cradle him in my arms.

"Yes, she was my priority at the moment because she used her safeword, but it was my scene, and it was my responsibility to make sure *everyone* had proper aftercare. I failed you, Elliot, and for that, I'm sorry. That's not who I am. You can ask Alaina."

He sucks in a breath when I use a name other than Meg. It wasn't a slip-up. She asked me to tell him. Meg was the catalyst for her trigger, and she didn't want to take a chance on it slipping out again.

"That's her name. My wife's name is Alaina, or Lai—"

"Lainey." He shifts in my lap to see me better and looks shocked by my words. "It can't be."

"Can't be what?" Now it's my turn to be shocked. I knew there was a good possibility he could know her, but he's acting like he *knows* her.

"Are you... Sawyer?"

# 27

# Lainey

"I have too much nervous energy." I sip the glass of wine in my hand, and Katy looks at me longingly.

"Feel free to share some with me." She pats her tiny belly bump, which she swears is just the extra donuts she's been consuming. I give her a funny look, and she laughs. "Not the wine, the energy. This baby is sucking the life force from me. Viktor has been a godsend with the other rugrats."

"As he should since they are all his creation."

"I swear I'm going to knock him out and get his balls snipped so he can't impregnate me anymore." I wince at the thought and shift uncomfortably in my seat despite my personal lack of balls. "He deserves it. I'm not his personal cow."

"TMI, woman!" I toss a pillow at Katy, and a wail comes from down her hallway. I admire Katy's parenting skills because the sound doesn't even phase her. I came to her house after work when Sawyer told me he was meeting up with Eli tonight.

213

Asked, not told.

He confirmed with me a dozen times that I was okay with him going out. I think it was close to two dozen when I told him I wanted Eli to know my real name.

"Do you need to check on the crying child?"

"Nope. It's Justine. She's a drama queen, and chances are Owen looked at her the wrong way. She'll come find me if anything is really wrong."

"I envy your ability to be carefree about this. I want to go hug her and give her the entire world to make her stop."

"Trust me, if Viktor were here, that's exactly what he'd be doing. Do you and Sawyer want kids still? I know you wanted to wait."

"Yeah. I think so. I mean, I do, but it isn't something we've talked about in a while." I wonder why?

"Does the boyfriend want kids?" I choke on the sip of wine I was taking and pat away the dribble that escaped the corner of my lips.

"Let's see what comes of tonight before planning our futures. I really hope I didn't mess anything up between them. Did I tell you he works with us? Well, in our building, apparently."

"No shit. Any idea who?"

"I wish. Sawyer knows, but I told him I didn't want to unless tonight went well." Leaning forward, I rest my elbows on my knees, get closer to Katy, and lower my voice. "Can you imagine having to see the guy you shamelessly fucked in a movie theater every day at work, knowing it could never happen again?"

"No, I absolutely can't because I'm not nearly as adventurous as you, Lainey. That's why I keep you around. I live for

214

your escapades, best friend."

"Fuck, Mommy." I feel the blood drain from my face as Emory, Katy's almost three year old pops up from behind the couch. Of course, the curse would be the one word he repeats in everything we just said.

"Duck, baby. Aunt Lainey said duck. Quack. Quack." Katy looks at me and rolls her hand to get me to quack with her. "Right Aunt Lainey? Ducks say quack, quack."

"Yep. Quack, quack. Just like a duck."

We quack several more times before Emory gets bored with us and wanders off, quacking to himself.

"I'm so sorry, Katy. I had no idea he was in the room, let alone right behind me."

She shrugs and shakes her head, dismissing my apology. "That child is a sponge, just like his Nana Spencer. He hears everything. Viktor and I have to play jungle animal sounds on the Bluetooth in our room when we have sexy time because he asked too many times 'why Mommy was yelling,' and it got too embarrassing."

"No way!"

"Yes, way. The little shit is nosey, but I love the snot out of him and the rest of them." She rubs her belly again, and the love radiates from her. "So, are you sure you're okay with the boyfriend thing? You've recovered from this weekend?"

I sigh and flop back on the couch, careful not to spill my wine. "I was never *not* okay about that part. It was the name that triggered me. The se—" I look around before continuing in a whisper. "The sex was incredible. Having them both take charge was... fuck. It was mind-blowing. I was never really worried about that part anyway. I've experienced it before. That's why I was so adamant that

Sawyer find someone first."

"I really do envy you. Viktor is such an Alpha male he growls when another man looks at me for too long. Forget how caveman he gets the more this belly grows."

"Fuck right, I do." Vik had walked into the room behind Katy and held a finger to his lips, wanting to hear what she was going to say about him.

I love their love. He walks around the chair she's sitting in and kisses her gently while caressing her tiny belly.

"Hey, Pepper. I missed you."

Katy beams at him and playfully swats his chest. "You were gone for less than two hours. Were you that lonely at the grocery store?"

"I'm always lonely without you."

"Take a kid with you next time. It will help with the loneliness." Katy gives him a saccharin smile, and I stifle a laugh.

"I'll get out of your hair so you can turn on your jungle noises, and Tarzan can meet Jane." I wiggle my eyebrows, and Vik gives Katy a death glare.

"What? She has best friend privileges. She gets to know everything." Katy pushes at his chest to stand and say goodbye to me. We hug at the front door, and I can't help but give one last jab before I go.

"Bye, Tarzan. I hope Jane has fun swinging on your vine."

"Pepper," Vik growls from somewhere in the house, and Katy pushes me out the door, laughing.

As I get in my car, I check Sawyer's location and see he's home. I deflate a little, not expecting to see him there so soon. It must not have gone well if he's back already.

216

Lainey: On my way home from Katy's. It was getting a little too Disney at their house.

Sawyer: Um. I'll need more info about that when you get here. I'm already home, and I have what I hope is a good surprise when you get here.

I double-tap the text and hit the heart response. I don't need to tell him I already know he's there, but I'm intrigued by what kind of a surprise he may have for me.

The anticipation makes the ride home quick, and my fingers drum on my legs as the elevator ascends to our floor. As I walk down the hall, our apartment door opens, and Sawyer steps outside, closing the door behind him.

"Hey, Baby. Everything alright? Why do you look nervous?"

When I get close enough to him, he pulls me into his chest and seals his lips to mine.

"I love you, Jitterbug," he says in a husky voice.

"Did you do something wrong?" I ask with a chuckle.

"I sure as fuck hope I didn't, but I took a leap of faith. What's our safeword?"

"Sawyer, why are you aski—"

"Alaina, what is our safeword?"

*Shit. Okay.* "Apple."

"Good." He runs a gentle finger down my jaw, and when he reaches my chin, he jerks my head up to look at him. "You were so brave when you used it this past weekend, and I don't think I told you how proud I was of you. When we walk through this door, I expect you to use the same judgment if you need to. We're always at your pace."

"We?" Who's here?

"Yes, *we*. Are you ready?"

I simply nod because I don't know what else to say. He looks serious but also sincere, and I trust him implicitly. I know what or whoever is on the other side of the door, Sawyer made the decision with plenty of thought.

He reaches behind him and turns the knob. The door opens with a gentle creek, and he steps aside so I can walk in first. There's someone sitting on our couch, and at the clearing of Sawyer's throat, that someone turns and stands.

Dark hair, bright blue eyes, and a devilish smile appear when he turns his head. I smile, making my way to Elliot and embrace him in a hug. I'm not sure who I expected to see, but it wasn't him.

"Hey! What are you doing here? I was just with Katy. You should have joined us." Elliot looks over my shoulder at Sawyer, then back at me.

"Lainey." My name sounds different than usual coming from his mouth. It's deeper. Darker. His hands flex on my hips and I realize we're embracing a little longer than is probably appropriate for a friendly greeting. I try to step back, but his grip tightens.

"Elliot?"

He's making me slightly uncomfortable. Sawyer and I have already had a strange week with the whole Eli situation, and I'd hate to make it weirder with this overly affectionate hello.

"Say it again," he whispers.

"Say... say what again?"

"My name. Call me Elliot again."

"Elliot."

"Fuck that sounds incredible."

218

My comfort level is almost to the floor, and I move my hands to Elliot's chest, ready to push him away. I look over my shoulder, expecting to see a completely different expression on his face, but instead of uneasy or anger I see expectation.

"Sawyer?"

"Jitterbug, meet Eli."

# 28

# Elliot

"Are you... Sawyer?"

To say he was shocked that I knew his name would be an understatement, but not as shocked as I was to learn my goddess crush at the reception desk is the same woman who changed my fucking world only a few days ago.

How did I not recognize her? The theater was dark. She was blindfolded. All excuses I can give myself as to why the woman I see every morning and most evenings, and whose tiny scrap of an excuse for panties were in my hand, is the same one who fooled me with a simple piece of cloth over her eyes. I had no idea.

Would I have done it if I did?

Fuck yes, I would have. I've fantasized about this woman since the day we met and I wanted to rail her under her office desk.

After Sawyer and I realized our connection, he insisted she needed to know, and it needed to be now. I knew she was at Katy's, and he said we needed to go to his house and meet her when she got home.

There was no objection from me as I followed him in my car to his apartment. I wanted to have my vehicle with me in case anything went wrong, and he agreed.

Now, the woman who has been the star of more late-night jerk sessions than I'd like to admit is in my arms.

"Jitterbug, meet Eli."

"Of course, I know, Elli…"

Slowly, Lainey's head turns back to me. Her eyes scan my face as she puts the pieces together.

Eli is Elliot.

I am Eli.

We've had sexual chemistry, albeit harmless flirting, because the line we've crossed is not something I'd ever do without Sawyer's permission. I had more than Sawyer's permission this past weekend. He was the fucking conductor. The producer and director. The Dom to our sub.

Lainey's head shakes, and her brows scrunch. She stutters as her brain misfires, and it's fucking adorable.

"You… you're. But. It can't be. Sawyer, are you serious?"

Her gaze bounces between Sawyer and me. As his smile grows, her confusion lessons, and I lift my hand to her face and use the pad of my thumb, attempting to smooth the lines between her eyes.

"He's serious, Cherry. Color me surprised when he told me his wife's name was Alaina. Honestly, if Katy hadn't name-dropped you this afternoon, I'm not sure I would have remembered you gave me that name the day we met. You've always been my Lainey."

"*Your* Lainey?"

"That's how I've thought of you since the day I walked into the building, and you were sitting behind the desk in your little navy dress, looking so fucking gorgeous."

Her body slowly relaxes in my arms, and the hands that were splayed across my chest in an attempt to put some distance between us are now brushing across my shirt absentmindedly as she takes in all the new information.

"Sawyer?" she questions him again, and he steps closer, sandwiching her between us.

I loosen my grip on her waist, and she spins to face him. I'm just as happy with this view. A few stray tendrils have fallen from her braided hair, and I push them aside and place a soft kiss at the base of her neck, where it meets her shoulder.

A low moan hums in her throat as I continue peppering her with sweet kisses.

"Talk to me, Jitterbug. I'm sure this is a shock. Remember you have a safeword. Elliot, what's our safeword?"

Grazing my lips to her ear, I whisper, "Apple. But I promise you'll never have to use it again, Cherry. You can trust me."

"I think I know that."

Sawyer kisses her forehead. "Talk to us."

"Can we sit? Being sandwiched between two sexy men is making my brain malfunction."

Sawyer and I lock eyes and smile before we step back. Lainey takes our hands and leads us to the couch. We sit, and instead of joining, she sits on the coffee table across from us. Sawyer and I scoot closer together so we can reach her, and each take a hand.

She looks at me. Really looks, as if she's seeing me for the first time.

"Someone explain to me how this happened." She pulls back her hands and starts ticking things off on her fingers. She looks at Sawyer. "This is the guy you bumped into at Midnight Moonshine months ago?"

He nods. "He is."

"So that means"—she reaches up and swipes at the faint pink mark on Sawyer's hairline—"Elliot was the voice that got you so hot and bothered you cut your head and made me come in the supply closet?"

"Fuck, hearing it all together like that is so goddamn sexy." I let my hand rest on her thigh and tuck my fingers under the hem of her dress, which keeps riding up every time she moves. I can't stop myself from wanting to touch her. I've wanted to for so long, and now that I have permission, it's hard to stop myself.

"So all of this was just pure, dumb luck?"

"Seems like it, Jitterbug. Is it a problem? I understand Elliot's already in your circle of friends."

I squeeze her thigh to get her attention. "I won't come between you and them, just like I'm not willing to come between you and Sawyer. The decision is utterly and completely yours."

"My decision?"

"Alaina, look at me." There's a sharpness to Sawyer's tone, and her head snaps to him. "You don't have to decide anything right now. I invited Elliot here because I thought it would be easier to do this in person. So you can associate Eli and Elliot. I knew you worked in the same building, but I didn't realize how often you crossed paths, and neither of us want to make having a relationship an issue for your work environment."

"Relationship." The word comes out in a barely there whisper, and I sense she's becoming overwhelmed. I sit back, removing my hands from her body, and she stares down at where my palm left her thigh.

"I'm going to go, Cherry. There's a lot to think about. I want you to take your time and know I will accept whatever decision you make." I move to stand and she grabs my forearm.

"Stay. You can sleep in the guest room."

The idea of sleeping under the same roof as either of them excites me.

Too much.

I need to give her space. They need to talk this over together without the influence of me being here. It's their relationship.

"Cherry, I want to, so fucking bad do I want to. But I can't. You deserve time to process; if I'm here, I won't be able to keep my hands off you. I'll come over tomorrow after work. And the next day, and the next. I'll come back every day that you want me to, but not tonight. Tonight, you'll have each other."

I can tell she appreciates my words, and despite wanting to protest, she relents and releases my arm.

"Can I walk you out?" Her hazel eyes look up to me with hope.

I glance at Sawyer, and he nods. "I'd love that."

Lainey takes my hand, and I shamelessly lag behind her so I can watch her ass sway. We reach the door and the air around us charges. She takes my other hand, and I feel like I'm sixteen again, standing on the front porch with my girlfriend, wondering, "Will they, won't they," but I'm a sure thing.

"Hey, Sawyer," I yell back into the apartment, not taking my eyes off Lainey.

"Yeah?"

"I'm going to kiss our girl goodbye. You got any objections to that?"

"Yeah, I do, actually." Sawyer stalks toward us, and Lainey releases my hands, stepping back. He grips my neck and pushes me against the wall, crushing his lips to mine. It's all dominance, and I fucking love it. I don't fight him, allowing his tongue to twist and turn inside my mouth. His grip tightens around my neck possessively, and I feel him hardening against my thigh.

Reaching down, I grab his cock, and he grunts while pulling away. "Let me kiss Lainey goodbye, and then let her take care of you." I give him a firm squeeze, and he closes his eyes, dropping his forehead to mine.

"Fuck. Are you sure you won't stay?"

No. Which is why I need to leave now. My resolve is waning.

"I'll be back."

"Tomorrow, Elliot. You'll be fucking back tomorrow. Understand."

"If that's what Lainey wants."

"It's what *I* fucking want."

I reach behind Sawyer and extend my hand, wiggling my fingers. Lainey understands and takes it. I pull her to the side and slip her hand under mine, and together we squeeze Sawyer's cock.

"Jesus fuck," he groans, and I suppress a smile.

Lainey takes over, and Sawyer's hand drops from my neck. I take the opportunity to switch places with her.

Grabbing Sawyer's chin when he tries to lean in and kiss her, he growls at the interruption. I ignore it and turn his face toward mine.

"It's a good fucking thing the decision isn't all yours, Doll. Now, I'm going to kiss Lainey and leave, and you're going to let her get on her knees and worship you. Understood?" I'm not trying to top him. I'm trying to focus him, and direct her.

Finally, Sawyer grunts his acceptance, and Lainey leans over, stealing the kiss I'm willingly offering. A large hand grabs my cock, and Sawyer's breath teases my ear.

"What about you?"

*Leave.*

*Leave now, Elliot.*

*Fucking. Leave.*

I step back before I can no longer talk myself out of staying, and my first thought is that I want the feel of his hands back on me.

"I'll wait to see if I'm invited back tomorrow. Besides, a little delayed gratification never hurt anyone."

"We'll see you tom—"

"Don't." I place a hand over Lainey's mouth. "Tell me tomorrow." Her head bobs under my hand, and I shift my eyes between them. "Goodnight."

I puff out a breath as I wait for the elevator. I could not have predicted when I woke up this morning, miserably single, that I could be going to bed with two potential lovers.

# 29

# Lainey

I never care what I wear to work. Scratch that. I always care, but I never put in much effort. I have my standard work dresses, and I rotate them. Today feels different. I want to impress Eli...Elliot.

Sawyer's Eli is Elliot.

The man who fucked me in a movie theater is Elliot.

I'm still wrapping my head around it. The two men are one in the same, and both...*mine*? Is that even possible?

"Stop fretting. You look beautiful." Sawyer's big arms wrap around my petite frame. A frame that felt much smaller last night with two men wrapped around me. What will it feel like to have them wrapped around me naked? "Where'd you go, Jitterbug?"

"Hmm? Oh. Just thinking."

"Your skin just flushed. Tell me what you're thinking about." Sawyer nips at my neck then blows cold air on the area. I feel the hairs rise on my nape, and apparently, so does Sawyer because he chuckles softly.

"You."

"And?"

"Elliot."

"Mmm. And?"

"Me, between both of you." I'm completely mush in his hands while he continues to lick and nip at my neck.

Suddenly, he stops and steps back. "Go to work before I make you late."

I turn and place my palms flat on his chest. "And I get to tell him?"

"Yes, Jitterbug." He kisses my nose. "You can tell him whenever you see him today."

I push his chest and spin out of his grip. "Okay, time to go. Get out of my way."

"Not so fast, woman." Sawyer catches my arm before I can get away and pulls me into his chest, searing me with a kiss of possession. I'm breathless when he pulls away. "Have a good day, and let me know how it goes. Love you."

My body vibrates with excitement as I sit at my desk. I've been practicing different scenarios in my head all morning, trying to decide how to ask him.

"Hey, Lain—"

"Tonight. Over. You. Sex. Fuck."

"Umm. It's not the craziest proposition I've ever heard, but okay, sure. Viktor can be a real caveman about sharing, though."

I groan and bury my face in my hands. Thank fuck, it was Katy. I can't imagine how mortified I would be if it were someone's client.

"Is there something else you'd like to tell me, best friend? I feel like with a greeting that terrible, you've got something, or someone, on your mind."

"Yeah, Elliot," I mumble through my hands.

"Um, what?"

*Shit.* I haven't told her anything about last night yet. After Elliot left, I did as I was told and knelt for Sawyer. Afterward, we showered and went to sleep. It was a bit of an emotionally exhausting day.

Katy peels back a few fingers, and I peek at her.

"Did you say…"

"Elliot. I said, Elliot."

"Talking about me, Cherry?"

*Fuck.*

I quickly stand from my seat, my rolling chair crashing against the wall behind me. It's the moment I've been waiting for. He's here. I run the palms of my hands down the front of my pink dress pants that I paired with a black blouse after changing five times.

*You've got this, Lainey.*

"Come. Sex. Tonight. JESUS FUCK." I cover my eyes again and plop back into my chair, except… "Ouch, fuck."

"Lainey." Elliot and Katy round my desk as I lay flat on the floor. I knocked the chair away when I stood and embarrassingly just landed flat on my ass.

I close my eyes, not wanting to see their faces. Whether it's concern or barely contained laughter, humiliation is all I feel.

"I've got her, Elliot."

"It's okay, Katy. I'll take care of her. She said a few choice words I'd like to investigate further. Annie will understand if I'm late; the kids won't if you are."

They talk over me as if I'm not feet from them.

229

"I wouldn't be too worried about what she said. She propositioned me when I walked up, too. Although, I think I got a few more words than you, and they were a little more coherent. How hard did you hit your head, Lainey?"

"Ugh, both of you go away and let me die under my desk. I'm not a praying woman, but I'm praying to the Heavens right now that the floor swallows me whole."

"Silly bestie. Down would be to Hell, and we're too pretty for that. You sure you've got this self-deprecating teeter totter, Elliot?"

"Go away, Katy. I'm revoking your gossip card in three... two—"

"Damn. Okay. You're mean when you fall on your ass. She's all yours, El. Good Luck."

The squeak of Katy's sneakers signals she's left, but the rustle of clothing on my other side and the heat emitting from his body let me know Elliot has gotten closer.

"I'm fine. You can leave, too."

"Not on your life, Cherry. You said, come, sex, and tonight, and I'm intrigued by all three words. Also, I think I take back my previous observation." I chance a peak, and Elliot is peering under my desk. "There would *not* be enough room down here for me to fuck you."

I sigh with more embarrassment and turn away from him.

"Come on. Let's get you off the floor before you hurt yourself." Elliot stands, and I hear the wheels of my chair rolling toward me. He extends his hand, and with much reluctance, I accept. He gently sets me onto the chair and doesn't let go until he knows I'm settled.

"You don't need to baby me."

"I'm not babying you. I'm taking care of you. Does

anything hurt?"

"Yeah. My ego." I want to rewind about thirty minutes and get the marbles out of my mouth. How could I fumble twice?

"Well, you look beautiful today despite your bruised ego. But are you honestly okay? Did you hit your head or anything?"

Now is my chance. I can do it right this time.

"Will you come over tonight, Elliot?"

"Don't answer my question with a question, Alaina."

"Fuck."

His lip twitches, and he knows what he just did to me. I squeeze my thighs together, wanting the pressure it induces. One word. He said my name, and that's all it took.

"I'll only ask one more time, Alaina. If you answer my question, I'll answer yours. Are you alright?" All I can do is stare as his hands innocently roam my body, looking for any injuries.

"I'm fine." His touch puts me into a trance I don't want to wake up from. When his hand reaches the nape of my neck, he tugs a little, forcing me to look up at him. People walk past the desk coming in to start their day, and I hope this looks more innocent than it feels.

Elliot leans in, and I panic with excitement, thinking he's going to kiss me. Instead, he moves to the left and brushes his lips against the shell of my ear.

"Good. Fucking. Girl. I'll be there tonight. Should I go home first and pack a bag?"

"Yes." I'm shocked I can even find the words to speak.

"Then I'll see you later, Cherry."

Elliot kisses my forehead and leaves me feeling exposed,

aroused, and excited. I turn in my chair to try and find some semblance of order when my phone lights up with a text.

Katy: WTF. I need ALL the details ASAP.

Lainey: If you wait until tomorrow, I'll have spicy ones for you.

Katy: DEAL!!!!!

# 30

# Sawyer

We're doing this. It's finally happening. Lainey is on her way home from work, and Elliot will be over after he packs a bag. My fingers itch to get my hands on them both.

"Baby, I'm home." I beeline toward Lainey and pick her up, throwing her over my shoulder.

"Sawyer, put me down, you caveman."

Her giggling is music to my soul, but I am single-minded at the moment. When we reach our bed, I put her back on her feet, and she attempts to wrap her arms around my neck.

"Strip."

She smiles at me like I'm crazy, but I'm not. I'm fucking famished, and only her pussy can save me.

"Strip, Alaina. I'm mad you're wearing pants today, and I don't have easy access to what I want. I may never allow you to leave the house again unless you're wearing a dress."

She must sense the urgency in my tone because she rushes to take off her pants, leaving on her panties like I know she prefers. Her blouse and bra come next, and my fucking goddess stands before me like a masterpiece painted just for me.

I slowly sink in front of her, peppering her body with kisses as I descend. When I reach her core, I wrap my hands around her hips and pull her close to me. With a deep inhale, I smell her arousal.

Hooking my fingers into her panties, I look up into her hazel eyes. They look more green than brown right now. "May I."

"Please."

I peel the pale blue lace off her hips and down her thighs. When I reach her feet, she carefully steps out of them. The only patience I had disappears with her panties. I place a flat hand on her stomach and push her down onto the bed. Before she's finished bouncing from the momentum, I have her legs spread apart, and I'm feasting.

Lainey's hands fly to my hair, and she tugs as her body convulses from my sudden onslaught on her pussy. Fuck she tastes good. All I could think about all day was hearing her moans; this is the quickest way to make it happen.

She doesn't disappoint. The flicking of my tongue has her moans damn near echoing around the room. With ease, I slip two fingers inside her, and her noises increase.

"Fuck, Sawyer. Are you okay?"

I hum into her pussy, and she gasps. I want her orgasm, and I want it now. I'm so fucking hot and bothered knowing that anything and everything can happen tonight. Eating my wife's pussy is like my fucking appetizer for the evening to come.

"Ohmygod, baby. I'm gonna... fuck... fuuuuuck."

I feel her orgasm pulsing around my fingers and her release as it drips. When her moaning stops, I pull my fingers out and crawl up her body. She watches my every move. With my fingers still wet from her orgasm, I smear them across her lips, and she parts for me. Lainey's tongue darts to lick away my artwork, and I stop her.

"Don't. That's mine." I suck my fingers into my mouth and clean them off before licking my way around her lips. Lainey pants and moans around my tongue while she squirms under me.

"Do you need something, Alaina?"

"You inside me."

"Does your pussy feel empty?" She nods and gives me her best doe eyes.

"Good." I kiss the tip of her nose and stand. "I want you wanting when Elliot gets here."

I leave the room without turning around, her growl of frustration following me.

Elliot: I'll be there in about 30. Should I bring anything special?

Sawyer: Just you, sexy. ~Lainey

I reread the text exchange between them and count down the minutes until he arrives. Lainey heard my phone buzz and grabbed it before I could. She's had a smile on her face since she responded to him.

"What if he's a vegetarian? Have I ever seen him eat meat? I think I have. Have I? We usually just have coffee together. What if—"

I stop Lainey's rambling by sealing my lips to hers. She

instantly melts in my arms and sighs into our kiss.

"Thank you. I needed that."

"I know, Jitterbug. Me too." I move her hair to the side, and my lips travel to her neck. Walking away earlier instead of fulfilling what we both wanted was as much of a tease for me as it was for her. I wanted nothing more than to sink deep inside her until she was screaming with another orgasm. The need for her is still strong right now, and I'm wondering if I have time to make her come again before Elliot gets here.

*Fuck it.*

Grabbing the waistband of Lainey's leggings, I pull them to her ankles in one swift motion. I lift her onto the kitchen island, wrap her legs around my head, and dive in.

"Sawyer, there's food on the counter." Her words may be protesting, but her hips grinding against me tell a different story.

"Mmhmm. I'm eating it." I nip at her clit before swirling my tongue the way she loves it, and all further protest dies on a moan.

We're enjoying ourselves when the doorbell rings. Lainey gasps and tries to sit up, but I lay my arm across her stomach, stopping her. With her leggings stuck around her ankles and her legs over my shoulders, she's completely at my mercy.

"Sawyer. It's probably Elliot at the door." She attempts to push my arm off her, but I'm not budging.

"Let's hope it is. Come in!" Lainey flops back on the counter with a long moan when I pump two fingers inside her and instantly find her G-spot. She's completely at my mercy now.

"Hello?" His fucking voice. It slides across my skin,

causing me to devour my wife even more. "Hell—*ooooh*."

"Hi," Lainey breathes out when Elliot reaches her on the other side of the counter.

"Hello there, Cherry. Don't you look stunning?" I peer over her body as Elliot gently caresses her face and neck.

"Fuck. Oh god, Sawyer. Yes. Ugggggh. No!" I chuckle to myself as I stand to greet our guest. "Hey. Come on in, Elliot."

"Sawyeeeer."

Elliot covers his mouth, trying not to laugh at Lainey's whining.

"Alaina, don't be rude. We have a special guest. Maybe he'd like an appetizer before dinner." I duck out of her legs and remove her pants the rest of the way.

Now that I've called her Alaina, she understands the dynamics in the room have changed, and she won't speak without permission.

"Let's let her calm down while we go over limits, Elliot. Maybe we should resume this after dinner."

Lainey whimpers at the thought of having to wait. She was on the verge of her orgasm, and I know she's anxious to finish.

"I am a little famished. If an appetizer is still available, I'd like to see what you have to offer." Lainey's chest rises and falls at his words.

Elliot walks around the island, and when he gets close enough, I grab his shirt and pull him in for a kiss. There's nothing chaste or soft about it. It's evident by the way Elliot nips and licks around my mouth that he's tasting Lainey.

"About that appetizer," Elliot purrs into my ear.

I pull away and grab his chin. "Rules first." I have his full attention, and he nods against my hold. "Alaina is my sub. Lainey or Jitterbug is my wife." He looks at her, lying flat on the counter, and smiles.

"It's a pleasure to meet you, Alaina."

"She won't speak without being asked a direct question or given permission."

He runs a hand down her inner thigh that's propped up on the counter. "So well trained."

"What's the safeword, Elliot?"

"Apple."

"Alaina, safeword?"

"Apple, Sir."

"Alaina likes to know what's going to be done to her body so she can choose to refuse if she's uncomfortable without having to use her safeword. I know it's unconventional, but it's vital to her trust. Lainey likes to be fucked upside down and sideways, and she could care less if it was a sneak attack or planned."

"Interesting."

It's my turn to run a hand on her thigh. "It took a lot of time and trust to get to where we are, and there are reasons we have these safeguards in place."

"I respect all of them fully."

"Good. Then, if you'd like an appetizer before dinner, you need to ask permission because I know what Lainey wants, but that might not be what Alaina wants."

I realize it's strange to talk about her as two different people, but there are two different trust levels in what we do. Our sexual behaviors are different, and while plenty of lines blur, she knows what to expect as Alaina, and I like giving her that security.

"Oh, and Elliot, one more thing. You can call me Sir, too."

# 31

# Elliot

The sight I walked into was definitely not something I expected. Hearing Lainey's moans of pleasure shocked me, but seeing Sawyer actively feasting on her in front of me made my dick instantly hard.

I respect and appreciate the base rules he laid out for me. I'm sure there's more, but he covered the immediate ones. Now I understand why she reacted the way she did when he called her Alaina.

While there were no expectations for tonight, the assumptions were there that sex would happen between the three of us. It was a pleasant surprise to see it had started already.

"Oh, and Elliot, one more thing. You can call me Sir, too."

His tone changes when he delivers his last statement, and it reminds me I'm not the current Dom in the room.

"May I kiss you, Sir?"

"You may." I close the distance between us. Our lips lock, and immediately, this kiss is different. I'm showing him my submission. Letting him control the pace.

A small whimper comes from the woman we've left alone on the counter, and Sawyer pulls away.

"She's waiting. Ask permission."

"Alaina, can I eat your gorgeous pussy and make you come all over my face?"

"Please, S..."

She looks to Sawyer, unsure if she should also call me Sir.

"You may call him Sir for now. We can discuss it later."

She nods at him and turns her full attention back to me. "Please, Sir"

As much as I want to dive into her pussy and drink my fill of her, I also want to worship every inch of her body. My hands glide up her inner thighs, and I pull her lips apart, exposing her to me for the first time. It feels like Christmas morning, and I'm opening the present I asked Santa for the most.

I look over my shoulder at Sawyer, who's watching us with rapt attention.

"Any requests, Sir?"

Fire blazes in his already wild eyes. He steps up behind me, fusing his chest to my back. His arm snakes up my front, and he wraps his hand around my throat.

"Limits, Elliot." It's not a question. It's a demand. His hand on my neck tightens when I don't respond quickly enough. "Limits," he says harsher.

"None that I've found yet, Sir."

"Good. We'll test that theory. Make her scream." Sawyer removes his hand from my neck, and I greedily dive into Lainey's pussy, hoping to drown. Her instant moan vocalizes her approval, and it's music to my ears.

Sawyer's body presses against mine from behind, and the

hand on my hip travels to the front of my joggers. He rubs it over the length of my cock, and I join Lainey in her moaning.

"No matter what I do, you don't stop until she's coming."

His command makes me shiver. I don't respond because I'm not sure what role I'm in right now, but not speaking unless I'm spoken to is enough direction for me.

Sawyer strokes me several times before his hand disappears, and so does his body. I whimper, the loss of his presence stronger than it should be.

"Fuck Elliot." Lainey's hands thread through my hair, pulling me closer.

I'm staring at her facial expression swirling from pleasure to relaxation when noise underneath me catches my attention. Without removing my mouth from Lainey's pussy, I peer around my shoulder to see Sawyer on his knees. His hands untie the string of my pants, and he stares back at me as he pulls them down my legs along with my underwear. My hard cock swings in his face, and he grips me with determination and spins his tongue along my head before sucking me in.

A long guttural moan escapes me, and Lainey pops up on her elbows to see what's going on. She can't see much from her angle, but it's easy for her to figure out what Sawyer is doing.

"Is our Sir taking care of you, Elliot?" She runs her fingers through my hair, and I purr into her pussy. Sawyer pops off my cock with a huff from me.

"Alaina, are you asking for a punishment?" He strokes me while he reprimands her, but I want his mouth back.

Lainey chews on her thumb, trying to decide her answer. It doesn't surprise me that she's a brat, but so am I. In one swift move, I plunge two fingers into her soaked pussy stopping any snarky remark she was about to make. A punishment for her right now would also be one for me, and I am single-minded and greedy at the moment.

*Nope. Fuck.*

Double minded. Definitely double minded as Sawyer puts his mouth back around my needy cock.

Lainey coming on my tongue and me coming down Sawyer's throat are my two focuses, and it's getting harder to decide which one is taking priority. I'm struggling to believe this is only the second blow job Sawyer has ever given. He moves his mouth in tandem with his tongue, and it's quickly driving me to the edge.

Lainey's internal walls constrict around my fingers, and I know she's as close as I am.

A timer goes off somewhere behind us, and Lainey screams, but it's not from pleasure. She slams her hands on the counter in frustration.

"Sawyer," she whines.

He pops off me again, and she scoots back on the counter, away from my mouth. I'm left confused and wanting in every direction.

"Go, Lainey."

Sawyer slowly stands, pulling my pants up, and I want to whine right along with Lainey. She spins off the other side of the counter, and I have no idea what just happened.

"What?" I shake my head, feeling lost.

"Dinner is done."

"But—"

Sawyer stops my protest with his lips and pulls my body into him. I can feel the outline of his cock against mine, and at least I know I'm not the only one feeling this turned on.

"It's time to eat, Elliot. There's plenty of evening left to play, but we need to fuel first. Lainey cooked Shepherd's pie. Let us take care of you. Okay?" My head bobs as I become entranced with his gray eyes boring into mine. "We can discuss things further during dinner. Then we can share dessert. How does that sound?" His gaze drifts further into the kitchen, and I follow it as Lainey pulls a casserole out of the oven.

"Sounds and smells incredible, Doll." Sawyer's eyes squint at the endearment, and I correct my mistake. "Sir. Sounds incredible, Sir." His finger sweeps across my cheek, and he leaves me to help Lainey.

We sit at the table and eat, and I'm not even sorry for the moans that come out of me as I inhale her delicious food. It's been so long since I've had a home-cooked meal, and it reminds me I have a trip planned in two weeks to go home. We're having a big party for all the kids with summer birthdays, and it's going to be a blast.

"How is this dynamic going to work?" Sawyer asks the question that's been running through my mind. "We all need to know our roles for everyone's comfort and safety."

"The two of you already have yours. I can be whatever you want me to be. So I guess the real question is, what role do you want me to play?"

"Lainey?" Sawyer runs a finger across her cheek and pushes her hair behind her ear. She leans into his hand and sighs. "What would you like, Jitterbug?"

"More."

"More? That's a very open-ended word. Care to elaborate?" They stare at each other for a long moment, and I can feel their connection. I want that. To be able to speak to someone without words.

As if understanding her, Sawyer nods, and Lainey stands, walking around the table. She stops next to my chair and motions for me to move back. The chair squeaks as I push it away from the table, and once there's enough clearance, she straddles my lap, draping her arms over my shoulder.

My hands hover in the space between us. I'm unsure where to put them as this is the first interaction that isn't being orchestrated by Sawyer and we haven't defined any rules yet.

"You can touch me, Elliot. It's okay."

"Doll?" I lock eyes with him over Lainey's shoulder. It's not that I don't believe her words, but all decisions are his right now.

"Listen to her."

That's all the permission I need. I wrap my hands around her small hips and pull her further up my lap. She looks down and smirks when she realizes I've moved her on top of my rapidly growing cock.

"Do you want to sub with me for Sawyer? Would you like him to have control over both our bodies?"

I swallow hard, and I'm sure she can see it because the thought of kneeling for him makes my mouth water. "I do."

"Do you know what I'd like?"

*Whatever it is, you can have it.*

"What do you want, Cherry?"

"You..." She slowly shifts her hips over my cock. "And Sawyer..." Back and forth. "Taking control of my body." I squeeze her hips, and she grinds against me more. "Together."

"You want the best of both worlds?" Her hips don't stop, and I'm still sensitive from Sawyer's mouth earlier. She's killing me. Getting to have her in the movie theater was incredible, but the memory is tainted with how it ended. I want to get back inside her and erase the negativity from my mind and hers.

"Do you think you could do both?"

"Cherry, I can be whoever you want me to be. I find pleasure in both roles. Sawyer, do you have a preference?" We both look at our Sir, who's leaning back in his chair, arms crossed over his chest, watching our interaction and looking hot enough to fucking eat.

"What my wife wants, my wife gets."

Lainey looks back at me with a triumphant smile. I trail my hands under her shirt, and my fingers tingle as they pass over her soft skin.

"And what exactly is it that you want?"

"I want a dommy sub boyfriend who pleases me as much as my husband because I want him to have a subby dom boyfriend who can work together to please me."

"I love it when a woman can tell me what she wants. I have a big question, though. How does this work outside the three of us? Obviously, Wes—Sawyer and I have been on a few dates already, just the two of us."

"The stumble was cute."

"I still need to get used to the new name. I think Sawyer suits him better anyway."

"I do, too. Should we deflect this question to Sawyer?"

I nod, and we turn our attention to the sexy man across the table.

# 32

# Sawyer

They look fucking fabulous together. I wondered if there would be any jealousy while I watched Lainey saunter over to Elliot like the sex goddess she is, but all I have are dirty thoughts. Dirty, depraved thoughts of having them both tied up and at my mercy to do with as I please.

"...question to Sawyer?"

"Hmm?" It's clear they asked me a question, but I didn't hear a single word they said.

"We were wondering about the dynamic with Lainey and I. How it works outside of just the three of us? Separate as pairs."

"Ah." I haven't thought of that. All of this is still so new. I thought it would be a while longer before we would get to this step. Elliot and I have had our solo times. The ideal hope when we went into this was to bring in a partner we could both enjoy. It never occurred to me that *both* could also mean Lainey and said partner without me. "It's obvious there's an attraction between the two of you. And I love the way you look together. I'm secure enough in our relationship to know Lainey would never leave me for another man..." I don't know how to answer the question.

Lainey must sense my hesitation and stands from Elliot's lap. She rounds the table toward me but so does Elliot from the opposite direction. Lainey straddles my lap, and Elliot moves dishes aside and hops on the table behind her, straddling his legs around her torso. It's a spectacular sight to see.

"Eyes on me, Sir." Her tone is soft, and as much of a command as it seems, it's a request that I won't reprimand her for.

"You have all my attention, Alaina. Always."

My hands travel her thighs, soothing her as much as myself.

"You're the reason this situation is even a possibility. You make the rules, and we'll follow them."

I'm temporarily distracted by the movement of Elliot's hands fluttering across her shoulders, giving her wordless encouragement. He's the exact type of partner I want for her.

They deserve an answer. I need to be true to my feelings. It's the only way anything between us is going to work. We have to be completely honest with each other at all times.

"No penetration unless I'm around. Hands and mouths are fair game when you're alone together, but no sex." My eyes flash to Elliot, and I almost miss the slight crinkle of his eyes. I'm sure that's not what he hoped to hear, but this is still new, and we need to have boundaries. "For now."

I reach out and take one of Elliot's hands, and he gives me

a tight smile.

"Elliot, I trust you. Please don't think it has anything to do with that. But as you know, I'm a Dom. Lainey has always been mine, and while the thought of sharing her with you is exhilarating, it's going to take some time for me to give her fully to you. I hope you can understand."

His beautiful smile slowly rises, lighting up his face.

"I understand and respect it. No penetration sounds like a wonderful compromise."

"None solo, for now. Obviously, it's a different story when the three of us are together. Alaina, how do you feel about that?"

"Anything you want, Sir." She chews on the bottom of her lip, and I know she has more of an opinion on the subject.

"And, Lainey? Jitterbug, how do you really feel about it?"

She pauses, adjusting between her roles and what she's allowed to say.

"I... honestly a little frustrated but also understanding." She cups my cheek and gently kisses the corner of my lips. "We have a lot to learn with and about each other. The two of you have my permission to explore with or without me. I want you to learn what you like without the pressure of me there. I know Elliot can take care of you however you need."

"Jitterbug, I—"

"Deserve to be loved and cared for, and it's okay if it's by someone other than me. I trust Elliot, and you do, too. You just told him you trusted him with me. You have to extend that respect to yourself too. Your self-worth is just as important."

Fuck. This woman gets me like no one else does.

"Elliot, are you okay with all of the terms?" Lainey spins in my lap, turning her attention to our third. I see doe eyes peering up at him, and imagine how it will be to have her on her knees for the both of us. Well, not her knees because that's outside her comfort level, but on the edge of the bed staring up at us, waiting for our instructions.

He runs a hand through her hair, and her eyes flutter at the contact. I know what his hands feel like in my hair and understand her reaction.

"Cherry, I'm fucking thrilled getting both of you in any way possible. Can we start right now? I'm feeling feral from all this talk."

*Me too.*

"Turn around, Alaina." Her head tilts when she looks back at me. "I want you to ride me while you show Elliot what you can do with this pretty little mouth of yours." I push my thumb against her lips, and she opens her mouth, sucking it in like my good girl. "Beautiful, Alaina."

Elliot sits back on the table and pulls his hands from her shoulders. Lainey stands from my lap and strips. Elliot's breathing increases as I watch each piece of clothing fall off. He's seeing her naked for the first time. What I wouldn't give to have the experience of seeing her exquisite body again with fresh eyes.

Once naked, Lainey smiles sweetly at me, and I motion with my finger for her to do a spin. I want to make sure Elliot sees the entire picture. As she turns, I hear a whispered "fuck" leave his lips, and I couldn't agree more.

When her rotation is complete, she stands patiently awaiting her next order. Elliot extends his hand to her in offering, and she takes it.

"I think you have a throne to sit on, princess." He gestures to my lap, and I push my pants down enough to pull my cock out. Elliot takes her other hand and helps keep her balanced while I line up, and she sinks onto me.

My eyes roll back into my head as the warmth of her pussy swallowing my cock feels like heaven.

The angle of the position arches her back, and Elliot releases her hands so her forearms rest on his thighs.

"Very convenient position, Cherry." He lovingly brushes her cheek, and as sweet as the move is, we need to keep boundaries.

"No nicknames during playtime, Elliot. There's a time and a place, and we need to remember our roles. There will come a time when we'll easily be able to decipher during scenes, but not yet.

"Yes, Sir."

Hearing him call me Sir stirs different feelings in me than when Lainey says it. There are things I want to do to him that I won't allow myself to do with her.

"May I move, Sir?" Lainey's innocent voice washes over me like the wings of a butterfly.

"Not until Elliot's ready. Help him out."

Her delicate hands reach out to the waistband of his joggers, and he lifts his hips to pull them down. She wastes no time taking Elliot into her mouth, and when he moans, so do I.

The sight of them together is even better than I remember. The movie theater was sexy, but the lights were off. There's no cloak of darkness in the middle of our dining room.

I'm not sure why she asked if she could move. She's at my mercy in this position. Her legs hang around my thighs.

251

The only thing keeping her upright are her hands on Elliot. I know he won't let her fall.

My first pump is gentle and controlled. I want her to get used to him before I let go and enjoy myself. I already know she'll have bruises on her hips when we're done since my hands will be in control of her movements.

I lift her a few inches and slam her back onto me. They both moan, and it's a fucking incredible sound. Elliot looks like he's in heaven with his hands planted behind him, head lulled back. His Adam's apple bobs when he swallows hard, and I want to lick it and feel it slide across my tongue. But first, I have a wife to pleasure.

I pick up my pace and meet her halfway between thrusts. She's letting my rhythm control her blow job, and knowing that I'm causing them both pleasure at once causes more dirty thoughts of the ways I can duplicate this scenario. Lainey on all fours. Both of them in front of me while I use my fingers to give them pleasure. Elliot fucking her while I fuck him.

"Lainey. You're fucking mouth."

"Alaina. And I won't warn you again, Elliot, or there will be punishment."

Heat flashes his eyes, and I know he's wondering what kind of punishment I would put him through. I'm sure he'll find out soon enough.

He nods and looks back down at our queen. She's looking up at him. I can tell by the way her head is slightly angled.

"God. Look at these pretty eyes. I can never tell if they are more green or brown, but they're incredible, Alaina."

I can't help but chuckle. Our dominant differences are already showing. He likes to give praise.

252

"Elliot. If you think her eyes are pretty now, just wait until she's looking up at you from her knees with her hands tied behind her back, waiting for instructions." His lip twitches at the idea, but I'm not done. "I can't wait to see *both* of your eyes in that position." My voice comes out more gravelly than I intend, but I can't help it. I need to make that happen. Soon.

"Fuck, I'm close." Elliot grabs her hair and looks at me for approval. A slight nod is all he needs before he bobs her head faster over his cock. I try to keep up with his rhythm, but I'm also close. I wanted to hold out and let them have their fun, but the sight of them is more than my restraint can handle right now. If I'm going to come, it's not going to be first.

I slow our pace to allow her to finish him. Elliot pants and curses under his breath.

"Sawyer," he barks my name through gritted teeth. It's not meant as disrespect. On the contrary. He's asking without words where he should come.

"She'll take care of you, Elliot."

His eyes slam shut as his head bobs. Long seconds pass, and I expect to hear his release, but it doesn't come. What does he need? I can tell how close he is, but he seems to be holding back.

Reaching forward, I place a hand on his chest. "Elliot." His eyes snap open to me immediately. I slide my hand up to the base of his throat—my thumb and forefinger squeezing just enough to assert my dominance. "Come for me."

That's what he needed. His mouth drops open, and like a bowstring snapping, his hips buck forward. Lainey gags at the unexpected shift but quickly recovers, and I see her throat moving as she swallows what Elliot is offering her. His moans are deep and guttural, and he empties himself into her mouth.

"Don't miss a drop, Alaina." I smooth a hand up her back as she rocks her hips against my lap, ready to come. I reach between her legs and give her the friction she needs. Within seconds, she's moaning her release while still taking care of Elliot.

"Fucking look at you. You're stunning. My pretty girl. Your orgasm is so beautiful."

Elliot pours praise onto Lainey while their orgasms subside, but now it's my turn.

"Back up, Elliot."

He looks at me confused but complies. *Good boy.* When he's far enough back, I tell him to stop and pull Lainey off me. I spin her in my arms and plant her butt on the table. I love that neither of them are questioning me but giving me their trust to care for them.

"Lay your head on Elliot's thighs." She does as told, and I wrap her legs around my hips and sink back in with one thrust. She gasps, but it turns into a moan as I pound into her.

"May I touch her, Sir?"

"You better. She's *our* concern now." With the one accentuated word, he understands his role has changed. With Lainey's hands wrapped around Elliot's thighs for leverage and his hands sliding down her chest to play with her breasts, I'm quickly losing the little restraint I had to hold back.

"You're taking him so well. Does his big cock feel good inside your pussy, Alaina?" Elliot rolls her nipples between his fingers, and it's almost my tipping point, but I want to give her another orgasm first.

"Fuck yes," she moans her response to his question.

"Let's give her one more, Elliot."

"I can't—"

"You can, Alaina." My tone is firm. Elliot looks at me. I see the concern for her in his eyes. "She knows her safeword. And she knows I know her body. She can take it. I promise."

His lip tilts into a smirk as he increases the pinching and twisting of her nipples. I reach between us and flick her clit while adjusting my hips.

Elliot grunts and I look up to see she's grabbed his semi-hard cock and is licking and sucking on it. Lucky bastard. She's incredible with her tongue.

The show doesn't last long. I adjust my hips one last time and when I feel her inner walls flutter around my cock I allow myself to come with her.

I brace my hand on the table as I fill her and look up when a warmth engulfs it. Elliot placed his hand over mine. We're connected as Lainey and I find our release. It dawns on me this is the first time I've come in front of Elliot, which explains the look of awe on his face. If I didn't know it would crush Lainey, I'd lean over and kiss him.

He continues to sing Lainey's praises, and I can't help but feel some of them are for me as his blue eyes sparkle.

# 33

# Lainey

I'm spent. I'm satisfied, sore, and spent. But above everything else, I feel loved.

This wasn't my first experience with two men, but it's never felt like this. I love Patrick and Chip in a real but very different way. Sawyer is my husband. The depth of his emotion supersedes anything I've ever felt. He knows me physically and emotionally. Sawyer knows my body better than I do most days.

I was worried adding someone to our already-established sex life would feel awkward. I assumed there would be a learning curve, but there wasn't. Sawyer and Elliot played my body so eloquently together, and the push and pull, the sweet and spicy, was delicious. The constant praise in my ears, paired with the punishing movements of Sawyer's hips, sent me on a high I never wanted to come down from.

Unfortunately, all good things must come to an end, but I can't complain. I find myself sitting in a fragrant bubble bath courtesy of Elliot. He packed a few extra little surprises in the bag he brought, including lavender bubble bath and massage oil if I'd like to indulge. And I do.

I've been sitting in the hot, fragrant water for about ten minutes when the boys come tripping into the bathroom. Their skin is flushed, hair ruffled, and I need to know why.

With the flick of my fingers, I slash water at them, and twin-hungry eyes snap to my attention.

"How's your bath, Jitterbug?" Sawyer sits on the tub's edge and glides his hand across my knee, where it just breaches the surface.

"Lonely. What were you boys doing without me because I might be jealous."

"Nothing much," Sawyer practically sings and glances at Elliot.

"Nothing much, Cherry. Just this." Elliot leans down and kisses me. It's sweet at first but quickly turns hungry, and I can understand how simply making out with him could cause Sawyer to look the way he does. Elliot kisses with a skilled tongue. Gentle yet demanding.

Sawyer moans next to us, and his hand on my knee dips into the water, traveling deeper until he finds his treasure. I spread my legs, giving him better access, and the movement almost makes me slip under the water.

Elliot's hands grab my arms as I giggle and gasp at the quick movement.

"I've got you, Cherry. You're safe with me."

Elliot's words have a depth of meaning I'm not sure he understands, but I believe him. I'm safe with him. With both of them together.

"Where'd that come from?" Sawyer's fingers have momentarily moved as I resituate myself in the tub.

"Where'd what come from?"

"Cherry. Why the nickname?"

I chew the corner of my lip as I look at Elliot and plead with my eyes to tell the story so I don't have to.

"Danishes," Elliot says simply as if that should explain everything.

"More information, Elliot." There's a hint of a growl to his words, and I don't know if it's his need for more of the story or his hands slipping back to my pussy.

"Lainey and I have had a little push and pull for a while."

"He's the panty snatcher," I blurt out.

Both men look at me like I've just said the most ridiculous words, and I guess, out of context, I have.

"The morning after the storage closet incident, when you took my panties. Remember I told you I had a run-in with a guy who helped with my spare panties?"

Sawyer's hand rises to brush over the faint pink mark left behind from the shelf.

"Wait." Elliot pushes Sawyer's fingers aside to look at the mark and seems to be putting some piece to a puzzle together. "You got this the morning you heard my voice, right?"

"Yeah," Sawyer smirks as if he understands the puzzle as well.

"After I left, you stole Lainey's panties, so I'm assuming something naughty happened. Then I ran into her in the hall, which explains why I picked up her g-string."

"Elliot is your panty snatcher. The man who made you wet after you were already dripping from my orgasm. The man that called you a good girl," Sawyer deduces.

"And I'm the reason you were so turned on you needed

258

release as soon as I left." Elliot looks smugly at Sawyer until he shakes his head. "No? Am I wrong?"

"Not entirely. I didn't allow myself relief, only Lainey. We had... plans for the evening, so I made myself wait."

"Plans? Do tell."

"Elliot. You're avoiding the original question. Why do you call my wife Cherry?"

"Sawyer," I hope he hears the warning tone in my voice because he's asserting his dominance in a situation that doesn't deserve it. He called me his wife, and not in a sexy way; it was possessive.

"It's okay, Cherry. I can handle him. I know my place, don't I... *Sir.*"

Everything happens so quickly; I barely register what's going on in front of me. The water splashes as Sawyer's hand whips out of the tub. Elliot disappears from in front of me, and I hear the air leave his lungs as Sawyer pushes him against the bathroom wall. I spin to my knees so I can watch the show. Sawyer's hand wraps possessively around Elliot's throat, and the sight turns me on.

They're in a staring contest for dominance. Although Elliot is in the submissive position, and I know he can back down if he wants to, he doesn't. I don't know if his challenge is stupid or admirable. Both men are bare-chested, and their delicious bodies heave against each other with their labored breathing. They're both tone and built, but Sawyer is broader, his frame encapsulating more of Elliot's.

The scene of testosterone-filled masculinity is almost too much to watch. I dip my hands in the water and continue what Sawyer started. Despite the obvious wetness of the bathwater, I can feel my arousal as I dip my fingers inside while watching the two men in front of me, wondering who will break first.

Other than a few shared kisses, I haven't seen them together. Sawyer was on his knees earlier, but I was a little preoccupied by Elliot's tongue, and the angle didn't allow me to see much. They look stunning. I can't wait to truly be sandwiched between their hard bodies.

Much to my surprise, Sawyer breaks their tension first, but it's not how I expected.

"You need a name." Elliot's brows scrunch in confusion, and I imagine my face mirrors his. "A name when we're in a scene. Like Alaina. She knows her place when I use her full name. Lainey and Jitterbug aren't used during playtime. You need a scene name so you know your role and your place."

"Oh. Why not stick with Eli? When I'm Eli, I'm yours. When I'm Elliot, she's ours."

*She's ours.* I like the sound of that.

"Alright, *Eli*, but let's get one thing straight. She's always mine." The growl in Sawyer's tone makes me pause. He's been so willing to share, but it seems he's struggling right now. "And so are you."

*Never mind.*

Sawyer's hand dips into Elliot's pants, and although I can't officially see his movements, I can tell he's stroking Elliot's cock. Sawyer wants to make sure Elliot knows exactly how "his" he really is.

I rest my chin in the crook of my elbow and watch the show they're putting on as if it's just for me. They are so fucking hot together, and my eyes flutter closed as I listen to them moan a moment before I give in to my own desires.

My skin flushes as my orgasm looms just at the precipice. I need something to tip me over the edge, but I'm too afraid to move and break the spell happening in the room.

"Fuck, Sawyer. Your hands feel incredible."

"No one gave you permission to speak, Eli."

That's it. That's what I needed. Elliot's praise and Sawyer's dominance. The collection of their words spirals my orgasm. I convulse in the water as my pleasure peaks, and I know I'm making a mess on the floor, but nothing in me cares right now. All I see are fireworks of color flashing behind my eyes.

I pant out short, shallow breaths as I come back to reality, and I realize my labored breathing echoes loudly in the bathroom. Too loudly. Where is the sound of Elliot's moaning and Sawyer's breathing? Did they leave me in here alone?

I lull my head to the side and crack one eyelid. Where my men once stood is a vacant wall. I turn my head to the other side, opening my eyes fully, and find myself staring at two pairs of ravenous, fierce eyes.

"Hi." I flutter my eyelashes in a vain attempt to appease their looks.

"Out of the water now, Alaina." I'm speechless when the commanding boom comes from Elliot and not Sawyer. I look to Sawyer for instruction but see a wall of emotions. "Don't look at him. He won't save you from your punishment."

"Punishment?"

Elliot crouches in front of the tub and grabs my chin. "Did you just come?"

"Yes?" Why is that a question?

261

"Did you have permission?"

*Oh fuck.* "But—"

"I didn't ask for excuses, Alaina. I asked a simple yes or no question. Did you. Ask permission. To come?"

*Fuckfuckfuck.*

Of course, I didn't. At the time, I didn't see anything wrong with my actions while they explored each other. In hindsight, I now see the errors of my ways, and if the look in Elliot's eyes means anything, I'm about to *feel* it, too.

"No, Sir."

"Sawyer is Sir. You can call me E. He was right. We need to make sure we always know our roles. Do you understand, Alaina?"

"Elliot, the man. Eli, the sub. E, the Dom. I understand."

He swipes his hand across my cheek. "Correction. Elliot, your lover. Eli, your partner. E, your Dom."

His words are so genuine, and I want to swoon, but he gives me no reprieve.

"I'll ask one more time. Did you have permission to orgasm?"

"No, E."

"Good girl," he croons, but I take it for what it is. My pleasure Dom still demands obedience, even through his sweet words. He's repeated himself enough already. Before he needs to ask again, I stand. Sawyer steps up with a towel and wraps it around me. As he leans in to tuck the front end between my breasts, he tilts his head so we make eye contact.

"Remember your safeword, Jitterbug. I'll make sure Elliot talks you through everything."

His words mean more to me than I think he even realizes.

The tiny seconds he breaks a scene to check in with me reinforces his acceptance of my past and his knowledge of my limits. My need to please has almost put me in situations in the past that pass my comfort zone. If Sawyer weren't an observant Dom who knows my body better than I think I do, our relationship wouldn't be as solid as it is.

"May I kiss you, Sir?"

# 34

# Elliot

My head still swims with the feel of Sawyer's dominant hands on my cock. He's touched me several times now, but the way he had me pinned against the wall while he stroked me was control. He was putting me in my place.

I wanted nothing more than to give in and let him take whatever he wanted despite trying to stay equal in his power play. Fortunately, the splashing of water and moans from our wonderful woman pulled our attention away from each other, and we became singularly focused on her.

"May I?" I gesture to Lainey's flailing body as I whisper in his ear. Sawyer smiles and sweeps his hand in a "she's all yours" gesture. On silent feet—not that I think she would hear it if an elephant crossed the room right now—we switch to the opposite side she last saw us.

Lainey looks stunning as her orgasm controls her body. Water splashes over the side, and even the mess she's creating doesn't pause her pleasure.

She's in trouble. While we weren't in a scene, I can already tell Sawyer understands why I asked his permission, and he's on board. Lainey's hazel eyes finally find us in the room, and whatever she sees on our faces, she knows.

"Out of the water now, Alaina." Her eyes flash to Sawyer. "Don't look at him. He won't save you from your punishment."

"Punishment?"

She looks both intrigued and concerned as I crouch down next to the tub and take her chin between my fingers. "Did you just come?"

"Yes?"

The question in her answer tells me she hasn't quite figured out her mistake. The assumption that because Sawyer and I were occupied with each other, she was free to do as she pleased.

"Did you have permission?" There it is. The realization that she fucked up. She tries to make an excuse, but I don't allow it. Now is my time to establish boundaries and find my place, my role in this relationship. It's unfortunate that it needs to start with a punishment, but I'll make it a pleasurable one.

She finally steps out of the tub, and Sawyer wraps her in a towel. They have a hushed conversation, and I hear him call her Jitterbug. He's checking in with her, and I love it. He's giving her a tender moment, and I'm not put off by it. This entire world is based on trust and understanding.

While we waited for Lainey to come home from Katy's yesterday, we talked about her role as a sub. They've made alterations from the typical role for her comfort and stability. I understand her aversion to kneeling at the beginning of a scene. I'd be lying to myself if I didn't admit I was a little disappointed to hear that. The desire to kneel next to her and give ourselves entirely over to Sawyer has my dick twitching just thinking about it, but maybe together, we can work on it.

Sawyer's patience with her is intoxicating. I'm eager for the day she trusts me enough to tell me her story. I won't push her to talk until she's ready. Lainey's boundaries are clear. Her resting stance is at the end of the bed with her panties on. Nothing begins until permission is granted by her, allowing me to take them off. Although, as I watch them make out, I hold back a chuckle because she's currently only in a towel. Will she put on panties to start the scene?

"Care to share with the class, E?"

Sawyer's voice startles me from my internal humor, and I realize I'm wearing a big smile. Also, his use of my newly chosen name shows his level of respect for me going into the scene.

"Shall we allow Alaina to get ready?"

He looks back at her, and they exchange their wordless conversation, resulting in Lainey nodding and stepping back from him.

"You have two minutes, Alaina."

"Yes, Sir. Yes, E."

I want to growl, knowing she's respecting me already, but I hold it back. That is until she reaches the doorway between the bathroom and bedroom. She stops and peers over her shoulder. With a seductive look and a wink, she drops her towel and strolls out naked.

A hand clamps my shoulder, stopping the growl.

"You gonna be good?"

"Fuck." I run my hands through my hair and puff out a breath. "She's... she's..."

"Yeah, she is. What did you have in mind?"

He's asking me? "Spanking or edging? Which do you think?"

"Dealers choice. Wanna rock, paper, scissors for it?"

"What," I laugh out. "Seriously?"

"Why not?" he shrugs and sets his hands up waiting for me. "Best out of three. If I win, it's a spanking; if you win, it's edging."

"Fuck. Why the hell not. Ready?" He nods. "Rock, paper, scissors, shoot.

Paper for me, rock for Sawyer.

"That's one for you. Rock, paper, scissors, shoot."

Paper for me again, scissors for Sawyer.

"One for me. Last one, E. Rock, paper, scissors, shoot."

We smile at each other, and he tilts his head toward the bedroom. It's time to play with our sub.

"I'll stay back and focus on her comfort. If you want or need me for anything, just ask."

My nerves jitter with excitement, and I grab the back of his neck and pull Sawyer in for a hungry kiss.

"I always need and want you. Don't forget that. Let's go punish our girl."

I knew how I would find Alaina, but knowing and seeing are two different things. She sits at the edge of the bed with her hands delicately folded in her lap. Her gaze stares down at the floor, her damp hair piled in a messy bun on top of her head. She chose to put on panties if you could call them that. Scraps of black fabric form a T between her round ass cheeks. Familiar black fabric. Did she put on my g-string?

Is that acceptance or more brattiness?

We round the bed and stop before her. Lainey's breathing is even but deep. Her rising and falling shoulders give away her nerves.

"Look at me, Alaina." Slowly, her head rises, just enough so she can peer at me through her lashes. "All the way." Her chin lifts until I can see all of her face. She nibbles on the corner of her lip. It's one of her nervous habits, and for the first time, I realize I can do something about it. Using my thumb, I pull her lip down, and her mouth pops open. I think she's expecting me to put my thumb in her mouth like I saw her do earlier with Sawyer, but I won't.

"Ask me the safeword." She stares back at me, and it takes me a second to realize I haven't asked a question. "You have permission."

"What's the safeword, E?" Her voice is low and drips with sweetness.

I caress her cheek and down her jawline, toying with her bottom lip until she sucks it in to scratch away the tickle with her teeth.

Smirking, I lean close to her ear. "Apple, Alaina. The safeword is Apple, and I want you to know that I know and respect the severity of the word. I've proven it once and don't want you to ever forget it."

She nods against my cheek, and I stand, taking her hands with me.

"Please stand for me." She obediently complies. "Turn around." Her bare skin from head to toe is tantalizing. I dip a finger into the edge of her g-string and rub back and forth.

"Are these mine, Alaina? Did you put these on to tease me?" Sawyer grunts beside me, realizing what she's wearing, and I see his lip twitch.

"Y-yes, they are yours, but I put them on to please not tease, E."

"Hmm. We'll see." I snap the string, and she inhales sharply. "May I take them off?"

This is it. Where she confirms or denies permission. I step back to give her room to choose without feeling like I'm intimidating her. Not that I ever would.

Lainey's head tilts slightly to the left, and her eyes shift to Sawyer.

"I'm here. I'm not leaving," he reassures her. I fall for these two a little harder with the respect they have for each other.

Lainey hooks her thumbs into the strings at her hips, but I stop her before she goes any further.

"Turn around."

She spins on her heels and resumes her removal. Seductively, she bends at the waist and pulls at the strings until they slip off her hips and fall to the floor.

"Sawyer, mind if I keep a party favor?"

"As long as you replace them. Her lingerie habit could put me in the poorhouse."

I'll buy her an entire fucking lingerie store when tonight is over if I need to.

Crouching down, I run my hand along her leg as I go, and tap her ankle to lift so I can grab my prize. I unashamedly do the creepy thing, putting the panties to my nose and inhale. Her fragrant musk makes my mouth water, and I can't wait to taste her again.

As I stand, I pepper kisses up her legs, the junction where her legs meet her plump ass, the dimples on her lower back. She's stunning. Her creamy skin erupts into goosebumps under my touch, and I can't help but blow cold air, causing her to shiver. Her body is so responsive. I haven't gotten to take her all in and worship her until now. It's almost a shame that she's here for a punishment.

"So Alaina, we played a little game to see if your punishment would be a spanking or orgasm denial." She sighs, waiting for the decision. "Sawyer, would you sit on the bed?" He listens just as well as she does, and I'd be lying if that wasn't a fucking turn on. "Naked," I add before his ass hits the mattress. He's hard. I'd expect nothing less with a naked Alaina answering to our every command.

"Would you like to participate, Sawyer?"

"Always," he responds, but there's curiosity to his response. As there should be. He's not going to be happy with me.

"Sit on his cock, Alaina. Backwards." She slowly turns and backs up to Sawyer. He grabs her hips to help guide her down, giving me a questioning look. I won the game. Her punishment is orgasm denial. It's too bad he's now along for the ride, or more specifically, the torture.

I bask in their collective moans as she slides down onto him. Watching his cock disappear into her pussy is mesmerizing. They get settled, and Lainey's hips grind against his lap. I let it happen for a few seconds before I stop it.

"Enough. Be still." Lainey immediately stops, and Sawyer glares at me.

*Sorry, big boy, You're along for the ride.*

I sink to my knees between them. Her pussy is pink as it stretches around his cock, and I smile, knowing that Sawyer will probably be the one punishing me next. Leaning forward, I lick the base of his cock straight up to her clit.

They both let out carnal sounds, and I know this will be fun.

"Here's how this is going to work." They stare at me eagerly, waiting after the taste I just gave them. "Alaina, your punishment is orgasm denial." She whimpers, and I hold back a smile. "Sawyer is going to stay inside you. Let me know when your inner walls begin to flutter, and I should stop. He knows your body, so we are making this a group effort. If by some chance he misses the signs, you have permission to speak up and tell me to stop, and I'll understand it means your orgasm is close. That is the only time you have permission to speak unless you are using your safeword. Do you understand?"

"Yes, E."

"If you come before I allow it, you'll also earn a spanking. Sawyer, are you good with all that?"

"It's your show, but why am *I* being punished?" There's no accusation behind his question. He's genuinely curious.

"I don't know if I'd consider having Alaina's pussy wrapped around my cock as being a punishment."

He pauses at my answer, and although it's not what he wants to hear, I give him a reasonable answer that he can't argue with.

"Let's get started."

An hour later, I'm sweating. Alaina's tears freely flow down her flushed cheeks, and Sawyer's jaw is tight with his need to come. I don't think he understood how much just being inside her would affect him.

"You've done so fucking well, Alaina." I sweep the dampened hair off her cheek, matted from her tears. "Just one more time. One more, and then I'll let you ride Sawyer's beautiful cock, and it will feel like you're flying. I promise.

"I-I..."

"Can she handle it, Sawyer?" We lock eyes over her shoulder, and I think the question I should be asking is if *he* can handle it. His gray eyes are nearly black, and his hands have been in fists, white-knuckled for a while.

"Yes."

Her body sags against him, and I feel her exhaustion. We're all exhausted, which is why I want us to endure one more before we find our pleasure. I say *we* because this has been as much torture for me as it has for them. I'm controlling my urge to let her come. Let both of them come. The pleaser in me wants them to have their pleasure. To give them every orgasm I've denied over the last sixty minutes. But I know the culmination will be so much more than they ever imagined when they finally get what their bodies need. I know Sawyer practices delayed gratification with himself, but I can tell even this is beyond his scope of edging.

"One more, and we can all have our release." I gently slide my tongue over her swollen clit. Her whimpering moan is music to my ears. It's pleasure and pain mixed. It won't take long. Her entire body is a live wire waiting to spark. When I swirl my tongue around her clit, Alaina squirms in Sawyer's lap, and he groans.

One circle... two circles... three.

*"Stopstopstop."*

I instantly move my mouth away and travel kisses up her body. "Good fucking girl." I reach her lips and kiss her tenderly. "I knew you could do it. Are you ready to come?"

"Please, E. I'm ready." Her words are full of need and want and desperation.

I focus my gaze on Sawyer and smile. "How about you?

Are you ready to come?"

"Say the fucking word, E." I crash my lips with his. He's full of pent-up energy spilling into our kiss, and I soak it up.

"Finish her, Sawyer."

Faster than should be possible, he pulls out and tosses Lainey onto the bed behind him. Her knees kiss her chest as he slams back in. I watch as his hips snap into her like a rubber band, and the noises they make are animalistic. Lainey screams her release seconds later. Even though I'm not personally responsible for this orgasm, it's still mine. They're both mine. Sawyer's back muscles tighten, and his hips stutter, and he comes deep inside her.

"Fuuuuck. God fucking dammit, Elliot."

*Me?* Sawyer said *my* name, not Lainey's.

He rolls off her, and they lay next to each other, panting. They're my beautiful masterpieces of exhaustion, and I couldn't be more satisfied.

"Eli," Sawyer barks, and I'm instantly alert. I drop to my knees and stare at the ground, aware of what that name means. He's done being used by me. The quick role reversal doesn't bother me. I told them I'd be whoever they wanted me to be, and I was serious. Dom, sub, partner—whatever they desire.

The bed creaks and Sawyer's bare feet appear at my knees. His fingers graze up the back of my neck, over my crown, and when he reaches the top of my head, he grabs a handful of hair and rears back. He stares down at me, and I can't decipher his expression. It's blank.

"That was very clever of you, Eli. I bet you're proud of yourself."

I lick my lips, attempting to hide the quiver of a smile

trying to force its way out. I feel *very* proud of how I controlled their bodies.

"Stand."

He releases my hair, and I follow his command. I gasp when he firmly grabs my cock. I need to come, but right now, that seems to be in Sawyer's literal hand since he flipped the script.

"Hey, Jitterbug." My eyes flash to Lainey. He used her nickname. Interesting. I suppose that means she's no longer in the scene with us. Not that she could endure anything else right now. She's curled under a throw blanket with her eyes barely open. She needs aftercare, and I'm itching to give it to her, but I'm not currently in a position to do it.

"Baby," she sleepily responds.

"What should we do about this?"

# 35

## Sawyer

Elliot feels like steel under my hand. I stroke him slow but firm, and I wait for Lainey to decide how we should let him come. *If* we should let him come. She taps a pink manicured nail on her bottom lip and hums as she thinks.

"Why don't you ask him?"

Elliot pants next to me as I continue to stroke him.

"Answer her, Eli."

"I want to come. If you'll allow it."

*Smart man.* "How?" I'll give him whatever way he wants, but I want to know if he's brave enough to ask for it.

"You," he whispers out.

He wants me. He didn't specifically say how. Blow jobs are as far as I've gotten with him. While the thought of bending him over this bed and fucking him sounds euphoric, I'm spent. My cock swings semi-hard between my legs. I've edged myself plenty of times during scenes with Lainey, but today was an entirely new level. And one I wasn't prepared for.

"You deny me an orgasm for over an hour, and now you want me to get on my knees for you? That's a very ballsy request, little sub." One I'm about to fucking fulfill, but I can't give in without giving him a little shit for the request.

Elliot swallows, and my eyes are drawn to his Adam's apple. I hope he doesn't speak out of turn. I'd hate to deny him the orgasm he earned, and he fucking deserves it. I've never come that hard before. Feeling Lainey squeeze my cock over and over again. It was blissful torture.

"Sit on the bed, Eli." I release my hold on his body, and he whimpers as he turns to the bed. He directs his head back to the floor, hands in his lap. I wonder who trained him because they've done it well.

"Sir," Lainey's melodic voice has my attention switching to her. I want her to relax. She's been through enough tonight. I need to get her in the shower, but I also need to take care of Elliot first. I feel like I owe him from the movie theater. I'll never shirk his aftercare again. I still feel like shit about it.

"Yes, Jitterbug." She smiles, understanding.

"Can I touch him while you do?"

Elliot inhales sharply, and I know he likes the idea. Does that blur the lines of what we're doing? Fuck no. I'm the one that makes the damn lines. There's no reason to overthink this.

"Why don't you ask him," I mirror her question from earlier, and she smiles. Removing the blanket, she crawls across the bed and stops behind him. I wonder which title she will use. Technically, none of them would be wrong. He's currently in the role as my sub, which would put her on equal ground with him, but she's no longer in the scene. She could call him E as a form of respect or simply Elliot.

"Does he have permission to speak?" I make sure he sees me and nods to them both. "Elliot, can I touch you?"

"Please do, Cherry."

Their comfort level warms parts of me I didn't know existed. Every time Elliot does something that just seems to fit with us, it's like he's connecting pieces to a puzzle that I had no idea was missing.

Lainey grazes her fingertips along the tops of his shoulders, and he shivers as goosebumps erupt across his chest. It's satisfying to see his body react to hers.

Slowly, I lower myself in front of him. One knee, then the other. His eyes remain cast to the ground, and I pinch his chin between my fingers and lift. With him sitting and me kneeling, we're almost the same height. His eyes ping-pong between mine, waiting for what comes next.

"I'm going to take care of you, Eli, and then we are going to take care of her, alright?" He nods. He could have chosen to speak his response since I asked him a direct question, but I appreciate his respect.

I trail my hands up his thick thighs and grab his cock. We lock eyes as I dip my head into his lap and flick the tip of his head. I still feel like an unskilled newbie when it comes to giving a blowjob, but Elliot hasn't complained once.

As my head bobs, Elliot closes his eyes, and his head lulls to the side. Lainey kisses up the side of his neck and smiles at me with her pink, swollen lips. I wonder what she thinks of her dominant husband on his knees for our boyfriend. I spend a lot of time on my knees for my wife's pleasure, but we both know a blowjob is about power.

A quiet "fuck" spills from Elliot's lips, pulling me back to the task at hand. I knew he wouldn't take long, and I increase my efforts.

"Fuck, Sir, I'm close. Fuck."

"Give it to him, Elliot," my temptress wife whispers to him. "Empty your come into his mouth and let him swallow you down."

Her fucking words make my cock twitch, but the groan and spurt of come that hits the back of my throat let me know they did exactly what she was hoping for him.

As she promised, I swallow every drop and suck until he's practically pushing me off him from oversensitivity.

"Kiss me," Lainey says, and I assume she's talking to Elliot until I see her eyes boring holes into me. He just came in my mouth, and she wants me to kiss her. What a dirty woman I have. *We* have.

I crawl up Elliot's body and crush him between us as I kiss Lainey over his shoulder. She moans as our tongues tangle together, and Elliot's hands begin to roam my body. I pull away before an entirely new round starts. We've been at this since before dinner, and I'm sure we could go all night, but I'm taking charge.

"Shower. Aftercare. Now." I smirk at their groans and feel satisfied with their reactions.

This is going to work. I've found someone who satisfies me physically and mentally. Someone who my wife already knows and accepts. Elliot fits right into a space I didn't even know was open.

After we shower, which wasn't as fun as it could have been because all three of us couldn't fit together, we stand in the bathroom doing our nighttime routines. An awkward feeling radiates off Elliot, and I don't understand it.

Stepping behind him, I rest my chin on his shoulder and meet his eyes in the mirror.

"What do you need?"

"I-What do you mean?" he asks, confused. His brows knit together, but I see the hesitation.

"Did we miss something that you're used to for aftercare?"

"No, I'm fine."

"Uh oh." I smile and bounce my eyes to Lainey's as she tsks at him. "That's a bad word, Elliot. We don't say the F word in this house." She turns and hops to sit on the counter next to us. I swallow hard as I peruse her body. Barely there panties, and a thin tank top are all she wears, and despite her nipples not being hard, I can still see their outline through her top.

"Oh, um. I'm f-okay. I'm okay."

Lainey brushes a hand down his bare chest. Elliot put on a pair of gray sweatpants, which made Lainey groan about "not being fair" and I'm only wearing my boxer briefs. He shudders under her touch, and my lips suck on his neck when his ass rubs against my cock.

"Talk to us, Elliot." Her voice is soft and reassuring. "The only way this works is with proper communication."

He sighs and places his hand over hers. "What now? Do I sleep on the couch? The guest room? Should I be preparing to go home? We didn't really talk about *after*."

"Aren't we all getting ready for bed?" I hate that he's feeling insecure.

"Yeah, but—"

"Aren't *we* all getting ready for bed, Elliot?"

He sighs again, and his shoulders slump. "Yes."

"Then *we* are going to bed. Together. Unless you don't want to, and that's a different conversation."

Elliot turns in my arms so we're chest to chest. Hardening cock to hardening cock. "I'm all in," he practically shouts inches from my face. "Fuck, that was aggressive. I'm sorry. I'm here, and I want to stay and—"

I place my hand over his mouth to stop his rambling. Lainey giggles next to us, and I shoot her a look to stop. Moving my hand from his mouth to his cheek, his eyes look so sincere.

"I'm not a hopeless romantic. I generally don't believe in insta lust or insta love, but for separate reasons, you both captivated me from day one. I... I can't believe I'm about to confess this." He dips his head and runs a hand down his face. "The day I came in for orientation and first met Lainey, I fantasized what it would be like to fuck her under her desk despite having noticed her ring. A few days later, I went to get coffee for Annie at your coffee shop, apparently, and Lainey smiled so sweetly at me when I walked by. She was wearing this skin-tight red dress, and there were cherry danishes in your display case. I bought her one, and she was thankful and excited." He looks over his shoulder at Lainey; her cheeks are pink, obviously remembering the memory. "She was so excited and took a big bite. There was a bit of cherry jelly left on the corner of her mouth, and instead of telling her, I reached across the desk and swiped it with my thumb... then licked it off my finger."

A glance at Lainey shows me the interaction also meant something to her. Her pink cheeks are now flushed red, and she's nibbling on the corner of her thumb. Should I be jealous that there was something stirring between them long before we discussed opening our relationship? Probably. But I know my wife. She told me about the panty incident, and if there were anything more, she would have told me that too.

"Cherry." The origin of his nickname for her dawns on me. "I get it now. Cute."

"Yeah. It kind of stuck. But not in front of Katy or the other girls. It's just been our silly little thing. Why Jitterbug?"

I huff a laugh. "The day I met Lainey, she was hopped up on coffee needing a coffee order for Ms. Poulsen, but she had lost the paper the order was on. When she touched me, it felt like she was going to jitter out of her skin."

"Sounds like Lainey."

# 36

## Lainey

Hot. Holy fucking hot. Not in the sexy way, either. I'm delightfully smushed between two bodies that were created by the Gods themselves, but they. Are. HOT! I can feel the very not cute sheen of sweat on my upper lip.

If it's not enough that their body heat is giving me a stroke, my bladder is also screaming at me. Carefully, I slither down to the foot of the bed, and as soon as I stand, Sawyer's arm reaches out to look for me. His hand finds Elliot, and he moves closer, wrapping his arm around his waist. I want to stay here and stare at them forever, but I really have to pee.

My body feels sore, but in the way you feel after a really good workout. I glance at the clock and realize it's almost time to get up for work. Since I don't need to shower this morning, thanks to the incredible aftercare I received last night, I decide to make my men breakfast.

My men.

*My.* Men.

Although it's not a new concept for me, I always knew Chip and Patrick were temporary. Sawyer is my husband, and we are adding Elliot, making them both mine. A giggle escapes me when I realize not only do I have a husband and a boyfriend, but my husband has a boyfriend, too.

I sigh when the smell of coffee fills the air while I begin cracking eggs. Sawyer keeps us stocked at home with all our favorites from Java Junkie. It's pretty special to have my own personal live-in barista.

As I hum and sway to the music playing quietly over the Bluetooth speakers, arms wrap around my waist from behind.

"Good morning... not my husband." They smell different, and I like that I can tell them apart just from their scents.

Elliot kisses the side of my neck and chuckles.

"Are you disappointed?"

I spin in his arms and glide my hands up his bare chest. "Not at all. Just caught off guard."

He smiles as he stares down at me with his piercing blue eyes. "May I kiss you, Cherry?"

"That depends."

His hold around my waist tightens. "On?"

"Have you brushed your teeth? Because we value good hygiene in this house."

Elliot's forehead tilts to mine. "Brushed *and* flossed."

I don't know what comes over me, but with a little hop, I fling myself into Elliot's chest, and he catches me by the back of my thighs as if it's the most natural thing in the world. Our lips meet, and I taste his minty toothpaste. I'm sure I taste like caramel and coffee since I've already downed half of my morning cup.

My hands trail to the nape of his neck then into his soft, dark hair. He moans when I tug at his strands, and I can feel the arousal pooling in my panties.

*Shit.*

"Eggs." I almost forgot I was cooking. I pull away, and he moves his lips to my neck. "Elliot, I'm going to burn the eggs."

"I'll buy more. I'll buy you an entire flock of chickens, and we can have fresh eggs every day."

"Elliot," I giggle. "Don't be silly. Let me cook."

He drops my legs but catches me before I fall. "Cook for me, wench." Elliot grabs my shoulders and spins me around before landing a playful smack on my ass.

Luckily, I'm making scrambled eggs, and we have excellent non-stick pans. I slide them onto the awaiting plate and toss the sausage in the pan I had waiting.

"Um, Elliot?"

"Shhh. Cook for me." I look down to see Elliot on his knees, removing my shorts I had thrown on before leaving the bedroom.

"But I—"

"Should I stop?" He slides a thumb through my wet pussy, and I'm incapable of denying him.

"No," I breathe out the word, barely a whisper.

"Then you make your breakfast while I eat mine."

And he does. While I attempt not to burn the sausage patties, he licks and sucks on my pussy. He moans like he's eating his favorite meal while I try to stay standing.

I quickly slide the food onto the plate with the eggs and brace two hands on the counter as my orgasm crashes through me. My hips ride Elliot's face, and he hums his approval.

Suddenly, there's clapping behind us, and I spin my head around to see Sawyer leaning against the kitchen island.

"Breakfast and a show. I could get used to waking up to this."

He rounds the corner and extends a hand to help Elliot, but I already see his ulterior motive. As soon as Elliot is on his feet, Sawyer dives in for a kiss. It's sloppy and all tongue as he attempts to taste me on Elliot.

Both men are panting when they pull away, and I am, too, just from watching them.

"Yeah, I could get used to this too," Elliot agrees with a smile.

"What do you need to get ready for work? I should have something you could borrow if you need it."

I plate our breakfasts as they discuss their morning. Elliot tells Sawyer he brought a bag with a suit but left it in his car because he didn't want to assume anything. After we eat, Elliot leaves to retrieve his suit, and Sawyer helps me clean up breakfast.

"How are you, Jitterbug?" Sawyer pulls me into his chest, and I melt into him.

"Happy. Content. Sore." I wiggle my hips, and we both laugh. "Can I give you a truth?"

"Always." He kisses the top of my head, patiently waiting.

"I had no expectations for, well, anything when you said you wanted to explore your sexuality with a man. After your several failed dates, I thought maybe this wasn't what you really wanted, and the phase would pass soon." He rubs my back as he listens to my confession. "I was hopeful for you but never for me. I supported you one hundred percent, but it seemed like a pipe dream that even if you found someone you were interested in, they'd also be interested in me. We're an established married couple. Things with Patrick and Chip happened because we all explored together. Our dynamic here is completely different."

"Is different bad?"

"No. No, not at all. I just meant I assumed different would mean difficult. But I think he's—" The front door opening cuts me off. Elliot walks in carrying his travel suit bag and sees us embracing in the kitchen, eyes on him.

"I'm sorry. I should have knocked. I didn't mean to interrupt." A look of guilt washes over his face, and I don't like it.

"Absolutely not. Come here." I extend my arm and wiggle my fingers at him.

"Elliot," Sawyer speaks up when he hesitates. "Thirty minutes ago, I walked into this kitchen to find you eating out my wife's pussy, and you're worried you interrupted a hug? Get your ass over here."

I bite my cheek to stop myself from smiling. I don't want Elliot to think I'm laughing at him. He walks toward us and drapes his bag over the kitchen counter. Sawyer opens one arm and pulls him into our embrace. He tenderly kisses Elliot's forehead, making me want to jump their bones right here and now.

"Is she mine too?" Sawyer looks confused by Elliot's question, but I understand it. Sawyer referred to me as *his wife* just now, and while it didn't have the same possessive inflection it did previously, I can't blame him for the question.

"Why, Elliot, are you asking me to go steady?" He chuckles

286

and glances at Sawyer.

"I think maybe I am. Sawyer, can I go steady with your wife?"

Bold move using his term against him.

"Maybe."

"Maybe? Are there terms?"

Sawyer switches his eyes to mine. "Finish the sentence you were about to say when Elliot walked in." *Crap.* He expects me to remember what I was saying. "You were telling me how you thought Elliot was different."

"Oh yeah! Well, it feels silly to say it in front of him, but I think he's our unicorn."

"Is that a good thing?" Elliot asks.

"Yeah. I was telling Sawyer that you were unexpected. A unicorn is a rare mythical creature, and that's kind of how I felt about us finding someone compatible for both Sawyer and myself."

"So I'm your unicorn? Can I also be... your boyfriend? Both of yours?" The raw vulnerability in his questions has my heart soaring. I want to wrap his adorableness into a bubble and never let it go.

"Maaaaybe," I tease while I move my hand down his back and grip his ass. He tenses under my hand, and I squeeze harder. *God, his ass is incredible.*

"How can I turn that maybe into a yes?"

"Sex." Before either of them get any ideas, I step back. "But there's no time for that right now. *Some* of us have a job to get to." I side-eye Sawyer. He knows I'm just picking on him. He works hard to support us even if Gus mans the coffee shop most days. There are a lot of behind-the-scenes things that Sawyer does daily.

"Well then, Cherry, I think we should get ready. Could I help you pick out your dress?"

My jaw drops. I've noticed Elliot's keen eye for fashion with his perfectly tailored suits, but it never dawned on me that this could be a perk.

I slap Sawyer's chest. "Baby, did you find me a fashionista boyfriend?"

"I thought I didn't have boyfriend status yet?" Elliot teases.

I grab the front of his shirt and tow him toward the bedroom. "Let's see how you do at picking out my outfit, and maybe you'll get an instant upgrade."

"Deal." Elliot anxiously follows with a smile, and Sawyer trails behind, laughing and shaking his head.

"Excuse me. Have you seen my best friend, Lainey? She usually works the reception desk, but it appears you've replaced her. You're much more smiley and chipper than she usually is."

"Shut your face, Katy. Am I not allowed to smile?" I can't deny her observation. My cheeks hurt from the amount I've done today.

"Also, you're dressed to kill, and my Lainey is usually fun and casually dressed."

"Says the woman in leggings and a t-shirt." I give her a deadpan look even though she has no choice in her attire. She's wearing the MAD Childcare logoed shirt and comfortable bottoms.

"Bitch."

"Brat." I open my mouth to rebuttal, but Katy sees my

cheeks flame red, and she slams her hand on the desk, causing a few heads to turn. "Explain. Now."

"I have fifteen minutes until my break. You'll have to wait, Nosey Nelly."

"Nope." She pulls her phone out of her crossbody and types away. "Viktor will be here in two minutes."

"But Katy, I—"

"Nuh-uh. No one is going to care what time you took your break as long as security is here taking your place. Aren't we lucky I happen to know a security guard that works in the building?"

"So lucky." My words are laced with sarcasm, and I know she hears it because she rolls her eyes and turns her back on me. I gather my things and put them in my purse just as Vik arrives.

"You needed me, Pepper?" He rubs her belly and places a chaste kiss on her forehead, and it's her turn to blush. Vik is already a strikingly handsome man, but when you pair his Viking looks with a suit, I can completely understand why Katy is knocked up *again*.

"Will you watch the desk so Lainey can take her break with me? We need to girl chat."

He brushes a stray lock of hair behind her ear that's fallen from her messy top knot, and there's so much love in that simple act.

"Of course. Are the kids good?" All four of their children are upstairs in the company daycare. I don't know how Vik is going to act next year when Owen, their oldest, goes off to kindergarten.

"They are wonderful. Lainey's relief should be here in about ten minutes. Thank you, Viktor. Love you."

"Love you too, Pepper. Have a nice lunch."

"Ugh. You two are giving me a cavity. Let's go, Katy. Thanks, Vik." I round the desk, hook my elbow into hers, and pull her away.

Katy manages to keep her interrogation contained until we get our salads and find a table. She's practically vibrating with her need to know whatever gossip she thinks I'm keeping from her, and I know she's going to freak out when I tell her.

"Lainey—"

"It's Elliot." I slap my hands over my eyes. Okay. That happened. I had no intention of blurting it out like that, but here we are

"Who? Wait. What about Elliot?" She looks around the dining room, assuming he's nearby, which is why I said his name.

"The boyfriend. Sawyer's boyfriend. My... boyfriend."

Katy stares at me with a blank face. No noise. No blinking.

"Elliot." She repeats his name in pure shock.

"What about Elliot?" My eyes snap to Blake, who somehow appeared behind me without hearing her heels click. "He should be down in a few minutes. He was updating an appointment for Annie."

Blake sits, and her gaze darts between us. She picks up a french fry and studies Katy's shocked face. When she turns to me, I look away. Blake may not be Elliot's *boss* boss, but she's still his boss. I'm sure he doesn't want any office rumors started.

"Katy, what's wrong with you?" She uses her fry to point between us. "There's something going on here. I want the gossip." Blake chews on her fry, waiting us out. "Lainey?"

"I—"

"Well, hello, ladies. What a beautiful group of women. Do you have room for one more?"

*Fuckfuckfuck.*

Katy coughs, choking on the iced coffee she's sipping, when Elliot appears behind me. I sat in the wrong damn seat. Everyone has snuck up on me.

Elliot reaches over and pats Katy on the back. She stares at me with wide eyes, and the pressure of everyone needing answers from me is too much.

I stand quickly, the chair scraping behind me. I need to get out of here before I say something that gets us in trouble.

"I-I've got to go—*shit!*" I spin too fast, and my ankle rolls out from under me. I squeeze my eyes shut and brace for impact, knowing it's going to hurt, but it never comes. Instead, I feel like I'm flying. I open my eyes to find clear blue ones staring back at me.

"Elliot," I say breathlessly.

"Elliot," Katy echoes behind me. I can't imagine what she sees right now. Elliot has me cradled in his arms, looking down at me with concern. I haven't given her any information about him other than the few words we were able to exchange before Blake showed up. Blake has no idea what's going on, but she's more perceptive than any of us give her credit for, and I know she's seeing something right now even though no words are being spoken.

"Are you okay, Cherry?"

I'm a fucking goner for this man. How did it happen so quickly? I'm lost in his eyes. I saw his lips move and heard his question, but my brain isn't working. It's like we are the only two people in the room despite knowing all eyes are on us.

"Lainey, oh my god. Are you okay?" Blake presses a hand on my shoulder, and I snap back into reality.

"Um. Yeah, I think so." I nod to Elliot, who gently lowers my legs and puts them back on the ground. "I think—*fuck*. Ouch. Okay, maybe I'm not okay." Elliot scoops me up again and sits me on the table.

"What's wrong?"

"Right ankle."

My skin heats as his hand slides down my leg. By the time he reaches my ankle, I'm biting my lip and suppressing a moan. He removes my shoe and presses his thumb into my skin.

"How's this fe—"

"Ah." I wince as he presses on a tender spot. I can already see a slight bruise forming in the area he pressed.

"I think you might have sprained it." He moves my ankle from side to side and watches for my expressions. There's mild pain in certain directions, and I agree with his assessment. It's probably sprained. It wouldn't be the first time I've sustained an injury from heels.

"Let me run up to the nurse at the daycare. I'll get you an icepack, and I bet she has something we can wrap it with."

"Thank you, Katy. I feel so stupid." Katy leaves, and I see Blake texting on her cell.

"Do you want me to take you home?"

*Yes. And do dirty, dirty things to me, please, Elliot.*

"I think I'll be okay to finish out the day, but I'll have to call Sawyer for a ride home."

"Nope," Blake objects. "I just cleared it with Annie. You're both free for the rest of the day. Take her home, Elliot. Let her rest that ankle."

Why would she assume he'd want to take me home? What does she know?

"I can call Sawyer. I don't want to be a burden."

Blake waves her hand, slicing the air. "Hush, Lainey. Annie was done for the day anyway. Elliot just cleared her schedule, so it's not like he has anything else to do for the day. Right, Elliot?" There's a twinkle of mischief in her eyes, and I'm wondering what she knows. I'm not sure how she could know anything since it all just happened last night, and I haven't even had a chance to tell Katy.

But Elliot...

I look between them as they exchange a look, and I know she knows.

I poke Elliot in the chest, and he rubs the spot.

"What?"

"You gossip. You told Blake."

His lips purse as he contains his smile.

"Don't blame him, Lainey. Something was written all over his face when he walked in, and I called him out on it. He caved too quickly, though." She side-eyes Elliot, and he looks embarrassed.

"I'm sorry, Cherry. I was planning to talk to Blake about us anyway. I wanted to make sure we weren't breaking any company rules."

"And you're not," she cuts in quickly. "The fraternization policy is only for superiors. Your roles are equal as far as the company is concerned."

"Sorry, Cherry. I should have spoken to you about it before Blake, but she's a damn shark and knew something was up the moment she saw me this morning."

Blake knows, and by the way she's acting, it doesn't seem like she cares. She knows Sawyer. She watched our love story unfold, and she approves of adding Elliot.

"Annie?" Her name rushes out of my mouth with worry.

"Lainey, relax. Annie is just as happy for you both as I am. Well, I guess all three of you. I don't know why you would even worry."

"Katy is going to kill me," I groan.

Blake looks around the room as if she's looking for Katy. "Why?"

"Because she's the last to know. Well, I sort of told her right before you showed up, but we obviously haven't had a chance to talk about it yet."

"Oh, yeah, that could be an issue. Well, remind her she knew before Nicole so she wasn't the last. Besides, Elliot told me, not you. So she can't be mad about that."

"This is Katy we're talking about. She won't see it like that."

"I won't see what, like what?"

*Dammit.* I guess I'm destined to be snuck up on today.

"I'm Lainey and Sawyer's boyfriend." Elliot's words are matter-of-fact with no hesitation.

I brace myself for the barrage of questions, but she's not looking at me. She's staring down at Blake.

"You knew?" she accuses Blake. "How could you not tell me, bitch?"

The laugh bursts from my lips without permission. I had no idea I was stressing over telling my friends about my new relationship with Elliot, but the relief I feel as I laugh says otherwise.

"Hey." Elliot swipes his thumb over my cheek, and I realize

he's wiping away a tear. "Happy or sad?"

"Relief. Stress. Happy." Elliot kisses my forehead, and the tears flow more. I'm a mess.

"Take her home, Elliot, before she causes more of a scene. We'll see you both tomorrow. Unless you need another day, Lainey. Don't stress if you do. Annie will understand." Blake squeezes my hand and smiles.

"Yes, please go. Your dramatics have taken up most of my lunchtime, and I'm starving. Text me later." Katy stares me down with those last words, and I know she's silently telling me she wants all the details.

"I will."

Katy hands me the supplies she collected from the nurse, and I try to slide off the table so she can finish eating.

"No, you don't." Elliot hooks his arm around my legs, and once again, I'm airborne.

"I can probably walk."

"And I can definitely carry you. I like my odds better. Let's get you home."

# 37

# Elliot

Lainey feels so good in my arms as I carry her to the parking garage. I wish it were under better circumstances and not because she's injured, but I'm not complaining.

"I feel like a child."

"I'm enjoying this. Don't kill my buzz." She huffs and crosses her arms over her chest until she sees me staring at her cleavage and uncrosses them.

"Perv."

"You love it." I step up to my car and realize I can't open the door unless I put her down, and I can't have that. "Hey, Cherry. Can I get your help? My keys are in my front left pocket. Think you can reach them?"

She rolls her eyes. "Just put me do—"

"Front pocket, Alaina." I need her obedience, and if this is the only way I can get it, I'll pull rank.

She stares at me for a few heartbeats before smiling. "Yes, E." Little brat.

Lainey shifts in my arms and squeezes her hand between us to my pocket. Her hand takes a slight detour and swipes across my dick.

"Watch it," I warn her. I already feel on edge. Being this close, smelling her hair, her perfume, the feel of her body on mine, is all too much.

She reaches into my pocket and pulls out my keys. Her brows pinch as she looks at the fob and finally looks at the car we stopped in front of.

"Unlock the doors, please." She pushes the button, and I maneuver us so I can open the door and gently place her in the front seat. "Thank you, Cherry." I kiss her forehead, and the use of her nickname makes the dam break.

"Elliot, you drive a BMW?"

"I do." I close her door and walk around to the driver's side. There are a few things I've splurged on since moving here. This car and my house being the main things.

"Why did I have to unlock it? Isn't this a luxury car with all the bells and whistles? Um, and how can you afford this? I'm sure Annie pays well, but *this* well?" She inhales deeply. "It even smells like a new car."

"Cherry, that was a lot of questions at once." I push the button to start the car, reach over the console, and place my hand on her thigh. She looks down and smiles. "Yes, this is a luxury car, but I have the keyless entry turned off. My garage is off the kitchen, and when I would walk around with the keys in my pocket, it would lock and unlock the doors. It smells like a new car because it is. I bought it when I got here a few months ago."

"It's beautiful."

"Just like you."

"Cheezy, Elliot. Cheezy." I wink, and she rolls her eyes. "Where are we going?" She finally notices the direction we're heading, but I ignore her and push a few buttons on the steering wheel. A ringing sound echoes through the car.

"Hey, what a nice surprise." Sawyer's voice fills the cabin and brings a smile to my face.

"Sawyer?"

"Lainey? What are you two up to?"

I can feel her staring at me, but I ignore it.

"Would you like to come to my house for dinner tonight?" Lainey's eyes light up, and she looks out the front window, realizing that's where I'm taking her.

"Dinner? Sure. What time?"

"Any time. Lainey and I are already on our way there. She had a little tumble at work and hurt her ankle. Annie gave us the rest of the day off. We're on our way to my house now. If that's okay with both of you?" I squeeze Lainey's thigh, and she smiles excitedly.

"Is she okay? Jitterbug, are you okay?" There's a panicked edge to his voice.

"I'm good, Baby. Elliot carried me out to his car like some invalid. It's just a little sore."

"Good. Okay, good. Yeah, I'll meet you guys there. I have a little more work to do, but—"

"Bring it," I butt in. "You can finish it while I make dinner."

"That sounds good. I'll pack up my stuff and see you in a bit." I can already hear him shuffling things around in the background.

"Baby, can you bring me a change of clothes," Lainey adds hastily.

"And overnight bags." Lainey looks at me, excitement

298

lacing her features. "And bathing suits… if you want. The hot tub is clothing optional."

Lainey shifts to face me. She hikes her knee onto the seat, and my hand slides further up her thigh.

"You have a hot tub? Sawyer, hurry up and get to Elliot's house. I want to use the hot tub."

"I'm on my way, Jitterbug. I'll see you both soon."

Lainey turns back to face front but leaves her leg propped up. I take it as an invitation and inch my hand further up her thigh. I glance at her through my periphery and bite my lip, seeing the dress I picked out. It's a form-fitting burgundy dress with cap sleeves that have a ruffle on them. The neckline is low and boxy and shows just a hint of cleavage. I had her pair it with gold jewelry and nude heels, which I regret after her stumble.

"How's your ankle, Cherry?"

She looks down and rolls her foot around. "Not bad. A little sore. I'll be oka—holy shit, Elliot. Is this your house?"

I push the button to open the garage door, and Lainey plasters her chest to the dashboard, looking around.

"This is me."

"You live here alone?"

"Yeah. Come on. I'll give you the tour. Don't open the door." I give her a stern look when her hand reaches out for the handle.

"You're frustrating," she yells at me through the window, and I round the front of the car. I open her door with a smile. "You don't need to carry me."

"How about a piggyback ride?"

Her eyes narrow as she contemplates my offer. "Fine. It's better than being carried, I suppose."

I take off my suit jacket and give her my back, crouching down. She grabs my neck, and we situate ourselves till she's comfortable.

"Mush, mush," she commands.

"I'm not a dog, Cherry."

"Oh yeah. Um? Yee Haw!"

"I like mush better. Let's go, trouble." I grab my suit jacket and carefully close the door.

Lainey "oohs and awes" as I show her each room of the house. She comments on how much Sawyer would love my in-home gym and how big my bed is. When we return to the living room, Sawyer is knocking on my front door.

"Come in," I yell as I place Lainey on the couch. I hear the door open, and Sawyer appears around the corner.

"Well damn. I was almost hoping I'd find you both in a compromising position."

"That can be arranged, Doll." I step up to him and slide my arms around his waist. Sawyer leans in and kisses me. It's a friendly hello kiss, slow and inviting. I love these kinds of kisses as much as I love the dominant ones.

"How's our girl?" He looks past me at Lainey, who's staring at us.

"Go ask her yourself." I release him, and he sits on the couch next to her. I let them talk while I head to the kitchen and pull things out for dinner. It's still early afternoon, but I hadn't planned for company, so I need to allow the meat to thaw for the baked ziti I plan to make.

I pull ground sausage from the freezer and hear footsteps behind me.

"Can I help?"

I close the door, and Sawyer waits for my answer. I push

aside a chunk of hair falling over his forehead and smile. "You said you still have work to do, and I don't want to get in your way. I planned to work out in the gym while you finished and the meat thawed. I was going to offer Lainey my bed to see if she wanted to nap and rest her ankle."

"Gym? You have a home gym?"

My lip quirks. "Yeah. Come see." He follows me down the hall, and I remove my tie as we go. I stop in front of the door and allow him to look in. His gray eyes sparkle as they roam over the equipment.

"Holy shit. Can I join you? Nothing I need to do for work is pressing?"

"Do I want to watch you work out? Is that really a question?" Sawyer smiles at me, and I want to kiss him, but I'd rather see his muscles strain. "On one condition?"

"What's that?"

"You have to be shirtless. I don't want any barriers between my eyes and the sweat I want to watch roll off your chest."

Sawyer reaches behind his head and pulls off his navy t-shirt. He drops it to the floor and reaches for the buttons on my dress shirt.

"As long as you're shirtless, too." My chest rises and falls quickly as he undresses me. "Do you have a pair of shorts I can borrow? If not, I'm happy to work out in my boxers."

I shudder as his fingers trace the newly exposed skin. They graze my chest and shoulders while he pushes my shirt off. It falls to the floor next to his, and I glance down to see the bulge in his jeans.

"It might be hard to work out with that."

He grabs the front of my slacks and feels my hardening

cock.

"I agree. It's definitely going to be hard."

My body jerks forward when he squeezes, and I moan.

"There's plenty of time for that later." I thrust into his hand, making him squeeze me again. "You get Lainey settled, I'll change and get you some shorts."

The heel of his hands rubs my length, and I want to say fuck the workout and take him to my bedroom, but as I told him, there's plenty of time later.

Sawyer finally steps back, and I already miss the feeling of his hands on me. He walks down the hall, and I pick up our discarded shirts. I can't help myself and I bring his t-shirt to my nose. My cock twitches at his rich scent. There's no cologne smell like I expected, only a hint of coffee, something musky and freshness probably from fabric softener. He smells like a man I want to roll all over and mark my territory on. He might not get his shirt back.

# 38

## Sawyer

Lainey eyes me curiously when I walk back into the room shirtless.

"Elliot and I are going to work out. Would you like to take a nap before dinner?"

"Oh my god, a nap sounds amazing." She plops back on the couch before popping back up. "I need to change my clothes. Will you help me?"

"Of course, Jitterbug."

I carefully assist Lainey with changing into the clothes I brought her and help settle her back on the couch with a throw blanket. When I walk back into the gym, there's music playing, and Elliot is already working out.

"Shorts are right there if you decide to wear them." He nods towards a chair next to the door as he continues his pullups. His back muscles move and flex with each rep, and I can't make myself look away. His skin already glistens with sweat, and his black basketball shorts sit dangerously low on his hips.

303

"Earth to Sawyer."

"Shit, yeah. Sorry." I have no idea how long I've been staring, but obviously long enough for him to call me out on it.

"Are you going to watch or join?" Elliot walks toward me, and I'm as stiff as a statue. His front view is even more stunning than his back. His muscles ripple as if he's already done a full workout. When he reaches me, his hands go to my pants.

"Can I help you with these?" I nod while trying to come up with coherent words, but none form. Elliot drags his finger along the inside of my jeans before popping the button. Each tooth sounds like fireworks to my ears as he lowers my zipper. With a gentle tug, my pants fall to the floor. He steps back so I can toe off my shoes and step out of my pants.

"You're beautiful, Elliot." The words are out of my mouth before I have the conscious thought to stop myself. He smirks and his eyes roam me from top to bottom. I'm standing in nothing but my gray boxer briefs, unashamed of my very prominent bulge.

"Thank you, but if you don't put clothes on, there's going to be a very different workout happening in this gym. *Sir.*"

Why does he enjoy being such a brat? I want to reprimand him for his sass, but he's right. I bend to the side and grab the shorts he left for me. Our eyes stay locked together as I put them on, but even they can't contain the now raging hard-on tenting them. Oh well. There's nothing I'm going to do about it. Not right now, at least.

"I warmed up for five minutes on the treadmill before you came in. How would you like to start?"

We spend the next hour rotating around his home gym. I

had no idea a man's individual body parts could be so sexy. I wanted to lick his abs when he was doing crunches, bite his calves when he was jumping rope, and when I spotted him during his chest lifts, I wanted to shove my cock in his mouth and watch him choke on it.

Even his ass, when he bends down to get us water from a minifridge, screams for me to take him.

"Ready for a shower?"

His question startles me. "Together?"

"If you'd like. Otherwise, there's a shower in the guest bathroom."

My hand flies to his neck, and I pull him into me, crushing our lips together. I try to convey how much I'd like to shower together through my kiss. Elliot steps closer so our bodies mold together, and I feel his reaction on my thigh. I think I've gotten my point across.

"Lead the way, Eli."

I'm not surprised to see a large stand up shower with several different heads. Elliot's house is modern comfort, and he looks like someone who enjoys a good shower.

As the room steams up, we strip without saying a word. He steps in and offers his hand for me to follow. We each have our own stream of water to wash and shampoo without much interaction.

I'm rinsing the soap on my face when Elliot's hard body presses against mine. Hot lips caress my shoulder, and his arousal is evident as he rubs his cock against my ass.

"Do you ever think you'll let me take you here?" His hips thrust forward, grinding into my ass.

Would I ever allow Elliot to take my ass? I have no idea. There's been a few occasions where I've allowed Lainey anal play. I'm sure he remembers the picture Lainey sent of my butt plug on our first date, but that's as far as we've gotten.

"Maybe. I need a different level of trust to allow myself that vulnerability with someone. I hope you can understand that."

"I do," he responds immediately, and I'm more relieved by his understanding than I expected. "Will you allow me to try something? Safeword applies to you, too."

What could he possibly want to try? Elliot's hands roam my body, massaging and caressing everything they touch.

"Please."

"Okay."

His lips on my neck are hypnotizing, and I hope I don't regret whatever I just agreed to.

"Spread your legs a little more for me." I look over my shoulder at him, wondering where this is going. "Trust me. And trust that if you say Apple, I'll stop."

My heart races, and I swear he can probably hear it. Elliot massages my ass cheeks as encouragement, and I spread my legs.

"Further," he whispers in my ear.

I spread them a little more, and he nips my earlobe.

"This is where I call you a good boy, and you don't slam me against a wall." He pauses, waiting for any objection, but I say nothing. "Good boy," he purrs in my ear, and I'd be lying if I said it didn't sound good coming from his mouth.

Elliot trails kisses down my spine, and I bite my lip to contain my moans. He reaches the small of my back, and his hand appears in the middle of my back, pushing gently.

"Hands on the wall, Sawyer."

"Elliot," I say with warning.

"Trust me. Say Apple if you need to, Sawyer. Otherwise, please put your hands on the wall."

His polite sass makes me growl, but I comply. I'm being vulnerable and giving up control. I hope he understands what this means to me—for him.

Elliot's mouth skims across my ass cheeks. He nips and licks, causing me to contract my muscles several times, and I hear him chuckle.

"Relax. I promise you'll enjoy yourself."

It's hard to relax when he's exploring uncharted territory. My body stiffens when he pulls my cheeks apart, but he doesn't let it deter him.

A gasp that quickly turns into a moan echoes through the room when Elliot's tongue swipes across my hole.

"What—Why does that feel so gooooood? Fuck."

His tongue swipes up and down, left to right. It swirls and fondles. Nerves I didn't know existed light up.

"Jesus fuck, Elliot." I rest my forehead on my arm and take in all the sensations he's creating in my body. My cock pulses as he applies more pressure, and he feels like he's trying to penetrate me with his tongue. It's unlike anything I've ever experienced before.

Elliot reaches between my legs and grabs my cock. His hand moves in tandem with his tongue, and I don't know where to focus my attention because it's almost too much.

"Fuck, I'm gonna come." The tingling sensation increases when he squeezes me harder and hums his approval into my ass.

The first spurt of come hits the wall, and so does my hand. I slap the wall, and pleasure floods my body. Elliot releases me to hold my hips when my knees threaten to give out. I grab my cock and stroke a few more times to draw out the rest of my orgasm and allow myself to collapse to the floor.

Turning, I face Elliot, who's wearing a smug smile.

"Thank you."

I'm confused by his gratitude. "Me? Why are you thanking me? Shouldn't I be thanking you?"

Elliot leans forward on his hands and knees and kisses me. "Thank you for allowing me the trust I know that took. I appreciate it."

I nod through my panting as I attempt to get my heartbeat under control. He stands and turns off the shower. Reaching out, he grabs a towel and offers a hand to help me stand.

"Let's go make dinner for our girl."

# 39

# Lainey

I'm woken by hushed words and metal scraping in pans. Rolling my ankle, I can tell it already feels better. I sit up and gently put pressure on it as I stand. There's mild soreness but nothing like the pain from earlier.

Following the sounds, I carefully make my way to the kitchen, where I see two damp, shirtless men flirting and cooking. Elliot dips a noodle in a pink sauce and feeds it to Sawyer, whose eyes roll back into his head as he nods his approval of the taste.

Sawyer goes back to shredding a block of cheese, and I silently watch them. You'd never know this is their first time cooking together because they look so natural. It all feels so natural. How can that be? I feel like the luckiest girl in the world.

I'm not sure if I make a noise, but Elliot looks in my direction, and his face lights up.

"Hey, Cherry. How was your nap?"

Sawyer comes up to me and wraps his arms around my

waist. "You should have called for one of us. How's your ankle?"

"My nap and my ankle are both good. Thank you for asking. I can walk just fine." Sawyer keeps a hand on my back as I walk farther into the kitchen and helps me sit in a chair at the island. "It smells amazing in here."

Garlic and sauce invade my nose and my mouth waters. Elliot joins me at the counter and kisses the top of my head.

"We're making baked ziti. Do you need anything while you wait?"

"Only a promise to use the hot tub when we're done."

"Anything you want, Cherry."

"Anything?" I run a finger down his bare chest.

"Anything," Sawyer whispers at my back. Heat floods through my body as I'm sandwiched between these two hunky men. "After dinner."

Insert a cold bucket of water.

"You suck."

"He does," Elliot croons. "Very well."

"Ugh. Go away." I put a hand on each chest and push. They chuckle and go back to their ziti making. A glass of wine appears before me, and I smile at Sawyer.

"Thank you, Baby."

Dinner was incredible—better than any Italian restaurant I've been to. I'm ready for a relaxing soak in the hot tub, as I was promised.

The guys continue to baby me and carry me to the backyard under a private screened-in room.

"Elliot, this is beautiful." Gauzy curtains cover any view from neighbors, and white fairy lights twine through the entire space, giving it the perfect glow for nighttime.

"Thanks, Cherry. My best friend and her husband put one in their backyard, and I knew I had to have one when I bought this house.

Best friend. Best friend. What's her name?

"Her name begins with an odd letter. It's not a Z, it's a... W. Right?"

He chuckles. "Correct. It's Wynnie. Short for Rowyn."

The three of us stand, waiting for someone to make the first move. I have the most clothes on, so I guess by default, it will be me. Reaching down, I grab the hem of my shirt and pull it over my head. Their attention turns to me as I wrap my arms behind my back to unclip my bra.

"You said clothing was optional, right?"

"I did." Elliot hooks his fingers in his black joggers and removes his pants. He removes the *only* article of clothing he was wearing and now stands naked.

His cock standing half mast as he steps to the platform and into the hot tub. I peel off my leggings, with Sawyer helping me to balance and Elliot assisting me into the soothing, hot water. Sawyer joins us with his gloriously naked body on display, and Elliot turns on the bubbles.

With my arms resting along the top, I lean my head back and enjoy the water. My leg bobs, and I bump someone's leg. I open an eye to see whose it is, and Elliot smiles back at me. He grabs my foot and massages a thumb into my arch. I moan, and Sawyer looks between the two of us.

"Foot rub," Elliot answers his curious look, and Sawyer smirks.

"Just to put it out there, before anyone gets any ideas, hot tub sex isn't as fun and sexy as it sounds. Water doesn't make for a great lube."

I burst out laughing because the thought hadn't even crossed my mind until he put it there. Sawyer shifts closer to Elliot, and his hand disappears into the water. Elliot moans and his head drops back onto his shoulders.

"But there are other things we can do that will feel just as good."

"Yeah. Yeah, there are," Elliot breathes out.

I don't have to see Sawyer's hand to know he's stroking Elliot. The expression of bliss says enough. Despite what's happening under the water, Elliot hasn't stopped massaging my foot. I use my free foot to find Sawyer's leg and trail it up his inner thigh. He shifts to give me more room, knowing what I have in mind. When I reach his cock, I gently brush it with my foot and wince. I forgot about my sore ankle. Sawyer releases Elliot to check on my ankle, and I see the disappointment on Elliot's face.

"How's it feeling?"

"I'm okay. I just twisted it the wrong way." I try to wiggle out of his hold so I can go back to what I was trying to do, but he holds me still.

"No more, Jitterbug. You need to rest your ankle."

I know he's right, but my hormones don't agree. I'm in a giant bathtub with two naked men, and I'm horny. Our relationship is still new, and everything is fun and exciting.

I pull my feet away from them and glide to their side of the hot tub.

"My hands and mouth aren't injured."

Elliot chokes on air, and Sawyer's mouth drops. I love that I can shock them both with one statement.

"I don't know, Sawyer. It's hard to argue with that logic." Elliot's hand moves through the water and caresses the top of my breasts.

"Sit up on the edge, boys." I bite my lip as I wait for them to respond. I don't ever take control, and while this isn't a scene, it's still outside our routine.

Sawyer plants his hands on the edge and lifts himself out.

"Okay, Lainey. We'll play your game." He nods his head in a gesture that tells Elliot to join him.

Once they're out, I realize this is the first time I have access to both of them, and I have all the power.

"Kiss."

Elliot's lip twitches. "Little missy here thinks she can give orders. Are we going to let her?"

Sawyer returns with an even more devious smile. "Yeah, I think we are."

"Well, then, let's give her what she wants." Elliot grabs Sawyer's neck and pulls him in for a kiss. It's fucking hot to see that small piece of dominance Elliot uses over him. Sawyer doesn't let it last long before he takes over the kiss, and Elliot's hand drops to his chest.

I watch them make out for a moment, but it's my playtime. I grab each of their cocks and stroke. Sawyer pulls away from their kiss and rests their foreheads together. My hands find a rhythm, and they moan and pant against each other.

I lick my lips and take Sawyer's cock into my mouth.

"Fuuuuck, Lainey. Just like that." He grabs a handful of hair at the nape of my neck and urges me to take him deeper. I love that he's allowing me to give him pleasure more often.

Elliot brushes hair off my cheek, looking down at me with affection lacing his features.

"You look so pretty with your mouth stretched around his cock, Cherry."

His words cause me to moan around Sawyer. I'm officially a slut for praise. Sawyer will tell me I'm doing a good job, but not the way Elliot does. Patrick and Chip were good to me—better than good—but I wasn't in the headspace to understand the depth of their words.

I switch my mouth from Sawyer to Elliot, and their moans make me feel powerful.

"I love your fucking mouth, Cherry." Elliot's head falls back, and his eyes close as I lick and suck on his tip. I'm still learning what he likes, but I've found some tricks he seems to really enjoy.

I rotate back and forth until I can tell they're both close.

"Who's gonna be first?" I look between them while I stroke with my hands, and they decide.

"Rock, Paper, Scissors?" Elliot asks while shrugging.

Sawyer chuckles and sets his fist on his hand, ready to battle. First round goes to Elliot with rock over scissors. Second to Sawyer with paper over rock.

"For the come," Elliot jokes.

"For the come," Sawyer echoes.

In unison, they chant, "Rock, Paper, Scissors. SHOOT!"

Sawyer wins, scissors to Elliot's paper, and widens his legs to offer me more space.

"Will you take over for me with Elliot so I can use both hands?" Sawyer reaches for Elliot's cock and gets brushed off.

"Focus on our girl and let her pleasure you. I'll handle myself while I wait my turn."

Elliot languidly strokes his cock as I shift between Sawyer's legs. I take him into my mouth and suck hard. He pulls my damp hair into a ponytail at the base of my neck, and I bob faster.

It isn't long before Sawyer is cursing under his breath and adding light pressure to the back of my head. I taste the salty pre-come moments before he shoots into my mouth with a low groan.

When he's done, Sawyer slips back into the hot tub and kisses me. "You're mouth should be fucking illegal, Jitterbug. Go take care of Elliot."

"Sawyer." We turn to look at Elliot as he joins us in the water. "Can I fuck our girl?"

# 40

# Elliot

Lainey is fucking incredible. Watching her finish off Sawyer had my cock swelling without being touched. I know I'm next, and as much as I want her mouth, I want something else.

"Sawyer. Can I fuck our girl?" I haven't been inside Lainey yet, and I'm dying to. Well, not officially, at least. I had "Meg" in the movie theater, and it was incredible, but I didn't know who it was at the time, and it feels like a completely different person. "If she wants, of course."

"I want," Lainey answers eagerly.

Sawyer chuckles and pulls her closer. "You do, huh? Do you think you deserve his cock?" Sawyer blindly reaches into the water and grips me firmly, making me gasp.

Lainey bites her cheek, holding back a smile from my reaction, and smooths her palms down Sawyer's chest.

"Don't you want to watch?

Fire blazes in his eyes, and he looks into the water as he strokes me. His hand is firm and demanding, and I have to force my eyes not to roll back into my head. I don't want to miss a moment of their interaction.

"Out. Now."

I don't know if he's speaking to Lainey or me, but we both react and quickly step out of the hot tub. I hand each of them a towel, and Sawyer follows us. He extends a hand to the lounge chair on the patio.

"Take a seat Eli." Mmm. I see where this is going. He can take charge. I'm more than happy to comply if the end result is Lainey's sweet pussy wrapped around my cock.

I settle into the chair and await my next instructions.

"Crawl to him, Alaina."

*Oh fuck yes.*

She hands Sawyer her towel and gingerly lowers to her knees. Her hips sway as she seductively crawls across the pavers. I know it can't feel comfortable on her skin, but she doesn't act as if it bothers her. When she reaches me, Sawyer gestures with his head for her to keep going, and she climbs toward me.

Her breasts sway as her body begins to blanket mine, and I reach out to touch them as she gets closer.

"Hands on the armrests, Eli. You don't have permission to touch her."

*Fuck.* I want to growl, but I know my place and grip the handles like I hate them. Right now I do.

"You're in control, Alaina. Ride him and show me how good you can be to my little sub."

My expression must tell Sawyer something because I see his lip twitch when we lock eyes. He's enjoying this, and I'm glad.

"Sir?" Lainey questions.

He steps up next to her, grips the back of her neck, and pulls back, making her tits arch into my face.

"Yes, Alaina?"

"May I touch him?"

Say yes, I want to feel her. Say no because it will be torture. I don't even fucking know what I want right now other than her.

"Touch him. Torture him. Do whatever you want to. Take your pleasure from him."

Lainey's petite hands caress my chest, and I suck in a deep breath when her nails scrape over my nipples. Most women don't think men like nipple stimulation, and maybe most men wouldn't admit to liking it because it makes them feel less macho, but I fucking love it.

My knuckles turn white, and I tighten my hold and moan at her touches. She moves one hand to my shoulder and uses the other to grab my cock and line me up to her entrance. Teasing us both, she rubs me through her lips, showing me how wet and ready she is. The feel of her heat sinking onto me has a loud groan filling the space around us.

"Fuck that's incredible to see." I hadn't noticed Sawyer step up to me as I watched myself disappear into Lainey's pussy. I have to agree with his sentiment.

When Lainey's other hand attaches to my shoulder, she lifts her hips and slams back down. Before I can react to the pleasure, she does it again and sets a fast rhythm.

Up, down. In, out.

My fists open and close with her rhythm, wanting more than anything to touch her. She leans forward, and her tits bounce in my face. She's taking this torture thing as a challenge and I'm loving to hate both it and Sawyer.

318

Just when I think the torture can't get any worse, Sawyer moves and climbs onto the chair behind Lainey. His hands engulf her breasts, and I've never been more jealous of someone else's fingers as they pinch and twist her erect nipples.

Sawyer sits on my thighs, and I feel his cock swinging against my legs.

Torture. Fucking torture. Sweet and pleasurable torture that I wouldn't change for anything.

"Let us hear you, Eli. I can tell you're holding back. Make your neighbors jealous." I lock eyes with Sawyer's grays, and he's enjoying this way too much. I've been biting my lip and breathing heavily, attempting to not disturb my elderly neighbors. His commanding tone feels like permission to let go and enjoy myself fully, but I still hold back.

"Don't disrespect me, Eli. You won't like it. I saw the levels you go to when doling out punishment. You've set a high bar to compete with."

Shit. I showed my hand too soon.

Sawyer pushes Lainey onto my chest, and the heat of our skin feels like flames between us. His hands disappear from her breast, and I quickly find out where they went when my balls are squeezed from under Lainey.

"Holy fuck." The words escape me without permission while he rolls and tugs my balls as Lainey continues hammering onto me.

"There it fucking is. I want to hear more of that. Let our girl know how much she's pleasing you. We wouldn't want her to feel disappointed."

Disappointed? She's rocking my fucking world. I can't imagine a scenario where she could ever disappoint me. My

Cherry is fucking perfection.

Despite wanting to be respectful of my neighbors, there's no more willpower in me to stay quiet. Lainey's new position has her clit rubbing against me, and soon she's coming around my cock. I follow right behind her with growls of praise and adoration spilling from my lips.

When I finish I look to Sawyer with silent question. He knows exactly what I'm asking as he steps back off the chair and nods. My fingers are sore as I peel them from the chair and wrap my arms around Lainey.

"That was perfection, Cherry. Thank you for the honor."

# 41

## Elliot

The last two weeks have been a whirlwind of stolen moments with Lainey and Sawyer at work. We've had sleepovers at our houses, and I'm beginning to dislike sleeping alone.

Sawyer has been spending more time at Java Junkie to be closer to Lainey and me during the day. His manager, Gus, rolls his eyes every time he sees me. I've heard him mumble that he needs noise-cancelling headphones, and Sawyer has promised to give him a raise.

Lainey: It's going to be the longest three days.
   Sawyer: Is there room in your suitcase for two more?

I smile as I read their text message from my seat at the airport. I'm heading home for the kids' summer birthday celebrations. The families decided several years ago that individual birthdays got exhausting with the almost dozen kids between us. Instead, we throw a big party sometime in the summer and spring and celebrate everyone within that half a year. I had no intention of missing it, especially since Wynnie is one of the birthdays we celebrate in the summer.

Elliot: I think you both told me how much you'd miss me last night. There isn't a drop of come left in my body.

Sawyer: Job complete. Have a safe flight.

Lainey: Let us know when you land.

Elliot: Will do. I'll miss you both. Don't have too much fun while I'm gone. I'll see you in less than seventy-two hours.

For the first time since moving here, I'm excited and sad about going home. Sawyer, Lainey, and I have spent so much time together that I can already feel the void of the next three days. They drove me to the airport and will pick me up, but the in-between hours already feel lonely.

I thought about asking them to come with me. I'm not worried about my family accepting me with two partners. Although with Sawyer and Lainey already being married, there is a small part of me that wonders how that aspect will be perceived. I know any concern will be from love, but I still worry.

The flight is uneventful, and instead of the minivan I expect to pick me up, there's a familiar pickup truck instead.

"Hey, Scotty, I didn't plan to see you. Everything okay with Wynnie?" I toss my small duffle bag into the back of his pickup and climb into the passenger seat.

"Yep, all good. Archie was throwing a tantrum, which set off Ella, and they wouldn't let her leave the house without them. I thought it might be easier for her to stay with them and for me to pick you up solo."

Archie, their two year old, is the biggest mama's boy, and it doesn't surprise me to hear he wouldn't let Wynnie leave without him.

"Archie, I expect, but Ella? I thought she had you wrapped around her finger?"

He huffs. "She's four. We've hit the mimicking stage. It's almost like having two toddlers. Thank god Tori does a good job distracting her most of the time."

"Speaking of. Why didn't my little monster niece come with you?"

He gives me a blank look before merging into the outbound airport traffic. "She spent the night at Hazel's house with DJ. There was no way she was leaving. God bless that woman. I have no idea how she handles four kids from four to fourteen. She's a fucking saint."

"Probably because she has three men in the house to help her. You're outnumbered, man." He grunts and rests his head back on the seat.

"Hey, do you mind if we stop by Tipsy Penny before heading to the house? I have a few things to wrap up before the party tomorrow, and if I can do it now while I'm out, it would make the rest of my day easier."

"Of course." I glance over and notice some new tattoos covering his right arm. When his daughter, Tori, was young, he covered his left arm in outlines of drawings and let Tori color in the pictures whenever she was bored. Over the years, the images have covered his back and chest. He's a living coloring book.

"New ink?"

He lifts his arm and rotates it around so I can see. It's been filled since the last time I was here. There are outlines of trucks, cars, and trains.

"Added some boyish things for Archie. After two girls, I thought he might like options other than butterflies and princess crowns." I arch an eyebrow at him, and he sees my expression. "Options. He can color whatever he wants and like whatever he likes. You know I don't judge, Elliot."

I keep him hanging for a moment longer before laughing. He exhales like he was concerned. Considering his best friend is one of his wife's three fathers, I know he is and always will be a safe space.

Pulling up to Tipsy Penny feels like home. I was coming here before it was legal. I can't wait to bring Sawyer and Lainey here and tell them about all my happy memories. As if she heard my thoughts, my phone buzzes and I see a text from my gorgeous girlfriend.

Lainey: Your flight landed ninety minutes ago. It's been two hours, and we haven't heard from you yet. Status check.

Crap. I totally forgot to message them in my shock of seeing Scotty.

Elliot: So sorry. I'll take my punishment for my delay when I get back. ;) I got distracted by a hotty, but I made it safely. I'm already dreading my lonely bed tonight. Miss you both.
   Lainey: A hotty? It better be an adorable puppy.

"Scotty, smile." He gives me a "what the hell" glare as I snap a quick picture and attach it with my next text.

Elliot: Scotty too Hotty, Wynnie's other (not better) half. He picked me up.

Lainey: LOL. I'll allow it. Glad to hear you made it. Text us when you can, and have fun.

Sawyer: This time. We'll allow it this time.

Sawyer: There WILL be punishment for not telling us you got there safely. Enjoy your weekend.

Lainey: We miss you too. «kissy face emoji»

"Which one?" Scotty's question startles me. He parked his truck in front of the bar but hasn't gotten out yet.

"Huh?"

"Or is it both? You're smiling like a love-struck teenage girl."

Am I? I hadn't even realized I was smiling. "How much do you know?" He looks at me for two entire seconds, and his face says it all. "Okay, yeah. I know who you're married to. My best friend tells you everything." I stare at my phone, anxious to know the answer to my question, but worried how he will respond.

"Fuck. You're worse than her. What's on your mind, Elliot?" His tone has the same inflection as a command from Sawyer, but there are none of the warm, tingly fireworks of anticipation.

"They're both texting me. I forgot to let them know when I landed safely." When I don't continue, he looks at me with raised eyebrows and tilts his head. "Shit, Scotty. You have that Dad look down pat."

"It's because I am one. And I'm old enough to be yours, so tell me what's on your mind."

"You're not—shit. You *are* old enough to be my dad."

325

"Uh huh. Talk."

"So she's told you everything?" Silence. I take that as my answer. "You know they are a married couple?"

"I do. And?"

"Well, *and* is my question. Does that elicit any kind of feelings or thoughts for you?"

He pauses to think and shifts in his seat. I notice his fist tightening in his lap, and his body language speaks volumes.

"Should it?"

"Please don't bullshit me, Scotty. You're the first person I've asked, and I haven't mentioned it to anyone else but Wynnie. Mom and Dad only know I've found two partners."

"Why haven't you told anyone?"

*For the same reason I'm asking you. I'm scared shitless of their reactions.*

"I don't know. It hasn't come up, I guess."

He scoffs at my obvious lame excuse. Even to my own ears, it sounds terrible.

"Elliot. You're a grown man now. You're allowed to make your own choices. We all just want you to be happy…" He trails off.

"Damn. There's a big but coming."

"But it's hard not to worry when you're entering an already established relationship. No one wants you to get hurt."

How could I expect anything less from the people who love me? A sigh of relief shifts me lower in the seat.

"I'm happy. Really happy."

"That's good. And you're *with* both of them?" He almost sounds uncomfortable with his question.

"Yeah, I am. Well…"

"Well?"

"Um. Sawyer and I haven't *crossed the finish line*, if you get what I mean."

"Elliot, I'm forty-two, not five. So you haven't fucked your boyfriend yet?"

"Oh god." I cover my face, feeling the heat rise in my cheeks. "Kill me now," I mumble through my fingers.

Scotty starts laughing a deep belly laugh, and I wish the truck was still in motion so I could jump out and end my embarrassment.

"Come on. Let's get inside so we can get back to the house before my wife thinks I've kidnapped you."

"That might be preferable to this embarrassment. Would you be wearing a mask? Eww. Okay, I just made it weirder. Forget I even exist." Grabbing the door handle, I swing it open and jump down. I hear his boots crunch on the gravel as we head toward the building.

As I walk through the front door, I see Wynnie's crystal hanging next to the door that she gave Scotty when she was fourteen. Despite the absence of rainbows reflecting from it, I still make a wish.

*I wish that Lainey, Sawyer, and I can find our happily ever after.*

A huffed laugh comes from behind me, and I realize I've been caught in my sentimental moment.

"Wynnie still does it every time. Tori does it now, too, and I'm sure it's only a matter of time before Ella starts doing it. Monkey see, monkey do."

I've seen Tori make a wish before, but she used to be secretive about it. The thought of Ella making a wish is adorable, and I want to make one with her tomorrow.

"So why haven't you"—Scotty lowers his voice despite no

one being in the bar just to tease me—"crossed the finish line yet?"

"I'm telling your wife you're being mean to me and deserve to be cut off."

"You wish you had that power." Scotty smirks, and I shiver at the stories Wynnie's told me about their sex life.

"He's never done it before, and I'm waiting for him to be ready. And I won't be the one fucking..."

"Gotcha. Good for you for respecting his boundaries. I have a serious question now, and then we can change the subject because I'm not sure your skin can get any redder."

"Appreciate it." I sit on one of the bar stools as he walks behind the bar.

"Do you feel like an equal in the relationship?" He stops whatever he's doing and looks at me.

I'm thrown off by his question. An equal. Do I feel equal? I've never even thought of there being inequality in our relationship. Does that mean I *do* feel like an equal?

Ugh. The word equal is sounding fuzzy in my brain, I've thought it so many times.

"I don't feel there's a power struggle. It hasn't been very long. Over a month for me and Sawyer and threeish weeks with Lainey. Honestly, it hasn't even been a thought. We've fit together so seamlessly like we've been doing this for years."

Scotty turns behind him, grabs a clear bottle of liquor, and pulls a shot glass from under the bar top.

"You better take a few. The girls have already started without you." He pours what I now see is top-shelf tequila into the glass and slides it to me. "Salt? Lime?"

My shoulders fall on an exhale. "It's going to be a long

night, isn't it." He pulls out a second shot glass, and I think he's going to join me, but he slides it next to the first and fills it.

"Drink up, Elliot," he chuckles, and I know I'm in for a long night.

# 42

# Sawyer

He's barely been gone a few hours, and I can feel he's far away. My body knows he isn't in the building next to me or on his way to his house to return with clothes to spend the night. It's the strangest feeling to be so in tune with someone who isn't Lainey, but not in a bad way. Elliot walked in our front door and we haven't looked back.

"Are you ready?" Lainey's voice in my ear brings me out of my internal musings.

"Am I ever? This won't end well for you, Jitterbug."

"That's my plan. Uppies."

She wiggles her arms in front of me to pick her up, and I set her on the bar top between Katy and Blake, with Nicole next to Katy. Blake insisted they needed a girls' night, and she didn't care how pregnant anyone was. No wasn't an option for anyone but Annie. The bartender hands each of the girls a shot, and they hand it to us. This isn't the first Kickin' Cowboy of the evening, and us men are prepared.

On the count of three, we chug, they splash us with a cup of water, then slap us across the face. The girls giggle, and there are various levels of growls from Viktor, Cole, Justin, and myself.

"I both love and hate you, Blake," Katy shouts over the music as Viktor devours her neck. Lainey slides off the bar top, and her body shimmies down me the entire way.

"Hey, Jitterbug. Having fun?"

She smiles and nods. "Can we send Elliot a picture?"

"Yeah. Of course." I pull out my phone and flip the camera to selfie mode. Lainey snuggles up to my chest, and I take several pictures, which I've been trained to do. In the last few, a set of bunny ears appear over my head, and I look to see Blake smiling. I flip the camera sideways to widen the angle and tell everyone to say cheese once I've gotten them in the frame.

Sawyer: Wish you were here with us.

I attach a few of the pictures, including a group one, and send the text. My phone is barely back in my pocket when I feel it vibrate. Expecting a response from Elliot, I smile and pull my phone out. My face immediately falls in shock when I see the notification.

"What's wrong, Baby?"

I flip my phone around to show Lainey what I just read.

"No, he didn't." Her hands fly to her mouth, and she gasps in shock. I click on the notification, and it opens my banking app. Along with a five thousand dollar deposit, there's a message in the note box.

*Make sure our girl is well taken care of, and treat everyone to a bottle (or several) of top-notch liquor on me. I miss you.*

Lainey reads the message over my shoulder, and I switch my app to the message screen. Before I can send a text of protest to Elliot, the phone dings.

Elliot: Don't freak out. Don't say no. Enjoy it, and I'll see you soon at the airport.

I don't know how to feel or respond. When we first started dating, he sent me two thousand dollars and told Lainey to buy herself a nice dinner. That was a lot of money, but five thousand seems unnecessary.

"What's going on over here?" Blake peers over our shoulders, and I drop my arm, holding the phone. "Secrets, secrets are no fun."

"She won't give up until we tell her something," Lainey says with an eye roll. "And he did say to buy everyone drinks."

"Oh, who's he? No. Wait, duh. It's Elliot, of course. What did he do this time?"

"He put five thousand dollars into our account and said to treat Lainey well and buy everyone bottles of top-shelf alcohol."

"Oh, hells to the yeah!" Blake whips around and flags down the bartender before we can stop her.

Cole approaches us, looking confused. His blond curls are matted to his forehead from the last cup of water splashed in his face.

"Everything okay?"

I sigh and shake my head in Blake's direction. "I don't think there's any stopping her at this point. Elliot gave us money to spend on everyone while we're here."

"Showoff," he scoffs with a knowing smile.

"What does that mean?" Lainey questions. "He gave us a lot of money. At least by our standards."

It's no secret that Cole, Lainey, and Annie are super mega-rich. Annie owns an entire goddamn building. Justin and Nicole are well off, too. I don't know where he got his money, but I know he owns a wing at the local hospital. Five thousand dollars is probably all in a day's work for them, but it's not something we can so easily bat an eye at.

"Do you not—okay, it's not my story to tell. I'll just say that Elliot isn't hurting for money and spends what he has wisely. If he sent it for the two of you, you're something special to him. Congratulations, because he's a fucking catch."

He turns to help Blake who has several bottles of liquor in front of her and I hear her yell to put it on the Hayes tab. Meaning mine and Lainey's.

"I feel like we're missing something." Lainey's green eyes stare at me as if I have the answers, but I'm as clueless as she is.

"So do I, Jitterbug."

Two hands shove into our faces with amber liquid in shot glasses.

"Drink up, bitches! The rideshares home are on Elliot." We take the tiny plastic cups from Blake, and she spins and whips out her phone. "Smile." We squish together with big grins while she takes a selfie and immediately sends it off. "Okay, now drink. Us non preggos have all night."

We cheers our little cups, and Lainey reaches for her

phone. She shakes her head before showing me the group text between her, Blake, and Elliot.

Blake: Hanging with your favorite people!!! Thanks for the drinks. I'll make sure they get home safely.

Elliot: ALL of you be safe. Send them my love. Don't fall apart on Monday without me.

"That's just a figure of speech, right?" It appears Lainey has fixated on the L word as much as I have. "Do you think he realizes she sent the text to me, too? He responded like he didn't."

"I honestly have no idea." The somersaults going on in my stomach are asking the same questions.

As we contemplate the use of such a simple word, a familiar scary-looking cowboy, adorned with a hat and a scowl, approaches our bartender, and they have a conversation over the ordering screen. He turns and calls Katy over to him, and she throws him a "what now" look before she grabs Vik's arm and drags him along with her.

They don't speak for long before Katy calls Lainey and me over.

*Did we do something wrong?*

"Hey, is everything okay?"

"It's all good," Tucker drawls. "I get alerted whenever we sell an entire bottle of liquor, and my computer just went crazy."

"Blake," I sigh. "Sorry about that."

"It's no trouble. I wanted to come out and see my grandbaby anyway." Tucker's eyes drift to Katy's noticeable baby bump, and she swats at him again.

"Um, hello. What about coming to see your daughter? Don't I count anymore?"

"Nope, you're Dempsey's problem now." Katy's mouth opens in shock, and Tucker keeps his face stoic for about five seconds before he cracks. "Of course I love you, baby girl." He leans over the bar and kisses Katy's forehead.

Tucker stares at me for a few long seconds, and I'm again wondering if I've done something wrong. His fingers tap on the bar, and I feel like a child in the principal's office. He turns to Katy and questions, "This is who Elliot chose?"

Katy rolls her eyes. "Yeah, Dad. Sawyer and Lainey are Elliot's."

He leans over the bar again and kisses Lainey's cheek.

"You've locked down a good man. I knew it the night of your first date."

Katy's mouth drops open. "Wait. Waitwaitwait. You knew? You knew they went on a date?" There's disbelief in her accusation.

"Of course I did. You had me watch out for Elliot that night. It was a pleasant surprise to see the two of them dining together."

"I can't believe you knew and never said anything." Katy crosses her arms over her chest, accentuating her baby bump.

"Sorry, Sweetheart. It wasn't my place. But I'm glad to see it all worked out." Tucker smiles and Katy scowls at him before turning his attention back to me. "Tonight is on me since you were able to drag my daughter out for some fun."

Lainey starts to protest, but Katy beats her to it.

"For withholding the gossip, I should let you, but nope, Elliot is funding our drinking and not driving tonight since

335

he went home for a family thing. Your bottom line is safe from Blake tonight."

We all turn to the brunette in question, who's licking salt off Cole's neck before chugging from the tequila bottle and sucking a lime from his mouth.

"On second thought, I'm charging you double."

The evening continues with more shots than are necessary for any of us, and I feel bad for Katy and Nicole as they deal with everyone and their drunken antics. The eight of us sit outside and wait for our rideshares to arrive, and my eyes drift to the side of the building where Elliot and I shared our first kiss.

Lainey giggles at the phone in her hand, and I snap my head too quickly to look at her, almost losing my balance. Planting my feet firmly under me, I lean to look at her screen.

"What's so funny, Jitterbug?"

Elliot: Truth or Dare?

Along with the text is a smiling picture of Elliot with a table full of empty glasses and beer bottles behind him. It looks like we are having similar nights.

"Is he playing or asking?" I pull out my phone and frown when I don't have a missed text.

Lainey strums my bottom lip, which I hadn't realized was poking out. "Aww, Baby. Don't be jealous he texted me and not you."

I wrap her against my chest with her arms stuck, folded between us, and kiss her firmly on her lips.

"He should be the one jealous that you're here with me,

336

and he's eleven hours away." Lainey tucks her head under my chin and sighs in contentment.

"I can't text him back if I'm stuck in your cage."

Just as I release her, my phone vibrates in my hand. My excitement spikes until I see it's just a notification that our ride is arriving. We say our goodbyes as our car is the first to arrive and slide into the back of a white sedan. Our driver smiles a greeting and leaves without another word.

Lainey checks her phone and quickly shows me a new text.

Elliot: Don't you want to play with me?

Accompanied is a picture of a pouty Elliot, and I want to bite his plump lip.

"He wants us to play. What should we pick, Baby?"

I take the phone and type Truth, then hit send. Eager anticipation floods through me at what he could ask.

# 43

# Lainey

"Truth. You're sure? That could be anything."

"Isn't that the point?"

Bubbles pop up on the screen as Elliot types his Truth.

Elliot: Tell me a secret.

"Is that for you or me, Baby? It wouldn't be fair if it was for both of us." My mind wanders, looking for a secret worth sharing if I need to.

"I'll answer. I typed Truth. It only seems fair."

Sawyer pulls out his phone and responds in the group chat.

Sawyer: I asked for the Truth, so I'll give you my secret.

Sawyer: I'm ready to move to the next step in our relationship. Both to give... and take.

My jaw drops, and I stare at my sexy husband, who just admitted he wants to fuck and be fucked by our boyfriend. Elliot has been happily waiting until Sawyer is ready. None of us wanted to rush him as it was the last and most significant step in their relationship.

"I'm proud of you," I whisper in awe. He looks up from his phone, apprehension in his eyes. Cupping his cheek, I give him a reassuring smile. "None of that. You were brave to admit that to him, and I'm proud of you." He smiles back at me as our phones buzz.

Elliot: That just made me so fucking hard. Wynnie threw a pillow at my lap and told me to cover up. Bathing suits don't hide much. I'm ready whenever you are, Doll. To give or receive.
    Elliot: Cherry, Truth or Dare?

"Oh, crap. I guess it's my turn. What do I choose?"
    "If you choose Truth, it might be your turn to reveal a secret. Are you ready for that? But also we are in the back of a moving car. I'm not sure what you could do for a dare.

Elliot: Tick, tock. Alaina.

Seeing him use my full name makes my stomach flip-flop. Even from eleven hours away, saying Alaina has the effect he expects.

Lainey: Truth
    Elliot: Tell me your secret.

"Told you." Sawyer gives me a smug smile, and I want to kiss it off his face.

It's okay. I was already prepared with my answer.

Lainey: I want Sawyer in your ass while I'm in his.

It's Sawyer's turn to look shocked. We've done anal on very rare occasions and have joked about a sex train between the three of us before, but it was always *just* a conversation—more of a concept or a what-if.

"You want that?"

"Yeah. Would it be something you're interested in?"

Sawyer turns his head to look out the window. A 'V' forms between his eyes as he considers. I know he just told Elliot he was willing to take it, but our dynamic is different. He would be giving up total control. He'd be in the middle.

"Baby, it's okay to say no." I lace my fingers through his and squeeze. My heart races so fast I can hear it in my ears. "Soy Sauce?"

Slowly, his head turns back to me, and his gray eyes bounce between mine.

"It's not a no, Jitterbug. I'd never tell you no, but I can't say yes right now either."

Our phones buzz before I can answer, and I look down at my lap to see Elliot's response. I snort a laugh and lift my phone so Sawyer can see.

Elliot: Anytime you'd like, Cherry. I'm yours. Every hole.

"Looks like you're saved by the switch."

Sawyer laughs at my ridiculous comment, and the mood

instantly lightens again. I never want him to feel like he has to compromise himself for me. Is it something I'd like to do? Yes. Would I allow him to do it simply because he feels obligated to me? Absolutely not.

Lainey: Truth or Dare?
  Elliot: Dare

"Not gonna lie. I was hoping he'd say Truth."
  "Me too, Jitterbug. What can we have him do?"
  We stare at each other while trying to come up with a dare he can do via phone.
  "Oh, I got it."

Lainey: I want a dick pic.

Sawyer's mouth opens like he wants to object but quickly closes it and shrugs.

Elliot: Deal. Let me excuse myself to the bathroom. It might cause a scene if I snap a pic down my pants in front of my parents and aunt.

"Oh shit. He's going to do it." Just knowing he's leaving his company to send us a racy picture has me squirming in my seat. Of course, Sawyer sees it. He sees everything about me.
  "Problem, Jitterbug?" His hushed voice breezes over the shell of my ear, making me shiver. The thumb of our intertwined fingers makes circles as it creeps further up my thigh.

"Not a single one."

Elliot: Incoming
Elliot: Thinking of you both. «image»

"Fuuuuuuck," hisses through Sawyer's lips like a prayer. I get it. I'm ready to worship at the altar of Elliot's hard cock.

It's clear he stroked himself before taking the picture. His cock stands at attention with his hand firmly gripping the base.

"He's beautiful."

Elliot: Where are you both?
Sawyer: Rideshare on the way home.
Elliot: What's Lainey wearing? Please tell me she's wearing a skirt.
Lainey: Sorry. Sawyer talked me out of the skirt, so I put on the daisy dukes.
Elliot: Dammit, Sawyer. I wanted a peek.
Sawyer: We'll be home in 10, and I can give you more than a peek.
Elliot: Get her ready for me. I want her dripping by the time you show me.

"What does he mean by that? We're almost home."

"I have an idea, Jitterbug." Sawyer shifts his hand and pushes on my inner thigh. "Open."

The look he gives me leaves no room for question. I flash a glance into the rearview to see our driver is oblivious. My thighs spread as I shift lower in my seat for better access, and Sawyer's thumb rubs the seam of my shorts.

"I bet you're already wet. Tell him. Tell him what I'm doing to you back here."

Sawyer puts more pressure on his thumb as he rubs directly over my clit.

"Tell. Him."

I pick up my phone with a shaky hand and obey his request.

Lainey: Sawyer is rubbing my clit through my shorts.

Elliot: Fuck me. Hold on. Now I need another excuse to leave.

I show the phone to Sawyer, and he laughs. His hand moves from my shorts, and I whimper.

"Shh. Let's make it more interesting." He undoes the button on my shorts, and even if I wanted to protest, I won't. I want this. "Wiggle them down a little and give me some room."

It's hard to wiggle inconspicuously, especially when you're pretty drunk. I'm sure I look much less graceful than I feel, but I'm watching the rearview, and our driver hasn't glanced back once.

As soon as I finish readjusting, Sawyer's fingers slide up my inner thighs and between the hem of my shorts.

"Tell him."

Lainey: Sawyer slipped his fingers into my shorts.

Lainey: He's rubbing my clit.

Elliot: More. Tell me how it feels, Cherry.

Lainey: It feels so good. I'm already so wet.

Lainey: I'm trying not to moan and alert our driver.

Elliot: If you can be our good girl and come before you get home, I'll let you have my ass when I get back.

Oh fuck. Oh fuck, ohfuckohfuck.

"Sawyer," I whisper-moan.

"I see the message. That's a challenge for me, not you. And one I don't plan to lose. Keep texting.

Lainey: Sawyer accepts your challenge. He's moving faster.

Elliot: I knew he would. Does your pussy need to be filled?

Lainey: So bad. It's empty.

Elliot: Sawyer will take care of you as soon as you get home. Don't worry, pretty girl.

Lainey: I'm getting close.

It's getting hard to type between my eyes wanting to close and having to keep my noises in. It's a sweet torture. Sweat beads along my forehead as my body heats up.

Elliot: I'm so hard picturing his hands on you in the back of that car. Are you biting your lip? Is it hard to stay quiet?

"Send him a pic. Show him where my hands are."

It's a strange angle and not very flattering, but I snap a picture aimed between my legs, showing Sawyer's hand half-hidden in my shorts. My shirt is blousy, so you can't tell my shorts are open.

Lainey: A party favor from Sawyer. «image»

Elliot: Holy fuck. I've never been so mad at a pair of shorts.

I want to see what his hand is doing in there.

Elliot: Record for me. I want to see you come on his hand. I want to see the face you make when you can't make a sound.

Elliot: Make it quick, Alaina.

"Sawyer, kiss me." I'm panting and struggling not to moan.

"Don't cheat, Alaina. E told you he wants to see your face. If I'm kissing you, he won't see anything. Hit that record button now because I know you're close."

I type and send one more message before I hit record.

Lainey: Record for me, please. I want to see too.

It's bold of me to make a request when I'm in this role. I hope adding the please will keep me from getting punished.

Elliot: Come for me, Alaina.

I quickly put the camera on selfie mode and rest it on my knee, angled toward my face. Seconds after I hit record, my orgasm crashes through me. Sawyer speeds up his fingers, and I taste blood—I pierce my lip, trying to keep in my moans. I'm not breathing, not moving. My eyes scrunch closed, and it's taking every ounce of willpower I have, from the tips of my toes to the hair on my head, not to scream my pleasure.

Finally coming down, I exhale a shaky breath. It's long, and my body deflates as I release all the tension. As Sawyer pulls his fingers out, he stops me when I move to end the recording. I pause and watch on the screen as he raises his hand to his mouth and licks me off his fingers. He's doing that for Elliot's pleasure. When he's done, he kisses my cheek.

"Send it."

# 44

# Elliot

oly fucking shit. Holy. Fucking. Shit. Holyfuckingshit.

"I...I... I have no excuse, guys. I'll be back. Again." I almost faceplant as I try to stand from the Adirondack chair I'm sitting in, and laughter erupts around me.

"Have fuuuuuun," Wynnie sings as I practically run into her house. Do I want to jerk off in my best friend's guest room? Fuck no. When I started the game of Truth or Dare, I never expected I'd be getting a play-by-play of what Sawyer is doing to her in the back of a rideshare.

"Love you guys. Don't wait up!" I gently close the door behind me so as not to wake any kids. I'm rock fucking hard, and there's a video coming my way soon. There was no way I'd be able to watch it while outside.

I close and lock my bedroom door behind me and strip naked. My eyes dart around the room. It's too quiet. I feel like my breathing is making too much noise.

347

*Noise. Noise.*

There's no TV in here. No box fan.

*My bag.*

I hop off the bed and grab my laptop. Pulling up my playlist, I click on the last one I listened to. Electronic music with a heavy base fills the room too loudly, and I scramble to turn it down. The last time I used my laptop for music, I was running on the treadmill. The playlist makes sense then, but not so much now.

Turning it down to a reasonable volume, I lay back on the bed and stroke myself. Long, firm strokes, knowing I want to record myself for them too, but I want to hold out so I can watch her video first. I want them to see what they do to me.

My phone finally vibrates, and my hands shake with adrenaline. With my earbud already in my ear, I know I won't have to worry about anyone hearing what I hope to see when I open the attachment.

Fuck!

They. Did. Not. Disappoint.

Watching Lainey come while I could see Sawyer's hand on the bottom corner of the screen was excruciating. I wanted to be in that backseat with them. But then that asshole stopped her from turning the recording off and sucked her come off his fingers. I nearly dropped the phone in my rush to turn the camera around and record myself coming for them.

Hitting send on the video, I realize this was a half-assed plan. My chest and stomach are splattered with my come while I lay in the middle of my best friend's guest bed, and there's nothing close by to clean myself up with.

Fuck it. It was worth the acrobats I'm about to do. I slither my ass to the end of the bed and slide down my back until I hit the floor. I reach out and grab the first thing I see, which happens to be my swim trunks, and realize that was a bad idea. The fabric smears, not absorbs, but at least I'm stopping the risk of dripping.

My phone chimes in my ear, and I look at the lit-up screen on the bed. How much more torture could I possibly endure?

I rest my head on the comforter and reach for the phone.

Sawyer: I had to carry our girl to bed, she's passed out. Between the alcohol and the orgasm, she's worn out. Sorry there can't be more fun.

Elliot: Don't worry, Doll. I've had plenty of fun and entertainment. I miss you both, and I'll see you soon.

He has no idea how okay I am with the lack of more activity tonight. I've already consumed too much tequila, I have a chest full of smeared come, and somehow, I have to clean up without any suspicious eyes. At least it's late, and I don't have to worry about running into kids.

Searching through my bag, I grab a pair of basketball shorts and throw them on. I walk out the door to head to the bathroom down the hall and crash into Scotty.

*Fuck.*

"Hey, El. Sorry about that. Archie was stirring on the monitor, and I was heading to che—um..."

To my mortification, he's staring at my stomach. I don't need to look down to know exactly what he's seeing. Not only does he now know I masturbated in his house, but the

349

evidence is still smeared on me.

My mouth drops open, but no words come out. I don't even know how to explain myself. Scotty is not only my best friend's husband, but he's old enough to be my dad, which makes this entire situation even more embarrassing.

His hand raises to clasp my shoulder, but he stops inches away and thinks better of it. Pulling back, he shakes his head and smiles.

"You know what? Good for you. I can barely handle Wynnie's appetite, and you have two partners waiting at home. The towels are in the bathroom closet. I assume that's where you were heading?"

"*Yeah.*" I drag out the word, my eyes darting everywhere but at his face.

He chuckles and walks around me without another word. Wynnie will give me hell about this. There's no way he won't tell her.

🖭 🖭 🖭 🖭 🖭

I went straight to bed last night, not wanting to embarrass myself more than I already did. I've spent the last several hours at the mercy of the bad-ass women in my life, bossing me around, telling me where to hang and place things around Tipsy Penny.

My mom is usually a force to be reckoned with, but include Aunt Hazel in the mix, and the two are like opposing storm fronts clashing.

"Hang this balloon arch here."

"No. That won't work there because of the flow of people."

"Let's put the gift table here."

ELLIOT

"We need a separate table for each person so there's no confusion."

Wynnie and I relish in their banter. Our moms are always good for entertainment value. She came to help, but since she's one of the birthdays we're celebrating, they haven't let her do much, so she's been my moral support.

"Heard you had a fun end to the evening." She wiggles her eyebrows at me, and I drop my head to my chest with a sigh.

"I can't believe you've been here for two hours before finally saying something."

She playfully pushes my shoulder. "I needed to let you sweat it out a little first. Scotty couldn't wait to tell me when he came back outside."

"It wasn't my fault. They sent me a video." My tone is whiny as I try to rationalize my actions.

"You're a big boy, Elliot. You don't need to explain yourself to me. But I do have one question." *Oh god, here it comes.* "Are you happy? Do they make you happy?"

"Ma'am, you have three children. Shouldn't you be able to count?" She gives me a puzzled look. "That was two questions, not one." She scoffs and rolls her eyes. "But, yeah. I'm so fucking happy. Almost irrationally so."

"Good. Then that's all I care about." I breathe a sigh of relief, knowing she could have busted my balls for the way Scotty found me. "But please know, I plan to burn all those bed sheets. And you're buying me new ones."

*There it is.*

"Send me the bill, bestie."

"Okay, I do have one more question. What was going on that got you all hot and bothered? Because damn, I might want some of that in my life."

351

I arch an eyebrow at her. "It involved a rideshare, hands in inappropriate places for the public... and a video showing the evidence. How does Scotty feel about mild voyeurism?"

Wynnie chokes on the soda she's sipping, and I pat her back while holding in my laughter.

"It's okay, bestie. I'll allow you to live vicariously through me. I know that man would never share you with anyone." As if on cue, Scotty strolls into the bar from the kitchen with two overflowing plates of nachos. He places one on the bar, instructs my mom and Aunt Hazel to eat, and brings the other to us with the same instructions. My mouth waters at the cheesy mountain of deliciousness. Scotty joins us, and we dig in while discussing the details for the rest of the day.

# 45

# Elliot

The party is as wild and crazy as I expected, and it makes my heart full but also a little sad. I wish I had invited Sawyer and Lainey. They would have loved meeting my parents and siblings, and I know Wynnie will love Lainey.

Before any introductions take place, though, I need to come clean.

I see my mom in the corner chatting away with Mac, Wynnie's dad. Knowing the relationship she has with all of Hazel's men almost makes me feel silly that I'm worrying about this. She loves me and has always accepted me for who I am... but they're married. I heard Scotty's concern loud and clear yesterday, and I know she will feel the same.

There's no time like the present. I know it's a party, but that just means she's had a few drinks and will be easier to talk to.

I stand from my seat and step toward my mom when a hand grips my shoulder. I turn to see my dad's bright red hair and smile as his hand slides across my shoulder, draping across the other side.

"We miss you around here, Elliot. Despite being the youngest, Paige now thinks she rules the roost."

"Don't lie, Dad. She's always been your little princess." His smile widens, and his eyes gloss over. My brother, sister, and I were dealt a shitty hand, losing both our parents, but Dellah and Collin stepped up and didn't bat an eye. There was never a point in my childhood where I felt anything other than love from them. As an adult, their love has turned into adoration and respect.

"Don't tell her that. She's already a monster."

We laugh together, and both watch Mom for a moment before I know I can't delay the inevitable any longer.

"Can I talk to you and Mom for a minute?"

"Now?"

"Yeah. I want to share something and don't want to wait any longer. I'm sure Scotty will let us use his office for some privacy."

"This sounds serious. I'll get Mom, and you can confirm with Scotty that it's okay to use his office."

Of course, Scotty says yes, and my leg bobs nervously while I wait for my parents to join me. A light knock has my head whipping to the door, and I stand as my parents walk in. Despite having seen my mom several times already, she approaches and wraps me in her arms. Some of my stress instantly melts away from her embrace.

"Dad said you wanted to talk, and it couldn't wait. What's going on?"

I motion for them to sit on the couch in the corner and pull a chair over from his desk.

*They love you and want the best for you.*

"I want to tell you a little more about the people I'm dating, Sawyer and Lainey." My mom beams her bright Dellah smile.

"You know we don't judge you for having two partners. Right son?"

"I know, Dad. But there's a small detail I've left out."

I sigh and close my eyes. Mom's petite hand takes mine and gives me a comforting squeeze.

"What is it, El? Tell us."

"They're… a married couple." No response, and I was too chicken shit to open my eyes before I said it, so I can't even gauge their reactions from their facial expression.

Mom removes her hands from mine, and I feel the disappointment. When I finally get the courage to open my eyes, tears are in my Mom's, and I instantly deflate.

"Oh my god, Elliot. No. Wait."

She's… laughing. The tears aren't tears of sadness; they're laughter. Mom leans over and pulls me into a hug. Her shoulders shake with laughter, and I lock eyes with my Dad behind her. I mouth, "What's going on?" and he joins her.

I pull away from her embrace, confused at their reactions, and allow them to compose themselves before speaking.

"What the hell?" Not the most eloquent words I could come up with, but I'm fucking confused by their reaction.

Mom takes my cheeks in her hands and smiles. "Do you honestly think we didn't know?"

"W-What?" How could they have known? Did I slip up and mention it without realizing it? No. I've been careful. Right?

One look into my mom's eyes, and I know how she knows.

"I'm going to kill her. Aren't best friends supposed to be secret keepers?"

"Not when her mother is your mother's best friend." Dad pulls me away to give me his own hug. "Were you really that worried?"

I sink back into my seat, suddenly exhausted from the myriad of emotions in the room.

"Well... yeah, I was actually."

Mom takes my hand again. "Why?"

"Well, since you're laughing at me, I can't understand why myself. It seems so trivial now, but it felt like such a big deal before. They're an already established married couple. That doesn't... bother you?"

"Does it bother *you*?"

"No," I answer without hesitation. "I knew what I was getting into when I went on the first date with Sawyer."

"I don't even need to ask if you're happy. I can see it on your face, Elliot."

"They make me so fucking happy. I feel like an idiot now. I wish I had invited them to come, but I was so worried about how you would react. How everyone would react."

"I have one question."

*Oh no.* "What's that?"

"Do they know about Annie? About your money?"

I can see it's a sore topic for her to ask about, but I understand why. She's concerned that their intentions are pure and not greed.

"They know about Griffin and the plaque out front, but as far as I know, that's the extent of their knowledge. I haven't brought it up. But our relationship started before he knew who I really was, remember? It's easy enough to look me up now that he knows, but there isn't anything to find.

Satisfied with my answer, Mom stands and reaches out for me. "Come on."

I take her hand, and Dad stands, too. "What's going on?"

"We aren't going to sit around in here and dwell over something that isn't even an issue when there's margaritas and cake in the other room."

"I see you have your priorities straight, Mom." She pulls me in for a final hug, and Dad joins in.

I don't know why I was so stressed about telling them. I should have expected this reaction—the non-reaction.

"You two go ahead. I want to make a call."

They exchange a knowing look and close the door behind them. I take my phone out of my pocket and decide which one to call.

"Hello?" Lainey's beautiful voice drifts distractedly over the line. She must not have looked at her caller ID to see it was me calling.

"Hey, Cherry."

"Elliot! Hi. How are you? Shouldn't you be partying right now? Is everything okay?"

"Everything is wonderful. I just wanted to hear your voice. What are you up to?"

"Hold on." There's rustling, and the water turns on and off before she responds. "Sorry, I'm baking. I needed to wash my hands so I could give you all my attention."

"What are you baking?"

"Peanut butter cup cookies. Trying to keep busy. I... miss you."

"Don't hesitate when you say that. Try it again."

"I miss you, Elliot."

"I miss you too, Lainey. You'll see me tomorrow afternoon. Is Sawyer around?"

"Yeah, hold on." She moves the phone away from her mouth and yells, "Baby, Elliot is on the phone." I hear the phone click over to speaker as the background noise amplifies.

"Elliot?"

My eyes close as his smooth voice washes over me. "Hey, Sawyer."

"Is everything okay?"

I chuckle because Lainey had the same reaction. "It's wonderful. I told my parents about you both." There's silence, and it takes me a moment to realize the confusion. "Sorry. They've known about you for a while, but I hadn't told them you are a married couple."

More silence, then Lainey finally speaks up. Anticipation lacing her single word. "And?"

"And I got laughed at. Wynnie had already told them. Big-mouthed best friend. All anyone cares about is that I'm happy and treated well."

"Are you?" Sawyer asks. "Are you happy... and treated well, Elliot."

"Yeah. Yeah, I am. Without a doubt."

"Good. Now go back to your party and hurry up and get your ass back here."

"Geez, eager to see me?"

"No, just your ass. You have a punishment coming to you."

*Just your ass.* That could mean a few things after last night's Truth or Dare confessions.

"Okay. I'll see you both tomorrow. I miss you."

They return the sentiment, and we hang up just as a knock

comes from the door.

"Come in," I call out, feeling stupid because this isn't even my office.

Scotty walks in, and whatever expression I have on my face makes him smile.

"I take it things went well with your parents?"

"Yes. And your wife is in the doghouse. She had already told them."

He chuckles and shakes his head. "Not my wife, her aunt's tequila. They had a girl's night about two weeks ago, which is when she told me. I bet that's when it came out to them, too."

"I'm revoking her best friend card. She's all yours, Scotty."

He grabs something from his desk, and we laugh as we return to the party.

# 46

# Lainey

The smell of cinnamon and pumpkin floods my senses. In my life, it isn't always an indication of fall since it's Nicole's signature flavors, but today, it is. The weather is turning. Autumn is my favorite season. I love wearing oversize sweaters and cuddling under blankets on the couch.

Life has been perfect lately, which I'm not naive enough to know means something bad is bound to happen soon, but I'll enjoy living in my blissful ignorance until I can't any longer.

Warm hands wrap around my waist from behind, and I immediately know who it is.

"What are you baking now, Cherry?" Elliot's lips brush against my neck, and I don't know how he expects me to answer when he instantly puts me under his spell.

He knows I enjoy baking, but I mostly do it to calm my nerves. "Apple and Pumpkin pies."

"Mmm. I knew I smelled something delicious. What's on

your mind?"

I lean my neck to the side to give him better access. Elliot is at our apartment almost every day now. It's easier for one person to pack an overnight bag than two. On Sundays, he brings over several suit bags so he doesn't need to drive back and forth. We tend to spend weekends at his house because he has the hot tub, and it's a change of scenery.

"I'm nervous about meeting your friends."

His best friend Wynnie and her husband Scotty are coming for the weekend, and I'm a nervous wreck.

"Cherry, they're going to love you. There's nothing to be nervous about."

I turn in his arms and wrap my hands around his neck, rubbing my fingers along his nape.

"They are okay with our relationship?"

"Yes."

I've asked him a dozen times in the last two weeks since he said they were coming. When he went home a month ago, he told us he confessed everything to his family, and no one cared. He's reassured me so many times, but until I see for myself, that doubt sits heavy in my stomach.

"Cherry, are you baking for my friends?"

"Maybe."

Elliot is picking them up from the airport tomorrow morning, but he needs to get back to work, so Sawyer and I are entertaining them until he's done for the day.

"They don't need to be entertained. Take them to S'morgasm, enjoy the back room, and I'll be back before you know it."

"You make it sound so simple." He pulls me in so I'm flush against him, and his warmth calms me.

"It is. They're simple people. You're overthinking."

"It was so easy with you. Without knowing, you already knew everyone in my life. There were no awkward introductions."

He kisses my forehead as Sawyer walks into the room. He sniffs the air as he approaches us.

"Jitterbug, are you stress baking?"

"I hate you both," I groan into Elliot's chest.

Sawyer moves up behind me and grabs my hips, pressing his into my back.

"I can prove that's not true." His breath fans across my ear, and I shiver at what he's implying. I slink away from them before I get caught up in doing something I really want to but shouldn't.

"Don't pout at me. I'm busy. I have to clean the kitchen and butter the crust every twenty minutes. You two don't need me to have some fun."

Sawyer steps forward and crashes his lips to Elliot's as if I gave them permission. I hear a zipper and see Elliot pulling Sawyer out of his jeans.

"Right here? In the middle of the kitchen?"

Elliot winks as Sawyer pushes him to his knees. "You don't want a show?" He leans forward and takes Sawyer in his mouth. I groan. Sawyer moans.

Why did I even ask? They don't need any encouragement to play together. The amount of times I've walked in on Elliot between Sawyer's legs is countless. I'm so proud of my husband. Giving up control is something he's always struggled with, but he so easily gives it over to Elliot, at least in the blow job department. In the bedroom, during a scene is an entirely different story.

I'm staring. I know I am. How can I not when my very sexy boyfriend has my very gorgeous husband's cock halfway down his throat.

The inevitable happens when Sawyer grabs my wrist and pulls me to his side.

"How wet are you, Jitterbug?"

"Niagara Falls."

"Can I help you take care of it?"

I should say no. I need to say no. I've already protested that I don't have time.

Fuck it.

"Please."

Sawyer's lips curl up into a devious smile while his hand sinks into my leggings.

"Damn, Elliot. The sight of my cock down your throat really has her turned on. You must be doing a good job."

Elliot moans, and Sawyer gasps. A giggle escapes, and Sawyer plunges two fingers into me without warning.

"It's not funny now, is it?" His thumb finds my clit while he pumps into my pussy. I rest my head on his shoulder and grab his upper arm to keep myself from collapsing.

"Fucking A, Elliot. If you want to come, you better do it yourself," Sawyer demands. He's getting close. I can tell by the husky tone of his voice.

I lock eyes with Elliot, who winks at me again while he adjusts his position and pulls himself out of his joggers. Elliot matches the rhythm of his hand with the rhythm of his mouth, and Sawyer matches the pace with his fingers.

We are a mess of panting and moaning, and I reach down to run my hands through Elliot's hair while I kiss Sawyer's neck. I knew they'd rope me into their shenanigans. Elliot knew when he was unzipping Sawyer's jeans, and Sawyer knew when he stepped in to kiss Elliot. The only clueless one was me, who made the comment that provoked this little orgasm session.

"Saaaawyer," I moan into his chest as my orgasm rapidly approaches.

"I'm right there with you, Jitterbug. Are you ready to come, Elliot?"

A mumbled "Mmhmm" sounds around Sawyer's cock, and everyone picks up their pace. I fall first, throwing my head back and tightening my grip on Sawyer's arm so I don't collapse from the pleasure.

Elliot's moaning starts my orgasm, but it's not until we're both done that Sawyer allows himself to come with a loud, guttural groan. He held himself back, whether for his pleasure or ours, I don't know, but as we all catch our breath, the timer goes off, indicating it's time to butter-glaze the pies. We laugh at the convenience of timing, and Sawyer helps Elliot up while I readjust my leggings. I kiss them both on the cheek and walk away. I have to finish my pies.

# 47

## Sawyer

Scotty is a big guy covered in tattoos and attitude—
until he smiles. We waited at Elliot's house while he
picked Scotty and Wynnie up from the airport, and
it's a good thing I never judge anyone on a first impression.
Their flight had been delayed and filled with turbulence,
and Elliot barely had enough time to kick them out of the
car, let alone introduce us.

Elliot: I'm so fucking sorry. I can't be late for Annie's
meeting. They are tired and might be a little grumpy, but
let them nap, and I'm sure everything will be fine.

That was the text we received right before the doorbell rang.
Elliot had kept us updated about their delay and arrival, and
at one point, we thought Lainey and I would have to pick
them up if their flight was going to be any later.

"Guest room," were the only two words the large man said
to us when we opened the door. Lainey showed them down

the hall, and it was another twenty minutes before their door opened. Wynnie, a pretty brunette with the bluest eyes I've ever seen, came from the hallway alone. We were sitting in the kitchen drinking coffee, wondering what to do, when she walked in and immediately apologized.

"Sorry, he's being an ass. He isn't a fan of planes, and between the delay and turbulence, he's threatening to rent a car on Sunday and drive the eleven hours home." She rolls her eyes, reaches into a cabinet to grab a mug, and pours herself a cup of coffee. She's familiar with the place, but we've never seen her here before. She must see something on my face because she answers my unspoken questions as she pours creamer into her mug.

"I helped Elliot set up the house when he first moved here. The coffee cup placement was important."

I extend my hand since we haven't officially met, and Wynnie looks at me like I'm being ridiculous. She puts down her coffee mug and steps forward, embracing me in a hug.

"Sawyer, I know more about you than you probably want me to. My best friend has a big mouth and no filter." She releases me and turns to offer the same greeting to Lainey, who returns her hug with enthusiasm.

"We've heard so much about you too, Wynnie." Lainey smiles at her as they separate; I can tell they will get along great.

"I apologize for Scotty. He's a great guy; he just needs a power nap and a shower. I heard we're going to S'morgasm? I'm dying to see what's behind that blue door."

"What have you heard?" Lainey asks while sipping from her mug.

"Blabbermouth best friend, remember?"

"Right. Well, then, I'm sure you know exactly what to expect."

"I made sure to leave room in our bags for any souvenirs we might find while we are here."

Yep. Just like I thought. They'll get along great.

Scotty napped for about thirty minutes before we heard the shower running. Wynnie waited until it shut off to go check on him, and when they emerged, the grumpy guy who originally showed up is gone.

"Hey, man." Scotty extends his hand to me, and unlike Wynnie, I accept it. "I'm sorry about earlier. Flying sucks. It's so good to finally meet you."

"No worries. I get it. You deserved a reset. Nice ink."

Outlines of pictures run up both forearms and disappear under his shirt sleeves. He releases my hand and lifts both arms to show me the patterns up to his shoulders while Wynnie explains how he's made himself a real-life coloring book for his kids.

"Just take your shirt off and show them everything," Wynnie encourages. He gives her an apprehensive look before conceding with a huff. The top half of his chest and most of his back all have the same outlines of images as his arms. The pictures on his back have more definition for advanced colorers. A wolf and a dragon take up most of his back, with smaller animals around them.

"These are incredible, Scotty." Lainey inspects the details of his back tattoos, and I can tell Scotty is comfortable with his shirt being off. He doesn't flinch when her finger reaches out and traces an intricate butterfly near his side.

"Thanks. The kids love them."

"I do, too," Wynnie chimes in. "The dragon is for me. I bought glitter pens to color it in."

"Glitter pens?" Lainey's tone is shocked as she looks at Scotty, waiting for a response.

"Not my finest moments when those get used."

The conversations flow easily, and Wynnie retreats to the bathroom to shower off the airport before we venture out of the house.

Elliot: How's it going? Again, I'm so sorry. Annie's afternoon meeting cancelled and she said I can get out of here early.

Sawyer: Everything is great. Lainey and Wynnie act like long-lost friends. I think we are in trouble.

Elliot: Oh shit. Abort. Abort mission!!!

I burst out laughing, and Lainey steals the phone from me before I get a chance to react.

"Rude."

She huddles up next to Wynnie while we wait in line to get lunch at S'morgasm, and her fingers fly furiously across my screen. When she's satisfied with her response, she hands me back my phone, and I'm almost afraid to look.

Sawyer: This is Lainey and Wynnie. You're in trouble, mister. Wynnie said she's going to give me all of your deepest, darkest secrets if you aren't nice to us.

The phone vibrates in my hand as Elliot's response comes over.

Elliot: I'd never be mean to my two favorite ladies. Annie has a card on file in the back room and said your purchases are on her since she kept me away today. I hope that makes up for my transgressions.

"Fuck." I didn't mean to curse, but it makes Lainey take the phone again, and she immediately shows Wynnie and the girls squeal with delight.

"What's going on?" Scotty questions me.

"Elliot's boss just gave them free rein to her credit card in the back room."

"Free rein?"

"Yeah. Elliot works for Annie as her personal assistant."

"I know of Annie."

Scotty's face has a haunted look, but it disappears as quickly as it appears. Does he not approve of Elliot's boss? I'll have to ask him about it after they leave.

# 48

# Elliot

With minutes to spare, I made it to Annie's meeting.

"I'm so sorry, Ms. Poulsen. I—" She raises a hand to stop me from going further.

"It's alright, Elliot. You're here. I'm sorry that I couldn't give you the day off. Today's meetings are important. I'll get you out of here as soon as possible so you may return to your family."

"Thank you. I appreciate everything."

My phone burns a hole in my pocket during the entire meeting. I manage to stay focused, but I feel terrible I couldn't stay to formally introduce my lovers and my best friend. They all know how important my job is to me and understand my dedication, but it doesn't make it any easier.

"Thank you all for coming today. Elliot will be in touch on Monday with the contracts."

I smile my acknowledgment and keep the confusion off my face. Monday? Originally, she wanted the contracts sent over today with any modifications made during this meeting. I wonder why the change.

We exchange goodbye handshakes with all the men in high-end, tailored suits, and I follow Annie as she sits at her desk and wakes up her computer screen.

"My afternoon meeting rescheduled."

My brows furrow, and I panic, thinking I've missed something. I frantically pull out my phone and begin to apologize again.

"Ms. Poulsen, I'm sorry I missed—"

"You didn't. They called before you got here. Blake rescheduled them for next week. I just need you for another hour, and then you may leave to be with your family."

My jaw drops. I'm speechless.

"I'm happy to stay as long as you need me. They are in good hands."

"Elliot, go spend time with your family and don't look a gift horse in the mouth. I didn't like having to deny your request, but it was imperative you were here today. The contract from this morning's meeting can wait until Monday. Type up the notes while they are fresh in your head, and then you may leave."

"Yes ma'am."

"Oh, and Elliot, I know S'morgasm is on your list of places to take them. Make sure you go to the back room, and you may put whatever you purchase on my tab."

"Your tab?"

"Yes. I keep a card on file there. It's one of Blake's favorite places. Please enjoy any purchases you'd like on me."

"Thank you."

I rush to type up the notes and leave within forty-five

minutes. I check Lainey and Sawyer's location on my phone and see they are at S'morgasm. It felt like a big step in our relationship when Lainey asked if we could share. One I was happy to do.

I park at the back of the building, knowing everyone will be coming out these doors when done, and walk around the building. Ordering a coffee, I show my ID to the barista and inform her I want to go into the back room. I quietly look around when I step in, hoping none of them notice me. I spot Scotty and Sawyer off to the side whispering and head to them first.

"Come here often?" I whisper into Sawyer's ear and run my palm over his ass. He spins around with a big smile, and I pull him in by his hips. "Can I kiss you?" I know he's been more open with PDA, but I don't want to make him uncomfortable. I'll still give him the option despite wanting to crush my mouth to his.

He looks to where Scotty stands, still watching the girls.

"Don't hold back on my account. If I can get used to my best friend kissing another guy, you two won't even phase me."

Sawyer looks back at me, and his eyes drift to my lips. He licks his, and I know he wants to say yes. I just need the word.

"Can I kiss you, Doll?"

"Yeah."

I stop myself from hungrily attacking him like I want and press my lips firmly to his, allowing him to lead. He opens his mouth to deepen the kiss, and I happily accept. This man is so easy to get lost in. We pull away quickly when a throat clears, and it appears we've gained an audience. Sawyer leans his forehead against mine, and I look to the side to see who's interrupted us.

"Why don't I ever get a greeting like that."

I pull my arms from Sawyer and outstretch them to Wynnie, puckering my lips. Scotty grabs her around the waist and hauls her against his chest.

"Don't you fucking dare," he growls, and I can't help but laugh at his possessiveness.

I raise my hands in surrender. "Hey, she started it."

"I'll happily take your offering." Lainey steps into my arms and presses her lips to mine. No hesitation. No permission needed. She took what she wanted, and I fucking love it.

"Are you having fun, Cherry?"

"It just got better."

"Have you maxed out Annie's card yet?"

"We're working on it!" I jump at the sound of Blake's bubbly voice as she appears from behind a clothing rack of lacy lingerie.

"Hey, Blake. I had no idea you were here."

"This is my home away from home. And Lainey invited me."

The woman in my arms shrugs. "I felt bad spending Annie's money, so I invited Blake. I hope you don't mind."

I kiss Lainey's forehead and smile down at her. "Of course not, Cherry."

"Good." Blake grabs Lainey's hand and turns to Wynnie, taking hers as well. "Our baskets are up at the counter already. I'm stealing the ladies for the next hour or so."

Sawyer, Scotty, and I begin to protest and Blake shoots us the "Mom look" shutting us up.

"Ladies, kiss your men goodbye. I've got something fun

planned for us. We'll meet you all back at Elliot's house."

With confused looks, we say our goodbyes and watch the girls leave.

"What the fuck is going on?" Scotty runs a hand through his hair and looks at me with a death glare.

"I just got here man. Sawyer, any idea?"

Sawyer looks at me as confused as I feel and shakes his head. "Nothing was said to me. This is all the girls' doing."

My phone rings, and I see Cole calling.

"Cole, your wife hijacked our women. What's going on?"

"Well, hello to you too, Elliot. Blake told me to entertain you guys, so I'm heading to your house with beer and pizza. Get your asses home."

"That doesn't answer my question."

"Listen, Blake used *that* tone on me. I didn't ask any questions. I'm sure you can understand."

A sigh involuntarily escapes me. I know all about the dynamics in their household. It's not too different from ours in the respect that there's role reversal. Cole is just doing as he was told, and I can't fault him for it.

"We'll see you in about twenty."

I hang up and look between Scotty and Sawyer with a shake of my head. "Sounds like our only choice is to collect their purchases and wait for them at my house. Cole is being sent over to babysit us."

"For fucks sake," Scotty mumbles. He's already had a shit day, and now his wife has been kidnapped for some secret outing. I can't blame him for his reaction.

# 49

# Lainey

"You aren't serious? Why are we here, Katy?" Wynnie, Blake, Katy, and I stand outside a tattoo and piercing shop, Savage Steel & Ink. My question is directed to Katy because she's the one with the devilish smile on her face.

"Wynnie!" Katy throws her arms around Wynnie's neck and pulls her in for a hug. It looks awkward with Katy's growing belly, but she doesn't hesitate to hug Katy back. "I've heard so much about you. God, you're gorgeous."

Wynnie's cheeks pinken from the compliment, and I understand why I heard Scotty call her Pinky earlier. The two of them are adorable.

"Okay, hear me out," Katy starts. Nothing good ever comes from her "*hear me out*" ideas. "Piercings. Piercings... down south."

"Okay." My head snaps to Wynnie, who just accepted Katy's idea without thought.

"Really? You're okay with getting a piercing? Will Scotty

375

be okay with it?"

"Annie and Cole will love it. I'm in!" Blake claps and bounces on the balls of her feet.

"Am I the only sane one here? You're both willing to put holes in your"—I lower my voice—"lady bits?"

The three of them laugh at me. It's clear I am the only sane one here.

"I should ask Sawyer." I reach for my phone, and Katy puts her hand over the screen.

"Lainey. It's your body, not his or Elliot's. You don't have to if you don't want to, but don't leave it up to them."

Oh my god, am I considering this? A vaginal piercing isn't anything I've even thought of before, but the idea isn't offputting.

"What's the healing time?" I say on a sigh. Katy knew she would get her way. I can see now that Blake was just a pawn in her scheme.

Katy grabs my hand, and we walk inside with various emotions written on our faces. As soon as she pops this baby out, I'm planning something as devious and ridiculous as this.

ooooo

"Katy, if you don't slow down, I'm going to have an orgasm in your front seat. I think you're intentionally hitting every bump and dip in the road."

"Who, me?"

*This bitch.*

After considering all the options, I went with a hood piercing. It felt like the safest option. Katy already has a triangle piercing, but after explaining all the options, Wynnie and Blake also went with the hood.

Now, with my southern region swollen and sensitive, every time the car jolts, it sends spikes of pleasure and pain through me.

"My guys are going to kill me." The piercer said everyone's body is different, and it could take anywhere from two to twelve weeks to heal. No oral sex for a while, and use condoms.

Katy reaches over and takes my hand. "Trust me. They will get over it as soon as they see it."

"I'm looking forward to the punishment."

I turn in my seat to stare at Wynnie and wince at the weird movement. As soon as I find a comfortable position, I question her sanity.

"Care to share with the class, Wynnie."

"What? Can't a girl enjoy a good spanking sometimes? Besides, there's other holes that can be used." Despite the confidence in her voice, the blush on Wynnie's cheeks tells a different story.

"I knew we'd like her," Katy says enthusiastically as she pulls into Elliot's driveway.

After carefully getting out of the car, Elliot, Scotty, Cole, and Sawyer step onto the front porch.

"Damn, that's a sexy group of men."

"Katy," I hiss loud enough for only us to hear.

"What? Tell me I'm wrong. The only way it could be better is if Viktor was here. Why didn't I invite Viktor?"

She's not wrong. The four of them staring at us look like models ready to walk the runway. Scotty and Elliot with their dark hair and Sawyer and Cole with their light.

"Yeah, okay. You're right. They're sexy."

"Welcome back, ladies. How was your outing?" Elliot smiles our way as if he knows something.

Blake pulls up behind us and jumps out of her car.

"Pup, I have a surprise for you." Cole meets her halfway, and she throws her arms around his neck, standing on her tippy toes to whisper in his ear. Cole's eyes widen, and he looks down then back at her eyes. Blake squeals when Cole dips down and lifts her over his shoulder.

"Gotta go. I'll be back later for my car. Nice to meet you, Scotty and Wynnie."

"By-eeeeee!" Blake giggles as she bounces on his shoulder.

Cole opens her door and gently puts her in the passenger seat. I can see the heated look on his face and how Blake bites her lip at whatever he says to her.

"Hey, Pinky." Scotty embraces Wynnie, and I watch, waiting to see if she tells him right away and what his reaction will be. She doesn't.

I finish walking to the front door, and two sets of warm arms wind their way around me.

"Do you have a surprise for us, Cherry?" Elliot's smile is still devious, and I think he already knows.

"You tell me. Was it Katy or Blake?" I look to the driveway and see Katy backing out and wiggling her fingers at us.

*Bitch.* I'll deal with her later.

"It might have been both. They are terrible about secrets." Elliot kisses my forehead, and it makes my stomach flip-flop. I shift my hips, and a small moan escapes me before I can stop it. Elliot snickers, and Sawyer looks concerned.

"Jitterbug, are you okay?"

"I think she's more than okay. Aren't you, Cherry?"

"Mmhmm."

"Excuse us." Wynnie pushes past us with Scotty in tow. "We'll be right back. I need to show Scotty something." She winks at me, and I can't help but giggle.

"Can someone please fill me in? I hate being in the dark." Elliot leans in and whispers into Sawyer's ears. His eyes widen and trail down my body. "No. Did you? You didn't?"

I bite my bottom lip and nod.

"I… bedroom. Now."

"Yes, Sir."

Sawyer growls and pulls me into the house. Elliot snickers as he follows us, and I shoot him a glance, telling him to behave. I hate that the surprise was spoiled for him, but based on the looks he keeps giving me, I don't think it matters when he found out.

The bedroom door closes, and Sawyer's hands pull my shirt over my head.

"The piercing is below the belt, Baby."

"I don't care. I want the full picture. Show me."

Slowly, I unbutton my pants and kick off my shoes. I make a show of bending over while I slip my jeans off, and Sawyer seems to vibrate with anticipation.

"Alaina," he warns, but I ignore him. I'm taking charge.

I sit back on the bed and slide until I can plant my feet at the end. Sawyer's eyes are trained on me as I spread my legs.

"Take a look."

He steps between my legs and gently pushes aside my pink panties. His growl rips through the room as he drops to his knees for a better look.

"How long?"

The look in his eyes is wild. He's asking how long before we can play with it.

"It all depends on how I feel. Several days at least, and then we need to use condoms for a few weeks."

"Weeks?" The word is strained. I knew the condom part would be the biggest disappointment. We haven't used them for most of our relationship.

Elliot steps up behind Sawyer and grips his hair, pulling Sawyer's head back.

"It will be worth it. If you have any doubts, ask Vik. Katy has had hers pierced their entire relationship."

"I don't want to know why you know that." Sawyer lifts his hand, and with a feather touch, he traces around my new piercing. Everything down there is so sensitive right now, and I want nothing more than to allow him to explore. "It's like a bullseye. Will this enhance your orgasms?"

"It could." Right now, I feel like if he looked at me just right, I'd orgasm.

"I want to fucking find out so bad." He shifts uncomfortably as he adjusts himself in his pants.

"You can help me clean it later."

Sawyer growls, and he's losing his composure.

"Baby, let me help you with that?" I glance down at the bulge in his pants, and there's no denying how turned on he is just by the sight of my new piercing.

"No. If you can't, then I won't."

Elliot whimpers, realizing that means he won't be getting any either.

"Sawyer, don't be irrational. My mouth and hands work just fine. And there's no reason to punish Elliot. He has all his working parts."

Sawyer looks up at Elliot, whose bottom lip juts in a pout. He grabs Elliot's belt and pulls him down on the floor next to him.

"Are you willing to allow me to take my frustration out on you?"

"Yes, Sir. But we have guests this weekend."

"Fuck." Sawyer hangs his head at the reminder we aren't alone. "Fuck. Okay. You two go back out there. I need a few minutes. Or a cold shower."

"Wynnie got the same piercing, so I'm sure Scotty's feeling the same way."

Sawyer stands and heads to the bathroom. I hear him mumble, "Goddamn women," before the door closes.

"You're naughty, Cherry. So, so naughty." Elliot extends his hand to help me up and pulls me into his chest.

"You wouldn't have me any other way."

# 50

# Elliot

It's been a torturous few weeks. Sawyer wasn't kidding when he asked if I was willing to let him take his frustration out on me. Despite Lainey finally feeling comfortable enough for sex, he's treating her like she's broken. As soon as she orgasms, he rips off the condom, puts me on my knees, and fucks my face until he comes.

I'm not complaining, but I know he's not completely satisfied, either.

Lainey: I need you. Our spot at lunch?

I've been staring at Lainey's text while attempting to keep my hard-on hidden under my desk. I don't know what she means by needing me, but we've been sneaking away for quiet orgasms in an empty office on the eighteenth floor for the last two weeks.

Sawyer is still afraid to hurt her and, in turn, won't allow me much access to her either. Lainey is frustrated. We need to talk to him about it, but in the meantime, she's been using me at work to take the edge off.

We're allowed to play without him. That rule was established right away as long as there was no penetration. We need to talk to him about that, too. I think we've been in this relationship together long enough that some new boundaries can be redrawn.

Elliot: I'll be there.

The minutes tick by slowly as I try not to think about our lunch date.

"Earth to Elliot."

"Shit." I practically jump out of my seat as a hand waves in front of my face.

"Sorry," Blake giggles. "You were really zoned out. I'm sure I can guess what... or who."

"You'd probably be right. Was there something you needed help with?"

"Nope. Just saying hi before Annie and I go out for lunch. Did you want to join us?"

"I have plans," I rush out, about as cool as someone caught red-handed in the cookie jar.

"O-kay," Blake says through a laugh. "I'll see you in an hour. I hope your *plans* are tasty." She winks, and I buzz her into Annie's office.

There are so many things wrong with her statement, but she knows exactly what she is saying.

I shut down my computer and wait several minutes after they leave so I don't have to get on the elevator with them. If I hit a number to an empty floor, there would be questions.

My heart races as I watch the numbers descend. We've done this several times, but something about her text makes this time feel different.

The elevator dings as it reaches my floor. When the doors open, there's an electricity in the air that has the hairs on the back of my neck standing up. I make a left off the elevator and open the third door. This office contains a couch that's come in handy.

My breath hitches when I see my incredible girlfriend lying on the couch, spread eagle, with her hand up her dress.

"Fuck, Cherry. You couldn't wait for me?"

"No. Get the fuck over here and finish what I've started."

Throwing off my suit jacket, I lay it on the empty desk and loosen my tie. Lainey hikes the hem of her dress so it bunches around her thighs and spreads her legs wider.

"No panties, naughty girl?"

"You'd just rip them off, so I thought I'd make it easier for you."

She's right. If I don't rip them off, I pocket them. I have a nice little collection going. I enjoy buying her new ones as much as I enjoy destroying them.

My hands smooth down her creamy thighs, and I spread her even wider as I go. The silver barbel with one blue and one clear jewel calls to me. She told us the different colors were to represent mine and Sawyer's eyes, and I thought he was going to lose it when he found out.

Lainey assures us she's fully healed, and I've heard her plead with Sawyer on more than one occasion to be rougher with her, but he still refuses. It's almost as if our roles have been reversed because he's been the sweet, loving one, and I've been the more dominant one. But only when we're in our little bubble on the eighteenth floor.

Her beautiful pussy already glistens from playing with herself before my arrival, and I dive right in. I'm still careful not to tug too much on the jewelry, but I use it to my advantage. As I flick it with my tongue, it hits her clit with a little tap each time, and her moans of pleasure urge me to go faster.

Using two fingers, I plunge into her needy pussy, and her inner walls flutter around me already. Lainey's hands come down and tug at my hair. I relish in the pain and quicken my movements.

"Fuck, Elliot. I'm so close. Keep going."

I can feel how close she is. Her pussy pulls my fingers back in with every pump. My tongue becomes more aggressive, and as much as I want to be careful, I trust that she'll tell me if something hurts.

Lainey's mouth drops in a silent scream as her hips buck. I spread my free hand over her stomach to keep her still while I drag out her orgasm for as long as possible.

"Enough. Stop. Please." I chuckle into her core as she pushes my head away.

She sits up and crashes her lips to mine while her hands frantically undo my belt.

"I need you, Elliot. Please," she begs against my lips.

"I'm right here, Cherry."

She pulls my cock out of my pants and strokes me as she straddles my thighs.

"No. I *need* you." She brushes the head of my cock through her wetness, and I groan at the warmth.

I grab her hips and squeeze in warning. "Lainey, we can't. It's against the rules."

"Fuck the rules. I can't take the condoms, the gentleness. I need to be fucked. Please fuck me."

She isn't leaving me with much choice as she lines my cock up with her entrance. I could easily push her off, but I'm as needy as she is right now. She isn't the only one who's been dying to fuck or be fucked. Sawyer has been holding us both back.

"If we do this, there's no going back. We have to tell him." She nods and stares into my eyes as she slowly sinks onto me. "There will be punishment, Alaina."

"It can't be any worse than not feeling either of you inside me for weeks." She bites her bottom lip as she fully seats herself on top of me.

"Fuck, I've missed you. We're in so much trou*uuuuugh*." My words trail off as she lifts her hips and sinks back down.

"Do you want to talk or fuck, Elliot? Because by the look on your face, I think it's the latter."

My brain snaps from her bratty comment, and all reservations leave my mind. Lifting her off me, I toss her on the couch and slam back into her. My hips have a mind of their own as they pump into her furiously. Lainey's nails, which found their way under my shirt, rake down my skin, and I soak up the pain they leave behind. I hope she makes me bleed.

"Did your pussy miss me? I fucking missed her. You're taking me so well. You're so fucking gorgeous. How's that piercing treating you?"

"I'm... it's... oh fuck." She convulses under me as another orgasm takes over her entire body. She's told us they seem more intense now, and based on how she's squeezing my cock, I believe her.

386

My phone beeps in my pocket, and Lainey whines my name.

"Shh, I've got you. We have ten more minutes. I'm almost there, and then we'll clean up. You're incredible, Cherry."

I reach behind me and silence the alarm. We learned the hard way that we need an alarm if we are going to get back to work on time. I have one set for fifteen minutes before we need to leave and another for five, so we have plenty of time.

Lainey grabs my shirt, pulling me down to her lips, and I hungrily drink her in. Everything about this woman consumes me. Both of them consume me.

I feel the tingle as my balls draw up. I start to pull back, and Lainey clamps her feet behind my back.

"Don't you fucking dare. I want to feel you inside me the rest of the day."

Her dirty words make me growl and slam into her harder. It only takes a few more pumps before I spill myself inside and almost collapse from my release.

I bury my head into Lainey's neck and say the words I've wanted to say for a while but haven't had the courage.

"I love you, Alaina."

I feel her breathing stop as she contemplates my words. "Say it again to my face. Don't hide."

My alarm beeps again, and I reluctantly pull out of her.

"Let me get something to clean you up. Don't move."

"Elliot?"

"I'll be right back." I tuck myself away, not wanting to remove her scent from me, and quickly run into the bathroom across the hall to grab some paper towels.

Lainey doesn't look happy when I return. She takes the

towels from me and wipes up my mess. She stands and fixes her dress without looking at me, and as soon as she settles, I pull her to my chest.

Brushing hair from her face, I look deep into her hazel-green eyes.

"Meghan Alaina Hayes." Her breath hitches at the use of her full name. I know Meghan has a negative history with us, but I want her to know how serious I am about my words. "I love you."

"Elliot…"

"I don't expect you to say it back, but I couldn't hold it any longer. You and Sawyer, I'm all in. Not that I haven't been all in, but I'm in. I'm here." I rest my forehead against hers. "We just fucked up and broke his boundaries, but I hope Sawyer forgives us for it."

"He will."

"I don't regret it. Not one second of being with you. Ever."

"I—"

I silence her with my lips. "Before you tell me, if that's what you were going to say, let's tell Sawyer what we did first.

# 51

# Sawyer

I'm ready. It's time. It's been months of Elliot and I together, and despite talking about it ad nauseam, I've been reluctant. Lainey and I have had anal sex before. I have no idea why I've been stalling to cross that line with Elliot.

My body vibrates with excitement for them to come home from work for several reasons. I've been so careful and gentle with Lainey and her new piercing. We haven't had a scene together since she got it done because I know she'll do whatever I ask of her, even if she's in pain.

I have something special planned that will have them both on their knees.

"Baby, we're home."

"I'll be right out," I call back as I check that I have everything we need for later.

I leave the bedroom, and Lainey stops in her tracks to stare at me. She bites her lip. I'm only wearing jeans, and they hang low on my hips, as I have nothing under them.

Lainey's body jolts forward as Elliot bumps into her.

"What the... oh."

My lip quirks. Lainey knows what my attire means, but Elliot hasn't been privy to a planned scene yet.

"Now?" Lainey asks breathily.

I shake my head. "No. Food first. I ordered Chinese."

Elliot's brows scrunch, not understanding our conversation. He points to himself, and his finger spins in a circle.

"Clueless. Other than looking fucking edible, could someone fill me in."

"He's planned a scene," Lainey whispers to Elliot over her shoulder. His eyes widen, and he licks his lips. "I'd plan on being the sub tonight based on his look."

*"His look."* Confidence. Determination. That's the look they're seeing. I'm done playing games, and I'm ready for action.

"Eat." They hustle to the table and sit, digging into the containers. I've already eaten, so I don't join them but sit and watch.

Lainey keeps sneaking glances at Elliot, and I get the feeling something is going on that they aren't telling me about.

Sitting back in my chair, I cross my arms over my chest, making my muscles pop. For this exact reason, I did a few sets of push-ups and sit-ups before they arrived.

"Alaina, Eli, what's going on?" Lainey stops with her chopsticks halfway to her mouth, and Elliot chokes on the food he's chewing.

Bingo. I knew something was up.

"Can it wait until after?" Lainey's eyes flash to the bedroom door. Whatever she has to say, she doesn't want me to know before we scene, which makes me want to know even more.

"No. We don't keep secrets, and we keep open lines of communication. Who'd like to speak first?"

"Sawyer, we—" Lainey cuts Elliot off.

"No. It was me. I'll take the heat."

Lainey drops her hands to her lap and bows her head. She's showing me her submission before she even speaks. This just got even more interesting.

"I seduced Elliot today, and we had sex. I swear it's the first and only time it's ever happened." The words rush from her mouth in one quick breath.

They both stop breathing as they wait to hear my reaction. *What is my reaction?*

If I'm honest with myself, I'm surprised to hear this was the first time. Elliot and I are the kings of quickie hand and blow jobs together. I made that arbitrary boundary when things were still new between the three of us, and a small part of me was insecure about what the future held.

"I also told her I loved her."

My eyes snap to Elliot then to Lainey. "And?"

"And?" Lainey asks meekly.

"Did you say it back?" I have no idea why I need to know. It doesn't matter who he says it to first. We are just as much individuals as we are a unit. We hold our own unique relationships within our throuple. Lainey is so easy to love, and I don't blame Elliot for falling in love with her.

"No. I wouldn't allow her to. I didn't want her to say it until we got our transgression out in the open."

*Good man, Elliot.*

"Do you regret it?" I don't know if my question pertains

to his declaration or if I'm asking if he regrets sleeping with Lainey without my permission. Does he regret breaking the rules?

"Telling her I love her? No. Giving her what she wanted? No. Breaking the only boundary you set for us? Yes. But I would do it all over again. She hasn't been satisfied."

"*What?* No. That's not… I mean, I'm always…" She sighs and looks at me with pleading eyes. "You've been so gentle with me, Soy Sauce."

Oh, this little brat is pulling out all the stops. Using that goofy nickname is a low blow. She's not wrong, though. I've been overly cautious and have not allowed Elliot to be too rough, either. I suppose I deserve them sneaking behind my back, even though I don't mind at all at this point. But I'll be damned if I'll let them know.

"How many, Alaina." She opens her mouth to answer, and I stop her with a raised hand. "On second thought. Eli, how many does she deserve?" I'm curious how many smacks he believes her rule-breaking earned her.

"T-ten?"

Mmmm. A stutter of fear and lack of confidence. That was sexy. Ten is a very respectable number for what she did.

"Alaina, how many does Eli deserve?"

"Five," she states with confidence.

She truly believes she seduced him and he deserves less. It's admirable.

"Fine. Eli will receive ten, and Alaina will receive five."

Lainey's eyes widen, and her mouth drops open, but she thinks better of it. Elliot accepts my words without even flinching. He almost seems happy to receive more than her.

"Finish so we can get started. I have plans, and despite

your misdeeds, they are still happening."

Elliot stands to clear his plate and offers his hand to Lainey to take hers. She looks down at her mostly-eaten food and makes a decision, handing it to him.

"I'll give you five minutes."

Lainey takes Elliot's hand once the plates are in the sink and leads him into the bedroom. A genuine smile creeps up my cheeks at what they see on the bed and nightstand. Lainey's Truth or Dare confession is waiting to come true, but first, I have punishments to dole out.

# 52

# Lainey

"That was too easy." I slap a hand over Elliot's mouth. "Be quiet and strip. We only have five minutes. Will you unzip me?" I give him my back, and he helps me out of my dress and unclips my bra. I toss everything on the armchair in the corner and sit on the edge of the bed. "Will you hurry," I whisper-shout at him.

It's obvious he doesn't understand the severity of the situation. An expressionless Sawyer is worse than an upset one. He had no comments about the I love you or the sex.

*How could he have nothing to say?*

Elliot finally joins me at my feet. He kneels naked, his cock semi-hard and I try not to stare. He's beautiful. His breathing is steady and even, compared to my erratic breath, as he wraps one hand around my trembling ankle and places the other in his lap.

My shaking body isn't fear. It's anticipation. Anticipation of the unknown. I know my safeword, and Sawyer knows my limits. I would never fear him.

I want to tell Elliot to place his hand on his lap, but his simple touch calms my nerves.

It's been more than five minutes since we were told to come in here. The clock on the nightstand says it's been at least ten. Sawyer sometimes does this to increase anxiety and anticipation. He wants to make sure I know who's in charge.

Sawyer's almost silent steps walk into the room, and I inhale a shaky breath. Elliot's hand squeezes my ankle in support, and I expect him to remove it, but he doesn't. Will Sawyer say anything about it? Elliot isn't in the proper waiting position.

"Aren't you two a beautiful sight." Sawyer's voice drips with admiration and awe as he runs his hands through our hair. I want to purr at the sensation until he grabs a handful at the base of our necks and forces us to look up at him.

There's the Dom I've been waiting to see. He was so passive in the kitchen. His gray eyes now burn with fire, and they dart between us.

"You're going to dole out each other's punishments while I watch. If I think you are being too soft, I won't count the hit. I want to see how truly remorseful you are about breaking my boundary."

Fuck. I've never handed out a punishment before. Sure, I've smacked Sawyer's ass in the past, but a punishment is different.

"Any objections, you know the safeword. Alaina, bend over the bed."

It's a good thing I'm already sitting because I don't think my legs could hold me if I had to stand right now. Elliot squeezes my ankle one more time before releasing me.

As I press my front against the comforter, I notice the things on the bed for the first time. How had I missed this when I came in? A folded towel with my strap-on lies near the pillows, and a bottle of lube sits waiting on the nightstand.

"Stand Eli. Alaina is owed five spanks for punishment. I'll count."

Taking a deep breath, I relax my body. It will only hurt worse if I'm tense, and I don't expect Elliot to go easy on me. I don't want him to. I know five isn't many, but it's enough.

The first crack sounds in the air before I feel the sting. I squeeze my eyes shut as the feeling spreads through my body.

"One. Oh, and Eli. Did I mention it's five per ass cheek?"

*What?*

It's not like him to change the rules. That means I'll have to give Elliot a total of twenty hits for punishment. My hands tingle at the thought when another smack comes down on the same cheek.

"Two. Good boy. Now, do it again. Stop delaying."

I hear Elliot grunt, and I can imagine what Sawyer did to cause that kind of reaction. Did he grip his hair? Tug on his cock?

*Smack.*

"Three. Faster."

*Smack. Smack.*

"Four. Five. Look at this delicious red ass cheek. It looks good enough to eat."

My body jolts as what I can only assume is Sawyer's hand smooths over my stinging cheek and squeezes.

"Praise her, Eli."

"Alaina, you did beautifully. Your cheek looks incredible." I relish in Elliot's praise for only a moment before the bubble pops.

"Finish, Eli. No stops."

Sawyer's hand leaves my body seconds before my other cheek stings.

"One." *Smack.* "Two." *Smack.* "Three." There's a pause, and Elliot gasps. "Again, Eli. I said no stops." Sawyer's voice is gravelly with lust. *Smack. Smack.* "Four and Five. On your knees, boy."

Sawyer is fully in the scene now. I fucking love it despite the tears I feel pooling on the comforter.

"Reset, Alaina."

Inhaling a deep breath, I roll to my back and sit up. My raw flesh stings, and I squeeze my eyes against the pain. I don't wipe away my tears because I know Sawyer likes them. I rest my hands back on my lap and wait.

The room is silent except for the very different tones of our breathing. Elliot is fully hard now, and his cock bobs thick on his lap as he kneels at Sawyer's feet.

Sawyer grips my chin and lifts my face to meet his.

"Check in."

A few seconds of my husband is all he gives me. Enough for me to nod before he releases my chin.

"Switch."

Elliot rises and bends over the bed while I stand behind him. Twenty smacks. I can't be soft. I know this will hurt me as much as him, but I understand Sawyer's reasoning for switching our punishments. As a Dom, Elliot should have known better and been able to resist me and control himself. He didn't, and Sawyer needs to remind him of his place and role in this relationship.

*Smack.*

"One."

Fuck that stung, but I need to get through this. I hear Sawyer counting, but I don't stop until I hear him say ten. He places a hand on my shoulder, and I realize I'm panting and crying again.

"Again. Other cheek." He doesn't remove his hand as a small gesture of support, but I hesitate, and he sees it. "Do you need to use your safeword, Alaina?"

"No." I can do this for him. For us.

My arm swings again, and by the time I hear Sawyer's voice say ten, I'm sobbing. I collapse to the floor and put myself in rest position at his feet. I know sitting on the bed is my usual position, but I don't have the mental or physical capacity to be anywhere but down here.

Elliot joins me, and his leg rests against mine. The warmth of his body makes me sob harder with... what?

Guilt?

Acceptance?

We both deserved our punishment. Boundaries are set for a reason, and we obliterated them without a second thought. I was impatient and inconsiderate.

With a deep inhale, I release a shaky breath and straighten my back. It's over and done. We survived our transgressions, and now we move forward. That's what a punishment is about.

"Stand when you're ready, Alaina."

I squeeze my eyes shut and will my inner goddess to get her shit together. Elliot's thigh pushes on mine with more pressure, and my first thought is he's pushing me to obey.

But when it doesn't move away, I realize he's showing me support.

Pressing my hands in front of me, I stand. My tears have stopped, and I'm proud of myself for withstanding what I did.

"Look at me."

I look into his stormy gray eyes and see the love shining through. He's just as proud of me. I can see it, but he won't tell me until later when we aren't in these roles.

"Have you seen what's on the bed?" I nod, and his eyes squint. "Words, Alaina."

"I have, Sir. Yes."

"Despite the punishment you've both received, my plans for the evening haven't changed. I believe you've learned your lesson, and going forward, there will be more open communication. Stand Eli."

Next to me, Elliot's shoulder brushes mine as he does as requested.

"Does anyone have any objections to what is on the bed?"

# 53

# Elliot

My ass is on fire as I stand next to Lainey. I am so proud of her.

"Does anyone have any objections to what is on the bed?"

I saw the strap-on lying there. I focused on it while receiving my punishment and imagined all the possibilities it could be used for. Is it for mine or Sawyer's ass? Lainey is going to look so fucking sexy with it attached.

Sawyer aggressively pushes up my chin to look in his eyes. My cock twitches at the power I see behind them. We've done plenty of scenes over the last several months together, but this is the first time I've seen him in full Dom mode, and it's intoxicating to allow this man to own my body.

"Do you remember Alaina's truth? The one she told you over text when you were home with your family."

I feel more than hear Lainey's quick inhale as she realizes what Sawyer is talking about.

"Yes, Sir." How could I forget? Sawyer in my ass and

Lainey in his was her fantasy. I never imagined he'd allow himself to be in such a vulnerable position. Especially now since we haven't crossed that bridge yet together.

"Any objections to making her fantasy come true."

*No. Fuck no. Let's fucking do this right now. I'm ready.* "No, Sir."

"Good. Do you want me to wear a condom?"

The question shocks me. The idea never crossed my mind when I thought about the day this finally arrived.

"No, Sir. Not unless you want to."

Sawyer pops my cheek, and I blink at the shock.

"I asked you a yes or no question. I wasn't looking for your opinion."

Dropping my head, I bite my lip. My cheek stings, but I want him to do it again. Harder.

"Up on the bed, Eli. Spread the towel out and present for me. I want to prep you. Alaina, get yourself ready." He turns his attention to her as I follow my instructions. "I've had a butt plug in for a couple of hours. When we're ready, I'll need you to remove it."

"Yes, Sir."

The shock that Sawyer has prepared himself for this quickly wears off as I hear the telltale click of a lube cap, and the cool gel drizzles down my ass crack. Sawyer's hands rub circles across my raw ass cheeks before he spreads them, and his thumb rims my hole. My already aroused body lights up like a firework.

It doesn't take long to prep me. Once he's slipped in one finger, my body eagerly responds for a second and then a third. Sawyer pants behind me, telling me he's just as excited about this as I am.

"Are you ready, Eli?"

"Yes, Sir." *So fucking ready.*

"Safeword?"

"Apple."

"Alaina?"

"Apple, Sir."

Sawyer removes his fingers, and I feel empty. I hear the click of the lube cap again, and the squish of gel as Sawyer lubes his cock for me.

Adrenaline courses through my body as I feel his head line up. I take a deep breath and release all my anxiety, relaxing for him. Thick hands wrap around my hips as Sawyer pushes forward. He uses short but quick thrusts to press himself further into me. Inch by glorious fucking inch, he sinks in. I keep my noises neutral, listening to his moans and grunts of pleasure. I want to soak up every sound he makes to remember our first time together.

Lainey gasps when our hips meet, and Sawyer is fully seated in my ass. Sawyer's hand brushes my spine and back to my ass. I peer over my shoulder and find his gaze staring at where we're connected. He pulls out slowly and back in. I drop to my chest, and he hisses as the position allows him to go even deeper.

"Elliot," he breathes out like a prayer. Not Eli. Elliot. He's so lost in the sensation he forgets his role. Sawyer's hips move with more purpose, and the moans I've been holding back refuse to be contained any longer.

I glance at Lainey, who's watching where we are connected with hooded eyes and biting her lip. The black strap-on attached to her sways as she involuntarily moves her hips in time with Sawyer's.

"Alaina." Sawyer catches her watching, and she looks guilty when she meets his eyes. "I'm ready."

His body drapes over mine as she steps behind him. Sawyer's hips push impossibly further into me as the butt plug is removed. Lainey takes the lube and prepares her dildo. I don't think I've ever seen a more erotic sight than Lainey stroking herself. I wish I could see what she's seeing when Sawyer begins to grunt over me.

I hope he knows how much this means to both Lainey and me. The vulnerability of the position he's allowing himself to be in isn't going unnoticed, and whether he likes it or not, I'll make sure I praise him when the scene is over.

As Lainey begins to rock into him, Sawyer pulls out, and they rock into me together. I'm being fucked by both of them. The woman I love is fucking the man I love, who's fucking me.

*Fuck.* I love them both.

I think I started falling for Sawyer the night I met him at Midnight Moonshine. The utter respect I had for him after the movie theater incident and seeing how he stuck with Lainey until she was comfortable only made me fall harder. She's the center of our worlds. Our Queen.

"Let me do it." Sawyer's gruff voice snaps me out of my love-sick trance. I gasp when his hips snap forward and back. He pivots between us, fucking himself and me at the same time. He's taking back his power despite being in the middle.

The noises in the room become animalistic. I need to play with my cock to come, but I won't ask permission. This is for Sawyer.

"In or out Eli? In or out. Choose fast."

"In." Fuck the Sir pleasantries. I want him to come inside me.

"Alaina, pull out." His voice is a commanding roar as she pulls out, and he punishes my ass with his thrusts. Sawyer's fingers dig into my hips, and I know I'll have bruises later.

"Fuuuuuuuuck, Elliot."

With a final slam, Sawyer comes deep in my ass. I can feel his cock jerking with each release. Too soon, he pulls out and lays flat on his back next to me, panting.

The room is silent as we wait for our next instructions.

"Jitterbug, take that off and take care of Elliot." *Fuck yes.* "Don't you dare come before her though."

*Shit.*

But he called her Jitterbug. That means the scene is over. My mind instantly goes into aftercare mode, but Lainey pushes me to roll on my back, and the sight of her crawling up my body refocuses my mind.

I grab the base of my cock as she lines up on top of me and sinks. She's soaked. Did she come already, or is she just that turned on?

Fuck it. I don't care.

Grabbing her hips, I pump up into her, and she pitches forward, bracing herself on my chest.

"Show me what I missed today. Show me how she wants to be treated, Elliot." Sawyer's hand brushes through my hair, and I take his words as permission to fuck our girl like she wants to be fucked. Hard and fast. I'll pull the orgasm from her before I come without any effort.

Sawyer continues to touch and stroke our bodies, never leaving contact as I bring Lainey to orgasm and quickly follow behind her.

We lay in a heap of sweat and come while our breathing returns to normal. I reach across Lainey between us and touch Sawyer's cheek. He smiles at me, and his gray eyes sparkle with satisfaction.

"I love you, Sawyer."

His smile falters for a moment as my words register. He pops up on his elbow and leans over Lainey to pull me in for a kiss.

"I. Love. You. Too." Each word is interrupted by kisses.

A girly squeal comes from between us, and we're pushed apart.

"Yes. Yes. We all love each other. You're crushing me."

"Do you love me, Cherry? You haven't told me yet." She knows full well I know how she feels. I stopped her from saying it back this afternoon.

"I'll love you more once you wash my hair in the shower and rub cream on my sore ass cheeks."

"Up. Shower. It was my scene, and I'm in charge of aftercare. Let's go." Sawyer stands and grabs an ankle, pulling us closer to the edge of the bed, and we laugh our way to the shower.

# 54

# Lainey

"OMG woman. What's wrong with you? You're such a buzzkill." Katy smacks my arm as my head bobs for about the dozenth time during our hour-long lunch break.

"Ouch. Don't be violent." I rub my arm as I yawn.

"See, that's what I mean. Are those men keeping you up too late? Sex is great, but a girl requires her beauty sleep."

"It's not them, it's me. I swear the second one of them walks past me, my nipples get hard enough to cut glass, and I could flood a pond. Most nights, I wear *them* out."

A throat clears next to us, and an elderly lady in a gray pantsuit stands and leaves while shaking her head at us.

Katy shrugs and turns back to me, lowering her voice. "How's that going, by the way?"

"Well, there hasn't been anything extreme since the night we all said I love you a few weeks back. Don't get me wrong. There's been lots of action, just nothing to that magnitude. But I have to admit, seeing Sawyer and Elliot together is fucking hot. I enjoy the show and don't need to participate to *participate*, if you know what I mean."

"Hi, one mother and four fathers. I get it. Probably have the t-shirt and wrote the book already compared to anything you've seen or done."

Katy isn't wrong. Spencer and her men are very active, and the older we get, the less they hide the adult stuff from her.

I yawn again, and she tisks at me. "Are you going to be this boring tonight, and are you going to eat that?"

Katy points at my half-eaten egg salad sandwich. It's all I could think about this morning, but after the first bite, I'd had enough. I shake my head and slide the container over to her.

"All yours, Mama. And I promise I'll be better tonight. I'll caffeinate up before we leave."

She lifts the sandwich into the air and motions it in my direction. "Are you sure?"

My stomach turns as the smell wafts my way. I sit back in my seat and nod my head. "Yep," I say with tight lips. "Eat up."

She eyes me suspiciously before taking a big bite.

All I want to do is go home and take a long nap, but I promised the girls, after confirming with Elliot, that they could come over and use his hot tub. He already reduced the heat to a safer level for the pregnant ladies, and we're going to relax and enjoy a kid-free evening.

"Do you need me to bring anything tonight?"

"Nope. Elliot said he would order us food and bring yourselves, and 'clothing is optional.' Ridiculous men shit."

We have a good laugh and finish our lunch break, with me trying not to watch as Katy finishes my now unappetizing sandwich.

407

⚏ ⚏ ⚏ ⚏ ⚏

"Cherry, is there anything else you need before we go?"

I'm still in shock as caterers flit around his living room, setting up catering trays of food.

"I... This... Why Elliot?"

He chuckles and wraps me in his arms, kissing my forehead. "Why not? Now you don't have to worry about anything but enjoying yourselves. All the servers have signed NDAs per Annie's request, so you can get as wild and crazy as you'd like."

"It's too much."

Sawyer steps up behind me, and I'm enveloped in my favorite place. Between them.

"It's everything you deserve, Jitterbug. Enjoy and stop arguing."

"I love you both, but if you don't let me go, very indecent things are going to happen, and Katy is in the other room."

They each kiss a cheek and step back. I instantly want to take back my statement and pull them close again, but my lady bits are screaming at me, and I have a girls' night to host.

"Leave before I change my mind." They each kiss me more passionately than is appropriate and leave.

"That was hot. I think I need a cold shower."

"Shut up." I toss a throw pillow at Katy, and she ducks as the doorbell rings.

Nicole smiles at me when I open the door and she looks over her shoulder and waves before I see their minivan back out of the driveway.

"*Dad* had to make sure I got in the house." Nicole rolls

her eyes over Justin as she steps into the house and I see Spencer's little black SUV pull in. I wait at the door but call for Katy. Of all the women, I know Spencer the least. She's never been one for conversation, but we always invite her to our girls' night. I was excited when she agreed to come, but I'd still like Katy here as a buffer when she initially shows up.

Spencer and Katy embrace, and there's an awkward moment of hesitation before Spencer leans in and hugs me, too.

The affection is unexpected but appreciated and brings tears to my eyes. I know Spencer's aversion to touch due to her autism, and her embrace means more to me because of it. When we pull away, I wipe my eyes, and Katy stares at me again.

Everyone crowds around the serving dishes when the doorbell rings again and my final guests have arrived.

"Hi, Blake. Annie."

"I brought party favors!" Blake's smile lights up the entire room as she holds up two grocery bags.

"Blake, you didn't need to bring anything. I told you I have everything handled."

"Trust me, Lainey. These aren't party favors." Annie walks past me, and Blake thrusts one of the bags into my hands.

"What's this?" My mouth drops as I look into a bag filled with boxes of pregnancy tests.

"I warned you," Annie's voice filters in from the other room.

"Blake?"

"Don't blame me. Katy told me to pick them up. Apparently, we are going to play pregnancy test roulette."

"We're doing what?" Nicole's blonde curls bounce as she takes a bite from a mini taco.

*That looks delicious.*

"Pregnancy roulette," Katy repeats as she takes the bag from me and opens the boxes. "Everyone pees on a stick, and we see how many positives we get."

"Um…" Nicole looks down at her large baby bump. Katy is still small in comparison, and I know Nicole gives her grief about it regularly.

"Yes. Yes. Of course, you and I will be positive, so we will see at least two plus signs. The fun is seeing if there are any more."

"Might I point out another flaw to your plan," Spencer chimes in. I'm forever envious of her auburn double braids and hope one day I get enough courage to ask her to teach me how to do them.

"I'm also aware that you and Annie are incapable of becoming pregnant. But if we don't all test, it won't be any fun." Katy pouts, obviously trying to guilt-trip us into her crazy idea.

"Okay, but if two of you are already pregnant and another two of you can't get pregnant, that only leaves Blake and me."

"Exactly." Blake boops my nose and takes a test from Katy, wandering down the hallway towards the bathroom.

"Here, go use Elliot's bathroom so we can do this two at a time." Katy hands me a test, and I stare at it like a grenade without a pin. Nicole hands Katy a plastic cup to hold all the tests while they process, so we can't see what they say until everyone is done.

I zombie walk to the master bath and slowly open the foil

packet.

*Just pee on the stick. It's as simple as that, Lainey. This shouldn't be hard.*

I shake my head to clear my errant thoughts. I'm on birth control; the shot. This is nothing. I need to check my calendar because I'm due for another soon, but if I were pregnant, I'd know. Right?

This has to be Blake's way of announcing she's pregnant. She likes the flair and pizazz of a grand announcement.

I pee on the stick, wash my hands, bring the test to Katy, and drop it in the cup. One by one, with a mixture of grumbles and giggles, the cup fills with the six tests. Katy sets a three-minute alarm, and everyone resumes eating and socializing.

My eyes wander over the food selections, but my mind mentally calculates one hundred eighty seconds. Only ninety seconds left.

Forty-five.

Thirty.

Fifteen.

Ten... Five... Four... Three... Two... One.

Silence.

*Fuck.* I must have counted faster than the actual timer.

When the timer finally sounds, I jump. Katy giggles next to me and gestures for everyone to take a seat. Once settled, which feels like it takes hours, Katy takes out the first test and lays it on the coffee table on top of a napkin.

"Negative." She takes out the next one. "Positive." Another. "Positive."

"Well, that covers us two preggers, Katy." Nicole rubs her belly, but I don't feel any better yet.

411

Another test is pulled out and laid on the napkin. "Negative."

Two and two. Only two tests left. Could one of those negatives be mine... or the positives?

Katy pulls out another test, and her eyes widen.

"Positive."

The room erupts into chatter.

"Blake?" I hear Annie say to her.

Her hands raise in surrender. "Katy told me to buy the tests. I didn't set this up."

"There's one more." Katy shakes the last test in the cup, catching everyone's attention. I hold my breath as she lifts the last stick. "Negative."

"Looks like it's you and me." Someone bumps my shoulder, and I see Blake handing me another test.

"What?" My brain is in a fog. This can't be happening. There's still a 50/50 chance it's Blake and not me.

"We are the only two who could be pregnant. I expected it was a possibility and bought two extra tests. It looks like we need them."

Blake walks down the hall. I turn to Katy and whisper her name. I'm not sure she's heard me until she takes my free hand and leads me into Elliot's room.

"Katy," I repeat. "W-Why? What made you ask Blake to do this?" I stare at the foil packet in my hand and see it tremble.

"Exhaustion, elevated libido, half-finished meal, feeling sick." She says each word with a tick of her fingers. "Is it possible, Lainey?"

"It's always possible, but is it probable?" I pull my phone out of my pocket. "I've been on the shot for my entire relationship with Sawy—*fuck*." I sink to the bed and stare at the screen.

"What?"

Katy looks over my shoulder to see my phone. I have my period tracker app pulled up.

"I swore I was due this month, but…" I swipe back to last month's calendar, where a flower shows my ovulation days, the blood drop shows my predicted period, and I made a note that my shot was due.

Was. Due.

As in past tense, by over a month. I do the math in my head and know exactly when it happened. The eighteenth floor. The I love yous.

"Katy, I think I'm pregnant."

# 55

# Elliot

Something is bothering Lainey. She's been acting strange for the last week. Sawyer and I have both noticed it, but she keeps telling us she's fine. The four letter F word.

Even this morning, we usually carpool, but she said she had an errand to run with Katy at lunch, so they were going to carpool. It didn't make sense to me why I couldn't drive her now, and Katy had to come all that way to get her, but nothing I said would change her mind, and I wasn't going to argue.

Lainey: Will you both be home tonight right after work? I'd like to talk to you.

Elliot: Of course. Am I driving you?

Sawyer: I'll be wherever you need me to be, Jitterbug.

Lainey: Katy will drive me home. See you around 5:30 at Elliot's house.

*What the actual fuck is going on?*

I switch text chats to message Sawyer, but my computer pops up with an alert to be in a meeting with Annie. I quickly put my phone on Do Not Disturb and pocket it. I found out the hard way that even on silent, it isn't quiet enough when I get stuck in a text group. The constant vibrating during a meeting almost got me in trouble with Annie.

I struggle through the next several hours, taking notes and scheduling meetings for Annie. At least the day has flown by. We even had a working lunch. The experience and opportunity that Annie gives me daily is invaluable. I'll never be able to thank or repay her enough for everything she's given me so far in my short life.

The moment Annie dismisses me for the day, I race to the lobby, hoping to catch a glimpse of Lainey, but the night security guard is already occupying the front desk. I glance at my watch to see it's only 5:06. She must have left at exactly 5:00.

I've never been so jealous of Katy and the time she's spent with Lainey today. I hope whatever has been bothering her gets resolved in the next twenty minutes.

When I pull up, Katy and Sawyer's cars are in my driveway. I know they are already inside because I gave them keys and codes well over a month ago. My palms sweat, and I rub them along my thighs, hoping to alleviate some of my nerves.

I feel a sense of dread as I approach the front door. It opens before I can reach the knob, and Katy gives me a weak smile.

"What's going on? Is Lainey okay?"

"She will be. I'm going to go. I got her here and made sure

415

she stayed. Just listen to her, okay?"

"You're scaring me, Katy." She looks over her shoulder into the house and back.

"Please, Elliot. Just listen."

"Okay." Katy walks past me, but I stop her when she's halfway down the sidewalk. "Katy." She turns and looks hopeful. "Thank you for being such a good friend to Lainey."

A half smile tilts her lips, and she nods before finishing the walk to her car.

I take a few cleansing breaths before stepping inside and closing the door behind me. Sawyer sits on the edge of the couch, his elbows resting on his knees, looking as nervous as I feel. Lainey sits alone in the armchair, looking guilty and anxious.

I remove my suit jacket and loosen my tie before sitting beside Sawyer. I kiss his temple and linger for a few extra seconds. It's obvious whatever we are about to go through, it's going to be together.

"Cherry, the anticipation is killing me. What's going on?" Next to me, Sawyer's leg bobs, and I place my hand on his thigh to offer him support.

"I... You know I love you both."

"Of course. And we love you." I speak for Sawyer because I don't think he can form words right now with as nervous as he looks. I can't imagine what's going through his head. This has been his person for over three years. They don't keep secrets. At least they didn't until whatever this is.

"I made a mistake. I got the piercing, and we were using condoms, and I wasn't paying close enough attention. Then there were the I love yous exchanged between us, and everything has been so incredible..."

416

Don't stop. Continue. The next word has to be a but, and I don't like the cliff that word leaves to fall off of.

"...but I can't do any of this anymore."

"...but I cheated on you."

"...but I only want to be with Sawyer."

"Lainey," I plead.

Even my hand on Sawyer's thigh isn't stopping his leg from bouncing. His hands are so tightly in fists that his knuckles are white.

"I'm..." Another pause, but that's not a but. "I'm pregnant."

Sawyer's body freezes. No bouncing leg, no breathing.

"That's it?"

Those aren't the first words I expect Sawyer to say when he finally speaks.

"That's it?" Lainey repeats incredulously.

"I thought you were leaving me or us."

"I—Oh god, no. I'm so sorry you thought that." Lainey stands and sits on the coffee table in front of us. Sawyer reaches for her and takes her hands.

Lainey is pregnant.

Pregnant.

It could be mine. She mentioned the piercing and the night we were all together. That was me. But we haven't used condoms since that night, so it could be Sawyer's, too.

"Elliot?" Lainey's sweet voice calls to me hesitantly.

I look at the two beautiful people next to me—the married couple who welcomed me into their lives.

Do I still fit?

Do they need me anymore?

I love them, but does a baby change things?

"Do I... Do you..."

A loud bang on the front door, followed by the push of the doorbell, disrupts the uncertainty in the air. The banging persists, and I hear a muffled but very familiar voice call my name.

"Mom?" I look back at Lainey and Sawyer before I get up, rushing toward the door to open it.

No sooner do I open the door than my mother crashes into me. She hugs me for two seconds before pushing me away.

"Why haven't you been answering your phone?!" She's erratic and emotional as she lifts her phone to her ear and resumes a conversation she was already having. "...He's here...We will be on a plane as soon as we can catch a flight... I know Hazel. I know."

Aunt Hazel? A plane? What the fuck?

"Mom. What are you doing here? What's going on?"

She looks at me for the first time, and I see her red-rimmed eyes. That's not jetlag. She's been crying. Where's Dad? Finn? Paige? Something happened.

"Mom?"

"Elliot, there's been an accident." I'm instantly panicking with flashbacks. Those are the exact words she spoke to Wynnie the day Scotty and Mac crashed their motorcycles. "Fuck. It wasn't an accident. He..." She pushes me again, and I see the rage fill every ounce of her body. "Why didn't you answer your fucking phone."

"Mom." I feel like a broken record. She hasn't given me any answers—only broken sentences. Tears stream down her face, and I can see whatever she's about to say is stuck in her throat.

Her knees give out, and I do my best to catch her in my

418

arms before she hits the ground. Dellah McLain has been through a lot, including the death of my parents, her best friends, and I've never seen her react like this before.

"Please tell me. What happened? Who's *he*?" My question seems to snap her out of her emotional state, and she pushes me away again and stands.

"We have to go—right now. I don't know when we can get a flight back home, but we'll wait until we can. We'll drive if it's faster.

I grab her shoulders and shake her from her rambling. "What. Happened."

"He's…gone. He was holding on, and I got on a plane to come and get you to bring you to her, but I had a voicemail when I landed, and…he's just gone."

I shake her again. "Dellah. Who is *he*?"

My mother looks me in the eyes with more determination and sorrow than I've ever seen. She takes a deep breath and says two words that rock my world.

# 56

# Sawyer

Lainey is pregnant. I've been a nervous wreck, wondering what she could want to talk to me about—to *us* about. She's pulled away from us all week, and I've had the worst-case scenarios running through my head.

Pregnant.

A baby.

We can handle a baby. We've wanted one but never talked about timing.

Elliot looks petrified. His eyes are wild.

"Elliot?" Lainey questions.

He begins to stammer when banging and yelling from the front door disrupts him.

"Mom?"

Lainey looks at me confused and mouths, "His mom." I shrug as Elliot opens the front door, and a woman collapses in his arms before violently pushing him away. She shouts about not answering his phone. She looks crazed like she's been crying, and she's rambling, not forming coherent sentences.

We've never met any of his family except his best friend and her husband, so having his mother here during such a critical time in our relationship feels monumental.

There was an accident. *He's* gone. She's trying to get him to go home on a plane. That's all the information I can gather until she finally focuses.

His mother looks him in the eyes and whispers words that make Elliot goes statue still. I didn't hear them, but Elliot pats his pockets, looking for his phone. I stand and grab his suit jacket, knowing he usually keeps it in there while at work. When I find it, I walk up to him and touch his shoulder. His entire body shutters away from me, and his head whips around. His face is stained with tears, and his eyes are wild. I raise the phone, and he looks at it, snatching it away. My eyes drift to his mother, and I give her a small smile. All I see in return is pain.

Lainey comes up behind me, and I tuck her under my arm.

"I'm Lainey. Is there anything we can do to help?"

With his phone to his ear, Elliot walks away from our conversation.

"Could you pack him a bag? A week—no, probably two weeks' worth of clothes and his toiletries."

"Of course."

Elliot walks back into the room. The sadness on his face has been replaced with anger, which seems to be directed at whoever he's on the phone with.

"… She's not answering her phone, so I called you…Well, put her on…Blake, I don't have time. I need it now. You know what? Never mind. I'll charter a fucking plane myself.

Tell her thank you for nothing."

Charter a plane? That takes Annie level money. Was he talking to Blake like that?

Lainey's phone rings as we walk to the bedroom, and the screen shows Blake on her caller ID. She answers and puts the call on speaker.

"Hello? Blake?"

"Are you with Elliot?"

"Yeah, but I don't know what's going on. Was he talking to you like that?"

Blake sighs. "I don't imagine he wants to hear my voice right now. Please tell him Annie has called her pilot, and they are getting her plane ready to take him home."

I pull clothes out of Elliot's drawer and look for something to put them in.

"Home? He mentioned chartering his own plane."

"I know, Lainey. And he could, but Annie's is getting ready. He just has to show up. Tell him he can have as much time as he needs. His job is safe. If you need to take time off, too, we understand. Just let him know we send our love."

"Blake, I'm sorry he spoke to you like that."

"It's okay. He's grieving. It's to be expected. Take care of him."

They disconnect their call, and Elliot paces back into the room, shouting at whoever he's on the phone with.

Lainey gently reaches up and pulls the phone away from his ear. His emotions are volatile, and I brace myself to react if he gets aggressive with her.

She removes the phone while keeping eye contact with him and disconnects the call. He's fuming. His breathing sounds like a bull ready to charge at the first flash of red.

Lainey touches his cheek, and his eyes slam shut. The tears begin again and stream past his lashes in rivulets.

With a soft voice more suited for a child, Lainey speaks to Elliot.

"Blake called me. Annie's plane will be ready to take you home whenever you get there. You don't need to waste money to charter your own plane."

He huffs at her words. "It wouldn't be a waste of money. I doubt I'd even notice the blip in my bank account."

Blip? Chartering a plane probably costs tens of thousands of dollars.

"Elliot?"

"It's a conversation for another day, but let's just say I have a very healthy bank account. Did Blake say how long?"

He's shutting us out. We still don't know what happened, and I think we deserve to know.

"How long will you be gone? Your mother said to pack for two weeks." I've stayed quiet up until this point, but I refuse to be cast aside.

"I don't know. I imagine longer."

"Blake said to tell you to take as much time as you need."

He nods and tries to step away from Lainey, but I close him in from behind and wrap my arms around his waist. He stiffens, whether from the foreign position or my nearness, but I don't care. He needs us whether he realizes it or not.

"What happened, Elliot?"

# 57

# Elliot

"What happened, Elliot?"

I don't know.

I don't fucking know, and standing here isn't giving me any answers.

"I have to go." I don't even care about packing anything right now. I just need to get home. I feel like a caged animal trapped between Sawyer and Lainey.

"Elliot." Lainey grabs my hand and places it on her lower belly.

*The baby.*

I still haven't given them any answers about the baby yet.

*Fuck.*

"It's probably not mine."

Lainey recoils back like I've slapped her; emotionally, it feels like I have. I'm dying inside and can't make any rational thoughts or decisions right now.

"I'm going to allow you to speak to my wife like that only once because something is going on, but you need to watch yourself. What happened, Elliot?"

I chuckle. He said *"my wife"* like she hasn't also been mine for the last several months.

I turn to face Sawyer, and he loosens his grip to allow me space.

"You're right, Sawyer. She is *your wife*. Maybe it's easier if we just say it's *your baby*, too. I don't know when or if I'll be back. It might be easier if I just walk away."

Lainey pushes at my shoulder, and I have nothing in me to stop her. Nor do I stop or even flinch when her hand slaps me across the face. I deserve it. Her tears only add to my pain.

I hang my head as I hear Lainey sob. Sawyer steps in and removes the space I left to embrace Lainey. I listen to them moving around, then their footsteps follow me to the living room, where my mother is talking on the phone. She quickly hangs up and looks at my empty hands.

"Are you ready to go? I got us a plane."

Her hand gently brushes what I assume is Lainey's handprint on my cheek.

"Your bag?"

"I can get anything I need when we get there."

I walk out the front door, needing some air, but not too far that I can't hear their conversation.

"Whatever he did to make you slap him, young lady, I'm sure he deserved it."

"We packed him a bag."

My mother thanks Sawyer, and I assume she takes whatever he packed for me.

"Mrs. McLain—"

"Dellah. Please call me Dellah, Lainey."

"Okay. Dellah, what happened? He didn't tell us."

"He didn't—oh my god. I'll take care of that for you. Now I know why you slapped him."

There's a long pause of silence, and I wonder if they are speaking too low for me to hear. When my mother finally speaks, I realize the pause was for her tears.

"You met his best friend, Wynnie, right?" Lainey gasps. "No, not her. Her husband, Scotty. Scotty died. He's dead. He was... murdered."

*Murdered.*

I hadn't even asked what happened when she told me. I was too deep in the emotional depths of her two simple words to me.

*"Scotty died."*

There isn't one reason over another that can make it any better. He's gone. My best friend lost her husband—the love of her life. And now, I have to leave the two loves of my life because family is more important to me than my own happiness. I survived my childhood because of Wynnie, and I will help her survive the loss of Scotty.

"Mom, we need to go." *Before* my words to Sawyer and Lainey catch up with me, I need to go. That *could* be my baby. Despite my turmoil of wondering where I fit in, there was a fleeting moment before my mother knocked on the door. A split second when I imagined Sawyer and me encouraging Lainey through labor. Bringing home our baby, and raising our beautiful family. Together. It was gone as quickly as it came.

Grief.

Heartbreak.

Despair.

Those are the emotions currently at the forefront of my mind. Getting to Wynnie, my best fucking friend, and holding her together because I know she's in pieces right now.

Fuck. I'll be happy to find pieces. Wynnie is probably shattered.

I don't care. No matter how long it takes, I'll sweep up her pieces and glue her back together.

"Dellah!" It's the last warning I'm giving her. I'll leave her behind and let her find her own way back. I have my wallet and cards. That's all I need.

🖭 🖭 🖭 🖭 🖭

When we arrived at the airport, Annie's plane was ready and waiting. I parked in long-term parking and wondered if I'd ever see my car again. I'll probably have someone come and pick it up for me, but that's a problem for another day.

My mother and I didn't speak the entire time. She cried herself to sleep, and I was happy for the emotional reprieve. The guilt was eating me up inside. When I finally looked at my phone on the plane, I saw all the missed calls and texts from different members of my family.

Mom: Elliot, there's been an emergency. Call me.

Dad: Where are you? Your mom is on a flight to come get you. Something has happened.

Aunt Hazel: El, we need you. Please answer someone.

Finn: Where the fuck are you?!?!?!?!?

Uncle Phoenix: Elliot

Dozens more texts awaited me, but I paused at Uncle Phoenix's, Scotty's best friend since high school. I've never had such an emotional reaction to seeing my name written in a text. Six letters is all he could manage to type before hitting send.

"Fuck!" The word hisses through my teeth as I slam my head against the back of the seat. There's nothing I could have done. Even from the first missed call, I was hours away. I chose to leave my family behind and pursue a career. I've never felt more selfish in my entire life.

Nothing. NOTHING can compare to the state I find my family in when we arrive at Aunt Hazel's house. The silence when we walk in slams me in the face. There's no joy, no laughing kids. Only quietness and the heavy weight of grief.

"Where is everyone?" I whisper to my mom, afraid to burst the noiseless bubble.

"Maybe at Wynnie's? I know the kids are supposed to be here. That's the last thing Hazel told me."

As if speaking her name, Aunt Hazel appears around the corner with Piper, her youngest, on her hip. Her eyes are puffy and laced with sorrow.

"Oh, hi. I didn't hear you guys come in." Her attempt at a smile barely lifts her lips.

"Aunt Hazel, I..." I have no fucking idea what to say.

"I know, Elliot. I know." Piper yawns and rests her head on her mom's shoulder. "Everyone is in the movie room. It's been a cartoon and electronic day."

"Is she—"

"No. She's home... with her kids." She glances at my mom, concern marring her face. "She came by a few hours ago and took them back. I tried to stop her, but she was determined.

Jude is with them."

"Go. I'll stay here with Hazel."

I kiss each of their cheeks, and my mom hands me her keys so I can drive to the other side of the property.

As I pull up to Wynnie's house, every light is on, flooding the area with brightness. It's close to the kids' bedtime, and the sight confuses me. Stepping out, I hear loud pop music permeating the air as if there's a party going on. If the lights and music weren't confusing enough, the sight I see when I open the door makes my jaw drop. I expect to see my best friend in a heap of tears. Instead, she's dancing around in the kitchen, bouncing Archie on her hip with Ella twirling and spinning in a sparkly pink party dress. The worst part, though, is she's wearing white. Specifically, the white of a wedding dress. *Her* wedding dress.

I close the door behind me and tentatively step into the room. "Wynnie?" Unsurprisingly, she doesn't hear me over the loud music, but someone else does. A blur crashes into me, and I immediately wrap my arms around Tori.

"Uncle Elliot." Her voice cracks as she sobs into my chest.

"Baby girl." I squeeze her tighter. I don't know what to say. What *can* I say? Her father is gone, and her mother seems to be having some kind of mental breakdown.

Wynnie still hasn't noticed me, so I lead Tori down the hall to her bedroom and close the door to muffle some of the music. I sit on the bed and pull her into my lap. She might be ten, but her petite frame curls into me like a toddler.

Her body shutters as her tears come harder. Rocking her in my arms is all I can do at the moment. I still haven't processed anything in the few short hours I've known, and she's known longer.

Fuck. She's only ten. I was young when I lost my mother, and over the years, my memories of her have faded, but I was only a few years older than her when my father died. I remember every second of grief and anger I felt. Wynnie is in the other room, ignoring...everything, it seems.

"I'm so sorry, Tori." I know all too well those words mean nothing, but I understand that any words are better than none. Especially when in this kind of an emotional state.

Kissing the top of her head, I look around her room and see the mess and destruction around us. This isn't a normal pre-teen type of mess. This is anger, aggression, and grief. Things are thrown around the room. Art supplies are upended and tossed around.

How long has she been stewing with her emotions alone while Wynnie has a party in the other room?

I want to be angry, but I can't. There's no wrong way to grieve, but I know avoiding is the worst way, and that's exactly what my best friend is doing.

"Tori, can I call Aunt Hazel or Dellah to come get you? I thought my mom said Grandpa J was here?"

She sniffs and nods into my chest, turning her head so I can hear her speak.

"He tried talking to Mom, but she ignored him. He's been sitting on the back patio. He didn't want to leave her alone but couldn't watch her act like... that." Tori's gaze drifts to her door as the music changes from one upbeat song to the next.

"How about I take you to him while I try and talk to her."

"Okay."

I find Jude exactly where Tori said he'd be. His face is just as sullen as expected.

"Uncle Jude?" He jumps up, his sandy blonde hair a disheveled mess.

"Elliot. Tori." He looks around, for what I'm not sure. His eyes drift to the kitchen window just as we see a bouncing Wynnie pass by the glass. He hangs his head and drops back to the chair.

Tori jumps in his lap, needing his comfort. "Take me back. Please, Grandpa J. I can't be here."

"Of course, Sweetheart. I'll take you to my house." Jude looks at me with pleading eyes. Their cinnamon color, the same as Piper's, almost looks black with the weight of his grief.

"I've got her, Uncle Jude. Let me see if I can get the other kids for you to take, too."

"She won't let them go easily." He wipes a hand down his face and through his hair. "Archie will fall asleep soon if she lets him. See if you can at least get Ella."

I nod and run a soothing hand through Tori's brown hair, the same color as Scotty's. She's his mini-me.

Stepping back into the house isn't any less shocking than the first time. In fact, it's worse. Ella's exhaustion is written on her face. Can she understand at only four that her daddy isn't ever coming home again?

Of course, she does. I remember the weeks after my mother died. Finn was similar in age to Ella, and while my father navigated his life as a single widowed dad with a newborn, I held Finn together when he would cry for his mommy.

"Wynnie?" I grab her shoulder mid-bounce and she gasps, turning in my direction with a huge smile on her face. It falters for one, two, three seconds before the fakeness is plastered all over again.

"Hey, bestie! Are you joining our dance party?"

Dipping down, I pick up Ella, and she smiles at my presence, clueless to the chaos around her.

"Wynnie, Jude is going to take Tori and Ella to his house. Can he take Archie, too?"

"Nonsense. We're having a party! Don't you want to stay with Mommy and dance?" She wiggles her fingers at Ella, who buries her head into my neck.

"Let me take her." Tori reaches across me, and Ella happily goes to her sister. Jude gives me a reassuring smile, and I try to get through to Wynnie again.

"Wynnie, let them take Archie. He's half asleep already." She looks down to see his droopy blue eyes, and her bouncing falters and slows to a stop. She hands him over to Jude's awaiting arms with a smile as if she's doing him a favor by allowing him to take her toddler.

"He was getting heavy, anyway. Tequila, Elliot?"

Wynnie turns toward the liquor cabinet, the tulle of her dress swooshing around her legs. The back lays unzipped, as the years and babies have changed her body, and it doesn't quite fit anymore.

"I'll take care of them; you take care of her. Thank you, Elliot." Jude looks at Wynnie and sighs. "Good luck."

# 58

# Elliot

Alone in the house, I take the offered bottle of tequila. No shot glasses or salt are needed for a night like this. Wynnie reaches in and grabs another bottle for herself. Apparently, we aren't sharing.

She's drinking and not talking. I need to get through to her. She's no longer dancing around the house but using the bottle like a microphone while sitting on the floor in a plume of white satin and tulle.

I remember the tears her dress brought to my eyes as she walked down the aisle. I helped her pick out her dress. I was there for every alteration, but nothing compared to the look she had as she walked down the white rose-covered aisle toward the man she loved.

Scotty is gone.

I still don't know how. My mom told Lainey and Sawyer he was murdered. A murder in our small little town is unheard of. Was Uncle Mac working when it happened? Did he have to respond to the scene?

Fuck, of course, he responded. Working or not, he would have been there as soon as he found out.

I need to know, and she needs to talk about it. With me. I sit on the floor next to her, pushing the dress aside and getting as close to her as I can. She watches me while tipping the bottle to her lips like she's drinking water.

"Wynnie—"

"I'm fine, Elliot. You didn't need to leave your cushy life to come dote on poor little me. I'm sure you have more important things to be doing for your big wig boss."

Shit. I deserved that. Although, of all the missed calls and texts today, not a single one was from her. She didn't reach out.

"Wynnie, will you—"

"Just go back to Chicago. You already took my kids away from me tonight. What more do you want from me?"

She's hurting. She's hurting so fucking much, and I'll happily be her punching bag.

"Rowyn, please—"

"Ugh. Give it up, Elliot. Whatever you have to say, I don't want to hear it."

I squeeze my eyes shut. *Fuck.* I hate to do this, but I need to get through to her, and she needs to listen to me.

"Pinky."

Wynnie flies at me. Her hand smacks across my cheek, and for the second time today, one of the other most important people in my life hits me. But Wynnie doesn't stop there. She pushes my chest until I'm flat on the floor and climbs on top of me. White swaths of fabric swallow her as her arms flail, and she hits any part of my body that her hands can connect with.

Arms. Chest. Shoulders. I take it all. I take it as her hits weaken. Her face morphs from rage to grief to desperation. Wynnie's dam breaks. Her body collapses onto me, and she screams into my chest. I wrap my arms around her, and she screams until she's hoarse.

She sits up and frantically claws at her body, tears still streaming down her face. She's trying to get the dress off, but she's so lost in her grief she's clawing at her skin.

"Let me help you."

"Get it off. I want it off." She's frantic. I sit up and help her gently remove the cap sleeves of the dress and lower the zipper the few inches she was able to reach when she put it on.

She stands, and the dress pools around us. She steps out of it and pushes the material to the side before climbing back into my lap and wrapping herself around me. I maneuver my hands between the two of us and unbutton my shirt.

"Sit back. Let me put this on you." She releases me long enough to help put her arms in the sleeves and drapes back over me. While I'm no stranger to seeing her in a bra and underwear, I'd rather her not be so vulnerable.

Getting to my knees, I stand and carry us toward her bedroom. When I reach the doorway, she shakes her head on my chest.

"Guest room," she hiccups out.

I walk us further down the hall and place her on the bed. There's no fight left in her. I go to the top drawer of the dresser, where I have a few spare clothes to change into, and take out a black t-shirt. Wynnie lets me switch her from my starched dress shirt to the soft t-shirt, and I strip down my boxers.

435

She's like a ragdoll in my arms as I place her into the bed and lay next to her. She curls into me like I'm her lifeline, and I am. I'll be here and be whatever and whoever she needs me to be.

Eventually, her crying stops, and her breathing slows. She's fallen asleep. The weight of the day pulls me under shortly after her.

The smell of coffee wakes me, and I smile, thinking of the perfect cup of coffee that Sawyer will have waiting for me as soon as he knows I'm up. I curl into the tiny body in my arms and take a deep breath.

The smell is wrong. My eyes fly open, and the evening rushes to my mind like a brick wall as I realize I'm holding Wynnie, not Lainey.

Who's making coffee? Maybe they have an automatic pot?

As carefully as possible so as not to wake Wynnie, I crawl out of bed and grab a pair of sweatpants. Hushed voices float down the hall as I head toward the smell of coffee.

Uncle Mac and Finn stand at the counter. Instant regret for missing their attempts of communication yesterday must show on my face. Finn charges toward me, and I brace for a hit, but he knocks the wind out of me when he wraps me in a hug instead. I only hesitate for a moment before I return it.

When he releases me, I open my mouth to apologize, and he shakes his head. "How is she?" His eyes drift down the hall, and I see the pain behind them.

"Sleeping."

"Has she cried?" Mac looks as tortured as the rest of us. He lost not only his son-in-law but a great friend.

"Yeah. After some tequila"—I rub my cheek, remembering

her assault—"and some fighting."

Mac's eyes trail to her wedding dress that someone laid across the couch. "And that?"

"When I got here, she was wearing it while dancing around the house like she was having a party."

"Jude said it was bad when he brought the kids over, but we were all so exhausted we went right to bed. Fuck, I didn't know it was this bad, or I would have come over here and given him back up." He runs a hand down his face. "At least she's cried some."

Mac is the oldest of Aunt Hazel's husbands but he's never looked it—until today. Somehow, the silver streaks at his temples look whiter, and his bright blue eyes, which Wynnie inherited, look dull. He's hurting like the rest of us.

"What can we do, El?" Finn pleads. It seems everyone is feeling helpless.

"I don't know. What I do know is no one has told me what happened other than... he's gone." Finn's eyes gloss over, and I pull him into my side. "I'm not asking you to tell me. Either of you. I want her to tell me." I look at Mac, whose face has gone blank. "Unless there's something I should know that she doesn't."

Mac shakes his head. "She knows everything."

"Good. Then on her time, I will, too."

"How long are you here for, kid?" Mac sips his coffee, wondering how long I have to help them deal with this situation. And yes, Wynnie is currently a situation.

"Indefinitely."

"But—" Finn questions, but I cut him off.

"Indefinitely. You know I don't need to work, but that woman back there needs me, and I won't leave her high and

437

dry. Ever."

"So… you're back?" Finn's voice is hopeful, and it breaks my heart even more that I left them.

"I'm back."

"Elliot, you've created a life out there. You have *people* there." I appreciate Mac's concern, but I can't think about it right now. I can't, or my already bleeding heart will cease to exist right on this kitchen floor.

"And they have each other. *She* needs me."

I can see he wants to protest, but his level of respect for my decision outweighs any objections.

# 59

## Wynnie

This isn't my bed. It smells like my detergent, but there's a smell missing. The lemony, earthy scent that is unique to my husband.

Was.

That *was* unique to my husband. I'll never smell it again. Him again.

Turning my face into the pillow, I sob while silently cursing Elliot for pulling me out of my dance party last night. I know it was selfish of me, but I wanted to pretend for just a little while longer. I was used to not seeing him until late. Even though he'd given away most of the responsibility over the years to his trusted staff, he would always step in whenever needed. Especially if it was after the kids went to bed and he knew his responsibilities for the day had lessened.

"Wynnie?" Elliot's voice breaks me even further, and all I can do is reach out an arm for him to help me. The air leaves my lungs, and I feel like I'm drowning. The moment he crawls into bed, I climb onto him.

"E-E-E-El…" That's all I can manage of his name through my hyperventilation.

"Breathe with me, Wynnie. Breathe. In"—his chest inflates under my cheek—"out."

"C-C-Can't…b-b-b-bre-e-e-e-th." My vision blurs with tears, and spots dance around the edges.

"Look at me. You're safe. I'm here with you. In and out."

I stare into his blue eyes and try to mimic his breathing. My chest hurts, and it feels hopeless. Everything feels hopeless, but I continue to try.

"That's it. I've got you. In and out."

Without realizing it, my breathing has calmed. I continue to suck in long, even breaths until Elliot pulls me back into him. My tears still freely flow, but I can breathe again.

I hear a buzzing somewhere in the room and know it can't be my phone because I put it on silent after I left the hospital yesterday.

"El, your phone."

"It's fine." His arms wrap tighter around me, and my sadness is momentarily pushed aside. His tone tells me he isn't "fine." Nothing, and no one is "fine" right now.

"What's going on?"

"Wynnie, this isn't about me right now. I'm here for you."

I know he is. I fucking know it, and that's the problem. I know my best friend, and I know he would, and probably did, drop everything in his life to be here with me right now.

"Elliot, talk to me."

He chuckles. "Shouldn't that be my line?"

I sigh heavily into his chest and pull back. "You still don't know, do you?"

He shakes his head, and his blue eyes are murky with emotion. I imagine mine probably look similar.

"How about we make a deal? I'll tell you mine if you tell me yours."

"Your dad and my brother are here. Your mom sent over food, and they made coffee. Let's get some food in you then we can lay in bed the rest of the day and commiserate together."

"I..." I love my family and know everyone will be here for me. We're all in pain, but no one can understand what I'm feeling right now. "Could we do breakfast in bed? I'm not feeling very social."

"Yeah, of course." Elliot kisses my forehead and gets out of bed. I look down at myself and realize I'm wearing an unfamiliar shirt and not much else. "Elliot?" He stops at the door. "I'd like some pants."

A small laugh escapes him. "I'll grab you some comfy clothes too."

While Elliot gets us breakfast, I sneak into the guest bathroom across the hall. I want to brush my teeth and wash away some of the aftermath of tequila and crying. Opening the bottom cabinet to grab a spare toothbrush, I freeze and cover my mouth to stop the loud noise from the sob that immediately escapes me. My other hand grips the counter to keep me upright while I take deep breaths.

I pivot my body and sit on the edge of the tub, trying to will the tears to stop. How can a bottle of saline solution pull emotions like this from me?

Because it's his.

Because no matter how many times you tried to convince him that his heterochromia made him unique and not strange, he still put in a brown contact every day to look his version of normal.

Him. His.

I can't even say his name.

"S-s-s." I huff. "You can do this. Sc-Sc-Sc...FUCK!" I ball my fists into my hair and pull. Physical pain is preferable to the gaping chasm in my chest. My body slumps to the floor just as the bathroom door flies open.

"Sweetheart. Wynnie, are you okay?"

"No! No, Dad. I'm not okay. Nothing is fucking okay!" Two more sets of feet enter the room while I scream at no one and everyone.

My dad crouches at my feet and gently touches my knee. I flinch at the contact, but he doesn't pull away.

"I know this sucks. This sucks so fucking bad. What can I do right this moment to help you?"

I point to the cabinet and mumble "contacts." Elliot immediately knows what I'm saying and turns his body toward me to block my view while he rummages under the sink. He hands things to Finn and tells him to get rid of it, then joins my dad next to me on the floor.

"Are you ready to eat and talk? We made a deal."

"Teeth first." I still need to brush my teeth. It seems like such a stupid thing to want to do right now, but I can't fall entirely apart. My kids need me.

One day. I'm going to allow myself only today to not be a parent. They need me to hold them together, but not today.

"Dad, are the kids okay? Can they stay with you today?"

He gives me a half smile and squeezes my leg. "Of course. They are happy and safe with us for as long as you need. We'll never say no to our grandkids."

"Come on, bestie. I think my brother has stared at your pink panties long enough."

"What? Oh god! Finn, I'm so sorry." I quickly scramble my legs under me, having forgotten I was wearing only a t-shirt. My cousin's cheeks turn bright red as I try to cover myself.

"I swear I didn't see anything, Wynnie. I would never—"

"Out, boy." My dad's commanding voice makes Finn turn on his heels and disappear. "I'll grab breakfast and bring it to you two... in the guest room?"

"Please. I love you, Dad." I throw myself into his arms. Maybe I was up for being a little social.

With everyone gone, I finally brush my teeth and change into the clothes Elliot brought me. When I return to the room, fresh coffee, muffins, and fruit sit on the nightstand, and Elliot stares at his phone with his fingers hovering over the keypad.

"It won't bite?"

"What?" His head tilts as he tries to understand my comment.

"The phone. You look like you're afraid of it. What did they say?"

He sets the phone face down on the comforter and pats the bed beside him. "You first."

I grab the coffee cup and sit on the bed. "No."

"I didn't say anything?" Elliot looks around the room to see if I was responding to someone else.

"No. I'm not going first. Tell me what's going on with you."

"Wynnie," he sighs.

"Elliot, humor the widow." He inhales sharply. "Too soon?"

My lower lip quivers as I attempt a smile, but it fails, and the tears fall. "Please. Distract me for a little longer before I have to relive it."

"Okay. Ugh. You're cruel." He picks up his phone again, unlocks it, and stares.

"Lainey is pregnant."

I gasp and almost choke on my coffee. "Elliot, that's... Is there a chance it's yours?"

He nods before he speaks. "A pretty good one if her timing is correct."

"Fuck. And?"

"And what? I found out about it two minutes before my mother knocked on my door. I yelled at my boss' wife in an attempt to get here to you, and I left. You're all caught up."

"Oh, Elliot. Have you spoken to them? What are you going to do?"

He hangs his head, and a moment later, tears drop onto the comforter.

"I pushed them away before I left. I told them it was probably better if they just considered it their baby."

I reach my hand out to soothe him. "El—"

"No." He aggressively wipes at his eyes. "No. Whatever you're going to say or tell me to do, if it involves me leaving you, the answer is no. I'm here. You need me." He grabs my hand and twirls my wedding ring around my finger. The yellow stones sparkle in the morning light, and my eyes well up. "I'm here because you need me, and I have nowhere else I'd rather be."

I want to argue, but I want to be selfish. Don't I deserve that right now?

"It's your turn."

I bob my head in acknowledgment. It bobs over and over. And over. My pulse increases, and my palms become sweaty. Just thinking about it makes my adrenaline rush, and I tremble. Elliot pulls me into his lap, and I curl into a ball and let him hold me.

"We heard the entire thing."

*"Yes, Pinky," Scotty says exaggeratedly. "I'll remember to pick up milk and Q-tips. Anything else? Why don't you text me a list. I'm sure you'll think of a few more things before this afternoon."*

*"You're such a jerk. I better add flowers to the list so you look like a good husband later when you grovel for my forgiveness."*

*The growl that comes through the line sends shivers through my body. "Someone will be on their knees, but I promise it won't be me."*

*"Prove it."*

*Bottles clink in the background as he continues counting inventory despite my teasing, and his next words come out hushed and gravelly.*

*"If you want to be a little brat, Rowyn, your punishment can be arranged."*

*"I love it when you threaten me. Go finish your counting so you can get home already. I love you."*

*"Uh huh. I love you t—Hey. Sorry, we're closed. We don't open until two."*

*"Scotty? Who are you talking to?"*

*"Put the phone down," a muffled voice tells Scotty in the background.*

*"Okay, yeah. No problem." I hear the thunk of the phone as it hits the bar top. "What can I get you? We're fresh out of avocados if that's what you came looking for."*

*Avocados? The bar barely sells food. We definitely don't sell avocados.*

"I don't want fucking avocados. I want the cash."

*Cash? Avocados? SHIT! Shitshit.*

*Our safeword is avocado.*

*Scotty is in danger. He's being robbed.*

*I run to the kitchen and grab the walkie-talkie we keep to communicate between the houses and hit the S.O.S. button. A loud screeching sound rings through the air, and I know someone in my parent's house will hear it on their end.*

"Open the drawer," *the intruder says.*

"We aren't open yet. There's nothing in there."

"Bullshit. Open the fucking drawer."

*Outside my house, I hear two motorcycle engines roaring in my direction. Seconds later, my dad and Phoenix barrel in, guns ready.*

"What's wrong?" *Phoenix stays with me as my dad clears the house.*

*With a trembling hand, I hit the speaker button and put my phone down.*

"There's a safe in my office. I can take you in there and get you the cash."

*Phoenix's eyes wide, and he mouths,* "What the fuck." *My dad walks back into the room and opens his mouth to speak. Phoenix raises a hand to stop him and motions to his ear for Mac to listen.*

"Do you think I'm fucking stupid? I'm not going anywhere. Open the register. I know you're fucking lying."

"Okay. I'll give you whatever you want. Could you put the gun down?"

*I clamp both hands over my mouth, and Phoenix catches me as I collapse to the floor. My dad leaves the room, phone in hand.*

*I know he's calling it into the station.*

*Phoenix pushes a button on my phone and looks me in the eyes. "I put it on mute. Is Scotty at the bar alone?"*

*Shaking my head, I barely have enough air to choke out, "Kristina." I take fistfuls of Phoenix's shirt in my hands. I'm visibly shaking.*

*"Mac," Phoenix calls. "We're muted. Kristina and Scotty are both there."*

*My dad returns to the room, barking directions to whoever is on the phone.*

*"They're on their way."*

*"You fucking asshole. Where's the goddamn money!" I startle at the rage in the man's voice.*

*"In the office safe. I'll take you."*

*I have no idea how Scotty is managing to sound so calm with a man wielding a gun at him. I'm not there, and I'm ready to crawl out of my skin with fear.*

*My hands hurt with how tight they're clutched in Phoenix's shirt, but he doesn't say a word as he holds me while we listen.*

*"Show me. Let's go."*

*Their voices trail off as they move toward the office, and I panic. I stand, picking up the phone and turning the volume as loud as possible. I'm frantic as I spin in a circle, feeling like I need to be doing something, but there's nothing."*

*"Dad?!"*

*"They're rushing, Sweetheart."*

*"Why are we just standing here? Let's go." I try to leave, but thick arms wrap around my body.*

*"Mac's guys will take care of him. Don't worry. Everything is going to be okay."*

*I want to believe him. I need to believe him, but I want Scotty* in my arms. I won't believe he's safe until I'm holding him.

"Okay... My guys are two minutes out."

A feminine scream pierces the room from the phone, followed by two loud bangs.

"Tell me those were fireworks. TELL ME THOSE WERE FIREWORKS!" I'm screaming. Or the person through the phone is screaming. Maybe both.

My entire body goes limp in Phoenix's arms.

"My guys are pulling in."

"Dad. We have to go. We have to go now."

A surge of adrenaline courses through me, and I manage to fight my way out of Phoenix's arms. Shouting comes through the speaker.

Police officers identify themselves.

Kristina's voice shouts. I only catch pieces of words.

"...office... shot... back door."

"No. Dad. Help him. Fucking do something."

Several more gunshots are heard muffled further into the room.

"Yeah... you got him? They got the suspect, Wynnie."

"Scoooootty," I whine.

My dad listens on the phone, and I hold my breath, waiting for any information. "Twice? Okay, we'll meet you there."

"Is he..."

"Alive, but... fuck I'm no doctor. Let's go."

Phoenix hugs me and kisses the top of my head before finally letting me go. "I'll stay and let everyone know what's going on. Keep me posted, Mac."

"You don't want to go? I can stay back. He's your bes—"

"No. I'm good."

The ride to the hospital takes an eternity. I'm squeezing my dad's waist so tight I'm not sure how he's breathing. The

448

*paramedics are pulling Scotty out of the ambulance when we pull up. There's so much blood covering the white sheets, and I practically jump off the back of the motorcycle the second we stop.*

*"Scotty." I run to him, and he's pale. So pale and fragile looking, but his eyes open for me, and his fingers wiggle. I grab his hand and squeeze.*

*"Pinky. You're here." His voice is weak, but his lip twitches in an attempt to smile. I place a gentle kiss on his lips and inhale his smell. It's wrong. There's no faint scent of lemon, only copper.*

*"Let's go," a stout paramedic yells as he slams the back doors to the ambulance.*

*"I'm here. And you better stay here too."*

*His eyes flutter closed, and I run along with the stretcher until a member of the hospital staff stops me.*

*"We have to take him back, ma'am. You need to step back." I can't even tell you who spoke because my eyes blur from tears. "Ma'am, please."*

*"Scotty, I love you. Tori, Ella, and Archie love you. Stay with us, okay? I love you, Scotty. Say it back." I squeeze his hand again. "Open your eyes and say it back!" I'm shouting at my husband, who's bleeding out in the middle of the Emergency Room, but he needs to know, and I need to hear it.*

*His left eye opens a fraction, and without his lips moving, I hear his labored breath and the whisper of words. "Love... you." The machine he's attached to beeps a steady tone, and strong arms grab my shoulders as Scotty's hand slips from mine, and he disappears behind double doors.*

*"Sweetheart—"*

*"No!" I scream. I spin in my father's arm and beat the sides of my fists against his chest. "No. No, he's going to be fine. They*

*are going to fix him up, and he'll come back to us."*

*A man in a jumpsuit puts his hand on Mac's shoulder. "Excuse me, Sir." He looks down at the floor. "We need to clean up."*

*I collapse into my father's arms from the sight in front of me. The floor is streaked with blood, leading through the double doors that my husband just went through.*

*It's his blood.*

*Scotty's blood.*

*"Shh, Wynnie. I've got you."*

*"Mom?"*

*"I'm here. I need you to stop screaming, or they are going to make us leave."*

*I don't know when she got here, and I had no idea I was screaming. All I know is the love of my life disappeared through a set of double doors, leaving me behind. The ache in my heart tells me he won't be coming back out.*

# 60

# Elliot

I'm crying so hard there's no use even trying to dry my face. Wynnie is cradled in my arms while I gently rock us. I think she fell asleep. She's been quiet for the last five minutes after telling me about the most horrific day of her life.

No wonder I found her dancing in her wedding dress when I arrived last night. I can't believe she was even upright after hearing how Scotty...

She watched him take his last breath. The doctor told her they could never get him back after his heart stopped. He had lost too much blood.

Not only did Wynnie hear Scotty get shot, but Uncle Phoenix and Uncle Mac did, too.

I must have drifted off to sleep because I'm jarred awake by screaming. Next to me, Wynnie is curled into a ball, crying and begging for Scotty.

"Hey." I gently shake her. "Wynnie, it's okay. I'm here. You're safe." No response. I shake her harder, and still nothing. Pulling her into my lap, she screams again, and I feel so helpless. "Please, wake up for me. I'm here. Shhh."

Wynnie's eyes pop open, but I don't think she sees me. She frantically scans the room when her wild blue eyes stop on mine.

"You stayed."

I open my mouth to respond, because of course I stayed, when she grabs my cheeks and locks her lips with mine.

I freeze.

Wynnie is kissing me. She's whimpering into my mouth. Warm tears splash across my face and I don't know what to do.

"You stayed. I knew you wouldn't leave us."

*Fuck.* She thinks I'm Scotty. Fuck.

"Wynnie," I mumble under her lips.

"I love you. You stayed. You stayed."

"Wynnie," I try again. I have to stop this. She's lost halfway between sleep and awake, and I know she's going to be mortified when she realizes what she's doing. "Wynnie." I grab her arms and push her away. Her hands grip my face tighter, and out of sheer desperation, I bite her lip to snap her out of her haze.

She jolts back, not understanding the aggression, when recognition washes over her face.

"Oh fuck." Her hands smack over her mouth, and she falls off the bed in her attempt to get away from me.

"Oh shit. Are you okay?"

Wynnie's shoulders shake, and I wait to hear her tears, but I'm shocked to silence when I hear laughter instead.

She's laughing, and it sparks a tiny jolt of joy in my heart.

"I...I...kissed you." She can barely get the words out

452

through her hysterical fit.

"Geez, Wynnie. Way to bruise a guy's ego." I laugh with her because her sound is infectious.

"Eww," she shoves my shoulder and wipes at her mouth, pretending to wipe away my lips.

Her hand pauses, and her fingers gently graze her bottom lip. I see it tremble, and the air in the room shifts from light to heavy as she remembers something.

"I didn't know," she whispers.

"Didn't know what?" I slide off the bed and join her on the floor.

"I didn't know it would be the last. I was running out the door to drive the kids to school and yelled goodbye. He jogged out to me as I was about to pull away and leaned into my window to kiss me goodbye. It was such a mundane kiss. I-I didn't know it would be our last."

For what seems like the hundredth time, I pull Wynnie into my arms and hold her while she cries. I don't care how many times I need to do this for her. I'll do it a hundred more times if it will help her heal.

When her crying stops, I glance at the clock and see we've slept most of the afternoon.

"Hey, your dad mentioned everyone was coming over there for dinner tonight. Think you're up for it? If not, I'll have someone deliver it for us."

She sniffs and lifts her head. "I should go. If for nothing else than to see my kids." Her face changes to panic, and she looks at the door. "Tori." Her daughter's name is pure pain as it leaves her lips.

While Wynnie isn't her biological mother, there has never been a day that she's treated Tori like anything other than hers.

"DJ has been doing a great job distracting Tori from what I've heard, but I'm sure she'd love to see you. Especially after the wedding dress dancing."

Wynnie groans and sits back, wrapping her arms around her legs. She rests her cheek against her knees and closes her eyes. Her lashes are wet with tears, and I brush a finger through her hair, moving it away.

"This may not be an appropriate time to ask this, but is all the paperwork in order for Tori? She's yours right? I'd hate a repeat of—"

"Yes." Her head pops up as she says the word with more conviction than I've heard her say anything since I got here. "Tori is mine in all aspects of the law. We crossed every T and dotted every I years ago. He made sure no one could take her away from me ever again."

"Good. I just wanted to make sure."

"I should shower before we head over."

"You don't have to if you're not ready." I want her to move at her own pace, and I know she's hardheaded. If I hadn't gone to such extreme measures last night, I wonder how long she would have danced in her wedding dress.

"I'll never be ready, Elliot. I'll never be ready for the looks, and whispers, and stares, but my kids need me. I'm all they have left."

"You're not alone, Wynnie."

"Aren't I? There's no other adult here but me now. I'm not like my mom. He was my one and only."

"I'm here. I'm with you." I can't...I won't let her feel like she's alone.

"Elliot, I love you with all my heart, but you have to go

back eventually. You could have a baby waiting for you."

My shoulders fall at the mention of a potential baby. "Can we not talk about this right now? I'm here for you for however long you need me."

Her eyes squint as she considers me. "For now, I want to be selfish. The next few days will be hard, and I'm going to need my best friend."

"I'm here, Wynnie. I'm not leaving you."

Her eyes glisten. "Everyone leaves eventually, El."

I won't argue because she's not wrong, but for now, I have no plans to go anywhere.

☺ ☺ ☺ ☺ ☺

Dinner is... strange. There's an inner joy at seeing everyone, but it's laced with sorrow. The kids laugh and play while the adults drink more than is probably necessary. It's an odd mix of chaos and despair.

I hate it.

Ella has asked where Daddy is several times, and Wynnie walks away while one of us tries to distract the curious four year old. Finn and I have been playing defense as much as possible because if anyone knows how to dodge the dead parent questions, it's us.

Fuck. Dead parent. I didn't think we would have to deal with this for another few decades.

I haven't taken my eyes off Wynnie. I've seen every shot of tequila she's snuck off to chug. Despite wanting to keep Archie attached at her hip, my dad managed to pry him from her to put him to bed.

Without the barrier of a toddler, she's going downhill fast.

455

"How is she?" My mom's voice startles me.

"About as despondent as you could expect. She kissed me this afternoon thinking I was him."

"Seriously?"

I chuckle. "Hopefully, we'll look back at it one day and have a good laugh."

We watch as Wynnie makes her rounds in the room, trying to make sure she speaks to everyone like she's the dinner host. I know she's just doing everything in her power to keep busy.

"Be prepared," she warns.

"For?"

She motions to Wynnie with her chin. "The emotional crash tonight is going to take on her. We've got the kids if you've got her. She's going to need you after this. Look at that fake smile." It's hard *not* to notice. "How much has she drank?"

"About half the bottle." I hang my head, feeling like I should be doing so much more for her other than watching her drink her sorrow away.

"Tonight, let her drink. Drink with her. Cry with her. Scream, shout, break stuff. Run naked through the woods if that's what she needs. But let her grieve and do it with her. Tomorrow, we need to make plans, and she needs to be a part of them. She'll never forgive herself if she doesn't."

"I'm scared, Mom."

She pulls me into her. I tower over her petite frame, so I rearrange us to embrace her better.

"We all are. The road ahead is long and twisty, Elliot. But she has us. She's going to push us away. She's too strong-willed for her own good, but we *will* get through it, and so will she."

I quickly wipe away the tear that slipped past my lashes and blow out a breath.

She pulls back and puts on her Mom face. "Elliot, promise me something."

"Anything."

"I know you, and I know the relationship you have with Wynnie, but you're both adults now. I saw those two wonderful people in your home, and I don't want you to forget about the life you built out there."

"Mom."

"Don't *Mom* me. Promise me you won't throw everything away you've worked so hard for. Professionally as well as personally. Wynnie is important, and I know you won't be leaving her side for a while, but eventually, she's going to need to fly on her own, baby. You'll need to let her falter a bit, but she'll grow her wings bigger and stronger for those kids. Know that even if she feels like it, she'll never be alone. We've got her."

I hear her words, and every one of them rings true, but right now, it's hard to see the forest through the trees. I can't focus on tomorrow. I just need to make sure Wynnie makes it through the next second, minute, hour.

# 61

## Lainey

How can someone who was in your life for so little time, compared to the grand scheme of things, have such a colossal impact? Six months ago, Sawyer and I were just any other happily married couple.

Now?

I don't even know what to say about now. Of course, we're still a happily married couple, but our couple is greatly missing our third.

Elliot.

I wipe at my eyes as I stare at the ceiling tile painted like an underwater scape. There's a little orange clownfish, and Dory's words pop into my head. *"Just keep swimming. Just keep swimming."*

"You okay, Jitterbug?" Sawyer squeezes my hand just as we hear a knock at the door.

A young blonde wearing pink scrubs and wire framed black glasses gives us a bright smile. She looks down at the chart in her hand and back at us. "Hi, Mom and Dad. How's everyone doing."

"Nervous," Sawyer chuckles out.

"First babies always are. We're just going to take a look and listen for baby's heartbeat. Based on your estimation, you're about nine weeks, correct?"

"I believe so. I missed my shot by over a month when I found out, so it was hard to tell."

She gives me a reassuring smile and sits on the rolling stool. "It's okay. We can get a pretty good idea as long as you're under about twelve weeks. Will you lift your shirt for me?"

I know it's too early, but I swear I already see a change in my body. There's a small pouch forming low down on my belly.

The gel is warm but startling. I've already seen our little bean. Katy took me to her OB the week I found out, but this is Sawyer's first time, and mine with this new doctor's office.

It's hard to understand what we're seeing on the screen, but the fast-paced thumping is unmistakable.

I gasp and cover my mouth. "Is that?"

"That's your baby's heartbeat."

Sawyer stares at the little flicker on the screen, and his eyes glaze over.

"You're incredible, Alaina." My stomach flips at the use of my proper name, but I know it's not being used for dominance. It's love, adoration, respect.

"Can we get pictures?"

"Of course," the tech tells him.

"Is it cruel if we do?" Sawyer asked if we should send Elliot a text with the ultrasound pictures, and as much as I want to say yes, I don't know if it's the right answer. "Or is it crueler if we don't? I know he said some things before he left, but I'm not sure we can hold him accountable for them based on the news he had just heard."

"Maybe not then, but how about the lack of communication for the last three weeks? He hasn't responded to any calls or texts. Does he get a pass for that? Did we mean that little to him? Was it that easy to forget us?"

The tears start at his words, and I growl, frustrated at these stupid hormones. Everything makes me cry lately. Sawyer snuck in for a quick orgasm while I was on break last week, and I cried at my desk for twenty minutes after he left. It was such a satisfying release. Apparently, my body felt like it needed to purge.

"No, Jitterbug. He's wrong and doesn't get a pass from us. Your frustration is valid, and so is mine, but I still think we should send it. He barely knew before he was ripped away. This baby is just a concept for him. Let's make it a reality and hope it helps him get his head out of his ass."

He's right. I'm the one growing the baby and still struggle daily believing it's real. I want Elliot to be a part of this life we're creating, but I'd never force anyone to be a parent who doesn't want to be.

Taking the pictures from my purse, I line them across the counter and take a photo of each one. I steel myself for the silence that will come once I write my message and hit send.

Lainey: We went to the doctor today and got a clean bill of health. Baby is healthy and thriving. We thought you might

want to see. «image attached»
    Lainey: I really fucking miss you.

The text takes a few extra moments to send because of the pictures attached, but when it finally does, I feel a ball of led lodge in my stomach. My heart flutters when the three dancing dots appear on the screen. I show Sawyer, and we wait, staring at the phone.

I can't focus on anything other than those dots that move up and down for what feels like an eternity. I tap my nails on the counter impatiently, and Sawyer takes my hand.

Finally, a long message appears in response, but it's not what I expect.

Elliot: I'm going to assume that "Cherry" is Lainey. This is Wynnie. Elliot is in the shower. I'm so sorry he's ignoring you. Please know it's not because of me. I've been begging him to reach out since he got here, but he's refusing to leave my side. I appreciate everything he is doing for me, and I will continue to encourage him that he needs to go back to you. But he's stubborn. And I'm selfish. I know I don't have the authority in your relationship to ask you this, but can I please have him for a little while longer? If not for me, then for his niece. Tori, my stepdaughter, is having a rough time. Elliot is keeping her together even more than he is me. She's only 10. I'm not sure how much of Elliot's past you know, but he's uniquely qualified to handle losing a parent at her age. If you'd like, I'd love for you to visit. He told me about how he left things with you, and I promise, that's not the man I know and love. He won't abandon that baby. I'd never forgive him if he did. He wouldn't forgive himself even more. He will do right by you. I'm going to delete this message so he doesn't see it, but here's my number if you want to reach out. I promise I'll respond. Thank you for sharing him with me.

A shared contact comes in a separate text, and a drop of water splashes the counter next to the phone. I didn't realize I was crying. I also didn't know I had lost hope until Wynnie just gave it back to me.

"I don't even know what to say."

"Well, at the moment, we wait to see if we get a response back from Elliot still. Save Wynnie's number, and you should probably respond to her so she knows you got it."

"Good idea." I'm honestly surprised we didn't exchange numbers when she visited.

Lainey: Your words mean more to me than you could possibly know. We understand your need and would never take him away from you. But we do miss him. I'm not sure about visiting since he isn't speaking to us, but I will consider your offer. Thank you.

Lainey: And Wynnie. There are no words to adequately express how sorry we are for your loss. We're sending all of our love and strength to you.

# 62

# Elliot

"How is she?" I look up from the paperwork I've been staring at for the last hour and smile at Kristina, standing in the office doorway. Tipsy Penny has been closed since the day of the shooting, and I'm trying to do what I can to help Wynnie get the doors back open.

"The first question is, how are *you*?"

Based on her posture, the weight of the world sits on Kristina's shoulders. She blames herself for Scotty's death. Having no idea what was happening, Kristina walked into the office that day, startling the robber. The guy shot Scotty and ran, leaving her behind.

"Alive."

I stand from the desk and cross the room. I haven't seen her since the funeral, and I was so wrapped up with Wynnie and Tori that I didn't get to speak with her.

Kristina is a beautiful woman. With her long black hair and green eyes, she has a rough-looking exterior that screams badass chick, but I've seen her with the kids, and she's a huge softie.

"Wynnie is...coping. Better than Tori."

Kristina's head drops to her chest. "Tori," she breathes out.

"Hey, stop that." I stand and cross the room, pulling her into my arms. "It's not your fault, and no one blames you."

She returns my embrace long enough to compose herself, then steps back. Looking around the office, she smirks at the pile of papers I was sitting in front of.

"When do the doors reopen?"

"Are you ready?"

"Elliot, I've been running this place for years. I can't allow the doors to close because of..." She swallows hard and shakes her head. "I'm ready. I owe it to him to keep this place going."

I can tell she feels an obligation to Scotty and to the bar, and if I thought there was something I could do to change that, I would.

"Everything is in order. We just need to call the distributors and get back on their delivery routes. Scotty kept impeccable records, so there isn't much to do here. I suppose we need to hire a person or two to pick up the open shifts."

"I'll take care of it. I can take care of everything, Elliot. You can trust me. Scotty gave me all the knowledge I need to run this place exactly like he did."

"Thank you, Kristina. Let me get your number so we can work out all the details."

We exchange numbers, and I go back to sorting through current bills.

Wynnie: How's it going? Wanna take the kids to the park when you're done?

Elliot: Of course. I'm wrapping up.

Wynnie: I'm only admitting this because it's in text. I opened a message from Lainey the other day on your phone, and I'm assuming you haven't seen it. You should look.

*What the fuck.*

Switching back into my messages, my hands shake when I see her name. I fucking miss them so much.

Lainey: We went to the doctor today and got a clean bill of health. Baby is healthy and thriving. We thought you might want to see. «image attached»

Lainey: I really fucking miss you.

My heart pounds in my chest as I click through the images. I've seen my fair share of ultrasound pictures and know exactly what I'm looking at. There's a little blob with nubby arms and legs.

A wave of heat courses through me when I realize that Wynnie kept this from me. This message was received two days ago. I know I've ignored all previous calls and texts from Lainey and Sawyer, but I wouldn't have ignored this one.

I need to reach out to them, but I said some really shitty things before I left, then went radio silent.

Fuck. This is all too much. I'm carrying around everyone's emotions, and I haven't had time to process my own. I've kept busy ensuring Wynnie and Tori are taken care of, but I left my potential baby mama and boyfriend high and dry like they meant nothing to me. Now, it probably looks like I don't care because I didn't immediately respond to Lainey's text.

"Fuck!" Papers fly through the room when I sweep my arm across the desk. There's so much destruction and chaos in my head right now, and I need my surroundings to match. Picking up a stapler, I throw it across the room. The sound of metal echoes when it hits the wall and floor. A box of paper clips goes next, and it sounds like rain as it explodes. A cup of pens, a calculator, tape dispenser. Each item makes its own sound as it beats against the wall. Each sound mimicking a feeling in my heart of complete despair.

Picking up the next thing within my reach I pause, arm reared back, when I look at what's in my hand. "World's Best Dad" screams at me from the coffee mug in my hand.

Falling back into the office chair, it rolls at my aggressive drop and slams into the filing cabinets behind me. The mug taunts me as I hold it, chest heaving from emotions.

Scotty was the world's best dad. *Was.* He's gone now. Archie barely knew him.

My eyes shift to my phone, and I swipe it open. The ultrasound picture stares me in the face, and the tears stinging the back of my eyes finally fall.

"What am I doing, Scotty? You'd give anything to be here with your wife and kids, and I'm hiding half a day's travel away from my potential future."

Putting the mug down, I lift my phone with shaky hands and pull up my call log. Where Lainey and Sawyer's numbers would be at the top, I now have to scroll to find them. That alone makes my heart ache more. It's been so long since I've spoken to them. Too long.

My finger hovers over Lainey's name. The need to hear her sweet, melodic voice overpowers any other emotion. With a deep breath for courage, I press the button. The phone rings once, twice, three times. After the fourth ring, her voicemail picks up. I deflate when I hear her encouraging voice to leave a message.

The tone sounds, and I open my mouth, but no words come out. My mind is overwhelmed but blank with everything I want to say. I *need* to say.

*I love you.*

*I miss you.*

*I need you.*

It's all right and wrong at the same time.

Finally, the only words that make the most sense slip through my lips,

"Please don't give up on me."

# 63

# Sawyer

Lainey has been a mess since she got home. Elliot called her. After weeks of no contact, he called when she was at work. Of course, she missed the call, but he left a voicemail, and she didn't want to listen to it until we were together.

The beginning of the message was silence. My rage boiled, thinking he didn't even have the decency to leave an actual message. After several long seconds, he finally spoke.

"Please don't give up on me."

Lainey sobbed. At his voice, his words, his request.

I don't mirror her emotions. As much as I want to feel her relief and sadness, all I feel is anger and betrayal. He's given us nothing to hold on to. Elliot left us high and dry after discovering he could be the father to the baby growing inside Lainey. In fact, based on her due date, it's more likely than not he's the father. I'm not mad about that aspect. I'm furious at the irresponsibility of his actions.

*Don't give up on me.*

Isn't that exactly what he's done to us? To the baby?

"Jitterbug, you need to eat. Our little coffee bean needs you to fuel your body."

Lainey lays curled in a ball in the middle of our bed, looking so tiny. She's clutching her phone, waiting for another scrap of communication from Elliot that I'm sure won't come.

"I'm not hungry."

"Alaina, you need to eat." She hesitates. She fucking hesitates, and that hurts me more than she could know. I never expect blind obedience, but she knows I always have her best interest in mind when I take on my role as her dom.

I can see her reluctance as she rolls and sits up. She places her phone on her knee, face up, so she can see the screen. I made a simple peanut butter and jelly sandwich with a few chips and an orange, and I watch as she eats the food purely out of habit.

Lainey's cheeks are flushed, and her eyes are bloodshot. This isn't my beautiful, vibrant wife, and the sight of her only fuels my growing rage. It was my idea to add someone to our relationship. I hand-picked Elliot. Pursued the random stranger from the bar. It was me who left my wife open and vulnerable to have her emotions crushed by another man. As much as I'm aggravated with Elliot, I'm furious with myself.

"Jitterbug?" Her hazel eyes, more brown than green at the moment, slowly rise to me. "What can I do?"

Her head shakes, and a glaze of tears fills her eyes. She moves her plate to the nightstand, only half her meal eaten, and shifts to wrap her arms around her legs. With her chin resting on her knees, she looks at me longingly.

469

"I need…" Her eyes squeeze shut like she's in pain. "I need to not think. I don't want to feel like this. Make me feel something else. Please."

Scooping her into my arms, I take us to the bathroom. I don't know exactly how she's feeling, but I can show her how much I feel for her. I imagine there's a hole in her heart like I have right now, and I can do everything in my power to fill that hole with overflowing love.

Steam fills the room while I undress Lainey, tenderly kissing every available inch of her body. She may not need sex, but I can give her intimacy until she gives me the green light for more.

In the shower, I wash her hair and massage her body with her loofah. She's pliant in my arms while I slowly dry the water from her hair and skin before bringing us back to the bedroom.

"I need you, Sawyer." Her sincere words are said through tears, and it rips me apart inside.

"I've got you." Pulling her into my body, I cradle her cheek to my chest and kiss the top of her head. She pushes me away, and I give her a confused look.

"No, Sawyer." Lainey sits up and straddles my waist. "I *need* you."

*Oh.*

"Take what you need, Jitterbug. I'm all yours."

She presses her mouth to mine, and I can taste the emotions on her tongue. Her arm slips between us, and she lines up my hardening cock to her entrance. I'll give her anything she needs; if it's my body, she can have it.

We groan into each other's mouths as she sinks onto me. Lainey sits up, pressing her hands to my chest as she rocks her hips against mine. Our love-making is slow and passionate as our emotions pour through our bodies. It's unlike anything I've ever experienced with her before and something I'm likely to never forget.

Even when Lainey begins to cry, I know she needs me to continue. Rolling us over, I take charge but don't change our pace. Slowly and passionately, I pump my hips while giving her all my praise and adoration. As unfamiliar as it is for me to be this gentle with her, it feels right because I'm giving her what she needs, and that's always my top priority.

"Sawyer," she sighs.

"I know, Jitterbug. Let it go. I've got you." Her inner walls flutter, and I know she's close. "It's okay to feel good." My words give her body permission, and I feel her tense under me. Her tears flow as she silently moans against her release.

When her body relaxes, I move to pull out, and she wraps her legs around my hips.

"No, Baby. Finish."

"I'm okay—"

"No." She pushes against my chest and I roll off her. With determination in her eyes, she puts me on my back and straddles me again. There's renewed vigor in her eyes when she mounts my cock and slams down onto me.

"Fuck." My back arches as she bounces like she needs me to come. Lainey's fists clench on my chest, and her nails dig into me. I relish the pain and grab her hips, encouraging her to go harder. Faster.

The tender sweetness in the room only moments earlier is gone, replaced with animalistic urges. Lainey's tears are gone, and her eyes are vibrant and green. She bounces on my cock like her only purpose in life is to make me come.

I don't let her down. With our eyes locked, she begins to pant, and I know she's close again.

"Are you going to come for me again, Jitterbug?"

"Only if you come for me," she replies through a panting smile.

I squeeze my fingers tighter around her waist and thrust up several times, grinding her clit on my pelvis.

"Oh fuck, Baby." Her inner walls pulse and suck me in, pulling me over the edge with her. Our joining is beautiful and carnal—the perfect mix of our needs.

Lainey collapses on top of me, her heavy breathing tickling my neck.

Once our breathing has calmed, I tap her butt to roll off me. I'm still semi-hard inside her, but I need to get her cleaned up.

"Roll over. Let me get us a washcloth."

"No. Stay right where you are." Her pussy squeezes around me, and I chuckle.

"If you keep that up, there's going to be a round two."

Turning her head. She kisses my chest and whispers, "Good."

We spend the rest of the night wrapped in each other's arms, renewing ourselves together.

# 64

# Elliot

It's almost Christmas. I've been back home, living with Wynnie for two months. There isn't a cheery bone in my body, and I'm beginning to wonder if I'm doing more harm than good while still here, but I feel lost in limbo.

Do I have anything to return to Chicago for? Annie told me I could have as much time as I needed. Blake has taken over my job and told me it's mine whenever I come back. I pick up my phone a hundred times a day to text or call Sawyer or Lainey, but I never do.

"You're worrying me, son." My dad walks into the office at Tipsy Penny, where I've been spending a lot of time. "You can't keep hiding in here."

"I'm not hiding. I'm working." *I'm fucking hiding.*

"Uh huh. And what exactly are you working on?"

There's nothing in front of me but a beer and my phone. Tipsy Penny reopened two weeks ago, and, as promised, Kristina has taken care of everything. She contacted the distributors and got us back on their routes in a day.

473

Business is better than before as the community pours their support into Wynnie's family. Everyone loved Scotty.

"Hiding."

"Exactly." He sits in the chair opposite the desk and picks up the mug that started my mental decline. "Talk to me."

"Who sent you?" I love my dad, but one of the women in my life sent him to talk to me.

"Who didn't is the question. Everyone is worried about you." I'm worried about me, too. "Are you running? From them? From…"

His pause speaks volumes. I haven't spoken about the baby, but everyone seems to know. I'm sure I can thank my best friend for that since she's the only one I've told.

"Fuck. I don't know."

He places the "World's Best Dad" mug back on the desk, and I breathe out a sigh of relief. That fucking sphere of ceramic feels like a stake in my heart that twists every time I look at it.

"Elliot. You aren't this man. What are you still doing here?"

Anger boils inside me. "I don't fucking know." I stand, and the chair flies back into the filing cabinets with a loud bang. My dad doesn't react.

"Couch." The demand in his voice has me obeying, and I move to the couch and sit. He joins me with his serious dad face on.

"Dad, I—"

"Nope. I'm going to talk, and you're going to listen."

I shut my mouth and nod. He takes a deep breath before starting what I'm sure will be a life-changing speech because those are the kinds he does best.

"I love you with every fucking shred of my heart, Elliot. I never expected to be a father." His voice cracks, and he pauses. "You, your brother, and sister are the best and most tragic things that ever happened to me, but I wouldn't change a goddamn thing about it. You have a potential baby waiting for you at home."

"I am home."

"No, you're not. Mountain Pines is a placeholder for you. Your home is back in Chicago. You're home is with that man and woman. Your *home* is where the people you love are. And yes, we all love you here, but we aren't in love with you. If you can look me in the face and tell me you don't love them, I'll shut up and let you be miserable."

Damn. He's swinging hard, and it fucking hurt.

"But Wynnie and Tori?"

"Have each other and us. Your aunt is getting her wish." He runs a heavy hand through his red hair and sighs.

"What does that mean?"

"Mac and I walked the property this week. Wynnie needs a place that's her own, and he wants to build her a new house. There are too many memories there for her."

"She's still sleeping in the guest room with me."

"Which only proves my point. We've already talked to Wynnie about it, and she's on board."

"So what does that have to do with Aunt Hazel?"

He sighs again, and it's heavier than the last. "Wynnie's house will be empty..."

"No way? You're going to move in?" He nods and runs a hand through his hair. I stumble over how to even reply.

Aunt Hazel has begged my dad to build on their property, and he's always been the one to say no. With over forty acres, they can be close but still feel like they have their own space, but my mom could never convince him.

"What changed your mind?" His eyes flash to mine, and I don't need him to answer. Everything changed. Scotty died. We lost a friend, uncle, father. "And Wynnie is okay with everything? She hasn't said a word to me about it."

"She was the one who asked."

Wow. I'm so proud of her and so pissed at myself. Why didn't she mention anything to me?

"You've been a little preoccupied lately with your own emotions. You need to deal with them. You need to go home, Elliot. Whether that means you tie up loose ends and come back here or you go be with them, the limbo you've left yourself in isn't fair. Ignoring your problems won't make them go away."

"Thanks, Dad. I'll figure my shit out. I think I have been hiding here, and based on what you just told me, it seems like I've overstayed my welcome."

He puts an arm around my shoulder and pulls me into his chest. "Never. You're always welcome here. But your heart isn't with us anymore, and we can all tell. Chase your heart, Elliot. We want to see you happy, but you're not."

🙂🙂🙂🙂🙂

"Are you sure?"

Wynnie places a hand on each shoulder and pulls me down so we're at eye level.

"Elliot McLain. Am I sure I want you to be eleven hours away from me *again*? Absolutely not. Am I sure that you're avoiding your life by using me as a crutch? Yes."

"But don't you need me?"

Wynnie wraps her arms around my waist and presses her forehead to my chest.

"Your support has been invaluable, and there are days that have gone by when I don't think I would have survived if you hadn't been here. But I can't be selfish anymore. We need to learn to heal on our own, and you need to go back to the people you love. They miss you."

"I wish I knew if that was true. I've messed up so bad by not talking to them." She pulls back and looks at me with guilt in her blue eyes. "What?"

"Don't hate me. I've been talking to Lainey pretty regularly."

I step back from her embrace.

"You what?" She's been talking to Lainey? "Why? How?"

She blows out a breath and sits on a kitchen stool. "Remember the text I told you about with the ultrasound pictures? I may have responded to it, and we exchanged numbers."

I have so many mixed emotions. How could Wynnie keep this from me? If they are talking, does that mean I still have a chance? Could they not be as mad at me as I expect them to be?

"I'm so sorry, Elliot. You've been going through enough. I didn't want to make things any more confusing. Please don't be mad at me."

"I'm mad, Wynnie, but not at you. I'm mad at myself." My feet carry me back and forth as I pace the room. "Does anyone still need me? I feel like I've been in purgatory, stuck in one spot between people who I think need my help, but I've been making all the wrong decisions."

"That's the problem, El. You've been thinking for everyone else but yourself. You came here for me. You stayed for Tori. Go home. We love you, and I'll miss you like fucking crazy, but you'll be back. I know you will. I love you for everything you've done and sacrificed the last few months. Now it's my turn. I'm sacrificing *you* for *your* happiness."

"I haven't been unhappy here."

"But you haven't been happy either. And neither are they. Go be with them."

I stop my pacing and shake my head. "It won't be that easy."

"Not with Sawyer. He's mad, and I don't blame him. You can't either. You abandoned them."

"I fucking did." Falling into the chair behind me, I bury my face in my hands. "I fucking did. *Fuck*. What if it's too late?"

I hear the stool move, and Wynnie leans on my bent knees. Her hands pull at my wrists, urging me to uncover my face.

My eyes meet hers, filled with sorrow and pain. "What if it's not? You owe it to that baby to find out. Go make things right. We aren't going anywhere."

I chuckle. "Except to the other side of the property."

Pulling Wynnie onto the chair with me, I hug her like my life depends on it. She will always be my home. My happiest memories are wrapped up with her and her family, but my future holds a different family. One I wasn't born into. It's a family I created with my own heart.

# 65

# Lainey

W hat's that saying? Another day, another dollar? It seems like every day blends in with the next. The only difference lately is my wardrobe and the ever-changing weather. Chicago winters are cold, and when the wind whips between the buildings, it takes your breath away and freezes you to the bone.

Big sweaters and skirts with leggings have been the only thing in my wardrobe keeping me warm, and I'm not upset I'm pregnant through the winter because I can be comfortable and stylish at the same time.

I'm counting down the minutes until lunch. Tomato soup is on the menu in the cafe, and my mouth has been watering all day thinking about it. I shiver as the revolving doors rotate and the breeze carries across my desk. The space heater at my feet works overtime today as it's particularly bitter outside.

Footsteps echo toward my desk as I look at the time on my cell phone—only five more minutes. My relief security guard should be here any moment.

"Cherry."

I pause. My body simultaneously freezes and burns to the core. It can't be. No. Nononono. I imagined his voice. My name on his lips.

"Cherry, please look at me." My eyes squeeze shut. This is the cruelest joke my mind could possibly play on me. I miss him so much that I'm hallucinating now.

I hear a sigh and footsteps walking away.

"Mrs. Hayes, are you alright?"

My eyes snap open to see Richy, one of the security guards, staring at me from the other side of the desk.

"Yeah. Sorry. Just having a moment." Standing, I grab my purse. "I'll see you in an hour. Thanks."

I don't give him the chance to ask any more questions before retreating to the elevator. Katy is meeting me for lunch, although I'm not sure I have much of an appetite anymore.

"Lainey?"

"Hmm?" I look up from my soup to a concerned look on Katy's face.

"Were you listening?"

"Sorry. I have a lot on my mind."

"I can see that. Want to talk about it?" No. I'm not sure I want to confess I'm hallucinating my boyfriend or maybe ex-boyfriend's voice.

"I'm just having an off day."

She hesitates before asking her next question. "Is it Elliot?"

My head snaps up so hard I think I gave myself whiplash. "What? Why would you ask that?" How could she know I'm missing him so desperately, I imagined hearing his voice?

"Do you not know?"

"Know what?" That I'm going insane? Yeah. Figured that one out.

"He didn't... Lainey, he's here." My head whips around on a swivel, looking for the man in question. "Blake told me he scheduled a meeting with them today. He's back."

"He's back." The words whisper through my lips not wanting to say them too loud. It can't be true. He's back, and he didn't reach out to us. "Wait. What time is his meeting?"

"She said lunch, so I'd assume now, maybe?"

"Now?" The chair falls back with an echoing crash as I jump up from the table.

"Lainey?"

"So he's here? Right now?" Maybe I'm not crazy?

"I would assume so."

I abandon Katy and my food and charge toward the elevator. Pushing the button more times than necessary, I stare at the numbers, and they descend to my floor. I rush in before the doors fully open and push the button to the top floor, flashing my badge to gain access. There aren't many people who have permission to Annie's floor, but being the receptionist, my pass allows me entrance to the entire building.

The doors close, and I stare at my reflection in the mirrored doors. I've been waiting and imagining what I would say the first time I saw him again. My body vibrates with anticipation just knowing he's in the building.

How could I have been so stupid to think I imagined his voice? Of course, it was him. What must he think of me that I ignored him? I didn't even look up to see if he was there.

As the doors open onto the top floor, I shield my eyes from

the glaring white marble floors. There's no receptionist waiting since it's lunchtime, and I walk straight down the hall to Annie's door.

Do I knock? Do I barge in? Do I even have the patience to stop myself from opening the door and putting my eyes on him?

My body answers for me when my hand grabs the handle and turns. For a split second, I worry it will be locked, but it opens right up. All the air in my lungs disappears at the sight of him.

Elliot sits on a couch across from Annie and Blake in a tailored black suit. His silver tie makes the blue in his eyes sparkle when he sees me. He immediately stands, and without thought, my body runs toward him.

I crash into his awaiting body, and he lifts me from the ground. My legs wrap around his trim waist, and I bury myself into his neck.

"Cherry." My name sounds like a prayer on his lips, and my body shudders with a sob. The feel of his body, his smell, his voice. Everything crashes into me like a brick wall, and I feel whole again for the first time in months.

As quickly as it all rushed toward me it falls to pieces. The man in my arms, this man I love, abandoned me. Abandoned us. Me, Sawyer, and the baby growing in my belly that has more of a chance of being his own flesh and blood than Sawyers.

"No." I release him and push away. Elliot instantly lets me go, and I slide to my feet.

"Cherry?"

"No. You don't get to call me that."

*Smack.*

My hand registers the sting before my mind does. I cover my mouth, shocked that I did that, and did it in front of Annie and Blake, who have been quiet during our entire interaction.

Elliot cups his cheek, and I expect to see disdain on his face, but all I see is understanding.

"I deserved that. I deserve so much worse than that, actually."

"We'll give you two a moment." Blake takes Annie's elbow, but I raise a hand to stop them.

"No, I'm leaving. You can finish your meeting. Annie, could I possibly have the rest of the day off?"

"Of course. I'll have someone take over the desk for you."

"Thank you. I'm sorry to have barged in. It was disrespectful and will never happen again."

"No apology needed. Enjoy the rest of your day."

I slowly walk backward toward the door, not taking my eyes off Elliot. I can see the pain in them and struggle not to run back to him, but I don't. Holding strong, I make it to the door, praising myself for walking away before he speaks.

"Alaina." Once again, I freeze. "Please turn around and talk to me."

I feel his presence as he walks closer to me. My body fights to obey E's command. His hand touches my shoulder, and a chill runs down my spine. Desire and despair war within me.

"Alaina," he commands harsher than before.

Tears well in my eyes. He's here. The other love of my life is here and wants me to talk to him, but I can't. My heart battles with my mind.

Elliot's hand squeezes my shoulder, urging me to do as

I've been told, but I don't. I won't. He hasn't earned my respect.

A single tear falls down my cheek as I turn my head to speak my truth.

The barely audible word slips through my lips, but he hears it. "Apple."

Elliot's hand disappears from my shoulder, and he steps away. I leave the room without any further hesitation, but I don't miss the thud from what I can only assume are his knees connecting with the floor.

# 66

## Sawyer

"Lainey, are you okay?" Gus' voice startles me as he yells my wife's name across the coffee shop. I jump from my chair and open the office door as Lainey crashes into me in a heap of tears.

"Lainey, what's wrong? What happened?" I try to pull her away to look at her, but she grips my shirt, not allowing me to. "Lainey, talk to me."

My words make her tears flow harder, and she melts into me. Bending down, I lift her legs, and she wraps them around me. Holding her like this feels so different with her baby bump between us. Every time I think I've gotten used to it, the baby has another growth spurt, and it feels new again.

"Are you hurt?" Her head shakes against my chest. "Are you safe?" She nods, and I let out a relieved breath. I'll hold her for as long as she needs until she feels ready to talk.

I rest back on my desk, letting her work through whatever made her charge in here. Eventually, her crying turns to hiccups, and she sighs a ragged breath.

"He's back." My muscles tense at her words. I hope I heard her wrong. I hope there's some other *he* she could be referring to, but I know there's not. Only one person could pull this kind of reaction from her; the heat of rage makes me itchy.

Lainey's head turns, resting her cheek over my heart. "He's back, Sawyer. I just saw him in Annie's office. I-I slapped him. He tried to get me to talk to him, but..."

"You don't ever have to talk to him again if you don't want to."

She pulls back, and I see the pain across her face.

"Don't say that. Don't ever say that again. He's a part of our future whether we want him to be or not."

"Maybe."

"Probably." There's conviction behind her word, and I know she's right, but I don't have to like it. "I used my safeword and left."

"I'm proud of you." Praise may not be my go-to, but I can't deny her my adoration when she does what's right for her.

My body may be with Lainey right now, but my mind is next door, beating the shit out of Elliot for all the pain he's caused the last several months. I don't know how else to help her through her pain, but I can remove her from the situation.

"Let's go home."

Our phones sound with a text. It's him. Elliot sent a message to our group chat. I know because Lainey set it to its own text chime. The sound of a train whistle used to make her smile, but I feel her body stiffen from it.

"Ignore it." Another whistle cuts through the air, and I

know she won't ignore a second text. "I'll look."

Grabbing my phone off my desk, I see notifications for two texts from Elliot.

Elliot: Lainey, it was incredible to see you. I earned your slap and more than deserved your safeword. I'm so fucking proud of you for using it. I will never fault you for telling me what you want. I'm back, and I'm planning to stay. I have no expectations of forgiveness from either of you, but when you're ready, I'd like to talk.

Elliot: I love and miss you both.

Lainey is crying again, but these are tears of heartache.

"I'm not ready." I run a soothing hand down her back and shush her tears.

"You don't have to be. Ever. Let's go."

She's quiet the entire ride home. I hold her hand and occasionally give her a reassuring squeeze. While we have equal heartache in this situation, I won't deny Lainey has a bigger stake in how all of this turns out. I'll love our baby no matter who the father is because half of it will be Lainey, but she's right. The other half could be his, and Elliot deserves the chance to be in its life. As for us, he'll have to earn it. If he's ever allowed the chance. The ball is in Lainey's court.

# 67

## Elliot

That probably could have gone better. Lainey ignored me when I approached her at the reception desk. She closed her eyes and didn't even acknowledge my presence. The last thing I expected was for her to barge into Annie's office and make a scene.

"Are you okay?" The sympathy in Blake's voice isn't necessary. I deserved everything Lainey just threw at me. "She's hurting, Elliot. I know you are too, but—"

"I'm fine." I don't need her words of encouragement. I don't regret how I chose to spend the last several months. What I do regret is my lack of communication, but that's not anyone's fault but my own.

Lainey used her safeword on me. While it's not officially the first time, we didn't have the relationship back then that we have now. She felt uncomfortable and didn't trust me. That's what that word meant to me, and fuck if it didn't hurt.

"Shall we get back to our discussion?" I look between

Blake and Annie, and they each nod.

I have a long road ahead of me, but I'm putting down roots here, and I want Sawyer and Lainey to know I'm serious about our future.

After my meeting, I force myself to drive home. I don't want to, but I have no right to show up at their apartment uninvited. I have no right to anything when it comes to them, but that won't stop me from showing them how much I still love and care for them.

After a workout and shower, I realize there's nothing to eat in my house. While I scroll through the food delivery app, I decide to make my first of many offerings. Lainey loves Chinese food. I find the restaurant close to their house and order all her favorite dishes to be delivered. Scrolling further, I order myself a salad and spaghetti dish and vow to go shopping tomorrow.

I watch the updates on my phone and know exactly when they receive it. They might eat it. They might throw it away—either way, I've made a gesture, and that's all I can do.

My sleep is restless. I had hoped to get a text message after the food was delivered last night, but I wasn't surprised when I didn't receive anything. I offered an olive branch, and I'll continue to do it until I'm told to stop.

Walking into the MAD Gaming Inc. building the following day, I stop at Lainey's desk. It's early, and I know she won't be in yet. I don't want to see her. I only wanted to deliver a single red rose. There's no need to leave her a note. She'll know it's me.

Wynnie told me Sawyer was mad, and I can't blame him. I disrespected the most important thing in his life. My hope is to win Lainey over first. I know Sawyer will be challenging, and I'll have my work cut out for me, I'm starting small.

For the next week, I come to work early and leave late so I don't run into her. I pack my lunch so we don't accidentally run into each other during break. I don't want to make her uncomfortable, but I still make my presence known.

Small gifts each morning show her I'm still here and I care about her. A cherry Danish, a keychain fortune cookie, a bigger bouquet of roses. Little meaningful tokens to express I'm still thinking of her.

After a week, I get my first sign that her exterior is cracking.

Katy: I'm Team Lainey, but also Team Throuple. Keep doing what you're doing.

I'm smiling at my phone when I'm startled by my silent stalker.

"That's nice to see."

"I swear you're the sneakiest person in heels that I know, Blake." She winks and perches herself on the corner of my desk.

"You can't hide up here forever."

"They can't be mad at me forever."

"Fair. What had you smiling?"

I turn my phone to show her the text from Katy.

"She's right. Keep it up." I see the gleam in Blake's eyes and know she's up to something.

"Spit it out."

"How do you feel about parties? We haven't thrown one in a while, but now might be a good time."

"Blake, Annie throws a party every time one of your kids loses a tooth."

"True, but I'm not talking about a kid's party. This kind is for adults only."

"I'm intrigued, and I'm in."

"Good. Now, to convince Annie." Blake stands and saunters toward Annie's door. She hikes up her skirt and fluffs her breasts before winking and stepping into the office. I can't help but chuckle and wonder when I hear Annie's door lock.

Elliot: Thank you for the heads up. I appreciate you.

Several days go by before Blake slides a black envelope across my desk.

"It was easier than I thought. This is an invitation-only party. We don't talk about it outside of our doors. Sawyer and Lainey have also received an invite, and I will do everything in my power to get them there."

I stare at the plain, unsuspecting envelope, and my heart races at the thought of seeing them.

"Before you come, there are some things you should know."

My curiosity is piqued as Blake takes a quick look around. Other than her stealth antics, no one walks down this hallway without being noticed.

"There will be nakedness, open sex, no phones, and inhibitions are left at the door. All invitees must wear a mask. If you don't have one, there will be extras at the door. A recent, clean bill of health needs to be sent to the email address on the invitation, as well as a signed NDA. There will be rooms available for activity if you aren't comfortable being watched."

"You're assuming a lot, Blake."

"Trust me. When there's this much sex going on around you, it's hard not to want to participate."

"Does that mean..."

"While Annie tries to keep herself more discreet, Cole and I like to indulge in some exhibitionism. Is that going to be a problem?"

"Not at all. Will I know anyone else there?"

"Maybe a few familiar faces from work, but we don't generally invite friends. If you're asking about Katy or Nicole, no, they aren't invited. Sawyer and Lainey are a favor to you. And you'll owe me a favor because it took some convincing to let Annie invite the three of you."

"Deal. Whatever it takes at this point, I'm in."

"I sure hope you mean that because this is a night you'll never forget."

<br>

🔒 🔒 🔒 🔒 🔒

<br>

I've never been to Annie's house before. There hasn't been a reason, and the more I walk around her house, the more I'm not sure this is the right one.

Nothing Blake said could have prepared me for the scene around me. Women in thongs and pasties and men with cock cages serve tiny food on silver trays. There are mini bars set up in several corners. The smell of sex lingers in the air, and moans of pleasure act as background music.

When I walked in, mask in hand, I was required to strip and turn in my phone. Clothing is optional but I had to at least be down to my boxers.

I stop at a bar, and I'm greeted by a good-looking man in a bowtie and cock cage.

"Beer, liquor, or champagne?"

I open my mouth to reply, but I'm interrupted by my name being called. Turning, I scan the room, looking for a familiar face, but no one stands out.

"Up here."

I trail my gaze up in the room to see Cole hanging upside down on a stripper pole, staring at me with a bright smile.

"Paul, give him the special. Make it two; I'm coming down." The bartender nods and begins making drinks while I watch Cole lower himself to the ground. I'm so mesmerized by the act itself it isn't until he's down that I notice he isn't wearing much. An electric blue Speedo that barely covers him practically blinds me when a light flashes across it.

Cole slaps me on the shoulder and reaches across to take one of the finished drinks from the bar. "You came."

"You pole dance."

Cole chuckles and runs a hand through his wavy blond hair. "It's how I caught Annie."

I ponder his words for a moment, knowing Annie as my slightly stuck-up boss. Somehow, I can see her being initially attracted to an almost naked Cole grinding on a stripper pole. He brings out a different side of her.

"Did you just get here?" He picks up my drink and hands it to me. It's bright pink, and I want to ask what it is, but I decide it's best to just take what's been offered.

"Yeah. Blake gave me a rundown, but... I could never have imagined *this*."

"My Princess can be a little hellion when she wants something. I hear this party is Operation Grovelling."

I almost choke on my drink because *what did he just say?*

"Um. I was told to come. I didn't realize my plight was the guest of honor."

Cole throws his arm around my shoulder and laughs. "You clearly don't know my wife that well."

Something about the phrase *"my wife"* makes my heart hurt, and I rub at the spot on my chest.

Cole walks me around the house, giving me a tour, when he stops in his tracks in the backyard.

"What's wrong?"

He points a finger inside, and I try to follow his direction. "They're here."

I'm sure my beating heart can be seen on my shirtless chest. Sawyer and Lainey walk hand in hand through the living room.

Sawyer looks fucking edible with his broad shoulders and trim waist. His runner's physique is on full display, and the cock I've been longing for is hidden behind navy boxer briefs.

My breath hitches when my eyes roam over Lainey. Blake must have warned her about the dress code because she's wearing a sheer flowy top with spaghetti straps and triangles covering her breasts. The fabric, which is a mouthwatering shade of red, has a slit down the front, and my eyes stop dead on her stomach. Her not flat, beautifully pregnant stomach. How had I missed that in Annie's office?

"You're drooling," Cole snickers.

"Fucking look at them. At *her*."

"Oh, trust me, brother. I like my women knocked up for

a reason—gorgeous, supple, and the primal Alpha need to possess what's mine."

Fuck yes to everything Cole just said.

"I-What the fuck do I do? I haven't spoken to Sawyer since I've returned, and the last time I saw Lainey, she slapped me."

"Give them some time. Let the high of the party sweep them up first. You'd be surprised how loose people become once they've been here for a while."

# 68

# Sawyer

If Lainey hadn't begged to come, I wouldn't be here. She told me how exclusive this party is and didn't want to reject the invitation. The STD test I had to send over was a little invasive, but seeing what I see now, I understand.

"Oh my god, you look gorgeous!"

Blake bounces to Lainey, and I try my best to avert my eyes. While I made sure Lainey's top wasn't sheer enough for her nipples to show, Blake doesn't seem to have had the same concern. Her lace top doesn't leave much to the imagination, and I want to be respectful of her modesty.

"Look how cute you are, Sawyer. If I was embarrassed about my body, we wouldn't have these parties. Everyone here understands the expectations. No means no, and if anyone happens to give you a blink of trouble, there's plenty of security here to remove them before anyone else even knows."

Lainey smiles, and I take a better look around the room. People are in various stages of undress and even more participating in acts worthy of being behind closed doors.

"This is a safe space." Blake taps my mask. "These don't offer much anonymity, but it's enough to let some walls down. Enjoy yourselves. What happens within these walls stays here. Everyone signs NDAs."

Blake kisses our cheeks, and when she walks away, I see her ass on full display underneath her thong.

It's hard not to get swept up in the hormones swimming around the room. I've pinned Lainey to a nearby wall a few times and ravished her with my mouth. My need to be dominant is raging with her baby bump on display. Whenever someone gives her a glance that lasts longer than I feel appropriate, the primal need to stake my claim takes over.

Blake told Lainey there were private rooms available upstairs if we wanted to avoid being in the open, and the thought of taking Lainey to one gets stronger with each touch and caress.

"Sawyer," Lainey moans in my ear as I feather my fingers over her little red panties. Her moan turns into a gasp, and I smile into her neck. When she steps back, I see the concern on her face.

"What's wrong, Jitterbug?" She's staring over my shoulder, and I turn to see what's caught her eye. I see a sight I never expected to see here, but I'm not sure why I'm surprised. Elliot stands no more than ten feet away, his eyes fixed on us.

"He's here." The pain seeps through her words, and I want to do everything possible to take it away.

"Let's go." I take her hand and move toward the front door, but she stops me.

"Sawyer. How long can we punish him?"

I know his gifts have been breaking down her walls. I've seen them coming down brick by brick. He's been smart with little things instead of grand gestures. He knows her better than I give him credit for.

"Tonight isn't the night."

"Why not? Why not *just* for tonight?"

I huff a laugh. "You think you can shield your heart for one night?" I shake my head. "You're ready to forgive him. I can see it."

"I'm ready to hear him out. I understand you aren't there yet. What if, just for tonight, we let our bodies talk." Lainey brushes my cock over my underwear. "Maybe you have some aggression you'd like to get out?"

She bites her lip when my cock responds to her words with a twitch. The idea of slamming into Elliot's ass with uninhibited aggression turns me on.

Lainey smiles and tugs my hand in Elliot's direction. As we walk toward him, he fumbles, trying to put his hands into pockets that his underwear doesn't have. I've never seen him look so nervous, and it puts a smile on my face.

"Hi," Lainey offers when we're close enough to hear each other.

Elliot speaks no words but stares at Lainey's bump, which is beautifully on display with her top.

The silence stretches between us, no one sure what to say.

"Do you want to find a room with us?" There's no inflection in my voice, and I hope he understands what I'm offering.

Elliot's eyes go wild as they bounce between us.

"We don't want to talk. Lainey made me an offer I'm

having trouble refusing, and it involves you."

"Yes," he responds quickly.

"Don't you want to know what it is before you agree?"

"No. Green. Yes. I agree to whatever it is if it involves the two of you."

I smirk at his eagerness but also the hell I'm about to rein down on him.

"Okay. Let's go find a room."

We follow the signs and are greeted by a security guard at the top of the stairs. He writes down our names, confirms with everyone they are entering the room of their own free will, and hands me a door hanger to place outside the door.

It's very efficient, and I'll make sure to tell Cole later how much I appreciate it. The room we are directed to has a massive four-poster bed with white bedding like a hotel. It's out of place compared to the rich greens and browns of the room, and I realize it's probably another party setup. They wouldn't want to ruin or keep sheets someone else used for their activities.

There are individual packets of condoms and lube in dishes on the nightstand, next to several bottles of water. I'm impressed.

"You look stunning, Cherry."

"Alaina," I correct him. "And in this room, you're Eli. I'm in charge. Do you understand and accept that?"

Elliot locks eyes with me, and my heart skips a beat at the depths of emotion in his light blue eyes.

"Yes, Sir." He dips his fingers into the waistband of his boxers, and they hit the floor. He strides to the foot of the bed and drops to his knees, falling into rest position.

The dominance rears its head, and I know I can do this. I

take care of my submissives, and no matter what or how I feel for Elliot, he's not who's kneeling right now. It's Eli. I am Eli's Dom, and I'll take care of his physical and emotional needs before mine.

"Alaina, join him." Her hands reach behind her to remove her top, but I stop her. "Leave it on."

Her eyes twitch in confusion before she wipes the expression off her face.

"Yes, Sir."

My mouth waters as her laced ass sways to the bed. As much as I want to see her beautifully naked body, that would mean Elliot could, too, and he hasn't earned it yet. I already saw the hunger in his eyes when he saw her baby bump for the first time. He will see what I allow, but I'm not allowing him that access yet.

Slowly approaching them, I lean my body over Elliot and lift Lainey's chin, kissing her passionately. My growing bulge rests on his shoulder, and I feel his chest heaving against my thigh. I feel the power over his body as it reacts to mine.

Stepping back, I look down at Eli and question my intentions. Elliot might have left us, but Eli still disappointed me, and my hesitation dissipates.

"Eli, look at me." His head snaps up, and I revel in his immediate obedience. "What's the safeword?" His eyes briefly shift to Lainey, and I know he's thinking of the last time it was used.

"Apple."

"Good. Now, let me explain my plans. You know that's not how I usually do things, but I want to give you the option of walking out before we start."

"No, Sir. Respectively."

"What?" No response. Only determination stares back at me. "Explain yourself, Eli." I try to keep the annoyance of his disrespect from my tone, but it seeps through.

"I don't need a warning. I'm here to stay. You have the green light. You have my consent."

He speaks with confidence and never breaks eye contact. As much as I want to protest, he gave his consent, and I'll respect it.

"Alaina, get the lube." My eyes leave Eli to watch Alaina as she crawls across the bed, swaying her ass in the air.

"Such a brat." Her head turns and she smiles before coming back, handing me a packet of lube. "Eli, lay on your back, feet on the edge of the bed."

Without hesitation, he lays exactly as I told him. I allow myself to peruse his nakedness. He's beautiful, and I'm not ashamed to admit I love his body.

Using my teeth, I rip open the lube pack and spread some on my fingers and the hole I'm about to use and abuse. I'm assuming he hasn't been with anyone since he left us, and I know that admission to this party was a clean bill of health. As much as I want to slam my aching cock into his tight hole, I'm going to give him some prep. In the long run, it will benefit both of us.

Eli watches my face as I rim him with my lubed fingers, and his mouth opens without sound when I slip the first finger in. Lainey's soft moan catches my attention, and I notice she's watching us.

"Take my cock out and get me ready, Alaina." She complies with eagerness, and I pause my pumping finger to appreciate her hot mouth.

With little warning, I push in another finger and see the crinkle around Eli's eyes before his expression becomes neutral again. He's quiet now, but I bet it won't last for long.

After pushing in a third finger, I pull out of Lainey's mouth and hand her the lube. Without instruction, she rubs the remaining gel over my cock.

"Sit on the bed next to Eli."

I wait for her to get comfortable before pulling my fingers out of Eli and lifting his legs in the air. His hole puckers at the emptiness and anticipation.

Resting one leg on my shoulder, I line up and push into him. Eli's abdominal muscles constrict, and a whoosh of air puffs past his lips.

He's going to make me work for his noises.

# 69

## Elliot

Sweet torture. That's the best way to describe everything going on right now. Lainey is so close to me, and Sawyer is pushing his cock into my ass.

Sawyer watches me intently as he inches in further. I know he's trying to make me moan. His goal is punishing pleasure, but I lived in a house in close proximity to my siblings, and I've mastered the art of being silent during pleasure. He'll need to work a lot harder than this.

I was speechless when they asked me to get a room with them, and I should probably be giving Sawyer any and everything he wants right now, but a part of me is mad at him as well. I was cruel the day I left, but he isn't without blame. He said the two words he knew would hurt me. *My wife.*

Two words that took everything we had built over the incredible months we were together and ripped them away. I won't give him the satisfaction of my pleasure if his goal is punishment.

The thrusts start hard and fast when he finally seats himself fully, but I'm prepared. I can read Sawyer as well as Lainey. I meet him with each snap of his hips. Sawyer folds me in half while leaning into me. He buries his cock deeper, and I taste the copper in my mouth from my bottom lip. I bit right through it while trying to keep in my noises.

Sawyer's voice, heavy with lust, fans over my face.

"You know good boys get rewards, Eli. Give me what you want, and I'll reward you."

The only thing I could want more than him right now is her. She sits inches from me, her eyes fixed on where Sawyer and I are connected. Lainey's fists tighten and loosen against her thigh, telling me how badly she wants to touch herself.

"That's right. She would be your reward. If you want her, let me hear you. Show me how much you're enjoying how deep my cock is up your ass. You're greedy hole keeps sucking me back in every time I pull out." Sawyer licks my bottom lip. He must have seen the blood. "Submit to me Eli. Don't disobey me, and you'll get your reward."

*Fuck.* He knows what he's doing to me. His harsh, demanding words. Dangling my woman in front of me like a carrot. All the need and desire piles on top of each other, and I'm lost in the pleasure.

A guttural groan starts low and rips through my vocal cords. My entire body reacts as my back arches, and the pleasure washes over me.

Sawyer laughs and pulls back. My legs fall on either side of his hips, and he holds them up.

"Climb on, Alaina. Use Eli's dick as your personal fuck toy."

Worry crosses her face, and she looks at me. I give her a

reassuring smile and a slight nod. I want this as much as she does, but she needed confirmation from me, and I fall in love with her deeper.

"Leave your clothes on, Alaina. Eli, no touching her."

She looks disappointed as she straddles my hips and lines up my cock with her entrance. It's no surprise to feel she's ready for me, and she easily sinks to my pelvis. Lainey leans down to use my chest for leverage, but Sawyer grabs her arms, locking them behind his head.

"I said no touching. I'll help you, Alaina." Sawyer grabs her hips, and they set a tormenting rhythm. In, out. Up, down. It drives me mad, and I let Sawyer know with every grunt and groan I make.

My eyes stay focused on Lainey's bump that bounces with Sawyer's hips. I ache to touch her belly. My baby.

*My baby.*

My. Baby...

My eyes slam shut, and the tears form. Tears for leaving them. Tears for the months I stayed away.

For the ignored and unreturned calls and texts.

For the anger I can read all over Sawyer's face and the disappointment in Lainey's.

For the time I missed since I've been gone.

"Ellio—" Lainey tries to console me, but Sawyer cuts her off.

"He knows the safeword. Don't baby him, and don't speak out of turn."

Lainey whimpers above me, and it makes my tears come harder. I open my eyes because I want them to see my pain, my regret. How much I've beaten myself up over the exact emotions they are feeling.

I know tonight, this moment, this connection, won't change anything. Sawyer is mad and deserves to feel that feeling for as long as he needs to heal. But Lainey's resolve is crumbling. Her sympathy has turned to empathy. I've got her. Now and after tonight.

Lainey's inner walls flutter against me. I can feel the tingle building in my balls

"May I come?" I ask for Lainey as much as me.

"No. Not yet. I'm not ready."

Fuck. Lainey's expression is one of pain, and she adjusts her hips so I'm no longer brushing over her G-spot. A no for me is a no for her, and she knows it.

"I see what you're doing." Sawyer chuckles in her ear. "Don't you want to come all over his cock, dirty girl?" *I fucking want that. Will he allow it?* "Don't you want to soak his stomach with your sweet release?" *Yes.*

"Yes, Sir."

"Then why did you shift? No one comes before you. You are our priority. Isn't that right, Eli?" I nod my answer a little too enthusiastically. "See, your fuck toy wants you to come. Now rub that pretty pussy all over his fat cock and come for us."

His words are filthy, but nothing compares to the word "our." Sawyer referred to Lainey as *ours.* Hope blooms in my chest, and I become reinvigorated.

I pump up again, meeting the rhythm, thrust for thrust. Lainey's clit slams against me with each move, and I feel her inner walls flutter around me again. Sweet moans dance around the room, and I hear her whispered question to Sawyer.

"Can I come, Sir?"

"Do it, Alaina."

The words are like a salve to my heated skin, and her hips twitch in sporadic movement as she squeezes me inside her.

"May..I…come…Sir?" Each word comes through gritted teeth as I hold back the orgasm that's begging to be released.

"Come for us, Eli."

It takes my mind a moment to relax before pleasure explodes through my body. My hands involuntarily fly to Lainey's hips, which are already occupied by Sawyer's hands. When I realize what I've done, I try to pull away, but he stops me by lacing his pointer finger over mine—a silent olive branch.

Sawyer's eyes close, and he grunts his release. I relish in the final moments of our connection, knowing this was transactional, and as soon as the scene ends, so will our cease-fire.

# 70

# Lainey

Leaning back on Sawyer, I release my aching arms and take several deep breaths. Elliot's blue eyes stare toward me, but he's not focused on me. He's in a heated staring moment with Sawyer.

My heart aches to return to what we had, but there's still a cavern of emotions between the guys, and they need to work on it together. Sawyer feels hurt and betrayed, for me and for himself. Elliot has been focusing on healing his relationship with me, but it's Sawyer's turn now.

"Don't move." Sawyer kisses my shoulder, and Elliot closes his eyes when he pulls out.

I mouth "Hi" to Elliot, and his face lights up. His hands still sit on my hips, and he squeezes his response and mouths, "Miss you." I want nothing more than to lean down and kiss him. Tell him everything is going to be okay. But I'll wait. I have to have a conversation with Sawyer first.

Elliot's thumbs shift and graze the very edge of my growing bump. I'm reminded he hasn't been part of this pregnancy yet, and seeing me like this has to be emotional for him. I believed Wynnie when she told me Elliot would do right by us and never abandon his baby. Everything I know of this man tells me he's compassionate and loving. We all go through hard times and grieve differently. It's how we deal with the aftermath that defines a relationship. Making the decision to stay, to fight. Elliot asked us not to give up on him, and I didn't. I haven't.

"Love you."

Two barely whispered words crack what little exterior I had. I fall forward onto Elliot's chest, and the tears flow. He's been through enough and doesn't deserve to be punished, at least not by me any longer.

He hesitates before wrapping his arms around me, but as soon as I feel the embrace that's so uniquely Elliot, I'm gone. I give over to every emotion built up since he left us.

Shock.

Pain.

Grief.

Doubt.

Acceptance.

Longing.

Everything floods through me.

Elliot whispers sweet words of praise in my ears, and it's almost too much to hear. The I love yous, I'm sorrys, and please forgive mes makes my heart ache.

Even when I hear Sawyer approach and know I should move, I can't force my body to leave the man I've been missing with half my heart.

I shudder when Sawyer's hand glides up my spine and brace myself for which persona he'll show me. Acceptance or defiance? I was told not to move, but I did. I was told not to touch, but I couldn't stop.

"Let me clean you both up." My body releases the tension I was holding while waiting for Sawyer to speak. Sweet, loving Dom Sawyer provides us aftercare. He makes sure we are both cleaned up. When he's done, I see the shift. Husband Sawyer takes over, and he's the man who isn't happy with Elliot. I don't fault him for it.

Kissing my forehead, Elliot tells me again how much he loves me, and I can feel his reluctance as he lets me go. Sawyer gave us more time together, which I'm sure he was uncomfortable with, but it was for me, not him.

Sawyer takes me in his arms when I climb off the bed, and Elliot doesn't move.

"This changes nothing between us, Elliot."

Sawyer's words are like a vice grip to my heart. Everything changed for me tonight. It wasn't the sex; it was the emotion behind it. The reconnection of our bodies that let me know he still cares. He still loves me. He's sorry he hurt me.

Their pain is different, and I can't expect a scene like this to change things between them. Especially since I selfishly encouraged Sawyer to take out some frustration on Elliot.

"I expect nothing less, but it's a beginning."

Sawyer guides me to the door, and I hear the bed rustle. I look over my shoulder before Sawyer shuffles me out, and Elliot is propped up on his elbows, watching me. He nods, and it's a wordless encouragement that we're okay. I follow Sawyer out with a newfound acceptance of our situation and a determination to help the two men I love reconcile.

Tension has been high in my house. Sawyer has tiptoed around anything Elliot-related, ignoring the small gifts he still gives me at work. Though now, to my delight, Elliot doesn't sneak in early or late. He proudly walks up to my desk and hands me my gifts in the morning. In the afternoon, he walks me to my car, and we exchange sweet words of love, but nothing else.

The Christmas holiday has come and gone, and I felt the weight of Elliot's absence. He went home for a few days and returned looking hollow. Their first Christmas without Scotty weighed heavily on everyone's spirits, and he brought the feeling back with him.

Christmas morning, there was a knock on our door, and a pile of packages awaited us when we opened it. Dozens of boxes, big and small, littered the hallway—each containing necessities for the baby. Elliot bought the entire registry I had created on his insistence.

A simple note accompanies the gifts.

*Because I love each of you, and this baby combines all our love. They will want for nothing.*
*~Elliot*

The reminder of many offhanded comments play on repeat in my mind. Elliot spends money like he has it but doesn't live a lavish life. His house is moderate, though it's surprising for someone his age to own. There's nothing too extravagant about his car other than being new. The gifts he gives me are coffee shop pastries and convenient store trinkets, not diamonds and designer purses. But he's put thousands of dollars in our account and was going to charter a plane to get to Wynnie.

There's more to Elliot than either of us knows.

"I want to invite him to the ultrasound."

"We can send him a video."

"Sawyer, that's not fair, and you know it. I've respected your feelings, but I won't budge on this."

"Alai—"

"Don't you dare. I won't be submitted out of this. If you feel so passionately about him not going, maybe *you* should stay home?"

I stand my ground as an angry Sawyer charges toward me. I'm not afraid of him or his reactions. He stops in front of me, panting like a bull. A firm hand grips the hair at the nape of my neck, and he tugs so I'm looking up at him.

"I won't be kept away from my child."

"I won't keep him away from his, either." Sawyer blinks several times, registering my words. We don't talk about the paternity of the baby because it doesn't matter to us who the father is, but shoving it in his face causes the reaction I was hoping for.

Guilt and acceptance flood his features, and his hand loosens. Sawyer knows I'm right, and as much as he hates to admit it, he can't argue. If the roles were reversed, he would feel the same way. Elliot had already been kept out of so much of my pregnancy because he wasn't here. This is the first time he's going to get to be involved. I haven't said anything to him yet because I know he'll drop whatever he's doing to be there, and I wanted to get Sawyer's final approval.

Sawyer drops his forehead to mine, and I see the pain in his eyes. It's not that he doesn't want Elliot there. It hurts him. He's struggling to forgive Elliot's actions as much as he's coming to understand what he did was out of grief and his own guilt.

"You're killing me, Jitterbug. I'm sorry. I'm trying."

I cup his cheek and rub my thumb over his stubble. "I know you are, but you need to find a way to let him in. He loves you, and it's hurting him as much as it is you."

"His betrayal cut deep. It's not as easy for me as a Danish and some roses."

"I know. And it shouldn't be, but you need to find some common ground. If you need to fuck it out of him, that man will bend over and touch his toes for you. If you need to throw punches, he'll take it and clean up your hands through his swollen eyes. Elliot's love is deep and boundless, but you need to hear it from him, not me."

"How did you let it go so easily?"

"You know my past. Love doesn't come easy for me. I guarded my heart until I could trust him. Did he hurt me when he tried to deny the baby? Of course. It hurt like hell. But grief is a bitch with sharp teeth and piercing claws. I had to decide if I was going to drown in it or fight like hell to make it to shore. I chose love. I had already chosen Elliot. Letting go of my anger was easier than letting go of the love he earned."

"He loved you first."

It's hard not to chuckle at his remark because it's absurd. "He may have said it to me first, but he loved you from the moment you bumped into each other at Midnight Moonshine. And you loved him then, too."

"I love you. You're pretty smart when you aren't being a brat." Sawyer playfully pops me on the ass, and I feel relief that we are one step closer to their reconciliation.

# 71

## Elliot

I can't stop staring at the text from Lainey. I'm convinced if I look away, her words will disappear, and it will just be some kind of a cruel dream.

Lainey: We have an ultrasound appointment to see the baby on Tuesday. We'd love for you to join us. We are finding out the gender.

The words that jump off the screen at me are "We'd love." *We*. As in plural. Lainey AND Sawyer.

*Sawyer.*

Thoughts of him make me ache inside. I miss him so goddamn much. I miss *us*. The us we created in the most unexpected ways. Three people coming together to love each other uniquely and wholly.

Elliot: I wouldn't miss it for the world. Maybe we can get dinner together afterward?

Lainey: I'll convince him.

I hate that she has to bribe and barter with him to spend time with me, but I'll take every chance I can to break his hard exterior.

Twenty minutes early, I'm waiting in front of the address Lainey sent me. I expected a doctor's office, but it's a private ultrasound business, and I wonder if she set this up just for me.

I see them approaching from the parking garage and can't help but feel lucky. Lainey looks beautiful in dark jeans, a dark green puffy jacket, and a white hat adorned with a poof ball. Sawyer looks just as delicious in a navy peacoat and matching hat sans poof ball.

Lainey throws her arms around my neck, and I wrap my arms around her growing midsection. Sawyer and I lock eyes over her shoulder, and he gives me a tight-lipped nod. Progress. It's not a scowl.

"Are you ready?" Lainey asks enthusiastically.

"More than ready."

The ride in the elevator is quiet, and there's a buzz of tension in the air. More than a buzz. It's a live wire flailing around, waiting for an unsuspecting victim. The question is, which one of us will it be?

The tension turns to anticipation when the gelled-up wand trails over Lainey's belly. Sawyer holds her hand while I caress her leg. I remember being in the room during my mother's ultrasounds with Finn and Paige. I went with Wynnie and saw Ella and Archie. But this? Nothing compares to seeing a life I created on the screen.

With Lainey halfway through her pregnancy, there are

516

fully formed arms and legs. The nose is prominent, and the baby can even be seen sucking its thumb.

There's no greater feeling in the world than right now, and I don't stop the tears that coat my cheeks. Lainey urges me to come closer and hold her other hand. Her fingers wiggle in the air, and I turn my gaze to Sawyer. The only way for me to hold her hand is to be right next to him, and I won't cross that boundary if he doesn't want me to.

A barely perceptible nod is his answer to my silent question, and I step forward. Lainey pulls me closer, making Sawyer and I stand shoulder to shoulder. A low groan slips through my lips at the contact, and I cover it with a cough. I see Lainey's lip twitch at my terrible attempt, but no one says anything.

"Are we ready to find out the sex?" the tech asks.

Yeses fill the room, and she moves the wand to adjust the baby and get a good picture.

I see it before they do because I know what I'm looking for. Biting my lip, I contain the sob as I squeeze Lainey's hand and lean a little closer into Sawyer.

"What is it?" Sawyer asks, trying to understand the screen.

"A girl," I whisper before the tech can respond.

Sawyer's head whips to me and back to the tech. She nods with a smile, and my heart breaks wide open when I see his eyes glaze over.

"*A girl.*" Those two words are said with so much reverence it's like a prayer on his lips. He pulls Lainey's hand to his lips and kisses her knuckles. I try to pull away and give them their moment, but Lainey holds onto me like a vice grip.

The look she gives me speaks volumes.

*"Don't you dare move."*

517

*"You're a part of this."*

*"She's your daughter too."*

She could be mine, or she could be Sawyer's. I don't give a fuck either way. If I'm allowed back into their lives, blood or not, she's mine.

I know what it feels like to be unsure of who you are. I was an orphaned pre-teen, and Dellah and Collin welcomed me with open arms. This baby girl will know every ounce of love I have to give. I'll spend every penny in my bank account to make her happy. But deep down, I know money doesn't buy happiness. It all comes down to love, and three people in this room are already unconditionally in love with her, and she isn't even born yet.

The elevator ride back down feels just as charged as the way up, but the energy is different. Lainey's hands twine together, wanting to reach out to both of us, but she's unsure. The doors open to the empty lobby, and she steps out first. I wait, allowing Sawyer to follow her out, but he doesn't move.

I'm fed up with his bullshit. I grab Sawyer's upper arm and pull him out into the lobby. I lead us into the men's room I saw while waiting for them to arrive. He puts up a minimal fight, but there's no conviction behind it. The door makes an echoing bang when it hits the wall from my force.

Sawyer finally pulls his arm from my grip, and fury burns in his gray eyes. Good. That's what I want to see. Fight for me, Sawyer.

"What the fuck, Elliot?" He steps toward me, but I stop his advance and slam him into the wall next to the door. My upper arm pins his shoulders down, and my hips seal the rest of his body to mine.

518

"I'm done letting you determine my relationship with the woman I love. I'm done letting you punish me for something I've apologized for a hundred times. You belong to me just as much as she does and just as much as that baby."

"Guys?" Lainey's concerned voice seeps through the door.

"We're all good, Cherry," I reassure her, and Sawyer says nothing to object. In fact, he says nothing at all. His chest heaves under my arm, and he looks like a bull staring at his mark.

"Are you ready to forgive me?"

"No." The conviction behind his word is admirable, but I feel him wavering. His body reacts under my touch. I have one chance, and I'm either going to get it very wrong or very right.

"On your knees, Wes." His nostrils flair, and I stop myself from smiling.

"What the fuck did you just say to me?"

There it is. The reaction I was hoping for. He didn't immediately tell me no. He didn't push me away. He questioned me.

"You heard me. You seem to not want to take charge of this situation, so I am. On your fucking knees, Wes. Don't make me repeat myself."

I see it. The flicker in his eyes. The moment that he accepts his fate. Dropping my arm, I take a small step back. He leans to the left, and I think he's going to run, but he locks the door, letting me know he's fully accepted his fate.

Watching this man sink to his knees is the most powerful thing I've ever witnessed. I'm rendered speechless when he bows his head, waiting for his next command. I plan to commit every moment of this to memory. There won't be another opportunity to see Sawyer this vulnerable. This is a gift he's giving me.

A soft moan escapes him when my hand runs through his thick hair.

"Take me out of my pants."

Sawyer's hands tremble as they unfasten my belt. He fumbles with the button on my jeans and eventually pulls my hard cock out. It hangs heavy and needy in front of his face, and I watch his Adam's apple bob. The power is intoxication. I'm all too eager to shove my cock down the back of his throat, but there are two levels to this.

Yes, he's currently on his knees for me, but it was his choice to give me this power. I have to also take from him, and I know that's going to be equally as hard.

"Do you want my cock?" He nods, and I smirk. He knows better. I run my thumb over his bottom lip before tugging it between my fingers, letting it snap back. "Words, Wes."

"Yes, E."

"Good boy. Now, take it down your throat, and don't stop until you make me come."

Sawyer sucks me in like a man starved, and I can see the tension melt from his body. He holds everything together. I know the stress of being the dominant in a relationship can hold, and he takes his role seriously.

His mouth is heaven, and I have to brace myself against the wall to stop my knees from buckling. I want this to last forever, but I need to finish this apology tour.

"Play with my balls. Make me come and swallow every drop." Sawyer takes my commands as law, and soon, I'm coming down his throat, trying not to scream my release in a public building.

"Fucking incredible. Now it's my turn. Stand."

Sawyer stands, licking his lips of any remnants of me. I want to devour his lips, but I won't give him the satisfaction.

As I tuck myself back into my pants, I purposely brush the front of his jeans. His cock strains against the front of his pants and my mouth waters, wanting to give him the same pleasure he just gave me.

"Pull your cock out."

"Why?"

Gripping his jaw with my hand, I get close enough to share breath. "Because I fucking said so, and I'm still in charge."

This is the true test. Will he give up his final shred of restraint? Will he finally forgive me and give in?

"You know your safeword, Wes. Use it if you need it." I know he won't. He'd rather use his last breath to curse me out than admit defeat. I'm not asking for anything but his forgiveness.

His hand pauses on his belt, holding onto the very last scrap as long as possible. It isn't until I hear the teeth of his zipper that I know I've won. He's forgiving me and letting go of the anger. The betrayal.

The floor is cold on my knees when I lower myself to give my final apology because that's what this is. Sawyer's body leans against the wall when I pull him in. Gentle hands hold the side of my head while I bob on his cock. I want to tell him to use me, but he knows he doesn't need permission. If he wanted to, he could fuck my face, and he knows I'd take it. But that's not what this is about. He's letting me back in.

I give Sawyer the best goddamn blow job of my life, but he's holding himself back. He's still gripping onto the last remnants of his dominance and not allowing himself to come. I need him to release the last scraps of his control. I think I know how.

# 72

# Lainey

I'm surprised I haven't worn a hole in the floor with my pacing. I heard the door lock. The occasional noises drifting through the door sound like pleasure and not pain. I trust them both to be adults and hope they are working things out as such.

The door lock clicks, and I hold my breath, waiting. Nothing happens. No one comes out. I tentatively knock and hear Sawyer grunt before Elliot's voice tells me to come in.

Nothing prepares me for what I see. Elliot is on his knees with Sawyer's cock deep down his throat. I understand the severity of this powerplay, but I don't know why I was invited in.

Elliot waves me over, and I lock the door behind me before joining them. They look beautiful together, and I realize how much I've missed their intimacy as much as my own.

There's a grunt and an audible pop when Elliot pulls off Sawyer.

"Cherry, Sawyer needs you." My eyes are trained on Elliot's hand as he pumps Sawyer's length. "He needs *us*."

I lock eyes with my husband and see a look of desperation. He's always a confident man, and seeing him struggle unnerves me. Taking his cheeks in my hands, I look into his beautiful gray eyes.

"How can I help you, Baby?"

Elliot sucks him back in, and Sawyer bangs his head against the wall several times. I see it now. He doesn't know how to let go. That's what Elliot meant by he needs us.

"Look at me." Sawyer's head lulls to the side, looking at me with desperation. "I've got you. It's okay." Pressing my lips to his, he takes over the kiss. He needs this. A feeling of being in control when Elliot's actions were making him lose it all.

I whisper words of praise and encouragement through our kiss.

*"You're safe."*

*"We love you."*

*"You can let go."*

*"We're here to catch you."*

I remind him we're both here.

I peek when I feel him shift and see he's gripped Elliot's hair and taken over the thrusting. Sawyer's noises change, and I know he's finally close to letting go.

"Give it to him, Baby. Come down Elliot's pretty throat."

Sawyer pulls away from me and slams his head against the wall again. Both hands thread through Elliot's hair, and with a roar, Sawyer holds him in place and comes.

When he finishes, he grabs Elliot by the neck and pulls

him to standing. Elliot doesn't fight him, and Sawyer's gray eyes ping pong between Elliot's blues.

In a heartbeat, Sawyer spins Elliot and pins him against the wall, reversing their roles. He jolts forward, locking their lips together. It's a struggle of power before Elliot's lips concede.

"Never." *Kiss.* "Fucking." *Suck.* "Put me." *Lick.* "On my knees." *Kiss.* "Again." Sawyer bites Elliot's neck hard enough to make him gasp, then licks away the sting.

"Yes, Sir," Elliot purrs.

"Fuck you. Fuck you, and don't you ever think of leaving us again. That was your one and only chance. Do you understand me? No amount of cherry pastries, roses, or even a fucking castle will get you in my good graces again. The choice is yours right now. Stay or go, but decide and stick with it."

The intensity of their stare-off sends shivers down my spine. Slowly, Elliot's hand reaches toward me and lands on my belly. I suck in a breath as he caresses our daughter for the first time.

"I'm all in. For all three of you. Especially her." All eyes fall to my baby bump. "Are we good, Sawyer?"

Sawyer's silence screams in the room, and an icy heat flashes through my body. He needs to say yes. We didn't come this far to still be stuck in limbo.

"You're staying? Even if she's mine?"

"Especially if she's yours." Elliot smiles, and Sawyer keeps us in suspense before he leans back in and tenderly kisses Elliot's lips.

"Yeah. We're good."

"Thank fuck. Can we please go feed our little girl now?"

"Anything you want, Cherry, it's yours."

🖥 🖥 🖥 🖥 🖥

I didn't think it would be so easy. The transition from anger and rage to love and affection was like a light switch. It's only been a week since the bathroom blowjobs, but it's as if the past several missed months never happened. All except Elliot's constant touching of my belly.

I hate that he missed half of my pregnancy, but with every caress and cuddle, he makes up for it.

Elliot: Buy a new dress and a suit and meet me at this address. A car will pick you up at 6pm.

Sawyer: That's a lot of money for a suit and dress, Elliot.

Lainey: Can I buy jewelry and shoes?

Elliot: Only if they are diamonds. I'd tell you to get red bottoms, too, but I don't want you to fall and hurt our daughter.

Sawyer: I repeat. That's a lot of money for some clothes and jewelry, Elliot.

Elliot: I'll explain tonight. The car will pick you up at six sharp. Be ready.

I hear Sawyer growl from the other room and pull up our banking app to see how much "a lot" is on Sawyer's terms. The phone falls from my hand when I see a ten thousand-dollar deposit.

"Sawyer!" He comes rushing in and immediately looks to my belly.

"What's wrong? Are you okay? Is she okay?"

"Ten thousand," I whisper as if there's someone who could hear me outside of our apartment.

"I told you it was a lot. I've given up. If he wants to send us money, I'm going to stop complaining. It makes him happy."

"Ten thousand." I know I sound like a broken record, but I've never seen that many zeros in our bank account.

"Where should we go shopping, Jitterbug?"

# 73

# Elliot

I've never been so nervous. I've made a decision that affects all of us, but I didn't consult them. What if they hate the idea? I don't expect them to help, but this is a commitment for me, and having their support would mean the world. This is a future I'm creating for our daughter and a legacy for my best friend.

Car lights pull down the road right on time. I step out in the balmy air and quickly open the car door when it stops.

"Come in. It's freezing out here." Lainey gives me her hand, and we quickly shuffle into the empty storefront. I arrived early to set up a space heater and warm the room. Currently, the only thing in here is a table with blueprints and my laptop.

"What's all this?" Sawyer looks around, and I admit it doesn't look like much right now. The space has already been gutted, but I've drawn chalk lines around the room for visual effect, along with the virtual tour my designer mocked up.

"My future. *Our* future, I hope."

"I don't understand." Lainey wanders to the table with the blueprints, and I'm sure she can't understand them. Even after having everything explained to me, it all still looks like lines on a large piece of paper.

Lainey gasps, and I wonder what she's seen to cause her reaction.

"Elliot, why is your name on here as the client?" Stepping up behind her, I wrap my arms around her growing bump.

"Because it's my project. I bought the building."

"For?"

"How about we step into the office? I can start from the beginning." I take each of their hands and lead them to the back of the space and through a set of double doors. The kitchen area is just as barren as the front room, but the office is the opposite.

A rug, couch, and small dining table are set up in the middle of the room. Next to it is a small buffet of food for us to eat and a mini refrigerator with drinks. The space heater in this room has more than done its job, and the office area is warm enough that I take Lainey and Sawyer's jackets.

"You both look fucking incredible." I run my fingers down the lapel of Sawyer's double-breasted charcoal suit with pinstripes. He's paired it with a white shirt and a silver patterned tie that reflects the gray of his eyes. "Money well spent."

I kiss Sawyer tenderly and sweetly because we have a lot to discuss. Turning to Lainey, I lose my breath. Despite the cold weather, her red dress covers only one shoulder. A silver belt sits over her baby bump, accenting the stretchy fabric that molds to her frame.

My hands have a mind of their own as they make circles over our daughter's protective house.

"Stunning, Cherry." I'm convinced she wears red just for me. I express in my kiss to her how much I appreciate her beauty. "Take a seat."

I wait until everyone is comfortable before I begin my story.

"I haven't shared much of my story with you because it's easy for people to take advantage of."

Lainey reaches out and takes my hand. "We would never—"

"I know that now. But we met on the internet. Not everyone is genuine."

"Go on," Sawyer encourages and takes my other hand.

"You know my father died in a car accident, but did you ever wonder why his name is on the fountain in front of Annie's building?"

"I assumed he worked there. Did he not?" Lainey questions.

I shake my head. "No. Annie's car was involved in the accident that took his life." Lainey inhales a sharp breath, and I squeeze her hand. "She wasn't driving. She was a passenger in the back seat. My dad ran the light, or her driver wasn't paying attention. I'm not entirely sure. Either way, I became an orphan that day."

"Shortly after Collin and Dellah adopted my brother, sister, and I, they received notice in the mail that Annie had set up trust funds for the three of us. She researched my dad and found out about us. She wanted to make sure we were taken care of."

"Annie did that?" Tears well in Lainey's eyes, and I know my eyes mirror the same.

"I promise I earned my job in her company with my own merit." I can't have them thinking I was handed the job because she felt some kind of guilt.

"We believe you, Elliot." Sawyer's smile reassures me they do.

"I was smart with my money. My parents taught me how to properly invest and save. I moved here for the opportunities the job afforded me, and I fell in love. Not once but twice."

"So, you have money? You know that doesn't matter to us. We don't love you for what you can give to us."

"I know, Cherry. You don't need to keep defending yourselves." I kiss each one of them before continuing.

"A few months ago, I fucked up. Big time. Don't try to defend my actions. I can look back now and see what a complete asshole I was and how much I deserved everything that came my way. Several lives were turned upside down by Scotty's death." I pause and take a deep breath. This is the part that will make or break us. "That brings me to this place."

"What is this place, Elliot? You said it was our future."

"Lainey, the day you barged into Annie's office, I was giving my long-term resignation and getting business advice. I was also asking her if she'd like to be an investor. The best business people understand they need a village."

"So this is an investment?"

"No, it's ours. Hers." I rub a hand over Lainey's bump. "I'm opening a Chicago location of Scotty's bar, Tipsy Penny."

Lainey's lip quivers as the first tear slips down her cheek.

"What did she say when you told her?"

I'm brought back to the memory of the day Wynnie helped move me here.

*"Are you ready for orientation?" Wynnie leans her head on my shoulder.*

*"Am I ready to follow in both my fathers' footsteps and conquer the business world? Yes." I turn and pull her into a hug. "Am I ready to live eleven hours away from my best friend, nieces, and nephew? Absolutely fucking not. Doesn't Scotty want to franchise and open a Tipsy Penny here? I can fund it."*

*"This is hard on me, too."*

"I haven't. I asked her parents, and they said I should keep it as a surprise. I once joked about him opening a franchise here. After... Well, it didn't feel like so much of a joke. It felt like something I could do to continue his legacy."

My tears drift down my cheeks and dot my pale blue dress shirt. Sawyer sniffles next to me, and I know none of us have been spared the sadness of Scotty's passing.

"I'm still not sure what this has to do with us?" I swipe a tear from Lainey's rosy cheeks and smile.

"Sawyer has the coffee shop, but Gus practically runs the place. I thought the three of us could run Tipsy Penny II together. Scotty's bar manager, Kristina, has agreed to come up for a week and show us the ropes once we get the place ready. I want to run it just like he did."

"But you and I have jobs. We can't just leave."

"Cherry, Annie is a businesswoman. She agreed to invest in us because she knows we will succeed. That includes replacing us when the time comes. But our jobs are safe until we don't need them anymore."

"You've really thought of everything, huh?"

"Sawyer, I know this is huge. I want to do it together, but I'll do it alone if it's too much. Neither of you have any obligation. I realize I did this without you, but we were on such rocky ground, and my realtor showed me this place. I had to take it. It's perfect. Actually, wait here."

# 74

## Sawyer

I keep a careful watch on Lainey. I understand the business side of things because of Java Junkie. She never wanted to be a part of my business, and it's always been okay with me. Elliot is offering us an opportunity that I'm happy to venture into with him, but I'm not sure how she's feeling.

Before I have a chance to answer, Elliot comes back in with his laptop.

"Let me show you my vision."

The virtual tour is an incredible mix of modern and rustic. There are side-by-side pictures of Scotty's bar and how he plans to mimic the decor. I can see his vision even better when we walk into the main space, and he points out where he has things outlined in chalk. Elliot really has thought of everything.

"Don't answer me right now. I've asked a lot of you. Think about it and know, whatever level of participation you're comfortable with, I'm grateful for it."

I can see in Lainey's eyes she's all in. I am, too. Elliot has a solid plan. The space and location are perfect. And if he was able to get Annie to invest, it means she is confident his—*our*—business will succeed. Our daughter will have not one but two legacies to build and grow with.

*Maybe we should have more than one kid?*

Holy shit. Let's get through one first.

Elliot brings us back into the office, where a meal of steak, potatoes, and asparagus waits for us. The dinner is delicious, though I don't know why we had to dress up for this.

"There's one more thing." Elliot pats the corner of his mouth with his napkin and lays it on the table. I can't imagine what more he could have planned. We are sitting in an empty building that he bought to turn into a bar for us, and apparently, he's loaded.

Elliot moves around the table and stands between us. He looks nervous as he reaches into his jacket pocket and pulls out a closed fist.

"I've been through a lot in my life, and because of that, I understand the importance of loving people with your entire being. The need to hold onto them with every fiber of your soul because you never know when they won't be there. I thought I lost you both once, and as much as it was my doing, it tore me up inside every day." Elliot drops to one knee, and Lainey gasps, covering her mouth with her hands. "I know the two of you are already married, and nothing could ever be legal between us, but I want to spend the rest of my life with you both. If you'll have me."

Elliot opens his hand, revealing three matching bands. They have what looks like diamonds and rubies embedded in the bands. Two are thicker, and one is thin and smaller.

Lainey looks at me with tears and anticipation in her eyes. "We're saying yes, right?"

I couldn't deny this woman anything. With a smile, I take her hand and hold it out to Elliot. He gently places the band on her left finger. It sits perfectly with the set I gave her, and I wonder how he got them to match.

Lainey takes my hand and offers it to Elliot, and he slides a matching ring to my left ring finger. As he reaches for the third ring, I take it from his hand.

"Let me. We would love to spend the rest of our lives with you. A marriage license is just a signature on a piece of paper. We don't need a piece of paper to make you our husband." I slip the ring on his finger and lace them together. I place my free hand over his heart and kiss his forehead. "Love makes a relationship—love, understanding, compassion, and communication. As long as we never forget that again, our marriage will be happy, healthy, and long. I do."

"I do." Lainey crashes into Elliot, knocking him on his ass as she peppers him with kisses.

"I do, too," he mumbles into her mouth.

"Alaina. Eli." They freeze. "Stand." Elliot helps Lainey to her feet, and they stand shoulder to shoulder. I lift each of their left hands and kiss our new rings. "I love you both. I want to go home and show you how much. Alaina, sit and wait. Eli, clean up whatever you need to so we can leave. Is your car here?"

"Yes, Sir."

"Tell me where, and I'll get it warmed up." Elliot hands me his keys and instructs me how to get to the back door where he parked.

The ride home is filled with tense anticipation. I sit in

the back while Lainey sits in the passenger seat. Several times, I've seen Elliot's hand move to hold Lainey's, but his eyes flash to mine in the rearview, and he pulls back at my expressionless stare.

It wouldn't bother me if he held her hand, but I find it entertaining that he's stopping himself, not knowing which role he's in at the moment.

"She's yours, Elliot. You don't need permission. Not unless I tell you otherwise." His shoulders fall in relief, and his hand grazes up Lainey's thigh before she laces her fingers with his.

We come back to our apartment, and clothes litter the floor as we make our way to the bedroom. Elliot strips and kneels at the foot of the bed with Lainey following behind him, sitting on the bed. It's incredible to see them get ready for me, but it's not what I want.

"I don't want to play. I want to make love to our wife and our husband. *My* wife and husband."

Elliot smiles as his eyes trail up my body, and he stands. His lips meet my neck, and I tilt my head to give him full access.

"What if I have an idea, Doll? I was thinking I'd like a little Cherry on top of my sundae. Would you care to partake?" Elliot's hand cups my cock over my pants, and I slowly nod. Whatever he has in mind, I'm in.

"Oh, fuck. Fucking, fuck, Elliot."

When he said Cherry on top, he meant it. My back rests against the headboard while Elliot's ass swallows my cock. Holding his hips, I kiss between his shoulder blades and lick a line down his spine while he bounces on me. Lainey's moans battle mine as she sits on top of Elliot, holding on for the ride. His hips seesaw between us, fucking and being fucked. I want to drown in the feelings of love, lust, and desire.

"Who's gonna come first?" Elliot asks while laughing, but quickly stops when I pitch my hips forward, and my cock runs over his prostate.

"Looks like it's going to be you."

"It's me. Oh fuck, fuck yesssssss." Lainey buries her head in Elliot's shoulder, muffling her cries.

"Fucking shit, Cherry. Your pussy is uuuuuugh."

"Another one bites the dust." I fuck into him hard and fast, chasing my release. Elliot's clenching seals my fate, and my orgasm explodes. Tears prickle the back of my eyes at the immense joy I feel in this moment with them.

We collapse in a heap on the bed. I try to regulate my breathing so I can get us all cleaned up, but Lainey rolls off the bed, telling us to stay.

"She's a bossy little thing, isn't she?"

Pulling him onto my chest, I kiss his forehead and pick up Elliot's left hand. My fingers twist his ring, and I smile.

"She's our bossy little thing."

"Ours," he repeats.

# Epilogue

## Elliot

*8 months later*

My mind is a whirlwind of chaos. Everything that could go wrong has. We had to find a last-minute caterer when ours crashed their food truck. The cake order got lost three times. Our liquor distributor delivered everything we needed except the blue curaço for Scotty Special Blue drinks. Fortunately, with everyone's help, it has all come together, and she's on her way.

Everyone managed to keep the new bar a secret from Wynnie and she thinks she's coming here to surprise me. Aunt Hazel told her I got a promotion, and nothing would make it more special than an impromptu trip to visit.

Her flight with Aunt Hazel, my mom, and the three kids lands in about an hour. Uncle Mac, Jude, and Phoenix are already here with their kids, Dean, Alex, DJ, and Piper. My dad, Finn, and Paige came with them. They all took a flight earlier this morning and, for the first time, complained about how inconvenient it was to live on their little compound. Sneaking around Wynnie and trying

539

to make plans with nosey kids proved harder than they realized.

Despite all the mishaps, we're ready. I have a car service set to pick them up at the airport with the guise that Sawyer and Lainey hired for them. I honestly don't know how, with so many moving parts, she still doesn't know.

I'm so proud of how she's been thriving since Scotty passed. She still has her hard days, but they are spreading out more and more.

"We're all set, Bossman. Are you ready? The place looks perfect."

Kristina has been invaluable these last few days, and I've tried to convince her to make the move to help run this place. She keeps telling me no, but I think she's wavering. Wynnie has taken on a bigger role at the bar, and I know the image of Scotty on the office floor still haunts Kristina. I can't blame her. I'd never take her away from Wynnie, but I wouldn't turn her down if she asked to stay, either.

"I'm as ready as I can ever be. Do you think she'll like it?"

"Elliot, you know she's going to love it. Expect her to bawl her eyes out. If she walks in the front door and doesn't immediately make a wish, I'll kick her ass for you." Hazel was more than happy to give me the crystal Wynnie bought for her as a pre-teen. I knew this place wouldn't be complete without a wishing crystal of its own.

"So the booze is free for *everyone* tonight, right?"

"Absolutely, Finny." I swing my arm over his shoulder. He's my height now, and it makes me sad that my little brother isn't so little anymore. "Free to anyone *over* the age of twenty-one."

"Big brothers are no fun."

"Aren't you glad you have two obnoxious ones, Paige?"

"I'm proud of you," she whispers, and I almost laugh, but I don't want to ruin the moment.

"What's that little sis? I'm the best big brother in the world?" I bump my shoulder against her to be obnoxious.

"Ugh. You had to make it weird. I said I'm proud of you, idiot. Wynnie is going to cry."

"I guess that's kind of the plan, isn't it."

A balloon pops, and a shrill cry pierces my ears. Uncle Jude picks up a crying Piper and whispers into her ear. He smooths her matching sandy blonde hair, and my heart swells. Uncle Phoenix and DJ are daddy's girl goals, but Jude and Piper are on another level. They have a connection with just a look. None of the kids are treated any differently in their house, no matter who their biological father is, but there are some things biology overrules.

"Hey, Daddy. Someone wants to see you." My incredible wife steps in front of me and hands me our beautiful baby girl. Charlotte Penelope could not be any more perfect. Two months ago, Lainey delivered our healthy baby girl. She came out looking identical to her mama with red, peach fuzz hair and wide blue eyes that wrapped us around her tiny fingers from day one.

We didn't want to do a paternity test. It didn't matter whose DNA ran through her blood because she belonged to the three of us in every way imaginable, but our lawyer convinced us it would make her safer to know.

Charlotte is mine as we suspected all along. But as soon as Lainey gives him the all-clear, Sawyer has called dibs on our next baby.

"I can tell you're nervous. Don't be. Wynnie has already

texted me several times today. I've convinced her you're clueless. She's going to let me know when they park so we can be ready."

"She's coming in the back door, right? I don't want her to see the sign out front and spoil it."

"Yes, Elliot. Relax." Big, beautiful hands steal my baby away, and I scowl at my husband. "You still have things to get ready. Don't give me that look."

I sigh and give him a quick kiss. He's right. As much as I want to snuggle my baby girl all day, today is the day I've been anticipating since I bought the building. Today, Wynnie gets to see what I've done for her.

"Hey, Elliot," Uncle Mac calls from the front of the bar. "There's a brunette with a baby on her hip, a Viking-looking guy, and four other little hellions waving at me right now. Do you know them?"

"Baby!" Blake flies past us and flings open the front door. She steals Lina from Katy's arms, and Lainey laughs.

"Cole, please knock that woman up before she starts stealing our babies."

He throws his hands in the air and shrugs. "That's what I keep telling her. Be my wingwoman, Lainey. Help me convince her."

"She's convinced." Annie's voice startles me, and Lainey and I turn to see our ex-boss smiling at us. Every person in this room has helped create this space to be what it is, but Annie's name made the most impact with getting everything done as quickly as it did. I had no idea the red tape I would have to cut through for a liquor license, building inspections, and a certificate of occupancy. "She's ready for another baby. Blake's just enjoying stringing him along."

"Sounds like something she would do."

"You've done an excellent job, Elliot. You should be proud of yourself." Annie's blonde bob swirls around her shoulders as she takes in the final product.

"I couldn't have done it without you, Annie. You've been invaluable to the start of this. Thank you."

"I take payment in the form of babysitting." She smiles again and saunters toward Blake, who looks like she's trying to eat baby Lina.

"We've got another lively bunch approaching," Mac calls again from the front door.

"Hey, Uncle Mac, do you need a new job? Seems like you'd make a good bouncer." He glares at my sister as she walks past him with a tower of coasters in her hand.

I see the disaster before it happens. In slow motion, a gaggle of girls tear through the open seating space. Justine, Piper, Rosie, and Ruth are giggling so hard they don't see Paige, and it's suddenly raining coasters with the image of shiny copper pennies on them.

The room is silent as Justin walks in holding their daughter, Frankie's hand, and Nicole carries baby June on her hip. They look around with confused faces, and I don't blame them. The chaos of the day has continued, and I have two choices. Fall apart or laugh.

I choose laughter. A big, boisterous laugh from deep in my gut fills the silence. How could I be upset? Everyone I love and respect is here or on their way. This place could be half falling apart and they'd still be here to support me.

I'm laughing so hard, tears stream down my face, and I have to bend over, bracing my hands on my knees to catch my breath.

Squeals of delight from Rory and Ruby break the awkward tension in the room as they run toward Hannah and Miles. Seth clings to Nicole's legs, unsure of what's going on.

Dean and Alex come in from the kitchen with paper plates full of tiny hors devours and inspect the fiasco around.

"I thought this was a party?" Dean's cheeks turn pink, and his blue eyes widen when his voice cracks on the last word. He clears his throat before repeating his question in a deep, manly voice.

Alex pushes past him, mumbling, "Didn't know I had another sister."

"Alexander," Jude's Dad voice booms. "Don't be disrespectful. Apologize."

Alex shifts uncomfortably on his feet, not liking being reprimanded in front of so many people.

"Sorry, *Gideon.*"

Mac turns from the scene, hiding his smile. He leans into Jude's ear, and whatever he says makes Jude punch his shoulder.

"I need to know who belongs to who." I look up into the silver-blue eyes of Katy's Viking. Everyone is always curious about Aunt Hazel's relationship. I know Vik's question comes from sheer curiosity and not judgment. "But before you tell me, I came over here to tell you Patrick and Chip are running a little late. Violet had a blowout. But they got whatever was needed for the blue drinks."

"Perfect. Thank you. So, the kids. It's in the eyes. Wynnie and Dean belong to Mac. Alex and Piper are Jude's, and Delilah Jane is Phoenix's."

"Do the three of you plan to have a basketball team, too?"

"Yes!" My wife enthusiastically cuts in over my shoulder.

"I guess you have your answer."

"Wynnie just texted me. They've landed and should be here within the hour." Lainey must see my panicked eyes and runs a soothing hand up my arms. "Here." She hands me Charlotte. "Have some baby snuggles for a few minutes, then get back to work."

"We got some more live ones. A pretty redhead, a cowboy, a goofy-looking guy, a cop, and…"

"Miller," Justin offers. "They pulled in next to us. No idea how we managed to get in before them with five kids. They are five grown adults."

I hear a throat clear and see Katy giving Justin an incredulous look. "One word. *Axel*. He's like three kids wrapped in one adult body."

"She's not wrong," Cole calls out while trying to wrangle kids that don't even belong to him.

My head swims as my past, present, and future collide under one roof. All around me, people who helped raise me mix with people who have helped mold me into the adult I've become over the last year.

Mac opens the door for our final guests. Spencer, Tucker, Miller, Lincoln, and Axel pour in the front door, and squeals of joy come from Owen, Emory, and Lexi as they collide with their grandparents.

I busy myself setting up the final details. Tonight may be for family, but tomorrow afternoon is our grand opening. I'm wiping my hands on a bar towel when a head of red hair blocks my view.

"Dad. Everything okay?" His eyes are red-rimmed, but I don't see any reason for him to be upset. He grabs my shoulders and pulls me in for a hug.

"Your parents would be so fucking proud of you. Their deaths were tragic, but I thank them every fucking day for allowing me to take over for them."

"Fucking shit, Dad. I was hoping I didn't cry until Wynnie got here. I expected this from Mom, not you."

He pulls back and looks me in the eyes. "Your mom and I are just as proud. I have no doubt you'll hear it from her as well. They're almost here. You're mom just texted me. Are you ready?"

"No. Yes. Fuck, how could I ever be? Will she hate me for this?" He pulls me back in and pats my back before finally releasing me.

"Wynnie could never hate you. You've done a fantastic thing here. She's going to love it."

"They just pulled up!" Lainey's voice alerts everyone to their arrival, and they all congregate in the bar.

The plan is to have her come in and see how long it takes her to recognize the people or the place. I don't want to shock her and yell surprise because as much as this is a party, it's also a new beginning.

I glance at the monitor I've been doing my best to ignore, and look at the corner of the screen showing the back entrance. A black limo covers half the picture, but the image of my mom and niece spikes my heart rate. Everyone pours out of the car, and I see the back door open. Lainey appears with Charlotte to greet them, and I think I might burst with excitement.

Aunt Hazel holds Ella's hand, and my mom holds Tori back so Wynnie and Archie can walk in first.

"Breathe," Sawyer says into my ear. He kisses my neck, and I take a shuddering breath.

546

"She's here," I breathe out.

"She's here. *You've got this.*"

We stare at the monitor as they walk into the building. I move to the next camera and follow them through the hall. My eyes shift to the entrance into the bar, and I wait.

My incredible best friend, with her long dark hair and unique blue eyes, recognizes what she's seeing the moment she steps into the room. Her eyes scan the space, passing over our family and friends. I know she's looking for me. I give her another moment to scan her surroundings before finally stepping through the crowd.

Her eyes find mine. Wide, blue eyes fill with tears. She passes Archie off to the first person she sees. Blake happily takes him, and Wynnie runs.

I brace myself for the impact when her body crashes into mine, and I lift her into my arms.

"I hate you so much. You're the worst best friend I've ever had. How? How did you keep this from me?"

"It was really hard."

"And you got everyone here. You're a fucking magician."

"Let me show you around." Wynnie squeezes me before relaxing, and I put her back on her feet.

She touches every surface and greets everyone as we pass. I tried to duplicate every aspect of Tipsy Penny that I could.

"You're fired." Wynnie's stern voice filters through the air, and I see her standing in front of Kristina, arms crossed over her chest.

Kristina shrugs and gives Wynnie a smug look. "Elliot offered me a job anyway."

Wynnie's jaw drops, and she swings at me, punching me square in the chest.

"Jesus fuck, woman. That hurt."

"Are you trying to poach my staff? She told me her aunt died. You're all a bunch of liars!" She yells the last part to the crowd, and everyone cheers and whoops. Several I love yous echo back, and my heart fills.

Wynnie looks so happy. I don't know why I had any doubt she would be upset. She's my best friend, my other half.

As the evening winds down, everyone slowly leaves to their respective homes for the night.

"I can't wait any longer." I hang my head at my mother's voice. I've successfully avoided her all evening, knowing she'll make me cry.

"Let's get this over with, Mom." I pull her into my chest, and she rests her cheek on my shoulder.

"What you've created here with your business and your family…" Her voice breaks as the tears fall. "It's incredible, and I'm so proud. So. Fucking. Proud. But I miss you." She pulls away and cups my cheeks in her palms. "I need you to buy your new family a big house so we can come visit all the time. I want to watch my grandbaby, or grandbabies if Lainey has her way, grow in real time. Ugh. Why did you have to move so far away?"

"I love you, Mom. Thank you for everything. You know you're welcome to come any time you want. Just tell me when, and I'll book your ticket."

"Okay. I need to find Hazel and Collin to take me home. I've had too many of Scotty's blue drinks."

I kiss her forehead and turn her toward my father and Aunt. That was a mistake because Aunt Hazel and a tired-looking Tori see I'm finally alone and walk my way.

"Thank you, Uncle Elliot." Tori wraps her arms around

my waist, and I smile into her hair. "It's so perfect. Mom keeps crying, but I know it's happy tears, and you did this for her."

"How about you, kiddo? Are you happy too?"

She nods into my chest. "Still sad some days, but the happy days are getting better. I love you."

"Love you too, Tori."

Aunt Hazel cups my cheek, and her lip quivers. "You've done something amazing here, El. She'll never forget this. It's perfect." Hazel's hug replaces Tori's, and it's official. My heart overflows. The praise from my family and friends is overwhelming.

"Thank you."

"We've got the kids. Send Wynnie our way whenever you're ready. We thought you might want a little more time together."

I thank her and give my final round of goodbyes.

Sawyer, Lainey, and Charlotte approach me as I close down the register. Everything was free tonight, but we still rang it all up as a trial run.

"We're heading out. Is there anything you need help with before we go?"

I step into Lainey, careful not to squish our daughter. "I'm good, Cherry. Take her home, and I'll be there in a little while. I love you." She kisses me with heat and passion, and I know there will be celebratory sex when I get home.

"Don't hog our husband, Jitterbug." Sawyer grabs my arm and tugs me away from Lainey's lips. Before I can protest, he crashes his lips to mine and wraps his arm around my waist.

*Definitely sex when I get home.*

"Eww. Don't make him horny before you leave him alone with me." I chuckle into Sawyer's lips and whisper I love you before giving my best friend my full attention.

Spreading my arms, I give her my biggest smile and shake my hips. "I'm all yours, bestie. Sans boner."

"Uugh. On second thought. Take him with you and leave me here with the tequila." Wynnie turns to walk away, and I grab her arm, spinning her into me.

Wynnie and I stay locked in our embrace as my family leaves.

"I did all this for you."

"You did all this for *you*. And I love you for it. Scotty would love you for it, although he'd probably hate it. He loved his hole-in-the-wall bar."

"He loved you, Wynnie. He loved you, and Tori, and those babies. He loved his bar and the life you created together. He was full of so much love, and it lives on within all of us." Wynnie sniffles, and I wipe my own tears away before they fall onto her head. "Let's make a wish."

"There's no sunlight."

"Has that honestly ever stopped you before?" She chuckles and shakes her head. "I have a solution, anyway."

I lead her to the front door where Aunt Hazel's crystal hangs and pick up a flashlight from a shelf. Clicking the button, I aim it at the rock, and rainbows appear around the room.

"Elliot," she breathes out. "It's perfect." I take her hand and squeeze. "Let's make a wish. One of our own and one together."

"Okay. I wish—"

"I wish that our family heals and everyone loves as deep

as the love that Scotty had for you."

"Have I not cried enough tonight, El?"

"Close your eyes and make your own now." She closes them, and her lips part and move while she makes whatever wish her heart desires. I close mine just as she's opening hers.

*I wish that whatever Wynnie just wished for comes true. She deserves everything good in her life.*

"I love you, El. Thank you."

"Love you, Wynnie."

The End

# About the Author

Casiddie is a single mother to five wonderfully feral children. When she isn't playing referee to them, she's creating worlds and characters and writing them down for your enjoyment.

Casiddie writes contemporary romance but hopes to delve into the darker side of writing soon.

**You can connect with me on:**

- https://www.facebook.com/casiddiewilliams
- https://www.tiktok.com/@casiddiewilliams_author

# Also by Casiddie Williams

**Hazel's Harem**

Curious where it all started. Join Hazel and her best friend Dellah and find out how her journey finding three wonderful men began.

**Annie You're Okay**

To learn more about Annie, Blake and Cole's relationship, check out their book.

**Caffeinated Passion**

Stella has been the focus of Penny's desire for almost a year. She watches her work while silently longing for her, wishing she could make Stella hers.

Though Stella is a down-on-her-luck waitress, she makes the best out of life with her son Cooper. She's desperately trying to get out of her terrible situation with her drunk boyfriend, one shift at a time.

When Stella finds herself in need of an extra hand, Penny takes the opportunity to swoop in and help her, offering a job to nanny her daughter, a safe place to live, and a relationship if she's interested.

Caffeinated Passion is part one of my single parent duet. Meet Toby and Christian in The Wrong Hookup and their unconventional meeting.

### Paint the Night Blue

After a decade of marriage, Jaycee finds herself in her mid-forties and newly divorced. At her sister's insistence, they go out for a night on the town, where she meets Ian, a younger man who seems far too good to be true.

A blue dress, a man half her age, and his desire to love every inch of her body is the recipe for a fun night of laughter and pleasure that Jaycee didn't know she needed.

Will one night be enough to satisfy their desires for each other?

Made in the USA
Middletown, DE
26 April 2025